Meta World 2
Neophyte

Meta World 2
Neophyte

A Novel by
LeRoy Smith

LeRoy Smith Publishing

IMAGE DESIGN AND COVER LAYOUT

CONCEPT ART AND COVER DESIGN BY
COURTNEY MCKEAND

COVER DESIGN ASSISTANCE BY
VICTORIA VALENTINE

Interior layout and advising by Gary Brin
Editing by Shenell Summers

This novel is a work of fiction. Names, characters, business, events and incidents
are the products of the author's imagination. Any resemblance to actual persons,
living or dead, or actual events is purely coincidental.

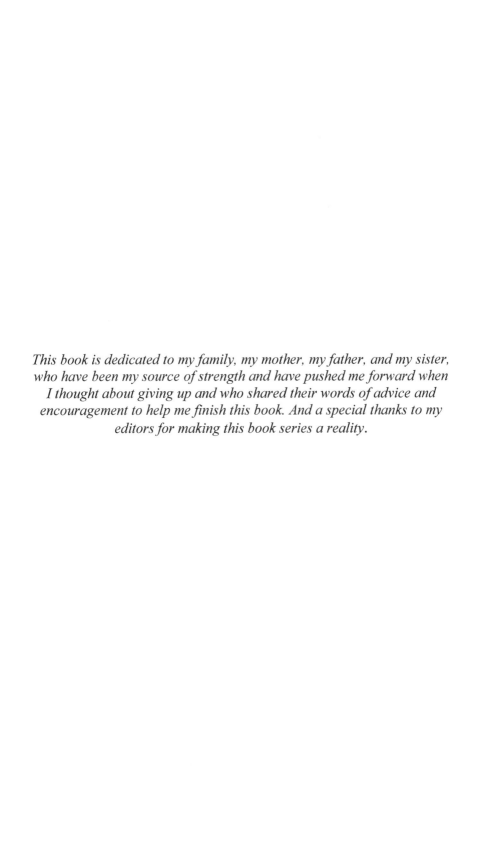

This book is dedicated to my family, my mother, my father, and my sister, who have been my source of strength and have pushed me forward when I thought about giving up and who shared their words of advice and encouragement to help me finish this book. And a special thanks to my editors for making this book series a reality.

Contents

Acknowledgments

This book was inspired by Stan Lee and *X-Men* who first introduced me into comics, as well as to Robert Kirkman who showed me how to balance grim and dark to adventure and hope. This book is also inspired by my favorite directors George Lucas and Steven Spielberg who helped mold my imagination.

Prologue

MAY 28: VALDOSTA, GEORGIA

As Samson looked out into the backyard he saw friends, acquaintances, schoolmates, and people, plus ones or twos. This party was supposed to be a graduation party for him and his best friend Bianca. They weren't valedictorians or anything but they received scholarships nonetheless. Bianca was hardly recognizable. Gone was the chubby tomboy who used to pick on him. She was now a statuesque Brazilian star of the volleyball team who had a couple of talent agents seeking her out. Luckily for Bianca, her powers were easy to control so she could play sports of any type. For Samson, the living embodiment of Newton's third law, it was difficult to find a sport where he would not have 'an unfair advantage.' Samson had the power of kinetic energy, meaning any and all forces of movement empowered him and also protected him. To instinctually shield himself from any blow would expose his powers, making them obvious to any observer. Therefore, any contact sports were out of the question. Tennis used to be an option until one time the ball went flying towards his face but mysteriously dropped two inches from his head, raising speculation and suspicion. Hence the only sport possible for Samson was swimming, which did wonders for his physique.

Samson and Bianca were suddenly surrounded by the volleyball team, the swim team, team groupies and team coaches. Samson's coach, Ms. Hortes, wanted him to continue his swimming career since he was the best anchor and long-distance swimmer that she had. While he would not outswim everyone, he would never tire out or slow down, resulting in several state title championships and quite a few trophies. One minor side effect of his power was the fact he had endless endurance while active. To test the theory, Samson actually ran for two days nonstop, ending up in Atlanta with only the minor fatigue a healthy, active person gets from a light morning jog.

As Samson watched Bianca, he found it hard to believe he was looking at the chubby girl who used to tease him. She was now the fit, athletic young lady who won State three times. She even wore a minor power dampener bracelet which kept her powers regulated so that all of her victories were earned. She became somewhat famous as a top tier athlete, and she was a nearly flawless beauty. Bianca had dark skin that hinted at her mixed-race origins, blended with European features and sandy brown hair, chased by a hundred guys. Samson would admit that he had asked Bianca out several times, but she always turned him down. After his third time hearing the 'friendship' spiel that every guy hates, Samson quit asking and moved on to date someone else. It's too bad that someone else was Anita.

If you asked Samson how he would describe their relationship, he would describe it as a cautionary tale of never letting a woman play with your friends or your mind. Anita had turned Samson into, for lack of a better term, a lapdog and a simp for almost a year and a half. At first, she was sweet and nice to him and his friends, worming her way into his trust, then she pretty much cut him off from most of his friends and pushed him into her personal circle. For a time, she was the cause of his grades dropping because she would accuse him of being neglectful. This went on until Samson realized Anita was seeing other guys. It was confirmed when the school's top running back got a video of them doing soft-core material, making the infidelity obvious and embarrassing. Instead of crying and weeping, Samson got mad and cut off all contact with Anita. Samson told her they were through and ignored her every attempt to speak to him. Anita claimed it was Samson's fault that she cheated on him. She found Samson weak, and she pointed out that he wasn't even truly black. Samson took that to mean she thought he was not man enough for her taste, but he retorted that not being ghetto or hood did not make him any less of a black man. Luckily, Samson decided he would never allow Anita to poison his opinion of women, though he always had a bit of apprehension. "Hopefully I will find someone to get the bad taste out of my mouth," Samson mused to himself as he people-watched by the pool.

"Hey, son, you think you can bring my spiked Arnold Palmer," Hakeem asked, seeming to be enjoying himself wading halfway into the pool.

"I'll have one too," echoed the mother of one of Samson's teammates. As Samson rose from the pool, a collective bunch of eyes admired the young man's body, sculpted by hours of swimming and, unknown to many, the Meta gene. As Samson walked towards the kitchen, which was connected to the backyard via a sliding door, he turned and asked, "Anyone else need anything?"

As soon as Samson saw twelve different hands pop up, he regretted it. Samson sighed, picked up his phone from the patio area and began to type in everyone's orders as if he were a waiter. Soon he was mixing two big pitchers of his dad's cookout famous cocktail and put several brand beers in an ice bucket. On his second trip he intended to bring out more sauce from the fridge when he overheard a heated conversation between Bianca and her mother, Luiza. Well, it was more like an argument.

"Mom, I'm not going to go pro. I'm not some ditz who's going to show off her body for some company," Bianca said, trying to get her mother to see her point of view.

"But, sweetie, there is a lot more money and security if you go professional," Luiza said, trying to get her daughter to see her point of view.

"And I will have a lot more restrictions to what I can do, not being allowed to be myself because it destroys a company image," Bianca pointed out.

"It's not all that bad. I'm sure they won't be that intrusive," Luiza countered, trying to downplay her daughter's fears.

"The fact is, I am a woman who hates fourth wave feminism and believes that everyone should be seen innocent until proven guilty, regardless of gender. That isn't Kosher nowadays," Bianca said.

"Just say it, but don't mean it. We know that it isn't who you are," Luiza pleaded, really hoping to get her daughter to reconsider.

"Papi almost lost his store because he didn't promote a woman instead of Jacob, who has been there longer and was actually liked by the other employees. And then she accused him of being a sexist pig. If the entire female staff didn't back him up that woman could have ruined him," replied Bianca, standing her ground.

"I know, I know, but you have the option to stay quiet about things." Luiza was grabbing straws at this point.

"No, I don't. I have to speak out or be forgotten, which is the drawback of being a celebrity. Not to mention, I could have some assistant in charge of my social media say things that I don't believe in and force me to correct myself—which means lie and encourage a façade, or tell the truth and be forced to apologize," Bianca explained as she remembered several celebrities going through the same thing.

"You are blowing this out of…" Whatever Luiza was going to say was lost on Samson as he snuck out of that conversation and headed back outside, while snagging a drink for himself. As he returned, he saw the last person he wanted to see at this party, Anita Pembrooke, his shallow, self-righteous ex-girlfriend. He remembered all the bad times they had together and all the crap he had put up with her. Then he saw her dark ebony skin, tall, elegant form, enchanting eyes, and full breasts, and he remembered why. Out of twelve hundred students in school, she was one of the top five beauties.

And as much as he hated her, he begrudgingly admitted she was still hot. But like some Hollywood celebrities, no matter how hot Anita was, she was still poison.

You know what, just forget her and move on, Samson thought, as he gave the adults their drinks. He made his way back to the pool. He decided to ignore her by joining in with the others horsing around, but Anita had other plans. As he was about to play some no-holds-barred pool basketball, Anita approached with Rayvonne, the star running back of their school. "Hey Sam, sorry I'm late, but you seemed to forget to tell me about the graduation party," Anita said innocently.

Most guys would be polite enough to excuse such an action, but Samson didn't feel like being polite. "We broke up," he remarked.

"Oh, come on, we're adult enough not to let such bad blood occur," Anita said, trying to act like the bigger person.

Samson, still refusing to look at her, "However you, Anita, take every opportunity to bad mouth me to anyone who will listen."

"Well, it was your fault that it ended the way it did," Anita accused.

"Yes. How dare I grow a spine and not cuckold myself so you can keep your side dog?" As Samson said this, Rayvonne moved towards him. He did not like being referred to as a dog, but Anita held him back from causing a fight.

"How about you say that to my face," Rayvonne said, more than willing to start a fight.

"How about you leave my house? Neither you nor Anita were invited or wanted. Besides don't you have a skanky cheerleader to cheat on Anita with," said Samson, who wasn't just talking trash. Rayvonne was the star athlete at their school and knew it. In the three years since he became the starting running back, he had slept with half the cheer squad, so Samson's insult was not hyperbole.

"Maybe if you took care of your woman better, I wouldn't have to," Rayvonne verbally struck.

"Considering I'm still a virgin, that's more on her than me." Samson rolled his eyes as he deflected.

"Wait, you openly admit that you're a virgin?" Rayvonne and several guys laughed at Samson's admission. But strangely, Samson was not bothered by it in the least.

"You're done, despite what the media tells me, I don't have to lose my virginity by fourteen," Samson replied, as he finally got out of the pool and stood eye-to-eye to the jock.

"Yeah, only hapless scrubs like you would say that, since no woman would be desperate enough to sleep with you," disputed Rayvonne.

"Not true, I hear your mom has serviced half the hood. I'm pretty sure I only need to drop my pants and that will solve my *so-called* problem." As Samson finished his zinger, Rayvonne attempted to punch him in the face. The scary thing about this was, if Samson wanted, he could have allowed Rayvonne to hit him, which would have broken his hand as if it were hitting a metal reinforced wall. Instead, Samson turned his cheek to cushion the blow from the idiot, then Samson let Rayvonne punch him three more times just to be in the legal right to fight back without using his powers. Samson then delivered a blow to Rayvonne's right side. Samson's boxing coach always told him that it felt like a taser to the midsection, which caused the oversized brute to collapse.

As a result, the running back flopped to his side, clutching his midsection. As an added bonus, it seemed Samson also knocked the air from his lungs, which made Rayvonne cough, grasping for air. There was a collective moan from Samson's fellow swim teammates. Anita looked shocked at her more muscled boyfriend getting knocked down with one punch. Instead of looking over Rayvonne, she started to slap Samson in anger, not only once or twice, adding a stream of profanity and insults about his manhood. Samson could not do anything, because even if he held her arms in place from hitting him, she could say that he was hurting her. It wouldn't matter if he was merely defending himself; society would side with her. That was until Bianca appeared behind Samson's wretched ex and knocked Anita into the pool.

"I know that a fat border-jumping bitch didn't just hit me," screamed Anita, her perfect image fell as her rage grew.

"First, I'm Brazilian. Second, if you think I won't knock your skank ass out, think again," Bianca was getting ready to fight, as she saw one of her school divas stand up. But before the two could get into a brawl, one of the parents intervened, separating the two. Hakeem wasn't a stupid or gullible TV dad, and he knew this was going to happen. The only reason she was allowed into the party was because the other parents peer-pressured him into it. As Anita had caused a fight, Hakeem felt justified to kick her out of his home without any blame.

"I warned you young lady. You and your boyfriend were welcome to eat and party with the rest of us. But it seems I was unclear, so please leave before I throw you out," Hakeem said as he stepped away from the grill, ready to usher the troublemakers out.

"It was your son." Anita tried to defended herself but was cut off by a tall, full-figured woman who happened to be Samson's mother.

"My *son* was attacked by your thug of a boyfriend and defended himself—and the only reason he didn't slap the crap out of you, after you started attacking him, is because I raised him better than that. And if Bianca hadn't stepped in, I would've ripped that rat nest you call a weave off your head," Aaliyah said, walking towards the little slut that had made her baby's life miserable for the past two years.

Anita, at this point, backed down from the angry parent. Even when she was dating Samson, his mother never liked her. Anita had seen enough of the woman to know that she would do as she threatened. As Anita helped her boyfriend back onto his feet, she gave everyone the stank eye and proceeded to guide him out the back gate of the backyard.

"That was a lucky punch, you little bastard," Rayvonne said as he gulped for some more air in the middle of his tirade. "When I see you again, I'm going to stomp a hole in you."

"Tell me that when you're not drooling on my front lawn," Samson said, as he turned his back on them, not wanting to deal with them anymore.

Rayvonne felt the anger fueling him to push past the pain, he wanted to start a fight again until Samson's dad got in front of him. While the running back may have seemed like the typical dumb ghetto superstar, he had enough wits about him to know not to mess with the older man. He heard from his uncle that Hakeem Brewer was a veteran and worked at a government job that was associated with US Marshals. So, calming his rage, he sucked it up and left. He could get back at that punk later without witnesses.

The party resumed as soon as Anita and Rayvonne left. Bianca was sitting on the edge of the pool next to her oldest friend. "So, what was that about?" she asked.

"If I had to guess, she wanted to rub it in my face that she dumped me for a better man," Samson guessed.

"Is that so?" Bianca looked in disgust at the direction of the two former party crashers as they left.

"What can I say? High school drama will have its way, whether you want it or not," Samson sighed.

"Seriously." Bianca could only roll her eyes and sigh in remembrance of all the bullshit she had to deal with, especially since she lost weight. While the boys are mostly willing to forget she was ever chunky, some of her more spiteful peers never let her forget. It seemed when most of her weight disappeared around her gut and went to her hips and butt, more boys took notice. And as soon as her body became mostly toned muscle with curves, her real friends stood by her while others began to make comments about her being on her knees.

"Tell me this ends once we head to college," Bianca moaned hopefully.

"It should, larger campus population, not as big a spotlight. You're the only one I know heading towards Everglades State College, so less peers to deal with, and if you need a friend I can be there," Samson said.

"Thanks. So, have you decided on which path you want to take?" Bianca asked.

"Not really," Samson tilted his head upward, looking into the sky as if the answer was there. "There are so many pros and cons. Though both my parents say they support me no matter which path, I think they want me to go Fortune 500."

- 19 -

"With your skills I believe it. Just watch out for-"

Whatever Bianca was going to say was lost as a couple of the boys from the swim team blindsided them and pushed both of them into the pool. While Samson was a little upset, Bianca was furious and started to chase them once she got out of the pool.

As she grabbed one in a headlock from behind and was grappling him to the ground Samson replied, "Bianca, don't break his collar bone. He has a swim scholarship."

"That only happened once, and he groped me," Bianca defended herself.

"Fair enough," Samson said, as he watched an almost college-age boy get his butt kicked by a girl almost as tall as him.

TWO YEARS LATER
JUNE 10: VALDOSTA AIRPORT

"Wasn't there a song that said that high school never freaking ends," Bianca groaned as she talked to Samson, who was relaxing a bit since he finally got enough credits for his associates degree.

Samson was waiting for a flight to Columbia, Missouri for the summer combine, where all the young perspective heroes show the scouts what they are capable of. It was a few days after Memorial Day, which meant they would have a late arrival this semester, but the classes were more like trade school than a university.

"What brought this on?" Samson asked as he looked up from his mystery book.

"I remember you saying that I could fade into the background because there are so many students. And the fact we're not allowed on   any   sport   teams   would   make   us   even   less on people's radars," Bianca said, accusing her best friend of lying.

Knowing the reply she wanted, Samson obliged her by stretching the first word. "Yes, but I have a feeling I was way wrong, apparently."

"Apparently on campus there is a fashion and designer club who loved my Brazilian fashion sense, put me on their magazine cover, and now I'm the object of a bunch of thirsty frat douches." Bianca emphasized her last few words.

"Don't sell yourself short. I know for a fact that the guys outside of fraternities are just as thirsty," Samson mocked.

"Oh, thank you, that makes me feel all better,"

"Bianca, you're talking to a guy you've known since the sandbox. You wanted to lose weight because you wanted boys to notice you. This is not your main gripe with this. So, what is it?"

"My   mother   is   pushing   even   harder   for   me   to   go the corporate route, saying my stardom on campus proves how marketable I am," Bianca groused. "She wants me on the skank squad."

The Magnificent Maidens were jokingly known as the "skank squad" by other Heroines. This was one of those situations where the organization started out as normal, but corporate and/or politics made it a sham of its former self. When WWI started, there was a squad of women from all over the globe, the Allied Entente, who were the first show of woman power in the modern age. Then, after the war, their mission transformed into a mixture of British and American women who used that same show of woman power to try to quell any further violence. But as time went on, the name stuck, and Heroines from age seventeen to twenty-eight became the faces of the future female Meta-humans. As times changed, so did their image. During the fifties and the early sixties, this was how they showed they were chaste. Then from the late sixties to early seventies, they had free will and were open with their bodies and beauty. This was when the super heroines began to be more risqué with their uniforms, which spread throughout the Heroine community. Then in the mid-to-late eighties until the year 2000, their mission became all about being a rebel and girl power. It had now become a mixture of the most self-righteous, egotistical, and almost man-hating group out there.

"The Magnificent Maidens know you're more moderate than what they usually aim for, right? Not to mention, you're not size four," Samson asked in a joking manner.

"I'm not a white woman either, but that's why they insist that I'm perfect for the team," Bianca joked along with him.

"I am beginning to see why you're so angry." Samson knew a quota count when he heard it.

"I refuse to be a token nobody," Bianca groused.

"I find it funny they say that their group will be more diverse, but the only thing they change is management to solely white women and one token gay guy," Samson commented.

"Hell—the team in the eighties were made of more women of color. Their idea of diversity is to bring in one lesbian and me—a Brazilian—to fill in the demographic," Bianca complained.

"So—is your mother pushing for it?" Samson asked, but he knew the answer.

"It's almost constant badgering every day, saying it's a great opportunity," Bianca complained.

"Look on the bright side - if society is like high school, then we're about to become the popular kids and trendsetters. And you got an invite to the nation's version of a bitch squad," Samson said, only to be punched hard in the shoulder. He had to wince, since the punch was hard enough to be heard by other people nearby.

Chapter 1
First Step in the Spotlight

JUNE 11: COLUMBIA, MISSOURI

As Samson and Bianca arrived at a hotel, both he and Bianca were put in the same room since both families trusted them not to do anything foolish. Not that it was anywhere near their minds, as the anticipation in showing the world what they could do was more important.

"Is it arrogant to say none of the physical tests worry me? Over the past two summers my dad and mom have been pushing me through drills to prep me with and without my powers. According to my stats, I'm equal to a NFL prime running back. Only the deductive reason test and quick assessment are my main worries," Samson said as he stretched out his muscles.

"Not really. All the physical tests are made for your powers to beat. And while deduction and aptitude tests are not the flashiest of the tests, they are essential. A lot of the top tier organizations find them vital," said Bianca, letting worry enter her voice as well.

"Physical skills are important also to major companies, but unlike most athletes, if you do something stupid or not see the obvious it could lead you in traction or dead. It could also lead to many others dying for your mistakes," said Samson, remembering the importance of the mental tests.

"Civilians dying because you're a dumbass would be bad for the corporate image," Bianca snarked.

"And yet we are blamed for dumbasses that get themselves killed. Or, the fact a villain commits a murder and we're not there to stop it, even though they know we're not gods," said Samson, remembering some of the bad press his parents had received.

"There are few cults out there who believe we descend from the old Gods as it were, and we Metas are the chosen people," Bianca replied.

"And those cults are one *Mein Kampf* away from a road that I really don't want to go near," said Samson, dismissing all the extremist groups.

"Oh, come on, you're exaggerating, right? There are nutjobs out there. We fight them most of the time," Bianca said.

"I'm just saying, ever since scientists named us Homo Excelsior there have been people thinking just because they won the genetic lottery that they automatically deserve to be treated better than everyone else," Samson replied.

"You worry too much. Anyway, you all set for tomorrow?" Bianca changed the subject.

"Uniform and name all set," Samson answered.

"Awesome, can I see it?" Bianca asked.

"I kind of want to wait until tomorrow to reveal it. You know, shock and awe," Samson explained.

"If you show me yours, I will show you mine," Bianca said in a coy way.

"I haven't heard that since we were ten and I showed you my ninja turtle underwear," Samson quipped at her poor choice of words.

"Were we ever that young and innocent?" Bianca lamented.

"It feels like decades, doesn't it," Samson reminisced about their almost forgotten past.

"What happened to us?" Bianca asked the same question everyone does at one point.

"Hormones, peer pressure, and having a sex drive," Samson answered with the usual culprits.

"Boys get really perverted when they reach that age, don't they," Bianca pondered, putting on an air of superiority.

Samson gave her a look that said he was going to call her on her bull. "You have three R-rated posters and a practically naked picture of an R&B singer."

"Fair." Bianca laughed a bit at being called out, then she waited for Samson to change into his new suit.

"Well?" she asked, as if it were obvious.

"You first," Samson calmly replied, as he started to scroll through his phone.

Instead of answering his comment, she just gave him a look and told him, "Oh shut up and put your uniform on."

"Uh-uh, you go first. You have a tendency to pull out of deals after you get what you want," Samson retorted.

"Oh, come on, would I really do that?" Bianca had the nerve to act offended.

"Yes, I've known you from the actual sandbox days, so please cut the act." Samson was not letting any false guilt get to him.

"You're no fun sometimes," Bianca complained.

As Bianca stepped into the bathroom, Samson looked towards the TV and saw various commercials and sports analysts talking about the big event.

Let's just hope I make a big enough splash, Samson thought as he heard the bathroom door open. Bianca's uniform was a mixture of sexiness and practicality. Her main colors were a deep blue with silver and gray highlights. Her mask was a half mask that covered everything from her nose up. Everything but her mouth and chin was concealed. Her eyes were lensed and looked modified; her top was something else. It was a choker corset combination that gave a view to her noticeable cleavage but short enough to show enough of her toned belly. She wore what reminded him of a female wrestler's pants—practical, but too form-fitting in certain areas. To add a bit of pain to her look, he saw that her gloves had metal caps and she wore steel-toed boots. Add the fact that she could make her body as hard as diamonds and could increase her mass to match a bus. Meaning, when she hit you, she would hit you hard.

"What do you think?" Bianca decided to show off as if she were a model with a few steps and spins to show her front and back.

"Let me guess, your mom designed the top," Samson said, knowing her tomboy tendencies.

"Though the corset doesn't cut off air to my body and they support the girls," Bianca said while teasing Samson with a bit of her cleavage. Samson, being a straight male with a sex drive, noticed but didn't shy away.

"It works like a wonder bra because it looks like you gained a size," Samson said in a matter-of-fact tone.

Bianca looked disappointed at his lack of a reaction. "Oh, come on. You're not going to react?"

"You've been doing this since your figure came in. I'm pretty sure you flashed me enough times not to be a blushing fourteen-year-old. I guess I'm desensitized by now," Samson pointed out.

"Eh, Papi always told me never to play the same hand too much," Bianca joked. "It's our turn."

Samson said nothing as he grabbed a suit carrier into the bathroom to get changed. After stripping down, he examined his uniform as he put it on. His pants were the typical spandex-looking affair, mostly black with five, large gold hexagons on his right pant leg. His combat vest was a stylish mix of practical and aesthetic blend. The vest was goldish-yellow with black highlights and had a bronze-like metal plate covering his pecs and the abs area of the vest. The surrounding material was Kevlar but a golden yellow in color and with three belt pouches on the side in black. Lastly, his face mask covered everything from the bridge of his nose down. It was black with the five golden hexagon symbols on the left side of his mask.

As he stepped out, he got a surprised look from his longtime friend. Bianca couldn't believe how combat-oriented he looked. She knew that both his parents were the more practical heroes. Hell, his dad was the Armory, but this looked like he was going to war.

"Were you drafted without me noticing," Bianca commented on how decked out he was.

"Eh, better be prepared than be caught dead," Samson said, remembering the old hero saying.

"Your power is kinetic force, what in the world can counter that?" Bianca still felt his attire was overkill.

"My face mask does more than hide my identity. It also has an air filtration system so gas attacks will be less effective. And the plates are special ones that protect against pure energy attacks. And I have a few hidden gadgets just in case I need to vary my attack," Samson pointed out his kit to her.

"Again—are you off to war," Bianca said, still in disbelief how strapped he was.

"If I was, I would be focusing on how I can turn a handgun into a Gauss rifle," Samson commented.

"Wait, you can do that?" Bianca was actually a little scared about that comment.

"Yeah, I can control kinetic energy—meaning the speed, force, and destructive power behind it as well. So, it would not be out of the question." Samson knew he could add power to objects to make projectiles.

"That's actually scary when you think about it. Only thing I can do is make myself heavier." Bianca felt intimidated by that aspect of his powers.

"And fade through walls, run about eight hundred miles per hour, become the literal immovable object, and you can punch out almost any Metas, period. And you had me help you train to fly as well. You're not exactly D-list when it comes to power," Samson said, trying to end her pity party.

"True but am I just a flying brick? You know—typical super strength, invulnerability—and can move through the air," Bianca questioned, still seeing only her flaws.

"So, despite the fact that's just the surface, as far as we know, you have the potential to grow to match or even surpass me?" Samson was trying to make her see her potential.

"Do tell." Bianca said, not really buying it.

"You control density which means you also manipulate mass to an extent," Samson tried to make her see the coolness of it.

"Again—how does that help," Bianca asked not getting it.

"You know this is the reason you should have paid attention in physics instead of drooling over Lorenzo Martino." Samson rubbed his right temple.

"In my defense, Lorenzo was the sexiest thing in our school that wasn't a jock," Bianca countered.

Samson just shook his head at his friend being so lazy about how her powers worked. He felt that she relied on him for almost anything that had to do with math and the harder sciences.

"Anyway, my handle is "K-Force" because I can control kinetic energy and others cannot call me black anything," Samson stated.

"Is that really a big concern?" Bianca was confused why that was even an issue.

"African Americans are often given black, ebony and Nubian, brotha or sistah, etc. as a moniker. My father first went by Rune Knight, but the media insisted calling him the Black Knight. Even his government liaison officially changed it, which he hated. But before he could change it, somebody had to say, 'I'm not black. I'm O.J. Simpson.' So not to have that heat dropped on him, he had to keep that name until the nineties." Samson stated his point again.

"Seriously you act like black people are the only ones who go through it," Bianca commented, thinking her friend was exaggerating.

"Give me three names whose race is the focal point, that is not supremacist of some type," Samson challenged.

"Okay Mexican Hyper-man, Lady Jaguar..." Bianca at this point was lost since she could not think of one. "Colonel Malaysia?"

"Colonel Malaysia and Mexican Hyper-man are named by nationality, not race, while Lady Jaguar is based off the Aztec

Jaguar warriors, which is part of her culture, so it doesn't count," Samson answered confidently.

"Oh, come on," said Bianca, not seeing the point of it.

"I'm just proving a point that no other people of a racial background have this problem," Samson said.

"Oh really, name three black people today who have that problem," Bianca challenged.

"Black Raptor, Black Volt—who is a legacy from her aunt, Soul Sistah, the second one, she got the legacy from her aunt. Ebony Flame and Chocolate Thunder are just a few examples," Samson counted off his fingers as he thought off the top of his head.

"Chocolate Thunder?" she questioned.

"R&B singer as well as a Meta-human," Samson responded.

"Are they any good?" Bianca asked.

"Considering you love the songs "Quiet Storm" and "How Does it Feel," I say yeah," he replied.

"Wait, that's him?" Bianca was in disbelief that one of her teenage celebrity crushes was a hero.

"Yep," he said.

"Huh, nice marketing," Bianca said with wolfish grin.

"I just realized you never told me what your name will be," Samson said.

"It's Azougue," Bianca said off-handedly.

"Wait, I know that word?" Samson scratched his head, trying to remember. "Quicksilver in Portuguese—right?"

"Very good, it is nice to see that my dad's lingua Portuguesa stuck," Bianca was impressed he was still in practice after all these years.

"Only because you liked to gossip without others listening in," Samson said.

As they began reminiscing about their past they also started to dress down for the night. The combine was going to start in two days and they needed to be prepared for the first step into superhero work.

The next two days was a mixture of training exercises, going over intro routines, and checking to make sure all their bodies were fit for the competition. Bianca did a full mix of boxing and BBJ in which she could use her full force of the weights advantage with her flexible stature, while Samson went full boxing, Muay Thai for striking blows, and full combat Judo to have impact ability. Given that they are both trained boxers, they had a small spar between the two of them. After Samson absorbed a couple of her blows, he slapped Bianca a couple of times if she let her guard down. To many outsiders it looked like he was beating on a girl, but superpowers make everyone equal or in this case removes any distinction between genders or race. Powers are the ultimate equalizer.

Then the big day came, featuring a specially made giant track and field used for Meta-human sporting events. To see the Tiger emblem and the six championships of Meta Ball were justified reasons for choosing this stadium. The ground and asphalt were made to have a resistance to Meta-humans. The best of the best young Metas ranging from ages eighteen to twenty-five were Beta level or higher. Some were first timers, and some were there for the final try out before they would be relegated as a part of the public hero sector, whether Professional or Government.

This would be the first step into either getting the major fame, money, and benefits or becoming a low tier hype man for a company as a glorified beat cop with a slightly better pay.

As far as competition goes, they were the typical combine events and atypical for the farther range of powers. For instance, there were the typical strength, speed, agility, accuracy, and power tests. The trials were altered to match what the average all-rounder Beta would achieve. This meant that the strength test was specialized hydraulic press with a cushion barbell which could withstand over four hundred tons of force. Once one surpasses the dead lift limit of three hundred, then he or she would automatically ace the test. Then they headed to a modified hydraulic bench press, which was set at five tons. Every time one fully extended the machine, a rep would be counted. Each hero prospect had three minutes to pump out as many reps as possible, though they would have to get past twenty to pass the test. Then the final test of the day would be the obstacle course in a Tetris Z-shape, where one must dodge traps and block or parry hidden blows, all while timed.

Bianca as Azougue was one of the first to start around nine in the morning since all the top picks and those with buzz were usually shown around noon, so they could be televised for the main audience on a Saturday. Many ignored her a bit because although she was a beautiful tomboy, they did not expect her to be a powerhouse. That was until Samson arrived to help warm up with her on the modified body bag. The loud and brutal pounding she gave the exercise equipment was impressive but not enough to peak anyone's attention. Little did they know, Bianca was going to be a showstopper. Bianca, or Azougue, proved the superpowers were the true equalizer when she out-muscled every guy by being the first to lift over three hundred tons, which shocked everyone. Next, she broke the all-time record by pumping out ninety-two reps, beating the old record by seven. Next was the agility test, which consisted of an obstacle course in which her performance was merely average. Azougue was hit by several traps, lost a step or two and was on the low side of the grading curve, so to speak. While she passed the average time of escape, she was slow compared to the sound breakers. While it seemed Azougue lived up to the name, she could move at adequate speed in a straight line. Sharp turns at running speed were a bit difficult for her.

There were a few faces Samson noticed as well that came before him. One was a young woman named Frigid; she was an Ice user who was not made for strength. First, she opted out of the repetition event, stating she only could lift three tons, which was nowhere near strong enough to participate. But she proved very skillful in the obstacle course where her reflexes were shown.

The rules of the timed obstacle course were to go through an area filled with traps and secret attackers. Participants could not destroy equipment of the course nor directly attack anyone that stood in the way. The point of the test was to show awareness, agility, and quick thinking to overcome an obstacle instead of just bulldozing through it. Frigid was able to quickly react to freeze or destroy all the projectiles, and the secret attackers were blinded by her ability to make a minor blizzard which allowed her to ace the obstacle course.

Next, was Nega Titan who was a Grower and Shrinker with some serious power, and in Samson's opinion, the most skilled he had seen so far. Though he could not lift the full three hundred tons, the two hundred-thirty tons he was able to lift was still an impressive feat, to say the least. His twenty-seven repetitions were respectable, but the main attraction was his obstacle course run. The obstacle course changed randomly to over twenty settings and they had computerized parameters to truly test every individual. Nega Titan went in slowly at first since no one knew which traps would be locked or unlocked.

Nega Titan cautiously stepped on each tile before him since he saw them activated by the previous participant, which was an amplified taser with a ten-second life span. That took the sidekick over a minute to recover, which not only ruined his score, but informed every enemy he had that he was vulnerable to such things. But Nega Titan was acting more aware of such traps while trying to escape the booby trap area of the room as quickly as possible. When Nega Titan made it halfway through, he stepped on a trigger that made several shock-staffs raise from the floor around him, but he was nimble enough to dodge them. This soon led to high-speed paint rounds firing as he stepped on another booby-trapped tile—but luckily, he only got nicked by one as he escaped.

The next area was where hidden attackers made of holograms filled a hallway, which was a virtual death trap to anyone that wasn't a Meta-human or skilled enough to pass though the blades and mud traps. The blades were dulled but still left some painful injuries if one was not careful. This second hallway was filled with a section of flipped tiles that were spiked with swing-blunt pendulum blades, and spinning blades, also rotating pillars with spikes and pit falls. Although it was all holographic in nature, most would feel sharp pain. This room would make or break most heroes. Here is where Bianca lost most of her time and gained penalties to her score. But because of Nega Titan's size-shifting ability and agile nature, he could easily move about with almost no hesitation. He could make himself so small that he could easily slip in between the blades, spikes, and large pits to hop over twenty-foot gorges. Nega Titan soon had the fastest time through the second area while most were still struggling halfway through.

The third and final area was the hardest because it was a combination of the second room with active shooters. One could skip over this room, like the five-ton weight petition test—but in doing so would lose all extra points to the final score. To some, it was better to fail this test than skip it. Nega Titan decided to try it as well. With the unseen traps and men firing rubber bullets that left traces of a special illuminate, it was the best test of awareness and reflexes for any hero. Again, Nega Titan had an advantage as he would frequently shrink down to a size of an ant every time a trap or hail of fire was pointed at him. Most would call it cheating, but just as in life, sometimes his power was perfect for certain situations.

Soon it was noon, and the best and most marketable future heroes were shown. The best example was the one media kept pushing for the next big thing—'Prime Time.' It was not a mistake that his name was Prime Time; he was the picture-perfect hero that the media loved to push. He had a pretty boy-band face, long dirty blond hair, green eyes. He had a football player body with a height of six feet four inches and looked like he had a heavy obsession with arm day. Broad-shouldered, broad-chested, built like a Calvin Klein model—Prime Time was the Top Draft pick, so to speak. All news correspondents just loved to hype him up, despite being, in Samson's humble opinion, a glorified jumping brick. Well, that was an understatement. The guy was conventionally invulnerable and had heightened senses. Prime Time's major selling point was the fact that his strength was one of the highest caliber, outside of Omega-class heroes. This simply meant that he was the most powerful hero there and he knew it. In a show of arrogance, he broke the hydraulic press which meant that he more than exceeded the four-hundred-ton limit. He also did ninety on the five-ton bench press challenge. The obstacle course challenge was difficult for him because his awareness was a bit off. Prime Time was caught by surprise and it showed. At least on the ground he was not agile, but because of how invulnerable he was, the blades and traps bent or broke. But he laughed it off saying that he need not worry since he had met nothing and no one that could hurt him.

And because of this fact, the points deducted only counted as half as they would on any other contestant. It was a new rule implemented to help the bruisers of the hero community, but seemed to be very selective of who would receive the exemption. Samson would argue that Bianca as Azougue was more durable than the Calvin Klein model, but the combine officials replied that his durability was a matter of record, while her durability was only speculated. Samson was not really annoyed by the guy; he was just showing the world what he could do. No, what annoyed

Samson was the press coming up and asking Samson variations of the same three questions just so they could hype up Prime Time even more. 'How impressed was Samson of Prime Time,' 'what does he think Prime Time's strong points were,' and 'did Samson think he saw anyone that could match Prime Time's skill?' And each reporter ignored anything else that did not fit their narrative.

"Unbiased media at its finest," Samson said under his breath as he watched Prime Time take the top spot only because he was given a handicap by the officials.

It would take an hour to replace the hydraulic press, so for the next eight or so contestants, including Samson, obstacle courses would be first. This upset some because they were bruisers just like Prime Time, but they were not given handicaps, which meant they would have a rough start. Any athlete will tell you that when they are being scouted, the first impression is hard to shake. There were a couple of complaints that they would rather wait until the hydraulic press was replaced. The officials were willing to let them wait, but they would be in the back of the queue. This was almost as bad since most scouts from the big companies would have left by then. So, the participants had to decide whether to wait for a better showing or bite the bullet. This sadly made the three participants before Samson falter worse than they should have. If Samson had to guess, it was because they were overthinking every move. While he did feel sorry for them, it was the way things were, and any advice Samson gave would be ignored. When Samson's turn came, he took in a deep breath, and let all the anxiety in him slip away. He remembered the facts; he had more skills than just his powers, and no matter what happened, he would be prepared for it. Secondly, his power was one of the best out there; he had trained it the best he could and even produced maneuvers that surprised his folks during his training. And third, even if he flunked, he did not care about being the top draft pick—he could build from the bottom up without the press hounding him.

Hell, that might be a good excuse to intentionally take a dive, Samson thought as he laughed. "Up next, a young man who says

- 37 -

he can take anything you throw at him and send it right back—K-Force," the announcer said.

K-Force was sure anyone who knew about this part of his life would be surprised that he did not mention his lineage. It was the easy way for someone in his line of work to gain fame by his lineage, if one's relatives were well-known. K-Force just wanted to see how far he could go without riding the coattails of his parents. So, as he started his first day of the trials, he was about to show the world what he could do without their help. As K-Force stepped towards the obstacle area the commentator's described his clothing to the television-viewing audience.

"As we see our next assistant Hero hopeful walk towards the Obstacle Arena, we see that he is responding well to the crowd and—" as the commentator observed, the young hero began his gymnastic tumble towards the Arena. It started with a cartwheel, then several hand to foot flips, then a strong finish by spiking the landing.

"Oh... oh, K-Force is more agile than he first appeared. I like his costume—it seems more practical with just enough flare to be memorable. But love the black and gold suit that seems to mesh well with his skin tone," the commentator mentioned.

"But we know from experience that just because he looks the part doesn't mean he will be able to survive the trials of the weekend," the head commentator said.

"True, but let us see how difficult the first room will be," the first commentator added.

K-Force pressed a button and the wheel spun, landing on nine, which was the highest setting for the hidden trap room. This meant there was only one path that would lead him safely across the room, but every other step meant traps would be flying at him. All of this would be timed, however there would be some leniency because of the high difficulty. It was still meant to push all applicants to do their best and weed out those that couldn't make the cut.

"Oh, nasty luck there, looks like he is going to need darn near perfection to make up for the first part of the test," the second commentator said.

"But you never know—he might have a surprise for us," the head commentator added.

K-Force just let out a small breath since he was hoping to hide some small bit of his skill. After all, villains would be watching the trials as well, and they would love to crush rookies like him. And these tests were a great measure of one's skills, while scoping out the competition. Right now, he was deciding what power to display if he wanted to have a few surprises ready when he got into a battle.

K-Force decided to use the least flashy but one of his most effective powers. As he stepped in, he disregarded the trap chamber and moved forward. Out of the floor a spinning buzz saw flew towards him from his left, but he calmly leaned out of the way and kept moving forward. The next step also unleashed jutting spears from the ground, but K-Force just danced out of the way. The young man in gold and black moved calmly at a brisk pace, only moving and shifting out of the way of the traps by the barest minimum distance. It was as if he knew where they were coming from. He dodged pitfalls, rubber tracer rounds, darts, and arrows, even a falling pillar which would have stopped at his hip height but would have been an automatic fail.

Unknown to the crowd, K-Force learned how to use his ability to feel all kinetic energy around him. This allowed him to react appropriately to anything that entered a minimum of three meters around him. K-Force could sense the size, shape, and speed at almost a third-party point of view, meaning he could effectively dodge anything thrown at him once they entered his domain of three meters. After sliding under a torrent of flame with nary a singed hair, he smoothly rose to his feet then quickly walked to the next area. K-Force did all this at the same time as those with super agility and reflexes or those with the lowest settings. This surprised many since his form spoke more power than grace. The second area was not much trouble as the first room, since he was able to flip and tumble across the room as if he were in Cirque du Soleil on the Las Vegas Strip. The only trouble he had was a sneaky second whirling giant blade. Its time was slightly off from the surrounding traps which would trick most people's timing and snag a strike on the would-be protégés. But to the surprise of everyone, it looked like he stepped on the second blade after jumping over the first one and used it as a platform to flip to the end of the second field.

The crowd was cheering wildly because they thought Samson was more of a bruiser and power type. The commentators were also blown away and tried to make up for the lackluster intro.

"Amazing, people, K-Force proved that he is a force to be reckoned with. Though his background seems sparse given that he was brought here by recommendation by Sunna, of all people," the first commentator stated.

"Oooh—is this the living Sun Heroine? Quite a bit of backing, but how did she find him?" asked the second commentator.

"Regardless, Sunna is still an Omega-level hero and if she sees promise from this young man, then we better watch out," replied the head commentator.

"Do not get too excited. He still has to go through the third area, and that has taken out more three-fourths of our contestants," countered the second commentator.

As K-Force walked in the third room, he finally saw why so many of his peers were caught off guard and blasted to hell. Inside there was enough lighting to see, but there were so many shadows that the enemy assault team could hit you from anywhere and they would lay paint bomb traps that took place of frag variety. And just like the second room, there were visible traps everywhere, though only one-fourth of what the other room had. While the attackers needed room to move around and fire at their target, this room was the most difficult; unlike the other areas, players could not stop, because upon doing so, they would be shot to hell. Therefore, K-Force had to keep moving or else.

Again, with his kinetic sensing abilities K-Force easily moved around the gunfire and the hidden shooters. He also remembered how his father told them to always underplay how truly strong he was, because this made enemies underestimate him, and this gave him room to fight back.

As K-Force dodged around, he allowed himself to be grazed by gunfire and tagged by a shot from behind. But only his shoulder was hit, so the points deducted were minimum at best. By the time he made it out, the crowd watching the whole event cheered loudly at the young man's performance. They saw him take the challenge head-on with no visible powers. The crowd watched a woman freeze everything in place and a man shrink so small that he could calmly run and walk through it. K-Force made his mark before the viewing audience and became noticed by a lot of scouts.

In the next ten minutes he showed what else he could do when he went to the deadlift area, which was now repaired. While he did not reach the max, he did top out at two hundred-ninety tons, which was more than he had ever reached. Again K-Force held back since he knew that he would keep everyone guessing, as it were. And he matched the top repetition bench press challenge, which made the scouts hunger for him more. He showed everyone that he had strength and a high level of agility. This irritated Bianca a bit because he was placed higher on the scouting chart than her.

"Great. First Prime Time, now you—I was supposed to take the combine by storm," Bianca pouted, but her eyes betrayed her.

"Wait, you scored lower than Prime Time? He got blasted more than you by quite a margin. You maneuvered like an SUV," K-Force teased.

"Hey," Azougue retorted mildly offended.

"But that means he moved like a literal tank," K-Force said, still not liking the results.

"Officials say since he is so invulnerable that the deductive points don't count as much." Azougue was repeating what they told her.

"If that's the case why not take the deductive points from your score as well? You are just as, if not even more, invulnerable as he is. You were measured taking a force equivalent of a nuclear bomb and moved on as if it were nothing," K-Force complained.

"Prime Time's abilities are proven, while my stats are not as verified," Azougue replied, not believing that for a minute.

"Meaning Prime Time is the media darling they hype up, and you beating him would be problematic since it would knock him out of the top five," K-Force said; he knew where this was going.

"At least it is not because I'm a woman," Azougue griped.

"We're Meta-humans. Superpowers negate any and all gender advantage men have. Look at the Omega-class Heroes. Last time I checked well over half were women," K-Force indicated.

"True. Does that mean you're the weaker sex?" Azougue joked.

"If that means I never have to buy a drink at a bar or pay for dinner again, I'm all for it," K-Force jested along with her.

"Oh c'mon you don't believe that, do you?" Azougue tried to retort his statement.

"Of the three boyfriends you had, how many gifts did you buy for them, and how many did they buy for you?" K-Force asked in a challenge.

Azougue at first wanted to retort but thought about it, then just shrugged and simply said, "Don't hate the player—hate the game."

They stayed behind to watch the other contestants, but few made an impression except for one gadget head. "Gadget head" was slang for a hero or villain who used gadgets such as tech suits or a variety of tools to help overcome challenges. But for them to be accepted, they must pass several minimum tests to be considered Heroes. To Samson, they were essential to any good hero team because without them it was a bunch of meatheads without a brain to guide more effectively. Not to say that super-powered Meta-humans could not lead a team, but it is better to have someone with ideas around to help think outside the box, when pure force cannot overcome it. There was one that was yelling at an official because he failed to pass the obstacle with an eighty-five percent score or higher, which was bare minimum for any gadget head.

"This is bull. I have to wait three full years to try again because I was off by five points," said a man by the name of Sleuth Hound. He was an example of a wannabe. Not because his costume was ridiculous; a lot of hopefuls could not afford top quality uniforms. Nor was it because he had no powers. Some of the best Heroes were men and women who pushed the limits of the normal human body and intellect. It was because he was a self-entitled prick that believed he should be handed everything, because he thought he was special. Occasionally, someone from a large town or small city saves the day a few times and thinks that he or she is the next big thing, only to find out that they are average at best. One of two things happen—they are humbled and learn from it, or they act like the system was against them in some way. Sadly, this was the latter category.

Eleet tried to calm the guy down—after all, everyone wanted a chance to be in the big show. But Sleuth Hound was going about it all in the wrong way. Eleet's costume was a mixed electric green suit top with a black stylized circle and the spread wings of a hawk in the center. He was of the few fully armored heroes from head to toe, not because he was not a superhuman, but because he was very cautious and thought ahead. Eleet was the perfect all-rounder balance. He was like the Delta Meta-human soldiers, but pushed all the way up to Beta levels, and all those physical skills together meant that he was high-level Beta or low-level Alpha.

"Calm down, Sleuth. There is always next year, or if you do well enough in the other areas people will forget those five points and pick you anyway." Eleet tried to calm the kid down.

"Don't give me that. YOU superpowered Metas have it easy compared to us who have to scrap for everything we need," said Sleuth Hound and smacked the man's hand away from him. "This test is biased against those without powers."

"No, it's not. Everyone has to take the same test. Even some of the powerhouses flunked with higher restrictions," said Eleet, pointing out how it was actually more fair than Sleuth Hound credited it for.

"Non-powered Heroes such as I have to score eighty-five or better or we won't get any fieldwork or try better next year," Sleuth Hound accused. "What this is, is privilege, whether you are an active part of it or not."

"No, it is a little boy who doesn't like the fact that he is not getting what he wants," said an aged voice from behind the complaining hero wannabe.

"Who are you to judge me? You're just another Meta like him," Sleuth Hound dismissed.

"No, I'm not, kid. I'm one of the few who went through the same test as you, but I had to score a ninety overall." The age-old voice belonged to a man who appeared to be in his late fifties or early sixties. He had a strong resemblance to an old television detective with a worn but well-cared for jacket, white dress shirt, and a black tie. He also wore dark beige dress pants and brown dress shoes. He also had messy gray hair with a few strips of brown and aged, strong, Italian features. He had no powers to speak of, but he had almost innate ability to know when someone had lied, with an analytical mind that could pull apart any false testimony with logic, common sense and forensics to back it up.

"When I was your age, I didn't have half the materials and ability to make equipment to fight crime like you do now," Detective Russo explained how things were actually better.

"True, tell what it was like to read by candlelight and have witch burnings as entertainment," Sleuth Hound jeered at the old veteran detective.

"Not as much fun as your grandmother was when your grandpappy couldn't get it up," Russo said calmly, as he lit his cigar.

"That is." Sleuth started to say before he got cut off.

"I'm going to tell you something your parents should have a long time ago. You don't always win or get what you want. Things will not go your way in life and you need to accept that fact and move on. You missed qualifications by five points. Big deal—you can try again next time" Detective Russo wasn't in the mood for the whining little snowflake.

"Sponsors don't pay attention to second time losers," Sleuth Hound declared.

"And that is your main problem—you care about contracts and sponsors, not what is going to keep you alive, despite how the media portrays it." Russo gestured his hands around the alethic field set up. "This is not a professional sport. We are celebrity soldiers. We fight to protect the public and have a high casualty rating."

"Like whatever Boomer." Sleuth Hound refused to acknowledge the old hero.

"Thank you. I'll take that as a victory," Detective Russo said as he turned to leave. He didn't feel like wasting his breath.

"What? You didn't win," Sleuth Hound protested.

"When you use a statement that ignores everything someone says because they are part of a certain demographic you disagree with— this means you are either afraid of what they have to say, or you cannot handle the truth," Russo again stated calmly because he knew he had the high ground.

Sleuth Hound was getting angry but instead he walked away from the older man, not wanting to justify his statement by responding. He swore he would show them that the combine was useless. As Sleuth Hound left, K-Force just shook his head, thinking that this guy either had very little experience in failure, or was the type to see his failure as other people's faults and not his own. Azougue just mumbled out what K-Force was thinking. "Casualty within two years I predict."

"That is if someone is dumb enough to pick him," K-Force agreed.

"They will. I know Sleuth Hound—he already has a connection with some people in the news networks, and he'll probably get a truckload of publicity," Azougue pointed out.

"And get tossed in a meat grinder without proper training." Samson sent out a silent prayer that the young hero didn't get himself killed because of his pride.

Chapter 2
Hard Skill vs. Superb Talent

As the combine went on, Azougue showed off more of her powers which surprised even Samson. When Azougue first started flying, it wasn't anything impressive. She could only float in the beginning, as reducing one's density only makes you lighter than air - not fly. Azougue learned to use mass fields to push and pull her in different directions. This allowed her to move more than sixty miles per hour. Samson was worried that she was going to embarrass herself in the aerial competition. First, participants had to complete ten laps around the stadium above sixty feet from the ground and under a forty-second time limit. Next would be a slalom run with a constant average speed of ninety miles per hour. Samson's expectations were blown away as Azougue floated up and was able to push and pull her body faster than he ever saw before. By putting waypoints around the course, she was able to zip from one place to another. The way Azougue flew was how a Gauss rifle operates. Instead of magnets she used mass fields, and each time she reached a point, she would be fired along the path she set. This in turn allowed her to keep up with the top five fliers. The slalom was handled as easily as the first test. Azougue's placement of waypoints around the course allowed her to zip through at a higher speed than other competitors. This kind of ingenuity was actually wanted by most scouts since it meant their prospect was not predictable or simple. Azougue made a name for herself by being able to outperform most of the natural fliers.

K-Force surprised Azougue as well since she knew for a fact that he could not fly. Jump high, sure, but flying was out of the question. Then Azougue saw her childhood friend unexpectedly enter the Aerial Competition as well. She saw the golden-yellow uniformed man jump up and stay mid-air, but instead of hovering or floating, K-Force was hopping on one foot which appeared to keep him stable. He began to stride along the fliers' route. Air-walking, as it would later be called, had been theorized about but

- 47 -

had never been done before. Despite barely making the top ten fliers' speed, he proved that he was more maneuverable in air. The slalom was even easier for him since his style of flight was made for quick turns. While his display of skill was impressive, Azougue wouldn't be denied as the far better flier. The last aerial event was called Dogfight, though everyone called it 'Keep Away.' There would be floating mines and drones chasing contestants inside the arena, which was a little over double the size of a football field. The object was to avoid being hit or tagged during a three-minute phase. The level of difficulty increased every thirty seconds, which meant very few made it past the two-minute mark.

Azougue proved once more that she was a very good flier and should be considered one of the best among the rookies. The first thirty seconds she had three plane-like drones chasing her with taser-like rounds which the perspective heroes had to dodge, or if they were hit three times they would be out. And the time they lasted was the time recorded. The next thirty seconds added floating mines around the arena, and if any flier was hit by one of these mines, the timer would stop. The following thirty seconds, they added three more drones, and the mines circle area was almost in an orbit. At the two-minute mark is where even great fliers failed.

The drones were replaced with faster ones, which were commanded by an individual Virtual Intelligence Program that would chase said fliers in a more intelligent manner. Dodging six fighter-manned drones while trying to avoid mines is usually too much for most inexperienced heroes to keep up with. The last thirty seconds was when all the stops were taken out, with seven manned drones and heat-seeking mines which would chase after you and blow up if someone got too close. Despite K-Force's ability to quickly dash around in the air at a fast speed, the drones coordinated him to fly too close to a mine, which meant his time was a respectable two minutes and twenty seconds. This was a great time, but that was nothing compared to Azougue whose mass fields allowed her to move around faster and in a more unpredictable path than those of K-Force. In the fifteen-year history of the event, Azougue joined the group of only four other people who had achieved the full three minutes. Azougue was so excited that she dropped her tomboy image and momentarily took on the excitement of a teen girl who had just received her first car.

This event should have been Azougue's time to shine because Prime Time could not fly; he could only jump great distances. They were measured from outside the stadium in a designated field where potential prospects could unleash their power without massive collateral damage. Prime Time's full-powered jump created a hole four meters deep and about nine meters in diameter. He was just shy of 9.8 kilometers, which was his personal best. This meant he was well in the stratosphere, as far as height was concerned. Despite the fact that Prime Time could not actually fly, the committee gave him more points to increase his overall score. At this point, anyone could see that this guy already had a sponsor, and the sponsors were pushing him to the forefront. They were going to make sure their new star was marketable enough to bring in all that money.

"Twenty says he goes to Los Angeles despite being the Top Prospect," Azougue commented.

"You're on, I still say New York. They have as much money as L.A. and they need him more," K-Force said agreeing to the bet.

Unknown to them, a group of other prospects were listening in on them. It should not be a surprise that they were both top prospects from the day prior, and they showed how skilled they were in the aerial competition as well.

"Why do you think that he would go there? Shouldn't he go to the most needed area?" a curious onlooking prospect asked.

Instead of ignoring the question, Azougue felt compelled to answer.

"While Top Prospects are supposed to go where they are most needed, this is like any sports combine. They go where they will shell out the most money," Azougue paused to sip the sponsor-approved sports drink. "If things were fair, he would go to the Midwest region where the most Meta-human crime is situated or northeast where there is the most crime-ridden city on earth."

"Though Fringe hasn't been seen for over six months, so that might change," K-Force added his two cents. The more dangerous the villains, the higher the Meta-level crime rate. And as dangerous and demented as Fringe was, he raised it by fifteen percent alone, whenever he escaped psychiatric care.

"True, but it will be a while before census will factor that in, since there is a chance he might show up like always," Azougue replied matter-of-factly. "Anyway, the Pacific region, more specifically California or North Atlantic aka New York almost always get the flashiest prospects."

"Because they have the most money and highest population overall," K-Force added in.

"Are you telling them, or am I?" Azougue gave her friend the stink eye.

K-Force waved his hands, placating her and told her to continue.

"Like he said, money and population play a big part in these drafts. Not to mention he went to Bellwether Academy—you know, the Ivy League prep schools for gifted individuals like us and over eighty percent have been sent to those two cities," Azougue finished her statement.

"Preppies always go to California or the New York and New England areas. It is their natural habitat," one gruff participant said in disgust.

"Where are you guys from?" Azougue asked.

"We are from non-specialized schools and had to learn by ourselves with help from our folks, friends, and local heroes— those who saw some promise in us," a more calm candidate said.

"That's good. Hopefully you'll knock down those kids for their own good," said K-Force, who loved seeing those stuck-ups get a shocked look on their face after losing to a supposed inferior opponent. It is also a needed lesson about never underestimating your opponent.

K-Force knew about this little issue in the Meta community that had been dividing them up. One division was with pure bloods and legacy versus the newcomers and commoners. There were heroes whose Meta-human bloodlines went back centuries when Heroes were Champions of Nations—or those who were trained by the elite Heroes who pass their name and title to the next generation. Then there were those families whose powers skip generations; they were not considered the elite by the old families who were the first to their name and rise to become symbolic Metas.

K-Force felt that his family used to be non-elite family. While his mother used to be a queen, they were not actual royalty in the Meta-human community. Their nobility meant nothing except maybe something interesting for parties—and the quickest way to become an 'elite' was having an Omega-level family member or have a family of high-level Meta-humans. Shaking off the introspection, he decided the best way to focus for the next competition was listening to music on his noise-canceling headphones. K-Force preferred his old headphones, but sponsors sent him ones from a rap mogul, so that he would not bring a non-sponsored brand.

Lifting the overpriced headset, K-Force began to realize that this wasn't new. Ever since the most powerful sports drink began sponsoring this event, it seemed that corporations had taken more and more control over it, including command of who would get the spotlight and who would be forgotten, despite being better skilled or more powerful.

As K-Force zoned out, he didn't expect much until he saw a genius in a super suit, for lack of a better term, reach the top ten fliers list. This was QuickTime, who had probably pissed off a few empowered individuals.

The next event was 'Projectiles' which was a mixture of skeet and movable drone target range. Because Azougue didn't have any range attacks except sending shock waves, she couldn't participate. K-Force, on the other hand, could concentrate his kinetic energy into beam-like energy, which allowed him to sniper targets from afar, while on the move. His score was not perfect—but it was above average. Prime Time tried to show off but almost destroyed parts of the unshielded stadium, since his eye beams were not as accurate as they should have been. The judges actually penalized him, since anyone could see that such ability would be dangerous to the public if it were used in a combat situation; though the media again ignored it and said the officials were overreacting. Sadly, the score hurt him more than if he had avoided the competition.

While there were other candidates, QuickTime caught K-Force's attention. QuickTime, who despite having no powers to speak of, was one of the super geniuses who had built a suit to overcome the deficit. His costume looked almost skintight, except for areas where he obviously put extra padding for protecting his vitals. QuickTime was also prepared with a utility belt of various gadgets and wings that helped him fly or glide. They also reminded K-Force of a flying squirrel. What caught his attention was the fact that he was being slept on, despite being one the better participants. QuickTime's suit allowed him to lift one hundred and twenty tons and perform forty-five reps—in the obstacle course he scored the best time outside of a super speedster. He seemed to slip and move just like a squirrel around all the obstacles and was untouched in all three stages. At the end result, he was second place in the agility competition, and twelfth place overall, but somehow he still didn't get any mention. It was not because he was a brainy-type hero. There was Mithril, a woman with a mechanized power suit that was being cheered as one of the most premiered women at this competition, but again she was from one of the prep schools.

However, the one event that made it impossible for him to be ignored was when he took over the Projectiles competition. QuickTime used projectiles in the shape of throwing daggers that had various effects such as explosion and taser. And with his suit he could throw them at machine gun-like speed. The scary part was the fact that he never missed once. QuickTime was able to hit near center on every shot, whether stationary target from up close or mobile target from afar. He never stopped to take aim like many others, and he could do this on the run, which added a whole level of expertise to his skills. The end result was that he took first place over everyone which made no amount of handwaving his accomplishments seem reasonable, though a few anchors tried to downplay him.

To K-Force, this was a good sign of what is most needed in any hero team. Therefore, if this guy aced the investigation and strategic test the next day, then he would be the perfect commander. While the majority of people think of the most powerful member as the one with charisma, in truth they are the faces. Each team needs a general who can make the right calls and direct the forces more effectively. They are the linchpins in making a good team into a great one. While many know this, they ignore it for the flash of the more powerful Heroes.

Definitely have to watch out for this guy. If he pans out, he might be a true top pick in this combine—not the overhyped muscled head they are trying to shove down the nation's throat, K-Force thought.

With the Projectile competition over and done with, the competitors were released for the day. Though most would walk about town hoping to drum up fans or paparazzi, K-Force preferred to change back to his civilian identity and go about peacefully. Azougue had other ideas; she wanted to bring up her clout amongst the press, and having K-Force along would help with that. K-Force refused because he wanted to go back to being Samson again, just so he could go out in peace. Mostly all the press that day was about how great some preppie was and how did it feel to compete against them, etc. As far as he was concerned, he would not be used to pump the media darlings when they had no interest in him.

Azougue told him he was exaggerating and begged him to suck it up. K-Force questioned what that had to do with him, but she just gave him a look that said not to argue about it and just do it. He agreed on the condition that they would eat in their normal identities so they could have dinner in peace.

After two hours of shopping and window-shopping, K-Force was unlike most guys and actually in a good mood. Just like he thought the press was only interested in their opinion on the top picks, and not their actual selves. Every time Azougue tried to promote herself or give her true thoughts, she was cut off or forgotten. On the plus side, Azougue and K-Force took a few fan photos, though he remembered to always use the hover hand over every female fan that wanted to take a picture with him.

The press tried to do the same thing with him, but K-Force got back at them by saying Mithril was better than Prime Time and they couldn't dismiss his claim. This was because both were being promoted. This was a good debate for the anchors. The press tried to gather more information from him and he laid it out.

"Prime Time is powerful but that's the only advantage he has. He has very little control and finesse, and he will most likely get someone killed if he does not stop showboating. Mithril, while not as powerful, has better control, higher skill, and is a lot more versatile," K-Force stated in a matter-of-fact way, before going in for the killer. "If I had to choose, I would feel safer with Mithril as my hero."

This comment made the reporters happy. They would most likely skew his words in a way to make drama for him and get ratings. But K-Force, at this point, refused to take any words back and decided to stick to his opinion. When Samson and Bianca were eating in civilian attire, most of the social media and regular media were showing his comment out of context. The comments were what one might expect, though he surprisingly received a lot of support.

Samson just shrugged and dug into a nice veal and eggplant parmigiana, which was very good.

"The way they mince the meat and pair it with the eggplant—very well made," Samson commented.

"Aren't you worried about your image? They are blasting your face all over the Internet," Bianca fretted, as she couldn't look away from her phone because she was worried about every social media reaction to his comment.

"Why should I care?" Samson had long since learned that trying to get the media to like you was almost never worth it.

"The media is going to bring you down, despite having some of the best scoring throughout the past two days," Bianca observed.

"And that's a bad thing," Samson stated calmly as he continued to eat.

"Can't you take this seriously," Bianca complained.

"I am," reluctantly Samson put his food down, so he could talk seriously with her. "Despite what people say, we are in a Draft pick. The fact you are so worried about your positioning proves that."

"And just like the Draft, the top picks are always put in the worst situations. With the exception of a few, the top three in any sport are always in hell where they are expected to do the impossible or have their talents wasted. No, the Meathead is going to NYC or LA. Me? I will be sent somewhere where I matter and work for a living. Southern California was over-saturated as hell, to put it bluntly. There is crime, sure, but they will be given to their favorites which means to stay you have to showboat enough to get noticed. If you don't, you will be used for nothing more than a trade tool for the next hot thing. In the meantime, just smile for the camera and wave." Samson drank to give Bianca some time to think about what he said.

"Getting paid a big fat contract is all some people want. Me? I want to make a difference," Samson explained.

"Okay I get it, but doesn't this hurt your image even after the combine?" Bianca not understanding his confidence.

"Not really. I got Incognito membership which protects me from most false narratives," Samson stated calmly.

"What is that?" said Bianca curious at his statement.

"Simply put, my folks pay monthly for protection from the press for me and my family. In which they will show full video of every incident that the media blows out of proportion and give actual truth of incidents. On 'In Depth Look', their personal news channel, if it is a slow news day," Samson started to get back to his meal until a notification noise from his phone got his attention. He looked down and grinned.

"Speak of the devil, it is going to be on *In Depth Look* tonight, which means I will get my side of the story shown," Samson grinned and went back to eating.

"You sure people will listen?" said Bianca, wondering if the service really helped.

"*In Depth Look* has over five hundred million views worldwide on average, and they are trusted and verified. I'm good," Samson tried to take another bite before he was interrupted.

"Samson?"

At this point Samson was getting annoyed. With massive metabolism, came the benefits of never gaining weight and a near perfect physique. The downside was he had to eat big portions from time to time or feel malnourished. This also meant Meta-humans hated having their meals interrupted.

"Yes," Samson said with a bit of restraint in his voice.

"How much for the Incognito Press protection?" said Bianca, very interested in the service.

Samson calmed down "Just the press—about eighty bucks a month. For the full package, it is going to set you back two-fifty."

Bianca had a contemplating look on her face before she began to eat as well.

The next day, the whole video was put out into the media, which forced the news anchors to place a more fair assessment on K-Force's opinion. And he got a lot more praise from Mithril fans, saying that he believed that she would make the better hero. This, on the other hand, gave birth to a rivalry between him and Prime Time. The media tried to make it seem they were equally matched, but in truth, with the exception of pure strength, K-Force had beaten him in every event.

Even in the third day of trials, it was shown that K-Force was in fact smarter than the average high-powered Meta. This trial was about investigation, adaptability, and decision making. Azougue did poorly in the investigation challenge, as she feared. Every year it was a mystery where each contestant must track and find clues to the murderer or thief of a certain crime. There were two different challenges; if you don't know who the culprit is, you must figure it out with a little help from the crime database. You have an hour to pinpoint the culprit. The other more difficult test was tracking said culprit. Just because you know who he is, doesn't mean you get to him in time to save the day.

These tests were televised since it was considered more the game show portion of the combine. They were more like logic-based puzzles, though crimes were placed for each contestant. They gave twenty possible choices to pick from, and players would get a chance to narrow it down by process of elimination. But if you chose the wrong culprit, or remove the right one, you fail. Azougue did poorly on this part; she could barely narrow it down to nine before she removed the culprit, thinking he was another false lead. The second half of the test, she improved by listening to clues and suggestions from the police. She found it easier to narrow the culprit to a section of the city.

Samson did better because his father was not only the Master of Merging Tech and Mystical but also the backup investigator on his own fed team, Storm Breakers. Hakeem drilled his children about how to do basic investigation and how to track someone down. Aisha was the better hunter than both her brothers—however K-Force did learn enough to determine the culprit after eliminating the three suspects. And he was able to figure out exactly where the culprit was hiding, with five minutes to spare. Many others failed, while others did circles around his score. Frigid and QuickTime solved the investigation in less than three minutes, and surprisingly Nega Titan completed it in five minutes. Prime Time was highly suspect, to say the least. First, he somehow found out the culprit after one minute, which was faster than most geniuses, but he couldn't for the life of him find the culprit's lair and failed the second half.

The next test was adaptability; it was a test meant to challenge participants by either restricting abilities or force through any perceived weakness. This test could be skipped, but this would draw a penalty. K-Force knew he was being paranoid, but he refused to showcase something that might reveal a weakness, or make his future opponents more cautious in their plans of attack. He knew this would count against him, but he figured that he would have to just make the top three of combat tournament, or it would not matter.

Azougue was so confident that she was immune to anything except a stronger force, which she was sure didn't exist outside the Omegas and a few Alphas. And she was confident that she could handle everything that was going to be thrown at her. Also, Azougue needed to bring up her overall bad investigation score.

Adaption tests would take place in the Tactical Field Room, also known as the Hazard Room. It was an advanced holographic technology and a tactical computer matrix. The Hazard Room could create immersive, interactive, artificial environments, simulating various situations, and only a few facilities in the US had these available outside of the military and pro Meta-human teams. These were as recent as the nineties, and created by one super genius Sooraj Bhatta, a second-generation Indian immigrant who was at the time one of the wealthiest inventors in the world. Every nation was clamoring for one of their own to train their Heroes.

The Virtual Intelligence Matrix made an actual difficult mission for Azougue. It gave her a mission to find and save three victims from a burning building. It seemed the VI knew that Azougue's skill was not mass manipulation, and unless she was a skilled user of it, it would be nearly impossible for her to pass this challenge. After all she couldn't become too heavy or she might fall through the floor. Or she could bash through the walls, and the whole building would come down on top of her head and kill the victims. So, this was going to require more finesse than what she had shown throughout the competition. Too bad for them that Azougue may not be the most graceful Heroine out there, but she had great control over her powers.

Azougue hardened her upper torso to punch the front door, which unleashed a torrent of flames upon her body. This did nothing to damage her skin, which was thick enough to ignore the searing heat. She quickly ran up the stairs, which would normally be a bad idea, if not for the fact that her body weight was somehow less than ten pounds of pressure with each step. It was the secret to her success in this event— perfect weight displacement. Azougue is a big fan of Fantasy where she got the idea from elves' natural ability to walk on top of snow. She learned from one nerd online that elves had a way to spread out their weight so evenly that it barely made a footprint. With this, she would go up and visit relatives in Ohio whenever winter hit so she could practice this ability.

It was difficult at first, but soon she could run on top of snow-like sand on the beach. The biggest test was when she saved her cousin from freezing to death after falling into a frozen pond. With perfect weight displacement, she was able to pull them out while simultaneously keeping both their weights as low as possible. This was something she did through adrenaline and survival instinct, which gave credence to the body and instincts sometimes knowing better what to do in a situation than your conscience mind. To practice the feat safely, she would go to the beach with family and bring driftwood barely able to float a small child. Then she would practice by trying to stand on it without sinking.

The results of her training showed itself. Azougue searched throughout the building to find her victims and bring them out to the holographic firemen. Then, for the last victim, who was a small child hidden in a closet on the fifth floor, she jumped out of the window and floated quickly down to the firefighters to get the child some help. This amazed many that she could be so resourceful and had such great control with her power. And for the first time, all in the combine came to witness how she stayed in first place, considering how high the difficulty rating was and how smoothly she completed the task.

There were two other impressive shows throughout the event. Frigid was placed in a fight against Format in the middle of the Gobi Desert during the summer. Meanwhile, QuickTime was not allowed to use any gadgets against Curb Stomp. Each situation was made to test them at perceived weakness. Frigid was put in an environment where she would have little moisture in the air and a harder time in the desert heat against someone whose power was unaffected by the heat. Format was a super genius turned evil, who was also a lazy fool who preferred to steal others' hard work to further his purposes. This was all done to keep up with his rival, Nathan Sparks, also known as the Chrome Champion.

His goal was to always take Nathan's idea and make better versions of it. The problem is he liked to cut corners, or get too ambitious, which led to failures. His battle armor was closer to a small mech suit. It stood ten feet tall and had digitigrades legs, or backward knees. Its purple shell was a special metal alloy which could take more damage than most of Chrome Champion armors. One arm was a cannon, that had a Gatling gun function and the other held a large spike Warhammer.

At first it seemed completely unfair since he held all the advantages until a shocking surprise appeared. Frigid's pale skin turned a deep blue color, and she charged forth, despite being in a ruin desert town where she could duck for cover. She dodged most of Format's barrage of high-speed bullets and RPG salvo, though she did get nicked by the hammer, which sent her spinning. All the while she slapped the mech suit repeatedly, though it seemed pointless, until the Mech started slowing down, and soon it came to a complete stop. The armor was covered in a frosty layer of ice, despite Frigid not having any use of her more famous big moves.

It didn't take K-Force long to figure out what she did. Frigid concentrated all of her cold energy to harden and enforce her body athletically enough to get in close and unleash said cold energy to the machine directly. Despite what comics say, most scientists have yet to figure out a way around extreme cold and extreme heat, so they still have to be cautious.

"I'm from the southwestern region of the US. This is just July back home," Frigid stated as she clasped her hands together and slammed them into the machine, which cracked open. This sent the viewers in the stands and on television cheering as she stood triumphant over her fallen foe.

The next was QuickTime who K-Force felt was given an unfair disadvantage, since the system wanted him to fight Curb Stomp. Curb Stomp was human, but made of white marble and invulnerable to most things outside of plasma and high energy weapons. And QuickTime had to win without using any gadgets directly against the brute, which seemed impossible. QuickTime dodged the big man's blows and tried to fight back, but the fact was his suit wasn't powerful enough to damage the bleached stone monster. The only saving grace was the fact that they were at a beach site. Curb Stomp wasn't an idiot, as many people made him out to be. Genius he was not, but he was careful enough to stay away from the ocean. So, QuickTime would move around and hide, it seemed. Though many were wondering why he went back to a single spot on the beach and used his gadgets. This process took about five minutes while he would jump and dodge and around the beach, throwing small boulders to keep the guy's attention.

QuickTime danced around and annoyed the brute without allowing the walking white wall to land a blow on him. Because despite what television and comics show you, if someone doesn't have the resistance to withstand a blow from a Meta with great power, there are only two outcomes—broken and twisted bodies or pulped meat. While Heroes are restricted by it so they can apprehend said criminal, most villains don't care about self-control and just try to crush everything. Then to the surprise of all, QuickTime threw some sand into the eyes of Curb Stomp. The stone-like villain, in the rage of being blinded, was lured to fall into a recently made sink hole, far too deep for him. Then to add injury to insult, QuickTime with his gadgets dug a trench towards the shore which brought on a rush of water which made the brute sink deeper while the water quickly rose. Since Curb Stomp would have drowned, QuickTime won the fight.

Again, people cheered at the display of wits and ingenuity, though K-Force was sure that QuickTime wasn't supposed to win, because there were some BS penalties against QuickTime, such as property damage and excessive use of force. QuickTime still impressed everybody with his fast thinking on how to beat someone with whom he had a clear disadvantage.

Prime Time was also challenged, though it was all in his comfort zone. He was to go against Purge, a four-arm villain who was considered one of the strongest brute force Meta-humans. The only reason he was considered an Alpha was because his powers weren't more diverse than his massive amount of strength and high durability. He was considered one of the most deadly villains out there because he was a big believer of Meta-human superiority. He saw regular humans as inferior beings who should serve at the will of the Metas, who were the new masters of the earth.

Basically *Mein Kampf*, except there was literal Übermensch around the world. It would be better if he was the typical all muscle and no brain, but the man was charismatic and had so-called data that proved that humanity would be better under Meta control. His rhetoric grabbed three types of people— the young and foolish, disenfranchised, or those who wanted power and control above all else. Add all that up, and the fact his brute power matched those in the Omega rank made him a threat to reckon.

Purge seemed like a great challenge at first, but how is power versus power going to test Prime Time to adapt? They made the setting in the middle of the street with a crowd of people fleeing. What happened then was a scripted fight that delighted the rowdy; they would slug it out in the center of the street. Neither moved as punches broke the sound barrier and the force broke glass around them. They even made craters in the ground since the colliding punches created a blast big enough to dig a hole. While Metas bend physics, they also have to abide by them to an extent. So, when a force equal to a train doesn't send you flying, it goes through your legs and into the ground. This was a great spectacle, but just a spectacle. Purge was a smart fighter, and he would grapple more. He would also pull a couple of dirty moves to take Prime Time down. This looked like a great battle, but it was too-tailored for those in the know.

The fight ended with a great finish—Purge was getting dazed and it ended with Prime Time knocking him out of the area, which ended the simulator; though in real life, Purge would have recovered in a few minutes unless one put him down hard.

Then, as a final cherry on top of that performance, Prime Time was searching the stands full of participants, then pointed towards K-Force with a glare, saying that he was next. Instead of backing down, K-Force gave the 'come get some' gesture.

Chapter 3
Brackett Run

JUNE 16: ST. LOUIS, MISSOURI
Sparks Industry Stadium

The fourth day of competition was a day of rest while the committee planned to meet in order to rank the applicants' total score and 'Judges' Choice.' The fifth day was the big day of the Upcoming Heroes Combine. The tournament is where the top thirty-two candidates fight each other until the Final Four. Then on the sixth day, candidates would fight for the ranking of most combat-capable Hero. This event was similar to college football playoffs compacted into forty-eight hours. The standings were posted on the fourth day during a ceremony where the awards for each competition were based on the top three of each competition. It was supposed to be important, but as far as K-Force (aka Samson) and Azougue (aka Bianca) were concerned, it was a day to sleep in. They laid in bed playing on their laptops, talking to friends and family before the award ceremony in full Hero outfits. Since this was the big venue, it was moved to St. Louis.

The standings were announced at 1 PM, while the awards were at 3 PM. Looking at the standings, Bianca was happy that she made ninth place overall, especially since she was independent of prep schools. Despite not doing the adaption competition, Samson was ranked sixteenth place overall because of high ranks in the other competitions. This was good, considering there were over fifty candidates this year, and most "non-preppies" were ranked twenty and below.

The ceremony wasn't all that special except for the awards, which were handed out by the Meta Ball Association President, Eleet, and Detective Russo. Most important were the specific placements in every competition. Azougue placed second in strength, sixth in flight and second in adaption. Everywhere else she placed lower than tenth place. QuickTime had placed second in the agility trials, eighth in flying, first in targeting, tied for second in investigation, and ninth in adaption. Prime Time placed first in strength, eighth in agility (which many participants disagreed with) tenth in flight (which was a stretch), seventh in targeting, third in adaption. K-Force did surprisingly well; overall fourth place in strength, third in agility, seventh in flight, and third in targeting. The Queen was Mithril since she never placed lower than fifth in every competition, except strength, and even then she held ninth place. Mithril also held fourth place in agility, third in flight, and third in targeting. She tied for second place in investigation and tracking, and first place in adaption. Her trial was where the technopath was forced to fight without her power armor using highly advanced sonic beams to defeat her opponent.

This made K-Force grin since it proved that he was right that Mithril was the better Hero, and competition proved it. This seemed to piss off Prime Time, who came in third place overall, and he glared at K-Force like it was his fault that he was not number one. K-Force just shrugged, knowing he had nothing to do with the standings, and he sat back with his awards from being in the top three of certain trials or competitions.

The next day they would be put in a Meta Brawl arena, Sparks Industry Stadium, to be precise. That is where Meta-humans from high-level Gamma to Alpha class would go out and fight in a MMA-style combat where the rules were looser than standard. Mostly because most blows that would cripple a normal person would be recoverable by Meta-humans.

The purpose was to show practical use of one's powers, skills and abilities. Despite it being essential, many super geniuses without a power suit of some type would not be able to enter. The sad fact is that's life. Villains or criminals don't care if a person's powers were not combat-oriented. They would maim or kill when given the choice or do anything to break you. The fact of the matter is no matter how much people howl in lowering the standards on Heroes, this would not make things fairer. It would only increase the body count when all rational contingencies were thrown away for some vague idea of fairness. Hence, the tournament is made for only those who can fight in frontline conditions. And that looked like it was not going to change anytime soon.

Thank God for some small sense of sanity, K-Force thought, as he saw the ceremonies close.

As they went back to their rooms, both he and Azougue dressed down and departed, which was normally difficult, since everyone carried cameras, and people had no concept of privacy, except when their own privacy became violated. So, most Heroes would visit areas that were government-made dead zones, where phones and the Internet simply would not work; these were areas where they could change and quickly escape any and all fanfare. This was ideal for those who did not have private security or sponsorship to protect them. However, this time one persistent middle-aged looking asshole demanded to be let through to expose the "so-called saviors who wore masks." This particular asshole was Jessica Jules Jennings, a blogger who harassed heroes relentlessly unless big corporate, tech giants, or government threatened her to back off.

If there was ever a citizen that Samson would refuse to save, it would be her. She exposed their Meta communities both Hero and citizens, and she was responsible for nine different murders when she exposed the Hero or Heroines families. She allowed villains and criminals easy access to their families. Would she get called on it or arrested? No, "freedom of the press" protected her.

During times like this Samson swore that he would never help a muckraker of the press unless he absolutely had to. As far as he was concerned, they were villains that needed to be arrested and locked away or left for dead when they got in over their heads. This was something they inevitably would encounter, since they seemed to think there were no consequences for them. Getting rid of such dark thoughts, Samson decided to talk to his family via video conference.

"Congrats, son, I'm so proud of you for making it so high in the standings," Aaliyah said proudly.

"You know you could have made top three if you did adaptation. Both you and Bianca have always been taught under such conditions," Hakeem told his son.

"I am too paranoid about having any weakness exposed," Samson replied.

"True, but you could have easily scored high on those tests." Hakeem understood their reasoning but was hoping to rub his son's success in his peers' faces.

"True, but I don't need some rookie killer taking notes about my limits," Samson told his dad.

"You really shouldn't worry about that. There is little chance you will run into those monsters," Aaliyah assured her child.

"Mom, as soon as people learned that Ratel was your daughter, three of your rogue gallery attacked her," Samson pointed out.

"Okay that's true, but it's all right. I beat them all anyway." Tamera aka Ratel tried to dismiss his point.

"You barely beat two, and the witch almost took you out, if not for your teammate saving you," Samson shot back.

Tamera did not respond to his correction, just glared at her baby brother for reminding her of her first big loss. And it was true

Michelle, or Lady Coyote, the chosen champion of the great trickster spirit, saved her. Lady Coyote had only recently recovered from her takedown by Chernobyl.

"Fair enough, but do you think you can keep quiet that you are related to us? You know as well as I do that the press will figure it out." Tamera was a firm believer of ripping the band-aid off approach to certain things.

"I know. I plan to tell them after I get picked. This way my standings won't be the top three picks, so to speak," Samson said.

"Wait, why not? Doesn't everyone want number one," Tamera asked, confused.

"Rarely being number one in the draft is a good thing. The top three are more than likely put in the worst teams with no plans or clue. They just end up ruining the athlete, while those who are fourth place or less have a better chance of making a championship because they have a better plan than to just get best player," Samson explained his reasoning.

"That is true, but that's sports, not Heroes," Hakeem retorted, not seeing the point.

"No dear, he is right. Samson you are trying to avoid the Pacific region, aren't you," Aaliyah asked, knowing the answer.

Impressed at his mother figuring it out, Samson said, "Good guess."

"Not much of a guess. You complained about how congested and scripted the Pacific region is. I know you're more like me and your sister. You hate to be sitting on the sidelines while you can help people, but instead you are told to let the more popular and senior Hero takes care of it," Aaliyah said.

"Oh God, you're right. And with your power they will send you to California, which is the worst environment for growth, unless you have the right backer," Tamera agreed.

"To say they are congested is ridiculous. It has excess of Heroes that they don't really need, and they keep trying to bring more in, like crime has grown more rampant. Though anyone will tell you North Central and the Northeast is where the crime rate is highest in the US," Hakeem added.

"Therefore, my need to drop my draft position. I'm more likely to be moved somewhere I will be needed. Instead of being put on the pine bench and only let out to make others look good," Samson finished his reasoning.

"Clever, very clever," Hakeem commented.

"Of course, he takes after me. However, Samson, are you sure it is a good idea to hold back so much?" Aaliyah asked.

"The less people know about me and what I'm fully capable of, the better," Samson said in finality.

"Alright, fine—we won't get on it anymore, but be sure that this is what you want," Aaliyah said.

After catching up with the rest of them, his sister asked him a very important question.

"Are you going to take a dive? Because if you are, I'd like to place a bet," Tamera asked.

"Tamera?"

"What? If he is going to intentionally lower his skills, I don't see why I shouldn't make money off of it," Tamera said. She didn't see the problem of earning some extra cash.

"No, I was going to give my best. Bianca won't forgive me if I took a dive before we had a chance to fight each other," Samson said as he rolled his eyes at his sister's antics.

"Ha! She'd probably sit on you again if you did that," Tamera said, knowing Bianca.

"Oh God, I remember when you used to rough house all the time when you were little. You two were so innocent—what happened," their mother lamented.

"Hormones and high school," Samson remarked.

"Definitely high school," Tamera said in agreement.

"Oh, hush you two." Aaliyah chided two of her children.

The next day bracket was drawn up and the fights were expected to be done around seven or eight o'clock. Why? Mostly because fights in real life don't last that long, and these were MMA-ruled fights—quick, efficient, and sometimes brutal. This was the catch 22 situation of being a Meta. What would take an average man days to heal, would only take about an hour for a Meta, with little lasting effects. This also meant less concern about health and welfare.

The Sparks Industry Stadium was one of the six large Brawl arenas in the US. They were smaller ones but this was meant for world level, top-class Brawl fighters. There was a reinforced tiled marble floor-like stage strong enough to be carpet-bombed and not get a crack. The stage was oval-shaped and sized twenty-eight by fifteen meters, big enough for a basketball court. There was a four and one-half meter pit where one could ring out if their opponent was knocked into it. The arena also had a force field that kept all powers locked inside. It was tested to withstand low Omega-level forces, so it would be safe for an audience to observe the battles. Hence, this is where the new up and comers were going to fight it out and jump higher into the standings.

K-Force was one of the first matches in the tournament, which suited him just fine. He had a game plan that would work against anyone except Frigid, Mithril, and Azougue. This was not because they were women; as he stated before, superpowers were the true equalizer. The civil rights and women's rights movements in the US were speculated to happen faster mostly because several of the US top Metas were black and women. No amount of threats would work against people who could literally wipe out towns.

No, Mithril and Frigid were better at zone fighting than him. K-Force's skills were more versatile than most, and his best skills were up close and personal. But this was just a long game plan where he could take a tough opponent by surprise from a full-frontal assault instead of a keep away game.

This was also why Azougue wouldn't be affected by it, mostly because they trained with each other and were both familiar with how the other fought. There were a few secret skills and techniques they had never shown each other, but his childhood friend knew what he was capable of.

K-Force's first opponent was Wild Claw, a rare triple power Meta-human who was a high tier Beta. Wild Claw was a young man in a red, skintight tiger uniform and had extended claws and teeth that could pierce steel. He had all of his physical abilities, including his five senses which were superhuman, and a heal factor which allowed him to take a licking and keep on ticking. Wild Claw was bred for the intimidation factor, and he had an almost seven feet tall pro-wrestler bod.

K-Force was more than ready to take on the feral tiger-like Hero, who seemed a big favorite for the fight. As K-Force walked across the gangplank into the arena floor proper he saw his opponent's entrance with music and lights. Apparently, they failed to inform K-Force that he could have an intro as well.

"Then again they do this crap every two or three years, so I should know that by now," K-Force sighed, as he loosened up by jumping on his toes and did practice strikes. He was trying to ignore his opponent's time to shine.

After Wild Claw finished waving to the crowd, K-Force finally got a good look at him. He looked to be Asian-American, though more rough and stoic than the boy band look which was more popular. The guy had a look that worked for him as the rough bad boy that was overly manly.

"So, twerp, ready to get cut to ribbons?" Wild Claw grinned in anticipation.

"Only if you're quick enough to catch me," K-Force grinned, as he bowed towards his opponent.

"Let's see how fast you move without legs." Wild Claw gave a sinister smile with his fangs showing, the claws on his hands and feet extended to fight.

At the signal, Wild Claw charged at him thinking he could get in close quickly, but K-Force seemed to slide away as if he were on ice. K-Force tried to hit him with a blast to the face, only for Wild Claw to dodge it in mid-air. This is how it went for about half a minute. They exchanged blows only to dodge them by millimeters, which the crowd loved. It was as if this were a brutal ballet to see who would land a blow first. Then, to the surprise of many, K-Force's beam curved and tagged Wild Claw in his side. While this shocked the feral fighter, K-Force knew he couldn't let up. K-Force came in with a concussive beam that crushed his opponent's knee. This was the death-nail for Wild Claw as he couldn't move as fast and agile on a busted knee. Soon K-Force showed that he could alter the shape of his energy blasts. Hence, he did a large sweeping motion that blew away Wild Claw to the edge of the ring. The tiger-striped Hero's claws sank into the stage, and was able to keep him from falling offstage, then, to K-Force's surprise, Wild Claw was able to jump right back to his feet. It seemed the healing factor was able to get his knee back in shape.

This is why I hate healing factor opponents, K-Force thought, as the agile fighter was back to jumping around, he got in close. K-Force allowed Wild Claw to get too close, and Wild Claw was able to get a few good swipes at his chest armor, resulting with a cut across his cheek.

K-Force didn't back down; he bulldozed towards the agile fighter and shoulder-checked him out of the ring. This received a mixture of cheers and boos, since it seemed some wanted a knockout or a tap out.

But a win was a win in real life and in competition most of the time. K-Force looked down towards Wild Claw who looked like he was raging a bit at his loss.

"Sorry for the ring out, but it was the only way I could beat you and make it to the finals," K-Force said.

"I read up on all my possible opponents, and you were one of the worst match-ups for me," K-Force extended his hand towards the feral young Hero once he calmed down. The big brute jumped upwards and grabbed K-Force's hand, and he did try to break it, only for him to strain his own hand. It seemed like he had forgotten that this particular Hero could lift two hundred-fifty TONS.

"How did you figure out I had a way from stopping you from flying or 'air-walking,' as your little trick is referred to?" Wild Claw questioned, showing that he researched him as well.

"Sure, I could air walk around you and fire my energy beams at you for over an hour, but you would still be standing and you have a knack for taking down aerial opponents with those gadgets of yours. So, I figured I should keep close and on the floor," K-Force stated.

"I would be less inclined to use them because you were in reaching distance, clever." Wild Claw grinned and gave a very rough pat on the back. While he wasn't above being a little petty, he wasn't going to be an ass.

The next fight of notice was the first big bout of the tournament— Nega Titan vs. Azougue, since both were considered top tier candidates for winning the whole thing. The other matches were almost squash mashes where one would get crushed by another Hero. It was almost always Home-Grown vs. Preparatory; an added wrinkle was the fact that they seemed to make it in favor of the Prep school students with a type advantage.

Of those matched, only three non-Preps made it to the next round—QuickTime, K-Force, and Phase, a kid from Dallas, Texas that could fade in and out on command and who seemed to walk through attacks to get up close and personal. There were few powers or devices to disrupt phase-shifting powers, and no one on the Prep side had one.

Azougue was the first heavy hitter from the Home-Grown variety. She was not given an easy match, to say the least. Nega Titan was expected by analysts to reach the Final Four and might be a match for Prime Time. Everyone was impressed by Azougue's performance, but few figured she would last long against the size-shifting giant.

Soon both of them reached the ring with walk-in music and the crowd cheering them on. Nega Titan had that million-dollar smile with an open face masked with a head plate. His uniform was a mixture of blue and yellow highlights that was form-fitting and he also had a side pouch for who knows what. He looked like he could take on anyone.

"Too bad for him Azougue is not just anyone," said K-Force as he saw them square off. At the signal, they charged at each other, only for Nega Titan to shrink and duck between her legs. Then he grew to twelve feet tall as he pounded into her, which did nothing to her as she merely grinned. He shrunk again to dodge her punch, but was quick enough to stomp on the ground, making the arena tremble a bit and causing Nega Titan to slip and fall into a roll. As Nega Titan rose to his feet and grew to his normal height, he had a shocked look to his face.

"Come on! Don't back down now. Woman up," Azougue gave a slight growl, but she grinned afterwards and got into a boxing stance.

"I was going to save this for Prime Time, but this could be a great test run," said Nega Titan as he reeled his arm back for an obvious straight punch, only for his fist to grow huge while the rest of his body stayed the same size. Having an arm about the size and speed of a truck rushing at you was nothing to sneeze at. It was powerful enough to slide Azougue back a few feet as she actually felt the blow. Soon Nega Titan was mixing in several blows where he would grow as tall as twenty feet, then stomp on her. Then he would shrink to normal size and give her a massive fist or kick. This was meant to confuse her and made it very hard to fight back.

This was the sort of action that everyone wanted to see. Azougue was being pushed and tossed around the arena, and it looked like the fight was winding down. Then, to everyone's surprise, Azougue knocked away Nega Titan's punch and tossed him to the floor. Then she began to display her BBJ skills by placing him in a hold. Nega Titan got out of the hold, shrinking to escape. Azougue merely clapped her hands and created a shockwave which nearly blasted him off the arena floor. Nega Titan had to grow twenty feet in order to avoid being knocked out of bounds. But he didn't know he had fallen into her trap until she tossed a mass field on him to make his body weightless. This negated any ability for the young man to move.

Then Azougue flew towards him using the same mass field. Despite being weightless, he was still over twenty feet tall and tried to meet her blow. Their fists met—then there was a slight break in the man's hand as if it was mashed by a hammer. Those who know about weight and inertia would tell you that if she did not hold back, that blow would have done more than just break his fingers. It probably would have shattered his hand. The pain shocked the pseudo giant into becoming normal-sized once again.

Azougue grabbed hold of him in a helicopter spin—then threw him toward the arena floor from over thirty feet in the air. While he did not crack the floor, you could see him bounce from the impact, which was never good for a normal person. A collection of gasps and 'oohs' were heard throughout the Arena, but many could not look away. It seemed this time Azougue had taken over as she landed and got into Brazilian jujitsu stance, moving forward.

Nega Titan recovered slower than usual and still grasped his hand while he looked at his fearsome opponent. It seemed all the cocky nature was knocked out of him, and he was more desperate to take her out. Though anyone could see, the only way for him to win was to get her out the arena and into the pit.

That was easier said than done as she seemed to figure out his fighting style. Every time Nega Titan tried to shift only his limbs, Azougue would use her obscene strength to grab his appendages and try to put him into a joint lock of some type. Being giant-sized wouldn't work because she would match him blow for blow, and he was still favoring his right hand, so it hampered his full ability. And sneaking up on her with his small size would not work either. Azougue would send shock waves just by clapping. Despite all this Nega Titan wasn't about to quit just yet.

Nega Titan got in close and feigned a punch for a giant-sized kick only for him to be pulled into a leg split. Azougue was quickly moving in for a leg lock, and he grew so she could not move into position. Then he tried to swat her away only for Azougue to pull his finger out of its joint. Reflexively, he brought his hand towards himself. This is what Azougue wanted to happen as she lightened herself to fly towards his face. Luckily, Nega Titan was fast enough to shrink, and he dodged out of the way. Then he rolled onto his feet and moved away from her, trying to get space between them.

It seemed he was cornered; that was until he reached into his pouch and pulled out one tennis-sized ball. Then he smashed it into the ground, releasing a giant smoke screen which at first Azougue thought was just an attempt to blind her. Much to her chagrin, it also caused her to have a coughing fit and made it impossible to keep her stance.

This might seem dirty to most people, but the rules only said non-lethal gadgets were allowed. It was a fair move, though the move meant nothing if one couldn't act on it. Nega Titan grabbed hold of Azougue in a pair of giant hands and tried to dunk her outside the ring while she was still recovering. But to his horror, at the last minute she made a mass field before she was sent hurtling towards the ground and pulled herself from his grasp. She was zipped to another part of the stage but still on the edge. Azougue was finally able to control her coughing fit, though she wasn't fully recovered. Nega Titan charged in a desperate moment by enlarging himself to knock her out of bounds, only for Azougue to grab onto that shoulder and spin him around again, tossing him into a mass field in one go.

This left him helpless as he was tossed above the ring while she composed herself. Then Azougue gave a look that stated that she was immediately ending this match. Nega Titan, exhausted, looked right back at her and was resolute to go out fighting. The pseudo giant was pulled rapidly towards Azougue as she prepared an attack. Nega Titan transformed himself to twenty feet tall barreling towards her, feet first. Azougue jumped up to meet him and nailed him into his gut so hard that he folded over her fist after having the air knocked out of him.

As he fell to the ground, Azougue floated to the ring floor with a flare of grace, and the referee began to count for a confirmed knockout. Once he counted to five, the referee examined Nega Titan then began to wave off the match. There was a cheer from the crowd, viewing this as the best match of the day. Many people call out Azougue's name in adulation. As she waved to the crowd in a show of appreciation, the ring doctor came in to examine the fallen rookie and saw that he would not be able to get up any time soon. A gurney was rolled out to carry him backstage where he could get better medical attention. As he was being carted out of the ring, the announcer came on.

"Ladies and Gentlemen, this match is over. Winner by knockout, the Brazilian Fury, Azougue," the announcer said, while stretching out her name to get the crowd hyped.

Azougue, in her excitement, clapped her hands quickly and did a little shimmy to express herself. The crowd and more than a few guys were eating this up. A ringside reporter came up to her and asked the same stupid question that they all normally asked.

"Too bad for them. Azougue doesn't have a modest bone in her body when she thinks she is top dog," K-Force said to himself as he just grinned and waited for the show.

"How does it feel to win your match?" the reporter asked.

"It feels great. Rarely do I get a challenge that actually pushes me," Azougue replied.

This took the reporter by surprise. It seemed he was expecting a different response. "Were you surprised that you won against Nega Titan?"

"My Papi taught me how to fight, and he always told me never get into a fight that I knew I couldn't win. And while Nega Titan was a great hero, he underestimated me, like everyone else—just because I was home-grown," Azougue answered.

Again, the reporter seemed a bit shocked by the young woman's statement but kept on going as if nothing had happened. "So, tell us how far you think you'll go, and who do you want to fight the most?"

"I'm going all the way," Azougue said confidently.

"Oh, quite confident," the reporter responded, feeling like he was getting somewhere.

"Why shouldn't I? Nega Titan was projected to reach the Final Four, and I took him out. No one on my side of the bracket is much of a challenge, and to answer your other question of who I want to fight the most—Prime Time," Azougue said, raring to go.

This actually visibly shocked the reporter but also excited him. This was the kind of drama that was worth gold if played the right way.

"So, a chance to fight against Prime Time is your main goal?" the reporter asked.

"No, my main goal is to win this tournament, and beating him would be just the spice to make it worth it," Azougue said excitedly.

"You think you can beat Prime Time?" The reporter was eating this up.

"'Never get into a fight that you know you cannot win.' Remember? And I'm not planning to back out of the fight. I know I can beat him, and if I do it will prove that I am the best, regardless of my informal training," Azougue stated. "You can't be considered one of the best unless you match or beat the best, so," Azougue pointed directly towards the camera, knowing Prime Time was watching. "Don't choke until I meet you - it would be a shame. I never had a chance to go all out with someone who could take it."

Chapter 4
New Challenger

"Well, if you wanted people to notice you, you definitely got their attention now," Samson said as they laid down for the night prior to the Final Four.

"This is going to be one of the best rookie hero combines in years. I have never seen such a group of talents pop up out of nowhere. Many of the home-grown this year are amazing. I can't believe we haven't heard about them in some way," Anderson Harp said to his co-host.

"Are you telling me you never heard of Frigid? She has been patrolling Albuquerque for two years under the state police, or Phase, the living ghost of Chicago? Both of them are not unknowns and they are home-grown," Trip Kayless replied, looking almost abashed by his co-anchor's lack of knowledge.

"It's true… they are well-known, but they are not the ones I'm talking about. K-Force is the quick and agile sharpshooter who seems to have more tricks than a Vegas floor show. I'm talking about Azouga—or Azouge? I admit I can't say her name very well, but her actions are easier to see, despite her name being difficult to pronounce. She is a veritable powerhouse and some of the biggest names out in Preparatory were easily taken out by her. Is she satisfied with that? Hell no. She is going after the big man on campus. She is chasing after Philadelphia's own Prime Time." Anderson was trying to hype up the audience with his usual style of dialogue.

"I know that, you know that, everyone knows that, and she told everyone on camera. She is getting a humongous amount of support from everyone, not just because she is from humble beginnings, but because she realistically can take on Prime Time.

If you look at the stats, she was the only other person who maxed out the hydraulic weight machine at over three hundred tons, and she tied in reps with him. She might be his biggest opponent in this tournament."

As Samson turned away from the TV he looked at social media reaction to their day of rising to the top. Many people were already questioning who they were. Since they were from the same region and were friendly towards each other, they were obviously a couple.

"Well, it's official, we're a couple, and apparently you have a crush on Prime Time. Oh, and me and Wild Claw are somehow a gay couple because I showed good sportsmanship," Samson joked.

Bianca could not stop laughing at the insanity some shippers go to at times. "Seriously, why didn't you tell me? You know I would support you."

"Honey please, while some like the big hairy bear type, I'm not one of them," Samson joked in an exaggerated gay voice. "In all seriousness, I think you're going to have to go all out tomorrow because if you don't even meet halfway on the hype, you're going to be worse than an unknown because you'll be ignored. You'll be a bust."

"Never say that word, never say that word, that's some voodoo crap," Bianca almost shuddered. Being a bust hurt a Hero's career more than anything. It takes astronomical work and dedication to bounce back from such a label because every time a Hero would do something special, everyone would say that it was a fluke or a flash in the pan.

"I'm just saying you want this kind of heat? Well, there is a price for it, and I hope you are well-prepared. Because you default on the audience interest, you'll be lucky you get mentioned on the six o'clock news somewhere," Samson warned, looking at her seriously.

As Bianca looked thoughtful for a minute she turned to talk to her best friend, who had a good and nasty habit of pulling her down to earth if she ever got too much into herself. Then she saw him look on his laptop at his next opponent. Mithril and her match against QuickTime was a good fight, but this girl was packing some heavy hardware where one would almost think that she was Nathan Sparks in female form. QuickTime's suit could go head-to-head against two or three Metas or maybe a battalion of armed soldiers, but Mithril was out to take on legions, as it were.

Mithril's strategy was battle zoning and she did it better than anyone else, though Frigid was a close match to her. And Mithril still outmatched her, just by pure variety and the payload that she possessed. The match Mithril had against Frigid pushed her several times because Frigid was able to get in close to do some damage.

"Trying to figure out how to beat the second leading lady," Bianca quipped as she tried to look at the last match.

"Yeah, this is going to require me to drop the long-range tactics," Samson said as he watched his future opponent.

"Really?" Bianca was surprised.

"Yep, I can fight long distance fairly well, but against her, I'm a beginner. So, I need a different game plan," Samson confirmed.

"Finally, I was wondering if you were ever going to use full capabilities or just baby step the whole tournament," Bianca said, excited to see how far Samson had come.

"It was more hiding info from my opponents. The less they know what I am capable of, the better. Mithril is the most dangerous type of opponent. She analyzes her future opponents and breaks them down. Watch how she beat Frigid," Samson said, as he showed Mithril's last match to Bianca.

At first, the match seemed to be even as both girls were good at attacking from a distance. Frigid began to reflect the laser away from herself and right back at Mithril, which shut down some of her arsenal. But the young woman had concussive cannon and repulse beams which were used to break it. Frigid used ice constructs in the form of melee weapons, swords, hammers, and arrows. This put the armor-wearing heroine on her back foot as she had to deal with the new assault. Mithril soon got hit by an arrow that froze part of her armored leg, which also destabilized her thrusters. The other arrow hit around her chest, which froze her jetpack. Soon she fell to the ground and was struck by two large sledgehammers made of ice. They hit Mithril relentlessly for almost half a minute, and then Frigid paused a few seconds to make sure she didn't do anything permanent. Then Mithril went on the attack with mini-missiles that were modified to again cause concussive force damage. But they were good at blowing up Frigid's ice constructs—she soon backed away from danger since parts of her armor were not frozen. The damage to her armor could be seen with dented metal, scraped paint, and some pieces that were torn off.

"I got your number now, so watch out Frostbite." Mithril soon unleashed a barrage of mini-missiles, lasers, and concussive rays. This became a one-sided fight as Mithril seemed to counter almost every move Frigid made. It was as if she could predict her movements. Soon after the comeback, Frigid was taken out with a massive beam that shattered her ice wall and knocked her out.

"How did the tech nerd bounce back and dominate so quickly?" Bianca asked.

"Frigid gave her too much time. She beat Frigid because she saw all of what Frigid could do during her other fights and trials, as well as during their fight. And with her supercomputer," Samson started to explain.

"Wait, she has a supercomputer!" Bianca knew the girl was a genius, but not that smart.

"She is a fifteen-year-old girl who graduated from MIT at age twelve and built armored suits like this for two years. Of course she has a supercomputer. And with the computer's help, she analyzed and came up with a game plan that suppressed any chance of a comeback," K-Force said as he put away the laptop and began to focus on a game plan.

"Okay that means the longer the fight, the easier it will be for her to beat most people," Bianca replied, realizing the problem going against this kind of person.

Samson looked at her in puzzlement. "Most people? Miss Marvelous' most constant and dangerous enemy is Multimillionaire Astrid Skrugg."

"The dusty old witch who is jealous of Miss Marvelous - how is she a threat to one the most powerful heroes in the world?" Bianca questioned, not getting his point.

"She's smart enough to find out Miss Marvelous' weakness, like radioactive Xenonite or magic which is why she has a robot that fires such energy. And has demonic henchman with magical abilities to keep her and her family at bay. Not to mention over a dozen plans and contingencies," Samson clarified.

"Okay, okay, so a genius with tech skills and a supercomputer means extremely dangerous," Bianca considered.

"Not all of them, but a person of Mithril's caliber, yes," Samson pointed out.

"So how are you going to beat her, Mister Mithril's Number One Fan," Bianca mocked, as she tried to figure out his battle strategy.

"Lure her into a sense of security. Then, to paraphrase a quote, 'Strike fast, strike hard, and no mercy,'" replied Samson.

"Don't worry, you're the best around," said Bianca, who couldn't help but laugh, and add a little to his movie quote.

The next day the first match was between K-Force and Mithril, which was talked about by many, but most thought it would either be a good fight with a clear winner or a squash match. And in both matches the Vegas numbers had the odds-on favorite, with Mithril at negative-455 while K-Force was at a plus-315.

Normally this would discourage most fighters who were discounted so much. But to K-Force this actually built confidence in himself because it meant they, including hopefully Mithril, would underestimate him. And underestimating an opponent, no matter how weak, will bite you in the ass. It is why you see upsets in many professional sports, games, or war. It was the one lesson his mother drilled into him since he was little. She saw a few of her comrades' die or end up critically injured because they underestimated their opponent.

"Whether they are weak or strong, always put your foot on the throat of those who wish to kill or maim you," Intercessor emphasized to her children. While he would not go that brutal on his opponent, the message was clear. Never let up and never let your guard down.

Mithril was coming into the ring, but instead of walking in, she flew in, showboating a bit. She was firing off fireworks while playing a power metal song about Valkyrie raining from the sky. This seemed like a good analogy for a flying woman in armor. When she landed, she did a little pirouette and bowed to the crowd. The crowd ate it up as this girl knew how to put on a show. Mithril's armor looked to be a mixture of practical woman armor from fantasy, yet form-fitting enough to show off her assets, which were her legs and hips. Her armor shined silver and white with green highlights. Her legs were in high-heeled boots that went to the top of her thigh and arched perfectly to her hips. Next was her battle one-piece swimsuit with a Queen Anne top, though it was metallically armored, it was made to fit her more comfortably.

Not wanting to be outshined too badly, K-Force had the stage covered in smoke then burst through with a spinning cannonball jump and landed in a squat position on all fours. The flames exploded up with a hard rock song about how you gain nothing without pain. Next, he walked calmly to the ring shaking hands and high-fiving with audience members near the walkway, until he was about fifty feet from the ring. He then did a tumble routine that would have landed him on an Olympic podium.

This made the crowd cheer for him, liking his display of skills and willingness to interact with them. This year, very few interacted with the crowd since three years prior a want-to-be villain tried poisoning the future prospects. For this reason, every stadium scanned food from the outside, and there was talk of banning all outside food during all events.

As K-Force entered, the force field came up and sealed them off from the outside audience. The only ones left were him and Mithril as they squared off, waiting for the bell to sound.

"Well, if it isn't my biggest fan." Mithril's voice sounded somewhat metallic because of her masked helmet.

"Eh, I just prefer competence over a flashy muscle-bound showboat, who assumes flexing is more important than doing your job," K-Force jested.

"Trust me, you're preaching to the choir. Try going to school with him for three years. But did you really pick me because I was better, or did you do that just to piss him off?" Mithril joked along with him.

"You're just someone I saw as the top pick over nearly everyone here," said K-Force, being sincere.

"While that is flattering, don't think that I will take it easy on you."
Mithril got into her stance.

"Wouldn't dream of it, however, could you do me a favor?" K-Force asked.

"Which is?" Mithril was wondering what he was going to ask.

"Promise not to go easy on me just because I'm a boy," K-Force quipped as he got into position.

Mithril just laughed out loud at the statement and got into a Tae Kwon Do stance, of all things. As soon as the bell rang, both young Heroes jumped back and began to fly and shoot at each other. K-Force with his energy beams of various sizes while Mithril used three different types of beams, mini-missiles, and so on. The battle looked like it was going Mithril's way since no matter what type of tactic K-Force put up, she would break it.

It was not completely one-sided, as many believed. K-Force was able to catch her off guard when he fired off more energy blasts from his feet and when he began to alter and change up aerial flight pattern. When Mithril used her mini-missiles on K-Force, he blocked them with his blasts which caused a dust cloud to disappear from sight. Then he dropped a beam straight from above, which was strong enough to drive her into the ground. This was a good effort, but Mithril shrugged it off as soon as he let up. The steel-clad woman charged forward and slugged into the chest with both fists, which should have knocked the air out of him. Then she gave him full blast to his sternum, sending him flying further across the arena floor which was a painful sight of him tumbling like a rag doll. At one point, he flipped on his head. After such a bad tumble, everyone thought he was out. In fact some thought he was in critical condition.

This gave pause to the battle for about five seconds. Though to many it felt like minutes, as K-Force lay unmoving. Then as if to defy logic, K-Force stood up and shook his head. K-Force looked towards Mithril and slapped his chest, "Come on hit me with your best shot. I'm not done yet."

While Mithril was worried about his health seconds ago, now she was irritated that he wouldn't stay down. At this point, she realized he had one of two things. One, he had a healing factor like Wild Claw; or two, he had crazy endurance like that blowhard Prime Time. This meant that she could go full force and not worry too much.

Mithril's suit hummed with power as she turned up the turbines. She unleashed a large amount of fire power and seemed to pummel K-Force into the ground. This would have taken down most Meta, even an Alpha level one. But when it was all done, K-Force still stood back with a grin that was irritating her. It was at this point she threw subtlety to the wind and charged up a massive power beam that was meant to take down Prime Time. The beam was so strong that it was able to burn a hole into the stage, something that survived most of the battles with a few dents and cracks, but no true damage was ever made.

And again, when the dust cleared, K-Force was on one knee but rose back to his feet with his armor singed around the edges. Next K-Force started to jump up and down slightly to loosen up his body and got into fighting stance.

"Sorry, don't have the time to play anymore," and with those words, he rushed towards her in the sky with a right hook to her face plate. Then he fired two more punches to her gut from his left. Then, faster than Mithril could react, a reverse straight kick to her gut sent her flying away into the force field.

Mithril recovered before she hit the ground out of bounds. She also stayed away from him but examined how that kick had actually dented her armor. "Shit," she gasped in pain as her body felt those blows. "If he could hit like that, then why didn't he?" Mithril felt a cold shiver run down her spine as the reason he hid this part of his abilities.

"Eden," she asked in a frantic tone. "How long will it be until you analyze his movements?"

"Not possible at this time." A posh feminine British accent replied back.

"What do you mean, not possible?!" Mithril yelled in her helmet as she tried to keep up.

"No data on this style of attack and his speed has increased, while its pattern has shifted tremendously," the female AI replied.

Mithril started to panic as she watched K-Force bounce in place in the air to keep himself afloat. Then she saw him charge at her at great speed. She was able to dodge his attack and fire point blank at him, but he sensed her and spun around her beam attack. Then Mithril dashed backwards in the air and tried to open up distance from K-Force as she tried to come up with a plan of attack. Sadly K-Force was not going to allow that to happen. This turned the match completely around. Blow after blow was unleashed upon Mithril as she tried to fight back. But nothing she did seemed to slow him down, and every attack that landed only pushed him harder. Then, as much as it irritated Mithril, she realized the only way to win was to outlast the young man. Even Eden said this was the right play, if she wanted to win. This plan went against her principles, but she knew she could not win a full-on assault against this young man.

She tried to stay away, but he was too fast for her to lose. He would strike at her vulnerable joints in her suit, which was the area she needed to bend easily if she wanted to move. Then, with only thirty seconds left, K-Force knocked her into the ground from the air and pounced upon her. The blow was powerful enough to cause critical failure in her suit as K-Force ripped the side of her suit open, and through a knife hand under her arm pit near her heart. It seemed all those attacks to her under arm area were a game plan, since it weakened the area enough for him to break through.

Someone like Prime Time would have never thought of such a way to attack, but it seemed like her first thought were true. Despite K-Force being a super powered Meta-human, he was strategic—a rarity among the high power Metas.

Mithril knew when she was beat and raised her hand in submission. The referee blew the whistle in announcement of the match being over.

"Ladies and gentleman, as Mithril is unable to continue without grievous injury, this match is declared unanimously a technical knockout. The winner going to the finals is K-Force," the announcer proclaimed, sounding a little in disbelief.

As a show of goodwill, K-Force helped Mithril to her feet as her damaged suit messed with her power system, so her legs were not getting the commands to move properly.

"I'm guessing I hit a vital system," K-Force said, easily lifting the two hundred-pound suit.

"Yeah, it took a while for the secondary control system to take over," Mithril said, as her backup systems came on.

"I know this is me telling you how to drink water, but you should look up a way to counter that problem. It might be your Achilles' heel," K-Force suggested, knowing how geniuses feel about their work being judged.

"Relax. You're just giving me some advice, which I need to fix as soon as I get back to my lab." Mithril tried to dissuade his worries.

"Yep, Heroes like you are usually the field commander, so if you get taken out your team will be in trouble," K-Force replied, sating what role she would most likely take.

"You really think I would make a field commander, don't you?" Mithril was surprised that someone of regular college age saw her as a leader.

"I can plan ahead and make quick tactile plans for myself. You're the big brain, big picture kind of person. Someone who puts people like me where I can do the most good," K-Force complimented.

Mithril surprised him by opening the mouth area of her mask and gave him a peck on the cheek, which was covered partly by his mask.

God, this is only going to make the shippers on social media worse, K-Force thought to himself as he saw the reporters double-time it towards them.

"Maybe kissing you was a mistake." Mithril realized her blunder.

"Maybe," K-Force replied, as the reporters looked at them like a younger sibling catching their older sibling doing something wrong.

Twenty minutes later they found themselves in an embarrassing interview, which mostly consisted of them explaining that they were not dating and that Mithril's kiss was just a friendly show of affection. While the reporters did eventually drop the subject, K-Force knew it was going to be a big topic in the news for a while. He also could predict the future rumors of him being a cradle robber because Mithril was a fifteen-year-old. He was eager to see Azougue give the world a big upset against Prime Time. While K-Force had full confidence in her, he knew this was going to come down to who could take the most punishment and who could dish it out. In his long practice sessions, if it came to toughness, his money was on Azougue.

Again, Prime Time came out into the arena with a couple of booming pyrotechnics, and as his theme music played, he swaggered to the stage. The crowd loved the last fight; it was more than they expected and had a great show of skills. Now it was the main event watching two powerhouses charge at each other. It was like watching the Orange Bowl with two great schools going head-to-head. Though looking at the way Prime Time was promoting himself, one might swear this was a pay-per-view wrestling match, with his showy entrance.

Though K-Force had no room to talk based on his own entrance earlier, he felt like Prime Time was pushing it a little too hard. Hell, his theme music was by a famous wrestling "Heel" from the '90s and 2000s from WWE, which made K-Force really worried about the state of the industry becoming even more commercial.

"Are they going to start scripting these things like wrestling?" K-Force prayed to God that wasn't going to be the end point of all this.

Then he heard a rap song bumping out the Arena speakers. Though it was a radio-edited version for the public view, listeners caught the gist of the song, which was 'Ride or Die (Trick)' proudly proclaimed as an uncut version. The song did match Azougue quite well as she never had been one to hide in the background or be subtle. She was loud and proud of what she was and wasn't going to hide it from the polite public.

As Azougue stepped into the arena, she struck a pose that showed off her muscles. Though lean and fit, they were quite visible when she flexed then turned to her long-awaited opponent. They gave each other a stare that said they would crush the other one for the thrill of a challenge.

"Thank you, for keeping it short and not being all hype," Azougue taunted.

"And now you'll know after I smash you into the floor," Prime Time gloated.

"Oh good, that just means it will be more fun when I beat you in front of everyone," she said as she slammed her fist into her palm in anticipation.

The referee called out to ask both of them if they were ready. They acknowledged that they were ready and waiting. As soon as the bell rang, Prime Time charged forward to end it in a quick and easy punch. There was a whip-like sound when his fist landed on her face, only for Azougue to grin, shrug it off and slug him back. When Prime Time stepped back, he was in shock, and it seemed that his punch didn't take her down.

Azougue tried to take control of the match by jumping forward and using boxing footwork to weave into the tanned brute's guard. He tried to knock her away with his immense strength, which had worked on everyone thus far, but she simply blocked it with her guard and slugged him in the gut, which actually made him wince in pain. Then she laid into him with a combination of blows that he had little ability to resist. Then, to the shock of many, Azougue knocked him to the floor with a straight right. Prime Time was sitting on the ground pole-axed and in shock.

This must have been the first time in a long time Prime Time had felt pain. The way he looked at his gut where the young lady had hit him, was a look of disbelief. Soon he was knocked back to reality as he heard the referee count to six, and immediately, he jumped to his feet, though a bit wobbly in the knees. But he refused to stay down when the referee asked if he could continue. He leaned on him a bit to get his own balance back, but he gave him a glare that said he would kill the referee if he interfered.

The referee slowly moved back away from Prime Time and looked to see if he could stand on his own. Once he saw that he was standing again, the referee quickly stepped away from the two and started the fight again. Azougue tried to rush in to finish it or knock him down again. Prime Time in a surprising show of resolve threw a hard right, which actually sent her flying a couple meters back. Unlike him, she had her guard up. To the surprise of the audience, Azougue's nose was bleeding which meant despite her guard being up; it showed that Prime Time was still dangerous.

Instead of charging towards her, Prime Time challenged Azougue to come at him, probably thinking since he injured her with her guard up, she would hesitate to come at him. But instead, it excited her since there was a real chance for her to push herself with someone outside of K-Force's family. She wiped the blood away from underneath her nose, grinned, and charged forward. Those with good perception or hearing would swear her steps had a heavier thud. As soon as Azougue rushed in, she huddled up for a few seconds as Prime Time unleashed another massive blow, although this one didn't send her flying as far as the other one. She was pushed back some, but she stood her ground. It seemed that was all the time needed for Prime Time to recover from his knock-down because he went forth and laid into the statuesque young lady in silver and blue.

Azougue was taking blow after blow with a more solid guard to protect her, but each blow sounded like a sledgehammer hitting a tire. A lot of people 'oohed' and cringed in sympathy pain, except K-Force, only because he knew from personal experience that it would take more than that to knock the Brazilian heroine down. This kept going until Prime Time wound up for a haymaker, only to have a left fired in his side, which made him miss his first blow. But before Azougue could capitalize on it, Prime Time recovered quickly and slugged her across the face. This made her stagger a bit, which allowed him several good blows to her body. It appeared like he would combo, but instead she parried a blow from Prime Time and gave him an uppercut that actually hurt him as he staggered. Neither fighter could capitalize on the fact that their opponent was wavering—but both were staggered as well so neither one could push ahead.

To many this seemed odd for superpowered beings to get into a boxing match-like atmosphere. But in truth, a lot of fights between people with similar levels of power usually turned into MMA fights. Mostly because neither wanted to admit the other was stronger than them. It always seemed to come down to who could take more. And as both fighters shook off the worst of their damage, they came back swinging only this time neither cared about blocking. They went into each other, and it turned into a premiere heavy weight bout. It was no longer about who was the better Hero; it devolved into who had the better punch. And the crowd ate it up, neither combatant backing down. As they exchanged punches, most were looking to see who would blink first. The difference in power was becoming more apparent as Azougue was getting pushed back. While her punches were strong enough to cave-in a train, they only slowed down Prime Time as he was pushing through.

As stubborn as Azougue was, she knew she couldn't match him in brute power for now. Like how she learned to fly or create mass orbs, it took time and research for her to find a go-around. There was a bit of pride in her, as she was sure she was tougher than the tan reject from *Jersey Shore*. While there were a couple of bruises showing, they were all superficial. Prime Time had twice as many bruises and looked worse than her.

"Higher endurance, my pert ass," she mumbled and changed her fighting stance.

Prime Time, not worrying or not caring about the fact that she changed her plan of attack kept on with his battle plan, he would take her down or knock her out of the ring. One more good punch and he would have her. Prime Time was furious this woman actually hurt him. She actually made him wince in a pain which he hadn't felt since he was thirteen. Now he was going to make her regret it. As his fist closed in on her face, he was caught off guard as she deflected his blow. Azougue seemed to worm around his upper body and had him slam into the ground into an arm bar. Normally this would not disturb him, and he could easily lift her weight. Prime Time expected to lift a pillow, but instead his body reacted as if a normal person were lifting four hundred pounds in that awkward position.

Prime Time had tried several times to lift her, but Azougue only added more mass to her form to make it impossible without him breaking his arm. Not to mention, she gave it a couple of twists to keep him in place, and the pain was actually rising. He tried to crush her shin into paste with his free hand when he grabbed it, but couldn't.

"What is she made of?" Prime Time mentally shouted as he tried to get free. He was not going to be tapped out by anyone. As he tried wiggling out, he noticed Azougue's foot was lifted enough to move a bit but not escape the hold. Then in a quick desperation move, Prime Time lifted her leg high enough with his free arm to move his head and unleash his eye beams, which burned like high-intensity plasma. This sent smoldering heat around her and made Azougue back off and let go in shock. Prime Time had finally found something that could hurt her, so he kept the heat beam on her for another ten seconds.

When it was done, there was a lot of smoke from something burning, though many hoped it wasn't Azougue. There hadn't been an accidental death in the combine in twenty years, but a lot of people watching thought it had happened. Then several heavy thumps and cracking sounds were heard. It was a female figure rushing out of the smoke, and it was Azougue, though her clothes have seen better days. The white silver color of clothing was charred, her left breast was hanging out, and her pants were lopsided daisy dukes, with one pant leg burned off above her knee, while the other almost reach her panty liner. The other thing people noticed was that the arena floor was crumbling under her feet with each step, as she delivered blows that made her opponent dizzy. Azougue put Prime Time into a standing arm triangle hold, which looked a lot tighter and painful for him.

This was something K-Force could sympathize with, mostly because he had been in those holds before, and when Azougue would lose her temper, she would make these holds as painful as possible. The bell rang to end the match, but it looked like Azougue wanted to pop Prime Time's head like a pimple. The main referee came on to the floor with three other referees, all with super strength of some level, and they instructed Azougue to release her opponent. They pulled at her arm, though at this point uncoiling a boa constrictor would have been easier. However, Azougue did let go after she realized who was commanding her, but not until Prime Time had turned a shade of purple. The bigger Meta-human was on his knees, trying to regain air with a referee checking on him and the other two referees moving her away.

The crowd was somewhat upset at the fight being stopped, and K-Force want to slap a guy complaining about not getting a free show, when the referee brought out a blanket to cover Azougue up. Soon many people were wondering why it was taking so long to announce the winner. As the two fighters were put on opposite sides of the ring, the referees were getting in between them.

"That's not good—it means whatever is going to happen will be controversial," K-Force sighed. K-Force prepped himself to jump in to stop Azougue just in case she got the short end of the stick.

"Ladies and Gentlemen, due to equipment failure and not heeding the referee call to release when asked, Azougue has been disqualified." As soon as the announcement was made by the referee, K-Force jumped down to the stage and helped the referees to stop Azougue from making a bigger mistake. After she threw a few punches into K-Force's body, she calmed down.

"Thanks," she said, then walk briskly off the stage with the blanket covering her ruined top. She almost stomped off in disgust, and the crowd's reaction wasn't much better.

"This isn't going to end well for you guys," K-Force commented on the referee's decision.

"This isn't going to end well for anybody," a referee stated as he sighed at how devolved this fight had become.

Chapter 5
Mama Told Me to Knock You Out

It was the next day after 'The St. Louis Screw Job,' as many referred to Azougue and Prime Time's match. Many of Prime Time's fans said that it was a fair call, and she shouldn't have lost her temper, which was a fair assessment. But the fact that she was taken out because of a wardrobe malfunction seemed kind of like bullshit since she almost beat him fair and square. Many said that her last hold would have won the match, and there was no way for Prime Time to escape. Social media was not nice on a normal day, and it turned into its special brand of hell after the interview with Azougue.

Azougue was still wearing her mask, though it was a bit damaged. She had a new sports top to replace her ruined one from the fight with Prime Time. The reporter obviously wanted to stir up trouble because of all the questions he could ask, so he asked the one that pushed Azougue.

"Do you think it was an unfair call?" the reporter asked.

"Hell yes, it was an unfair call. I heard no bell. The press themselves said they barely heard it over the crowd, so I shouldn't have been disqualified. And the very idea of a wardrobe malfunction being the main point of disqualification is bull," Azougue passionately expressed.

"It is true. Extenuating circumstances had made the Combine committee not disqualify you, because you were in the heat of battle, and the crowd practically drowned out all sound from anyone hearing the bell. And when the referees got your attention, you pulled back away from him," the reporter said to explain the change to the ruling, though he was acting like that friend that always tried to start crap for the enjoyment of seeing a fight.

"Exactly, uniform being destroyed—that sort of thing happens to both Heroes, male and female. We get our clothes torn, cut, ripped, melted, and in my case, burned off because the villains go at us with everything available. It's not my fault my clothing is not as resistant as I am," Azougue argued.

"So, you're saying if this situation happened in a fight with a culprit, you wouldn't care that your clothes were damaged exactly like tonight?" the reporter quipped, loving it when the athletes spoke their mind.

"I'll go topless in the middle of Times Square, but as long as I am saving people, it should not matter. If my clothes are ripped to shreds, it is up to me to decide on how I should feel." Azougue didn't like showing off her body, but she had her priorities.

This got certain groups rooting for her online, and it somehow became an issue regarding how a woman's body was her own business. Some pointed out it was more about how certain Puritan views shouldn't matter in combat situations, whether life and death, or competitions. Being her best friend and roommate, K-Force had to listen to her vent about how full of crap the judges and the Combine committee were. It was 1 AM before she finally relented and let him sleep.

Now Samson as K-Force was sitting in a private meeting room near the Arena as they put in new flooring for the next day's fight. It seemed that quite a few were cheering for him now. But a lot wanted him to take out Prime Time because of what had happened to Azougue.

Two men walked in with a tall, almost white-haired woman, who seemed to be in charge, at the front. The men he believed were the scouts for companies during the Combine event. He also recognized the woman as a Heroine from the '70s; her name was

Bedazzle. She had retired after she hit the age of forty because her company wanted to promote a younger, prettier girl who was barely of legal drinking age. Instead of becoming desperate or becoming a crabby recluse, Bedazzle became a Sky-High Industry company woman and later a member of the board. Two years prior, she had passed down her name to another girl with similar powers as a show of making her own legacy.

"It is a pleasure to meet you Ms. Colson," K-Force said in full costume as he shook her hand. He couldn't help but be impressed by her Meta-human genes which made her look in her mid-thirties, despite having just had her sixty-third birthday a month prior. Her permanently white hair was not from age but a side effect of her powers. And despite being officially sidelined, he knew she would go out and fight a superpowered villain when the need arose. The one thing that seemed off was her chest. K-Force was by no means any more perverted than the typical male, but he was sure those were bigger than they were in the '90s posters he saw as a kid.

"Ah you've heard of me, good. Do you know who I work for?" the former Bedazzle said as she sat in front of her perspective employee.

"Sky High Industries, the company that had you as Bedazzle, made famous for almost thirty years. And one of the biggest names in Hero representation in the country," K-Force answered.

"Yes, very good, and do you know why I called you here?" Bedazzle asked calmly.

"Ever since I beat your rival company's star Mithril in a match, the Harrison Brothers have been eager to sign me up. You see value in me also," K-Force quipped.

"Yes, that and more. You see, we do know who you are as well, Samson Brewer," Ms. Colson said as her grin widened because she saw the mild shock on the young man's face. It always made her feel good to shock and upend the fragile world of these young upstarts.

"Yes, we know who you are and we were surprised that you didn't announce this to the public. May we ask why? Being Intercessors and Armory, son, is a big draw," Ms. Colson grinned at the young man's shocked face.

"I didn't want the same crap my sister had to deal with for five years of media saying that 'she is so and so's daughter.' They dismissed all her triumphs because she came from someone's blood line. It took three years for 'Ratel Saved the Day' to appear in the headlines instead of 'Intercessor's Daughter,'" added K-Force, putting it out there plainly.

"So, you will want to start off with your own name before you reveal that little tidbit. And trust me, in this game people will figure out your family sooner than later," Ms. Colson warned.

"I know, but if I make a good showing here then maybe my name will shine through quicker than it did for my sister." K-Force knew that this was a long shot, but it was possible.

"That is a good attitude to have. Sky High has been more about moving forward with the new, while respecting the legacy of those that came before. We were interested in you before we found out about your family. Your overall skills have been in the top ten in each event, and your combat skills were even more impressive." Ms. Colson moved in closer than what seemed comfortable for K-Force. K-Force knew about this tactic; his dad warned that they usually throw beautiful women at guys like him, and while she was older than him, she was still very attractive.

"But I must ask if you are still holding back," Ms. Colson queried.

"Yes," K-Force said in a matter fact way.

"And you are not going to tell us how much?"

"Always leave people guessing, it makes living as a Hero a lot easier and longer. And when you-" K-Force started a quote from one the oldest premiere Heroes.

"And when you run out of tricks, refine your old ones or create new ones," Ms. Colson finished for him, grinning as she remembered the old quote that most knowledgeable Heroes lived by. A smoky chuckle escaped her lips while her two associates grinned as well.

"When your big fight with Prime Time is over, keep us in mind. We loved having you with us. Though I have to ask, is there anything you want specifically, or a request?" Ms. Colson was curious about the young man's desires.

"Yeah, keep me out of the Pacific region. That place is a career killer," K-Force bluntly stated.

"What?" Ms. Colson and one of her male companions said as one.

"You're serious? Everyone wants to go to the Pacific. It's where most of today's Heroes get their big start," Ms. Colson stated.

"And it is where I will be on the bench for three years while being called a bust," K-Force countered, making his feelings known.

"That's an exaggeration, don't you think?" Ms. Colson was surprised that he didn't want to go where they paid more and have the biggest media center.

"Not by much. Look, I was raised in the Hero lifestyle because of my parents and I heard the horror stories from my dad about California," K-Force raised his hand in forestalling the same drivel they give the public. "It's California, not Pacific region. I'm calling a spade, a spade. The headquarters are in San Francisco not Eureka, which by charter should be *headquarters*, as each regional office headquarters must be in a well-developed city near center point of the region. Not center of the most populated and wealthy state."

"Fair point," Ms. Colson conceded.

"My main gripe is if I go to California, I'm most likely going to be put somewhere between LA and San Francisco which already has an excessive amount of Heroes, despite crime levels have dropped significantly since the '80s," K-Force pointed out.

"They still have a high crime rate, in fact lately it has risen over thirty percent," Ms. Colson argued.

"Regular crime such as robberies and murders, yes, for people like me, our purpose is in saving lives and helping police in major shoot outs and drug busts where extra muscle is needed. Not to mention LA is overcrowded by Heroes as it is. One A-Class Hero or two B-Class Heroes for every three hundred thousand in a city or a Hero team which handles 1.2 million. Los Angeles has the Hyper Squad team, a team of eight A-Class Heroes and over fifteen other Heroes who were not associated with them. San Francisco has eleven for its own city, despite not having a million people," K-Force stated.

"It houses the headquarters of the Pacific region as you stated, so they need extra power for protection of the city. Any villains who want to take over the region need to take that area out first," Ms. Colson indicated.

"True, but only five extra which circulate between the top Heroes of the area. San Francisco should have eight at most, not eleven. While San Alonso has a larger population and barely has four at any given time," K-Force rebutted.

"Okay, they are overcrowded, but that's not a real problem." Ms. Colson was grasping at straws here.

"It's when the priority list is in effect," K-Force fired back.

"You know about the priority list." Ms. Colson looked surprised now.

"His father protested the damn thing. Of course he knows about it," answered the sandy brown-haired man who looked to be in his late twenties.

"Yeah I'm not in favor of waiting to be handed scraps or standing by and letting the bad guy get away because a Hero higher on that list has dibs," K-Force said in an exasperated tone.

"It's not like that. You are allowed to protect the citizens and chase off the criminal," Ms. Colson said, knowing how weak her excuse was.

"And not stop and capture him because that is the big Heroes' job. I'm with the kid—that policy is asinine and gets people hurt," the sandy brown-haired man couldn't keep quiet about his hate for the policy.

"It is to make sure rookies don't get in over their heads and let the professionals take charge." Ms. Colson was getting upset that this man was interfering with her meeting.

"That's what the mentor program is for and you know it. If the kid wants to make it big, he has to toe the line and follow the inner circle. And even if he follows all their policies, they still might ignore him for their major constituents or the elite who decide who rises or falls." The sandy haired man stood his ground.

"Sounds like a personal experience," K-Force commented as he watched his two agents argue.

"Worst eight years of my life, my career was dead until I got moved to Minnesota and could show what I was worth," the older man said in a voice full of regret.

"Pathway?" K-Force guessed the man's identity by the company, hair color, and similar body shape.

"Good guess kid, but yeah, it's me. Me and Mazer Gal working together in a new region helped me rise to the top. So, I get the reason why you do not want to go there. They seem to punish you if you try to do anything without their permission in California," Pathway explained his reasoning.

"And as much as I hate to admit it, New York is on its way becoming exactly the same way," lamented Ms. Colson as she saw the decline of her old stomping grounds in the recent years.

As the representatives whispered to each other for a bit they all seem to come to a speedy decision.

"If you join us in the next twenty-four hours, we will do our best to get you drafted to the other regions. Though you might get sent to the Rocky Mountain region," Ms. Colson warned.

"Vegas, Denver, and Casper are hot spots and Dire Beasts was a danger to the more remote regions of the country, so I will always be challenged. I'd rather wait three years to get to a better area with a great foundation than waste my time being a superpowered model, just smiling and waving for the California elite," K-Force pointed out.

"Fair enough. Call us when you have decided," said Ms. Colson as she and her associates left the room.

K-Force decided to wait for his next agent representative from Enteriagey Industry, aka Prime Time's company. He was surprised that they wanted him, but K-Force figured that they wanted to hedge their bets and get a prize unsigned Hero. He decided to decline Enteriagey Industry since they had some policies that he refused to co-sign. The sad truth was, in the current world, if you worked for a company or for an individual, you were a terrible person by association. So, he would rather avoid all that if he could.

The man who walked in did not look like someone who wanted to see K-Force. When the business suit individual entered, he gave off an appearance of someone who was annoyed by the fact that he had to talk to K-Force. Said agent had a pointed face and a beak of a nose, as well a receding hairline. He walked in with a suit that probably cost over six hundred dollars and was on the phone with someone else. This was a power play he heard about from his mother who had to deal with people like this as result of a long life and being a woman in less enlightened times. Make the client feel that they are less important, so when you low ball them, they feel like they are being generous, which again made it easier to say "no thank you" to their company.

"Sorry, important call but nothing that concerns you," the Enteriagey agent walked in with the smile a shark would give to its prey.

Ignoring the minor insult, he focused on what the Agent was going to say.

Two hours later Samson was furious at what the little rodent-faced bastard had commanded him to do. It seemed Enteriagey demanded that he take a dive for their star, or they would let private information about him and his home life slip, not caring that it would cause collateral damage. This was an obvious lie, but for most people unaware of the laws and punishments, such actions would be devastating for any company. Not to mention, this was something that they used to either make others take a fall or frighten to sign on with them. And who knew what they would do to make them stay signed on. The agent also made it clear that even if he still defied them, they would make sure he could never win. So, they were rigging the match for their benefit, meaning he would have little to no chance of defeating Prime Time.

The rodent-like Agent, whose name Samson didn't catch because he didn't care to remember, left the room and told him that they controlled his future. If he defied them, they would make sure that no one would ever sign him, as they had enough pull and he was not that big enough for their word to be ignored.

Bianca, who was listening in on Samson's video call to his mother, was also getting angry. She has gotten subtle threats herself from anonymous people, telling her not to get too cocky and to quit complaining about her loss or she would have no sponsors.

"Those jerks threatened me as well. It seems I shook a beehive when I pointed out how ridiculous my foul was. At least I know which company not to sign up for, since I got over twelve offers as well," Bianca smiled proudly.

"Just make sure they are not in association with Enteriagey unless you want to be under their thumb," Samson cautioned.

"Duh, I'm not an idiot. My dad taught me how corporations make pseudo monopolies by making agreements to work as one without combining," Bianca sassed her longtime friend.

"So which offer are you taking?" Samson's mom, Aaliyah, asked her son's oldest friend.

"I don't know. I will have to research all of them just to make sure I'm not entrapped by them," Bianca responded.

"You can pick Enteriagey competitors to make it easy," K-Force offered.

"Sure, Sky High and Lunglomerate but I want to know all my options before I make one," Bianca replied.

"Nice to know you are making an informed decision," Samson complimented her foresight. "I don't really have as many choices as you do. I could join my mom's company. Which wouldn't be that bad; it would be cool to be a mother and son duo."

"Isn't that kind of corny," Bianca asked, making sure that was a wise choice.

"Not really, family working together has always been a big draw and liked by the public. Plus, me and Mom would be the first mother and son team," K-Force defended.

"Mama's boy," snarked Bianca.

"It is only an insult if I considered that being a bad thing. Besides we have eight father-daughter teams and no one calls them daddy's girls," he defended.

"No, but a lot of people are not going to be okay with the idea," Bianca warned.

"We are getting away from the main point. Son, how are you going to respond to their 'offer,'" Aaliyah asked her youngest again.

"Simple. I'm going to take down their so-called prized Golden Goose, Prime Time, in such a way that they can't call any fouls, or put the match in his favor," K-Force replied with an eager tone in his voice.

"How?" Aaliyah sound eager as well.

"Simple, I know his main weakness," Samson answered.

"Which is?" Bianca asked.

"He can dish it out but he can't take it. You proved that by the fact that he was so disturbed by the very idea he could be hurt and he couldn't handle fighting through pain," Samson explained his observation.

"How is that going to help you in a fight with him?" Bianca asked.

"Rumble in the Jungle," Samson replied cryptically.

The next day K-Force was in the ring waiting for the bell. He got an anonymous text before the match reminding him of the consequences if he didn't take a dive like he promised. Laughing at the arrogance of those people, it warmed his heart at how angry they were going to be. As Prime Time seemed to walk in with even more pyro behind him, K-Force rolled his eyes and stated that Prime Time needed this ass whooping.

K-Force knew that they were somewhat like athletes, but they were also a mixture of cop and soldiers. *And that there are people out there who can kill him if he is not careful*, K-Force thought, as the referee went through all the rules. Bianca only started the lesson that there were bigger fish in the ocean, and it was up to K-Force to finish it.

Prime Time looked eager to begin the fight, and it was because there were a lot of comments about him winning because of a bogus call or that he got lucky. There were comments about him losing to a girl, but most people didn't see gender when it applied to Metas, except for a couple idiots. When a woman can crush a man's skull like a soda can with a twitch of her hand, gender advantages go out the window.

So, when the bell rang, Prime Time rushed forward swinging into K-Force's guard. The punch was a bit sloppy, but the following hits were not. It seemed that Prime Time was coached to keep close to K-Force. It would be the best advice if not for the fact that up-close combat was K-Force's specialty. The punches that were landing against K-Force were strong enough to fold a truck, but all that power would come back and bite Prime Time later.

"Come on, is that it? I'm waiting to be awed by Prime Time not bored to tears," K-Force tried to push his opponent.

That did get a reaction as the punches had a lot more power, but still it wasn't enough. *Looks like Prime Time wasn't trained for trash talk*, thought K-Force, as he stepped back, dropped his guard and waited for Prime Time to attack him.

"What are you doing?" Prime Time was getting confused now.

"So far nothing you're throwing is remotely dangerous to me, so I am not going to waste energy blocking." As K-Force said this, a heavy blow was struck equivalent of a wrecking ball, but K-Force actually stood there and only moved his head slightly as if Prime Time's punches were more of an annoyance. While it was a bit of a gamble, K-Force knew he had to do something to get the powerhouse Meta-human to really unleash his power.

"Maybe what people say is true. You only won by luck, because Azougue hits a lot harder than this," K-Force taunted.

That seemed to be the button to push because for three punches Prime Time was actually able to move K-Force back. The fact that the blows stung was odd since anything other than crushing force had never been able to hurt him before. He had experimented to test the limits of his powers. K-Force had been stabbed, punched, shot at, strangled, even set on fire one time. His mom grounded him and his sister Tamera for a month for that little stunt, but it did show that he had a high resistance to flames, though plasma seemed to burn off all the hair on his body. It took his brother to regrow his hair and eyebrows back. Luckily the plasma shots were not hot enough to give him any burns. The only thing that could hurt him was crushing or squeezing forces and sustained extreme temperatures.

That meant Prime Time's blows were ballistic missile level at least. Each blow seemed to shake the Arena and rattle the windows despite the force field's ability to mute such forces. The crowd winced and was in awe of such force being unleashed. Prime Time's blows were getting faster and more vicious, and he even unleashed a straight kick into K-Force's midsection. The blow was the most powerful one yet, as it made deep grooves into the floor as K-Force slid across the ring floor. Prime Time was actually happy as he felt this was what he needed to get the taste of the last bout out of his mouth; a squash match to prove that he was not lucky or weak, but that he could take on anyone—even a dangerous underdog with unknown limits.

Then as another haymaker was about to land, K-Force disappeared from Prime Time's eyes, which were used to seeing bullets in flight as leaves falling from a tree. Then Prime Time felt his opponent before he saw him, as he felt his entire body shift and collapsed to his left side. Prime Time felt another blow to his side that seemed to break his ribs, which he thought was impossible. K-Force wasn't done yet, as he unleashed a sharp, low kick to Prime Time's leg. This caused Prime Time to lose his balance, and then he felt a brief, intense pain before blacking out.

The world watched in shock as this all occurred faster than the normal eye could see. The onlookers saw Prime Time pounding away into a squash match, where they worried that K-Force would be the first Combine death in twenty-seven years. Then, in a flash they saw K-Force crouching over Prime Time within a large crater two meters deep. K-Force rose from his downed opponent with his fist, buried in the temple of Prime Time's head, which was a perfect spot to land a knockout punch.

K-Force quickly moved back and away before any false calls could be made against him. As the referee rushed to the down fighter, he hesitated for a few seconds before he started counting.

"You can count to a hundred—he is not getting up for a while," K-Force muttered as he scanned the crowded for the Enteriagey agent and grinned widely.

K-Force just waved with a grin as he waited for the decision. Soon the referee stopped counting at six, since Prime Time wasn't moving at all. They had to get a stretcher to carry the much-hyped

Hero out of the ring, while many were shocked that K-Force pulled an upset.

I can only imagine the uproar I created, but it was worth it for now, K-Force thought as he played up to the crowd and danced a small pop and lock routine that he usually danced his friends.

Over a month later, the threats were coming through until the company realized they were stepping on big shoes by messing with Armory and Intercessor. With Samson's father being in charge of the entire southeastern region and the other being on the National Defenders Squad, it would be a losing battle to threaten them. There was a weak attempt to say he cheated, but everyone saw that fight in specialized slow motion. They saw him slip under Prime Time's guard and nailed him twice in the side, which broke two ribs. Then K-Force kicked Prime Time's back leg out to make him fall towards the floor, with his fist knocking into Prime Time's temple, slamming his head into the floor.

Every fight commentator said it was a clean chain of attacks, although some said K-Force was lucky. And, just as Samson figured, all the talk about how no one would sign him up was full of crap. Samson went from four to twenty offers, especially after his interview with Tripp and Trevon.

"K-Force, my man; how are you doing today?" Tripp asked his guest.

"Pretty good, considering all the attention I'm getting now," K-Force said, showing off for the people.

"I would think so, since you took out two of the heavy favorites, in spectacular manner," Tripp commented.

"Any thoughts on who you're going to sign up with," Trevon asked.

"I narrowed it down to five at the moment, and I won't tell you which company I'm signing up with. But I can tell you it is not Enteriagey. I feel a lot of hostility after what I did to Prime Time," K-Force said.

"Boy, you ain't telling us anything we didn't already know. But in all seriousness, that's what we called you here today for. Everyone wants to know—was your win over Prime Time planned or luck of the draw?" Tripp asked in his colorful, blunt way.

"Going straight to the point, okay, y'all remember Rumble in the Jungle?" K-Force asked both hosts.

"I don't want to brag about it since it shows my age, but yeah I remember seeing that legendary fight," Trevon gloated.

"Like me saying how old I was when that fight happened is going to make me look any better. But yeah, I saw the match as well," Tripp being sly.

"I pulled the rope-a-dope strategy on him to take him out," K-Force honestly answered.

"Rope-a-dope," Trevon said with a chuckle. "I'm surprised anyone from your generation even knows what that is."

"Blame my dad. He used to watch old boxing matches like Thrilla in Manilla or Sugar Ray versus Hitman Hearns," K-Force added.

"I love the fact your father decided to take personal interest in your education in tactics and classics. But could you look at the screen and show us how you used that strategy," Tripp played to the crowd while complimenting the young Hero.

"Sure," replied K-Force. As he waited for a commercial break to end, the television crew that set up the video conference proceeded to set up and synchronize him with the studio feed. When they came back, they went through minor sports highlights of the week, then they turned it over to the fight K-Force had with Prime Time.

They started the fight out with Prime Time rushing into K-Force to keep him from fleeing, by pounding him down. For twenty seconds, it looked like K-Force was just trying to escape.

"Here, I let Prime Time pound me to gauge his punches and see if I could take what he could dish out. I felt him hold back a lot compared to what he was throwing at Azougue and realized that he was pacing himself," K-Force explained.

"Yeah, I remember that some of the blows he unleashed rattled my teeth when I was in the stands," Trevon commented.

"Exactly, and at that strength the punches were effective as a nerf ball. So, I goaded him by opening up my guard to show that he would actually have to put effort in beating me," K-Force described the scene before them.

"I saw you talking to him. What were you saying?" Tripp asked about the scene where K-Force dropped his guard.

"He asked what I was doing, and I told him I was not going to waste my time blocking his soft punches," K-Force stated bluntly.

"Oh, I bet he didn't like that," Trevon guffawed.

"He took it well, until I said that he got there by pure luck against Azougue. That set him off," K-Force said with a grin.

"To his face? Oh no, you didn't!" Tripp was shocked by the audacity.

"I was trying to get him angry," K-Force explained, just telling them like it was.

"From the rush of blows he unleashed on you, we all heard and felt how much power and force he used to crush you into paste," Trevon still gesturing for the audience at home.

"Which is where I wanted him, so I drew him into thinking he finally had me cornered and practically felt his overconfidence, I let him land the first haymaker to build his confidence, then ducked under his second incoming blow," K-Force displayed for the audience.

"Which you made him swiftly pay for, textbook Ali," mentioned Trevon, who loved it when Heroes and athletes used skill and technique over power.

"Young man, when did you come up with his battle plan?" Tripp asked.

"Never give me time and knowledge on my opponent. It gives me time to analyze a game plan and execute with efficiency," K-Force came out and said.

"Ruthless efficiency. I like that Mamba mentality," Tripped added.

The rest of the show was commentary about how he felt about his opponents and who he wanted to fight the most. The final point of conversation was his family, or more of the reason he did not mention them.

"Heck, man, both your dad and your mother are great Heroes. I believe Tripp has Intercessor in his yearly top ten," Trevon asked.

"Top five, Trevon, top five," Tripp countered.

"What he said, I'm surprised that you didn't announce that bit of background information." Trevon was trying to answer the audience questions from the live stream.

"I'm trying to make a name for myself, not my folks," K-Force stated bluntly.

"You ashamed of them or something," Tripped asked.

"Don't try to build drama since both my parents and I had this conversation before I came to the Combine," K-Force said, trying to avoid this line of thought.

"I'm not trying to start drama. I'm just asking the question why you don't want people to know you're related to Armory and Intercessor," Tripp said, asserting his question.

"Let's add my sister Ratel there as well, and that is, the reason for almost four years my sister had to deal with being the daughter of our parents. No matter how great a deed she did, it would always be a reflection of our parents, and she hated that. And after every mistake, it was always about her bringing embarrassment to our parents, which drove her up the wall at times," K-Force clarified.

"You're saying that as if that didn't help get you here," Tripp accused.

"My family name didn't pave the way for me. I got here to the top stage by myself. As you stated before, I was nobody until I took down Prime Time. Did I get some high-level training? Yes, but he had a whole freaking Ivy League school that cranks out quality Heroes like a construction line," K-Force replied, justifying his decision.

On and on this small discussion went, but it got his point across to many out there in the viewing audience. People who heard the fight plan agreed that it was a good plan; some even called it the perfect plan.

JULY 12th
AUDITORIUM THEATRE
CHICAGO, ILLINOIS

Over a month after the Combine, K-Force was at the draft celebration where all this drama could be put to rest. While his fight victory over the heavy favorites was phenomenal and pushed him higher on the rankings, he was still not top three. Though many online protested that he had proven to be more versatile, this didn't really matter to him in the grand scheme of things. He was sixth place overall, which meant he would not be dragged to the Pacific region, since they only had two first round picks, and they were not going to waste them on him.

The night was going fine with food and drinks for the Heroes and agents. The lucky few had mentors of friends who were Heroes to wait with them. Bianca's parents could not attend due to safety issues for the family. She was very aware that the press would do anything for a scoop, such as exposing their identity and location.

This had happened before, and most of those reporters were tried and jailed for their actions, especially after the first few only had to pay a fine for accessory to murder. In those instances, Heroes were so enraged that they either killed the reporter or destroyed the entire news building. So, the next best thing was her best friend's family, who came in and sat with her and Samson.

"Thank you for coming Intercessor. It's nice to have people cheering me on since my folks couldn't make it," Azougue said. She was wearing a formal version of her attire.

"*Please*, you're practically family," Intercessor responded. She was wearing her own formal version of her super suit.

"Plus, you two made me money on the bets this year," Ratel said, grinning as she looked at her red sole high heels, which were bought with those winnings.

- **119** -

"Ratel," Intercessor chided her eldest's antics.

"Relax, Mom. I spent no more than a thousand and got thirty to one odds in both of their first fights. Though I did lose some when she lost to Prime Beefcake," Ratel commented.

"Really, sis, don't you have a boyfriend," K-Force rolled his eyes.

"Yeah, but there is no rule that says I can't look at pretty boys," said Ratel, feeling no shame.

"Fair enough, but you know how paranoid some significant others get when most of your co-workers are model material," K-Force said, pointing out how some various relationships drop.

"Jesse understands that I'm only interested in him. In my workplace there are only three types: Married, Players, and Scrubs. Married and Scrubs are self-explanatory, but Players, yeah, I'm too old to believe in changing or save-the-bad-boy crap," Ratel said, laughing it off.

"So, you're saying you're just window shopping," Azougue said. She knew where the woman was coming from.

"Exactly, it is like looking at a dress you can't afford, too small, or far too risqué for your taste. It is nice to fantasize about, but no reason to waste your time and money on it." Ratel snapped her fingers for emphasis.

"The first Meta Hero draft pick is Northeastern United States region," the head of the United Hero Association paused for effect, "...Mithril." This received a loud cheer since the draft announcements were taking place in Cleveland this year. A lot of spectators came from the New England area to be at the event. Mithril, being a bit of a showoff, wore a power armor more elegantly paired with a form-fitting evening gown.

"Thank God, I was slowly losing faith in humanity if they picked Nega Twat as the number one pick," Azougue sighed in relief.

"Look, Azougue, I know you're not happy with him hitting on you all the time, but you got to let it go. We are on the same side, and you can't carry that animosity with you. On the off chance that you two begin to work together, that animosity would be a detriment," warned K-Force, trying to lower her aggression towards another Hero.

"Enough of the five-dollar words, twerp," Ratel laughed lightly at her little brother. "But he's right. As much as I play vicious Hot Head, I save that anger for villains and crooks. I keep all my beef away from, not only my work, but my personal life as well."

"Easy for you to say, you don't have some sleazy Argentinian who thinks I'm his woman because I'm the hottest Brazilian in the whole draft," Azougue argued, still not liking it.

"That and I think he has an S&M fetish, since this infatuation started after you decisively whooped his ass," Ratel commented.

"Oh God, don't remind me. That creeps me out a bit," Azougue said with a shudder.

"I figure that you would like a little boy toy under your control." K-Force was remembering some of the guys she had dated.

"While some girls like the idea, I need a man who will stand up to me and pull me down to earth when I need a wakeup call," Azougue stated before the announcement for the second draft pick.

"With the second pick in this year's Meta Hero draft, Pacific region of the United States pick. Prime Time!" the Chairman stated calmly, as Prime Time walked to the stage, shook the Chairman's hand and hugged him. Then he put on the Pacific region logo, which was a very large capital "P" and a rolling golden wave. People cheered, of course, but it was more of a confirmation.

- 121 -

"How did California get a draft number that high? They are overcrowded and don't have enough of threat level to warrant a number that high in the draft," Intercessor said, slightly disgusted by the obvious bias.

"California traded about three Heroes, with one being Alpha Level, to the Rocky Mountain region," K-Force said, none too surprised.

"I swear to God, they're turning this into a sports league," groused Intercessor, as she rubbed the bridge of her nose.

"No offense, Mom, but we have a Combine and a draft and they are trading Pro Heroes like baseball cards, this is what happens when you allow big money into events like this," K-Force pointed out.

"I know, but I hate hearing your father say 'I told you so,'" Intercessor sighed.

"Mom please, Dad never says that to you. If he did, I'm pretty sure you two would have divorced a while ago," K-Force quipped.

Intercessor laughed at her son's comment as the other draft came and went; they were approaching the announcement for the fifth place pick.

"With the fifth place pick in this year's Meta hero draft, the Central Region of the United States pick... K-Force!" the chairman of the Meta-human Association announced.

At those words, K-Force went through three emotions very quickly. Shock, disbelief, and utter joy with the fact that he would go to one of the biggest trouble centers in the US. The Great Lakes area was just swimming with crime and had some of the best opportunities for young Heroes to make a name for themselves. K-Force walked proudly towards the stage with his mother acting like the typical mom, clapping her hands loudly and saying, "That's my baby." Azougue low-fived him as he walked by her and cheered him onward, and when K-Force shook the chairman's hand, he felt like everything was coming together and could visualize the next five years, imagining fighting crime and gaining a name for himself, and being able to get past the shadows of his parents. He saw himself earning enough money from advertisements to set himself up for a couple of years. Then, he could see himself earning a heavy reputation when he finally made it to Federal level, which would set him apart from the others. He saw himself writing his own ticket, and going anywhere he wanted, as a part of a mother and son team. He knew once his siblings heard of this, they were going to probably call him mama's boy. But he knew what sold, and family teams were always big sellers.

All of the hard work is paying off. The first step of the rest my life is now, K-Force thought as he grabbed the cap with a large capital "C" embossed from wheat and the image of the Great Lakes.

Soon afterwards, Azougue also was called to the stage as the eighth overall pick, which made her actually jump out of her chair. She Samba-danced across the stage as she shook the man's hand and grabbed the Central's hat as well. It looked as though K-Force and Azougue were going to be wreaking havoc on bad guys in the Midwest, especially if they would get to tag team like they did when they were young. The night got better and better, until a last-minute trade was announced right before the twentieth place pick.

"For exchange, two first draft picks and Nega Titan. Central is trading K-Force to the Pacific region of the United States," an announcer said over the speakers. K-Force was dumbfounded when he heard the announcement, but he only had one response and didn't care if his mother heard him.

Chapter 6
California Dead Zone

To say that Samson was pissed was an understatement. He had a clear route to his goal of being a great Hero. Now he would be bogged down in a place where he would be benched until he was 'taught' to be more of a corporate whore for the masses. So, eighty percent of his time would be promotions, then he would be put in the background, just so that their big names could grab the spotlight. K-Force told his sponsors how he felt about it, and he also told them he would go to Canada or Europe if they put him anywhere between Los Angeles and San Francisco. They tried to dissuade him in telling him that it was not that bad. Samson mentioned Night Haze which shut them up. She was an example of how the current system in the Pacific was absolute garbage.

During the five years Night Haze was assigned to California—San Francisco to be more precise—she barely had any chances to prove herself. When she got permission to stop a villain or crime, Night Haze would break down her villain; then right before she took him or her out, a more popular Hero would spring out of nowhere to take her glory. This happened to almost half of her takedowns for three years. When she was Federal, she actually started to gain real skills in fighting crime and helping people, something that should have been done in her first two years, but somehow being a cover girl model was more important, according to her handlers. When she chose to be Federal instead of Professional, the villain-snagging became blatant, and they practically drove her out the state.

At that point, they understood how much Samson loathed the idea of going to California, and how much of a waste of talent it would be if they didn't at least send him to a less cluttered area of the Pacific region. Washington and Oregon were out because most veteran Heroes who don't have major media attention move to greener pastures and were not going to give it up unless they had the star power to shine. Northern California was also out, as well, because of the same problem—not to mention they seemed determined to keep K-Force out of the area. So, after three days of negotiation and threats to take an offer from Liverpool, England, he was sent to the only southern California city that wasn't cluttered to hell; San Alonso—also known as Silicon Beach or Border City was only seventeen miles from the border of Mexico. This was considered a crap job by some since many believed it was a jump up from being border patrol, but this couldn't be further from the truth. In the recent years, villains started to feel cluttered in the Los Angeles area as well. So, they moved to San Alonso to build their own criminal empire, without having to deal with the Big Four of California.

The week before Samson and Bianca went their separate ways, they decided to have a night out together as a celebration of both of them getting big corporate jobs. While at a bar, they noticed a certain scene all over the TV sets.

Soon Samson was watching his brother killing Chernobyl on live television while Omari was on his last legs. Then Samson and everyone in the bar heard or read in captions Fringe's confession of his frame job and implications of Senator Cannady.

"Wasn't that your brother?" Bianca looked in shock as she watched Omari tearing through some the deadliest villains on the East Coast.

"You know it is," Samson said in a tone that spoke of slight disbelief.

"Did he just kill Chernobyl?" Bianca winced slightly as she saw the villain's head get caved in.

"You know he did." Samson grimaced.

"Does this mean he's 'out' now?" Bianca asked, genuinely worried.

"You know he is." Samson shook his head in resignation.

"I guess we know what the big topic will be for the next month." Bianca knew that Heroes, whether "wannabe's" or registered, loved gossiping about those kinds of things.

"What do you think?" said Samson in a "no duh" expression. Then, as if on cue, his phone started ringing.

"It's your mom, isn't it?" Bianca knew very well how Samson's family acted, from being around them for so many years.

Samson sighed in a final resigned tone, as he pulled his phone from his pocket.

"Hey, Mama," Samson said as he continued to watch the insanity unfolding before his brother. "Yeah, I'm watching it right now."

They watched the news and saw craziness spiraling throughout the rest of the evening. The news was itself one-sided, fighting accusations against Cannady and stating that words of a madman should not be taken into consideration. Meanwhile others showed actual proof that backed up the claims and pointed out Anonymous had never lied or sent false information, despite how many people tried to disprove it.

In spite of this, there was political intrigue of a plan to turn Metas into private armies for the select political elite. This had happened before. There was an inner circle of government politicians who controlled the Meta population and tried to use them to commit a coup. While not as blatant as the 1950s attempt, it still showed why no one person or group of politicians should ever have that much power. Bianca and Samson could see that the laws were either going to be reinforced or changeed entirely to prevent such an event from happening again.

There was another observation that went around most social media. His brother's ranking had to be increased at this point, which was a big deal in the Meta-human society. Omari was considered only a Gamma-level Meta, just because his powers were that of a mediocre healer. Healers were more valuable than many other types. With his skills in combat and increased strength of his healing ability on display to the world, he might be considered a high-level Alpha. This also meant that every corporation and government agency was going to go hunting for him. And to end cap it all, the girl his brother was dating was Red Banshee. Omari had always been rational in relationships, and now he was caught banging some chick from the other side of the law.

"Red Banshee? Your brother is shacked up with Red Banshee. Oh, I can't wait to see what your mother is going to do to him." Bianca looked almost impressed.

"Having been on the receiving end of her tirades, I can tell you he will be walking funny for a while," Samson said. He looked bewildered by the news playing before him.

"Think he will be put in jail?" Bianca asked.

"Strong chance any of the Alphabet soup agencies are willing to pull the 'we will keep you out of jail, but you have to work for us' card. That is, if the corporations don't pay someone to force him to work for them," Samson replied as he scratched his head in frustration.

"Oh, I forgot that, and they will make him take shitty pay for his work instead of being paid what he is worth," Bianca responded, remembering all the Metas with useful powers that were known to break the law.

"That depends on what they can charge him with. Which is a good thing since coming out this way gives him a degree of protection." Samson was already brainstorming his brother's defense, if needed.

"How?" Bianca was confused. He was caught associating with a villain.

"He found the real murderer, took out one Beta- and Alpha- level villain, and was attacked by a corrupt politician. If they try anything egregious at his trial, they will be hounded by the public, and it could be thrown out as obvious trumped up charges," Samson said. At first he was grabbing at straws, but the more he thought about it, the more it made sense.

"So, he has some protection," Bianca said, wanting confirmation.

"Some, but who knows what bullshit they will pull out just to ensnare him?" Samson said as he felt doubt creeping in.

"Oh, our lovely American justice system," she said in sarcasm.

"You say that as if any justice system is perfect. Let's face the facts, no nation's justice system is incorruptible. Even in the socialist countries the one percent is merely replaced with bureaucrats who breaks the law more blatantly," Samson retorted, pointing out facts he had learned from the history of Cubans who escaped from their own country.

"My family is from Brazil; we had an official who molested my aunt. And our nation has a history of police brutality, so trust me, I get it," Bianca sighed, recalling the horror stories told to her.

"Well, we are not getting anything more for the rest of the day, so let's focus on something else, before I lose my mind," Samson said, turning away from the TV to focus on anything else for a while.

SEPTEMBER 9th
SAN ALONSO, CALIFORNIA

When Samson arrived in San Alonso, he was glued to the news as he set up his temporary home. On his laptop in his room, he had his whole family, except his brother who was still under investigation by the FBI. Since the incident involved a politician, a few people in government were exposed as being in on the whole Senator Cannady conspiracy. The press was having a field day with Incognito exposing every link between the senator and Fringe. There were attempts to ban everyone who posted it on social media, but as a big middle finger, they instead posted it in the advertisements. The website could not be brought down, mostly because it was self-funded. And the organization, Incognito, was created by the best hackers in the world. There was little to nothing anyone could do to hide it. There was talk of dangerous misinformation being spread, but very few people believed it. Especially with John Doe testifying the whole plan to congress in the next couple of weeks.

"What is happening with Omari? It seems they are trying to keep him and his new squeeze hidden from the world," K-Force asked worriedly.

"The press tried to put your brother in the spotlight but he can talk rings around reporters and use their words against them," Aaliyah said proudly.

"Meaning they don't want to go into a losing battle, since every conversation being recorded will be scrutinized by Incognito. So, they can't edit it to make them look better." K-Force knew how these things worked.

"Exactly, as bad as the press are now, imagine how they would act if there was less accountability," Hakeem commented on the terrible practices.

"Accountability for thee, and not for me, I imagine. But that's beside the point. Despite some efforts, this incident will not be swept under the rug. Cannady has been caught and there is not enough backroom dealing that is going to save him," said Aaliyah, grinning darkly. She loved seeing politicians get their comeuppance, since you usually see them slide out of trouble.

"A lot of Metas, Pro and Fed, have threatened to quit or leave the country if he is let go. Helen has promised that she would go to Sweden or Denmark if they let the orchestrator of Jacob's murder free," Ratel added her own information.

Samson knew that was a serious threat on both accounts. Meta-humans, whether Hero or private sector, were basically vital resources for any nation. If a large portion of them were to go on strike, quite a few portions of the country would grind to a halt. Omegas were a major part of national defense, to the point that losing one was a detriment that would be very hard to recover from. Nukes were dangerous still, but firing missiles across great distance could be easily countered. Losing her would get a President or a lifelong politician voted out of office easily.

"So why is the government still saying that there is an investigation?" Samson couldn't believe how long it was taking.

"Because Cannady is giving names and statements to keep himself out of jail. Though at this point, he better hope that his info can keep him out of the hellholes that traitors are sent to," Hakeem said.

"It doesn't matter how many big names he is connected to. Cannady won't live long enough to testify to anyone," Aaliyah said in a hopeful tone.

After hearing the minor details of what was happening to his older brother, Samson ended the video call and closed his laptop. He decided to clear his head of the drama by playing some games on his V-Box. As he was settling down for the day, Samson thought about his own current situation and why he had come to this city. In this bad situation he found himself in, San Alonso was the best option available to him, with only 4.3 million dollars instead of the 5.8 million that he was promised. He, like all sidekicks, or 'Hero assistants,' which was the PC term, would share a condo apartment with a roommate named QuickTime - the Pacific's third and final Pick. This proved the Pacific region was way too overcrowded; it had traded away nine Heroes, gained four Heroes, and they were still overloaded.

When K-Force left his home for the first time, his mother actually cried because her youngest and final child was leaving the nest. She held him for a long time, since they would be more than a state away from one another, which to people who can fly is the equivalent of an hour drive. As much as Samson hated to admit it, he felt scared. He was truly without his parents' immediate guidance. As much as Hollywood liked to portray adulthood as college age, it is not. You are still under the protection of parents even though they are not physically there. No, when you get a job, and pay bills and taxes, you are truly an adult. To Samson, the amount of responsibility one shows defines adulthood, not age.

The condo he moved into was a small, gated community with two beds, two-and-a-half baths, and 1164 feet in space. There was a pool out back, shared with the neighbors, and it was surprisingly half the size of an Olympic pool, which was nice for someone who was once on the swim team.

The move in wasn't as arduous as he thought. He found that when doing the heavy lifting himself, there was less of a chance of anyone wrecking his belongings. Outside of a TV and bed, which he had to supply, the place came furnished. After two hours, the place was finally settled, since he left most of his things back home. He only brought what he considered his essentials: his game system and PC Rig his brother had built for him. While he wasn't an avid gamer, he loved to play when he was on down time.

As he booted up his game system, there was a rattle from the front door as a young, wiry white guy with shaggy, brown hair walked in with a backpack, along with the movers. Judging by his height, and the fact that Samson knew he was supposed to share the condo with QuickTime, he figured that this was probably his new roommate.

Deciding to be a good roommate and make a good impression with someone he was supposedly stuck with for the next couple of years, Samson decided to help him move in.

"Hey, the name is Samson, your new roommate. Need any help with your stuff?"

"Huh, uh sure, thanks," the shaggy, brown-haired young man seemed to say as he saw the large black man around his age help the movers with the bed frame. The movers were also surprised by the fact that Samson wasn't a weakling, until they saw the muscles under the loose T-shirt he wore.

As Samson and the movers walked past the brown-haired young man to carry the bed frame to the other bedroom. "Oh snap, my bad the name is Avery. Sorry, didn't expect you to be here so soon."

"Don't mention it, just hope we get along," Samson said as he slowly put the headboard of the bed to the ground while the other mover just dropped it on the carpeted floor.

This is why Dad says movers have to be spoken for before you hire them, Samson thought, as he looked towards the slightly muscled but overweight man who walked back towards the moving truck.

The week following the move-in was not spectacular by any stretch of the imagination. There was no drama of Samson and Avery butting heads and becoming friends. Nor were there any epic battles in which they formed a brotherhood, unless it counted for them being on the same L-shaped couch eating nachos from a nearby restaurant and playing Mission of Honor together. It took a couple of days, but since they were new around each other, they started talking to one another. Neither of them was happy to be there in the Pacific. Avery wanted to go to his old stomping grounds in the Midwest corner of the US, since he was a Minnesota native. And he wanted to help clean up the city from the ground level. It turned out that the Heroes rarely went after people who actually affected the average man's life, unless the press was nearby.

Avery turned out to be the son of a top-class lawyer who saw the corrupt get off scot-free, because of small mistakes committed by the police; or a district attorney who believed that 'people shouldn't have their life destroyed because they assaulted or killed a guy.'

"I wish that I had something as noble or goal-worthy as that, but it is my family business in a way, which I love to continue. And my other motive is a bit of vengeance since a dear aunt of mine was killed because someone like your D.A. released some asshat from jail with a list of murder victims. I want to be Federal, so I can make sure that those who are too dangerous to be let back into society lose their ability to harm anyone again," Samson said, remembering his Aunt Gabby.

"You're not going all castigator, are you?" Avery said worriedly.

"No, but I am going to do everything in my power to make sure that they never become a reoccurring threat. If someone breaks out of prison repeatedly, it is obvious they don't want to change," Samson stated candidly.

"I understand where you're coming from. Just don't let them turn you into a monster. Some criminals like these people need help." Avery tried to dissuade his new roommate.

"After the third or fourth time they step out of a prison or asylum and end up killing another group of people, do they still deserve help?" Samson said, adding his own belief.

This became a small division of opinion, of which they would come back to repeatedly. But it was not a make-or-break decision between them. For the most part they got along well. Samson explained the basis of his power to Avery as it wasn't the whole story.

"What, you control kinetic energy? As in the very concept of force?" Avery was shocked by it all.

"Not control, per se, but I can manipulate the energy around my body," Samson replied, not wanting to give everything away.

"No wonder you took out Prime Time. You absorbed all his energy and threw it back at him. You pretty much made him defeat himself," Avery assumed.

"Got it in one go," Samson confirmed.

"Do you have any weaknesses," Avery asked a bit nervously.

"Sorry, you're cool and all, but we're not that close." Samson ended that line of questioning.

"Fair enough. I guess it's my turn, ever heard the old adage that humans only use ten percent of their brains?" Avery offered.

"Yeah, it was made up by some pothead probably from the '50s or '60s. I think it is more like our brains don't work at complete optimization, like we are only running it in first gear, even though we can reach fifth gear," Samson replied.

"Exactly, good analogy. Well, I, on the other hand, can go to fifth gear for about six hours a day. Perfect recall, instant learning, instant analysis. Give me an hour and I can speak any language fluently," Avery explained.

"How does that translate to skintight power suit," Samson asked.

"That I will admit comes from my grandpa, who was a regular super genius. I improved the technology to match modern times and found solutions that weren't available in his time," Avery revealed.

"Guess I'm not the only one with family support," Samson acknowledged.

"Yep," Avery verified.

"Question? I talk to some super geniuses; you don't use every twenty-dollar word in the book. They try to explain everything in the most scientific way possible, and that leaves most people scratching their heads and feeling stupid," Samson was curious about his genius roommate's behavior.

"I repeat, I'm only that for six hours of collective overtime; the rest of the time, just someone with above average intelligence who coasted through college by the skin of his teeth," Avery explained.

"So, you have an on and off switch for the technical mumbo jumbo," Samson summarized.

"Yep," Avery verified again.

"Cool. So, who is your mentor going to be for the next two years?" Samson decided to change the subject, since this route of questioning had ended.

"That would be Faultline. They want me to pair up with the most back-breaking vet in the Pacific," Avery groaned lightly.

"Wow, lucky you. You are actually learning something, opposed to me, who will probably be getting the smile and wave training." Samson was a little envious.

"Oh, come on, it can't be that bad." Avery was sure Samson was blowing it out of proportion.

"My mentor is the Bronze Bomber," Samson stated with no joy.

There was silence after that little exchange of information. "Um, at least you got something pretty to look at."

"If that's the case, I feel I have a better chance of learning from Porn Hub," Samson quipped.

At that comment, Avery busted out laughing and was rolling on the floor. "Oh, come on, you didn't need to go that hard."

When Monday rolled around they met up at the city center in the municipal building which housed an area where most of the Heroes met. There was no hall of justice or secret hideout; that was for national teams. For the rest of the unofficial teams of Heroes, they worked out of a branch of City Hall. In K-Force's case, he and his new coworkers were in charge of San Alonso County, Imperial County, Riverside County and Orange County. If that wasn't enough, they also patrolled the border when needed. It might seem a lot of ground to cover, but major crimes that required their help was not that widespread or frequent. They could be thought of as SWAT-sponsored teams that went in shifts but had 24/7 service, mostly on call. If a situation was too dangerous for one or two Heroes, more were called in to combine their forces in order to take care of it.

This was material they gave everyone to read about beforehand, and it was distributed in the orientation because some people hate reading instructions; they believed they could do without it. Hence, K-Force and QuickTime were experiencing this at that moment. As bad as it was to sit through the PowerPoint presentation, it must have been painful for a guy who had photographic memory to feel spoon-fed as if he were a toddler. While it felt like a waste of time, it did introduce them to Heroes in the area which they would have to work with. One woman was the youngest one there, besides them, and she decided to become Professional after she served her time as a sidekick.

This was someone K-Force remembered from six years ago when she was in her own class, Gyges, the curvy Psyche Powerhouse. What made Gyges stand out, besides being considered the best in class and despite being tenth pick, was the fact that she had a mild mutation to her body, namely her skin being a light violet or lilac color. While she had a more voluptuous figure than the standard Heroine, she had once admitted that if she hadn't obtained her powers, she would probably weigh over five hundred pounds. But, like all who gained the Meta gene, she gained the most perfect body possible, and she loved showing her body off in her icy blue evening dress-like apparel. Her top was wrapped around the back of her neck, but was left bare back with a flowing dress that had slits on both sides of her full hips. It was a mixture of flaunting her body while making her look classy. She took full advantage of this because of her exotic skin color and background. She had been with several rappers ever since she moved to California.

And as much as K-Force hated to admit it, despite being kind of shallow, she was very attractive, which she knew. K-Force remembered how their first meeting went.

K-Force was finally finished with orientation and introductions to most of his coworkers. Gyges sashayed towards him and started to play with her black hair. Her suit emphasized her assets, her larger than average breasts, as well as her thick but well-put-together hips. Though she was only five-feet eight-inches, K-Force felt like he was in the grasp of a predator.

"Hmm, well it's been a while since we had new blood around here. Maybe with you here I won't be called Rookie or Kid anymore," Gyges said as she touched his chest.

Calm down, though every sign says she is interested, it also could mean she is just flirting and being friendly. Though, I sure as hell am not going to act like a high school virgin, K-Force thought, as he kept control over himself.

"I seriously doubt anyone would mistake you for a Kid, but that's how every organization works. Even if you prove yourself, you will always be the baby of the group until someone else comes along," K-Force replied.

"Sounds like you had some experience," Gyges said.

"Nah, heard enough crap from my friends when they first started working," K-Force half-jested.

"So, tell me, you nervous?" Gyges teased.

"About working here, yes and no. It's mostly when I'm called to do something and not mess up," K-Force replied honestly.

"Oh, don't worry sweetie, we all have those first mission jitters. But I'm not going to lie, if you mess up, the press will not be kind," Gyges assured him and noticed he winced at the mention of the press.

"Not a fan, are you?" Gyges had never met a rookie so disgusted with the press.

"Nope, but I am going to have to deal with them regardless," K-Force rolled his eyes at the thought of dealing with the glorified paparazzi.

"The price for fame and fortune," Gyges repeated a mantra that got her through the tough times.

"True, but I swore if they went after me, I would not give them the satisfaction of ignoring their crap," K-Force said candidly.

"Oh, sound dangerous if you want to be a Hero," Gyges warned him.

"In the forty-five states, exposing a Hero or information on his or her family is fifteen years in prison or twenty to life if someone gets killed or hurt. California is one of the states where it is just a fine," K-Force said to emphasize how much he had to keep to his vest.

"Still seems extreme." Gyges owed a bit to the press herself.

"If you watched the trial, Sunna's husband and home was exposed by a reporter who wanted a major pay day. Senator Cannady paid for said information. I'm lucky. My family are all Metas which means full protection. Sunna's family, on the other hand, have to have their identities changed, face wiped from records, and move into an entirely different region to stay safe. All because some press junkie could not keep his mouth shut and mind his own business." K-Force was only stating facts.

"Okay, but they can also be your greatest asset, so don't burn them all with one brush. If you want to make it big, you are going to have to play nice." Gyges saw his point, but was trying to reason with him.

"I'm more than willing, but I refuse to sit back and take attacks against people I care about. Turning the other cheek doesn't work with paparazzi," K-Force said, making his feelings on the subject known.

Gyges could only shake her head at the young Hero who seemed way too combative. *What a waste of potential*, Gyges thought. Having been in this business for almost six years, she knew that if you wanted to make it big, you had to turn the other cheek.

Too bad, he was cute though. But I can't waste my time with guys like him, Gyges thought, with a little extra flip in her hips to draw the eyes to her ass.

"Making friends already," QuickTime jested as he walked over.

"Maybe, but we already had a disagreement about how much we need to bow to the press," K-Force replied.

"Oh, those rats who only speak about free speech when it benefits them," QuickTime dismissed.

QuickTime was a lot more vicious against the press than K-Force. K-Force openly admitted that having the umbrella of Incognito to protect him from assaults by the media was a major blessing. QuickTime didn't have that, but he did have a super genius intellect, and just enough pettiness to utterly destroy any press that went near him. K-Force found it odd that QuickTime was merciful towards criminals, but for the press he had absolute hatred. Obviously, there was a story there, but he wasn't going to pry since they barely knew each other.

Today wasn't much of anything except becoming officially Assistant Heroes, though everybody and their grandma still referred to them as sidekicks. The orientation consisted of an introduction and having them posing for the camera. The photos would upload to their official web page and magazine cover. Both newcomers felt that they were wasting their time. QuickTime openly admitted that he would have had a more productive time sitting on the couch and playing some Battle Royale.

While the first day was less than impressive, the rest of the week was interesting, to say the least. The day he met his mentor was the day he got a full dose of the modern Hero industry. Bronze Bomber, like her name suggested, was not the most practical Hero one might meet, but was infamous for being a lot of flash and flare; her appearance alone made that self-evident. To say she was top heavy would be an understatement, and to the dismay and joy too many, they were natural. The Meta-human gene was a natural mutation that optimized the human body and sometimes it exaggerated certain aspects of the body as well. There was a reason some people called the Meta gene the porn star gene at times. But that's not the main reason why she seemed risqué to some people. Her outfits or uniforms always went to the edge of lewd and appropriate. For instance, what she was wearing then was her favorite uniform, a white one-piece leotard-like suit that stretched down into her shin-high boots. A white, sleeveless, turtleneck top with full coverage, and she had black highlights in the belt around her waist, gloves, and boots. At first glance, despite being tight to her body, it didn't seem all that lewd. That was until she turned her back, which was bare all the way to her small of her back. Her breasts were seemingly stretching the material. This covered her bronze, metallic-like skin, which happened to contain her interstellar power, the closest thing that humanity had to near infinite energy source. Add the fact that this girl was blonde, and you can get why she was considered a bimbo Hero.

The press for the first week was absolutely annoying, trying to make this a big deal, when it was not; Bronze Bomber, a liberated woman, training a hot prospect for the future. The press tried repeatedly for K-Force to work with them in saying something political, but he refused. Politics were the main dividing factors for people currently, and he wanted nothing to do with it. He would only talk about causes and charities with which no one could disagree, and this, in turn, made him boring to the press.

Sorry, I have no interest in being a firebrand or a mouthpiece for whatever movement, K-Force thought, as he patrolled the area of Orange County with Bronze Bomber. The area he was responsible for was the southern part of California, which was decided by population density and land mass. Hence, he and fourteen others were spread across Orange County, San Bernardino, Riverside, Imperial, and San Alonso. The highest population of Heroes was in the coastal region which included, LA and over thirty-five Heroes. The Bay Area had a smaller population and size than

Southern California, but had twenty-six in total, while SoCal only had eighteen at most.

It seemed this was the case of patrolling those who would give the largest donations. Though it might seem like the dream patrol for most people, it was terrible for Heroes. For those of a Heroic profession, the best route was the crime-ridden areas of cities or communities. That is where you show your worth by busting robberies, murders, shoot outs, and drive-bys. If a Hero stopped a rape, as disgusting as it sounds, the Hero would gain much praise in the press for a while. In plain English, smile and waving only works when in the spotlight; out of it, Heroes had to show their worth.

As he followed behind Bronze Bomber through the air, it seemed that she was contemplating something, until she finally spoke. "Why did you ignore that reporter?"

"Which one?" K-Force had spoken with several before they began their first patrol.

"The one who asked you about the Meyers vs. Catlin trial," Bronze Bomber asked.

"Because I'm not allowed to have an actual opinion or be a nuisance about it. He wanted confirmation of me siding with his political views," he stated flatly.

"You will be asked those kinds of questions all of the time. You will have to answer them," she said.

"Despite what concepts modern athletes and celebrities forced down our throats, no I don't," K-Force answered.

"Don't you think we have a responsibility to the public. People look up to us, and they want our opinion," Bronze Bomber stated.

"Not when an honest opinion can get you canceled. That man killed a child and should go to prison, but because he's a celebrity, they are arguing that he should be put on probation or house arrest for a few years," K-Force said, disgusted that it was even a debate.

"I agree, and I said that no child death should be overlooked as a simple mistake," Bronze Bomber agreed with him.

"You have enough clout in this business to buffer you from too much damage. I'm relatively a nobody, and there are people looking for an excuse to crucify me for knocking out their golden goose Prime Time," K-Force said.

"Please tell me you're exaggerating." Bronze Bomber didn't like what she was hearing.

"An agent from his company said, and I quote: "The downside about being at the top is the fact that when you fall, it is three times as hard to stay above water," K-Force explained.

"Okay, I can see why you're weary about doing anything that could come back at you. Enteriagey has gone after me, as well. They say I'm stealing Wraith Queen thunder, when I only saved her life," Bronze Bomber admitted.

As she mentioned Wraith Queen, K-Force remembered the Heroine who in many ways held the opposite image. Azougue compared them to the Cheerleaders and Goths as far as demographics appeal went. Though that is somewhat true, Wraith Queen was the bigger sellout, as her former fanbase whined about on forums. Wraith Queen was less gothic and more corporate businesswoman at that point in time. K-Force had no problem about these changes, as time and age naturally change people. And he knew that every Hero whose identity sticks to a fad either changes or becomes forgotten.

Shoot, the only reminder from their early 2000s image was their rivalry. Well, the media portrayed it as a rivalry, but who knew whether that was true or not.

"It's the image thing. If your client is saved by the opposing team's client, it makes them look bad in the public eye. So, to save face they have to say you interfered," Bronze Bomber explained, showing she had history with Enteriagey.

"That is something you got to learn in the professional world - some companies will try to upstage or sabotage each other," Bronze Bomber added, showing that she was more than a well-endowed metallic woman.

"Is this the reason we see Heroes fight each other sometimes?" K-Force was surprised that his parents forgot this in their lessons.

"Exactly, people play it off as misunderstandings, but in truth it is resentment and rage between a group of Heroes that are often pushed by their backers. If there was ever a reason to join the Federal side of things, it would be they don't deal with that crap like us pros," Bronze Bomber clarified.

"Wait, you encouraging me to choose the Fed side?" he asked.

"I believe in being honest with you and letting you know what you are getting into," she answered.

This actually surprised K-Force, who thought she was a shallow corporate mouthpiece. "Huh, shows I don't know people as well as I thought I did."

Less than five minutes later, they heard sirens. They also saw a speeding armored truck with a lot of gunfire shooting back at several police vehicles.

"Should we help?" he asked

"No, we can't solve all the police's problems, and I'm sure your parents will tell you to leave the mundane problems to the police. Since, like us, they serve a purpose, and we can't be everywhere. They can handle this level crook easily," Bronze Bomber replied.

Soon they heard an explosion which turned out to be one of the robbers blowing away one of the cop cars with a rocket launcher. This made the following cop car crash onto the sidewalk, almost hitting a pedestrian, as it went through the store front window.

"Stop them," she commanded. Not wasting time to question her orders, K-Force flipped upside down and kicked his body towards the ground. Then he expertly landed in front of the armored truck, not giving them time to turn or swerve out of the way. He simply placed his hand out towards the truck, and as soon as he touched it, all the force and momentum were absorbed into him. It was as if the world's greatest brakes activated as K-Force instantly stopped the car. K-Force didn't just absorb all the momentum of the car but also the impact on the occupants inside, because such a sudden stop would snap some bones and spines. Though he wasn't merciful enough to make it completely safe, given that they had killed several officers already.

When the armored truck stopped, the man standing in the op hatch of the armored truck greatly injured his back and ribs as he slammed into the unforgiving rim. This caused him to misfire the RPG into the air away from the police helicopter. K-Force saw the missile and waited until it was far enough away to shoot it out of the sky. Next, he jumped on top on the armored truck to apprehend the occupants inside. When he stopped it, he sensed six people inside. So, when he slipped through the roof, everyone was either rolling in pain or dazed by the sudden stop and impact. Moving before they could react, K-Force grabbed every gun within his reach, taking them away from any itchy trigger fingers. Soon K-Force spotted a comely woman tied up and gagged who was dizzy as well. He also spotted a hand reaching for her with a knife. K-Force fired a concentrated beam from his finger which broke the man's hand. Then K-Force moved quickly to push the man away from the hostage, which sent him flying towards the wall.

"Hold on, Miss, let me get you out of here before more come around," K-Force said as he cut through the restraints with his finger vibrating like a knife through them. The woman hugged him tightly as if her life depended on it. This was a typical reaction being in a life and death situation. Most people would be distracted, but K-Force had it drilled into his skull to always be on guard until the enemy was in police custody or dead. Luckily, he did, and he saw the passenger criminal was awake and pissed, preparing to fire off an automatic shotgun. K-Force spun with the woman in his arms away from the gunfire as he took five shots to the back. Normally, this would be stupid to do in an enclosed metal area since most Heroes who were bulletproof had bullets bounce off of them. K-Force just robbed the shotgun rounds of all their momentum when they hit his skin and dropped to the floor. Once he heard the man ejecting the spent magazine, K-Force, without looking, fired a concussive blast that most likely cause broken bones and a concussion.

Looking around for anyone else wanting to continue the fight, there was one guy who purposefully laid there with his hands up in surrender. The woman in K-Force's arms still had a death grip on him, which made him sigh in frustration as he moved her to his side, so that he could begin tying up the crooks.

It took fifteen minutes for the police to get the woman to let go of him. The woman was still in shock and wanted to be near the safest and strongest protection available, namely K-Force. Bronze Bomber tried to make her move, but only got her name, Giselle Flores. Giselle clung tighter every time Bronze Bomber tried to move her. When Giselle finally was able to move her, she kissed his cheek repeatedly and thanked him.

Next came the reporters, who K-Force was prepared for.

"Ms. Bomber, Ms. Bomber, wonderful job appending the culprits today. I must say this is the cleanest take down I've seen," one reporter stated.

"It was my rookie here who did all the work. All I did was stand back and supervise," Bronze Bomber said, giving credit when it was due.

"Was that a good idea? He is still green," another reporter asked,

"Hence the term 'supervised.' I needed to see what he could do and what I had to work with," Bronze Bomber replied.

"Isn't that a risk? Normally most Heroes work side by side with their assistants," the second reporter asked again.

"And I was right there if anything went wrong. I am the type of teacher who watches her student perform, then helps to correct any mistakes they may have committed. I will also stop him before he does anything drastic. Besides, from what I have seen, he did everything almost seamlessly," Bronze Bomber smoothly answered.

"Speaking of which, we have seen several suspects being wheeled to the hospital. Do you think that your use of force was excessive?" A third reporter began questioning the rookie directly.

"When I and the boss lady spotted them, they were shooting at police officers and doing ninety-plus. And from what I heard from the police, there will be three funerals, maybe four if the one in critical condition doesn't make it," K-Force replied.

"You think that excuses your vicious act on the suspects?" the third reporter accused.

"Yes, since none are dead," K-Force replied in an uncaring tone.

"They might be criminals but they are," the third reporter tried to start.

"Subjected to the same laws as you and me, which means lethal force used against law enforcement calls for retaliation in kind," K-Force interrupted, pointing out the law.

"That's for police officers, not you," said the third reporter, acting like he had caught the rookie.

"Professional Heroes are allowed to use any means necessary outside of lethal force, and the commanding police officer judges if such force was excessive," K-Force emphasized that point.

"Hey Lt. Nash," K-Force called out to the supervising officer in charge of the crime scene.

"Yeah, Kid," the officer in question replied.

"Did I use excessive force on these culprits?" K-Force asked the only person whose opinion mattered.

"Two bank employees are dead, one injured. Five people were injured when they bulldozed their way through traffic, and I lost three officers, with one in critical condition. So no, I believe you were more than reserved in your actions," Lt. Nash said, making his feelings on the matter very clear.

K-Force gestured toward the commanding officer who validated the sidekick's action. This irritated the reporter enough that he walked away in anger, grumbling probably something inappropriate underneath his breath. While other reporters seemed wary to question him, a young one rushed up to him.

"Hey, sorry about Gary. He is a firebrand type who loves to start crap," a young reporter said.

"My parent told me the best way to deal with his type is to ignore them when they seek confrontation," K-Force stated, saying nothing the press didn't already know.

"Sage advice. Hector Ramirez, KPZN Channel 8. So, are you opposed to answering a few questions?" the reporter introduced himself.

"I'm fine with it, but if the boss lady says I have to go, then…" K-Force gave half apologies in case he had to leave.

"Got it. So, first question, are you excited about being in California?" Hector asked.

K-Force knew he couldn't be completely honest about his situation, but he could answer without insulting anyone. "I'll be honest about California not being my first choice. I wanted to prove myself by going to a more hostile area in the North Central region or the Northeast. Pacific region, particularly California, is so well-guarded that I will struggle to prove my worth." K-Force was being careful to not sound like he was dissing the state but making sure his feelings on the matter were clear.

"Wow, you're admitting that," Hector asked in shock. He was expecting him to give the same spiel they all gave. 'It is an honor to be picked. I think it's great they chose me,' et cetera.

"Yeah, I think people appreciate me being real with them. Besides, it doesn't mean I will slack in my duties. It just means it will be a while before anything really exciting happens." K-Force knew people would prefer real opinions rather than scripted ones.

"Okay, if you don't mind me asking, how do you feel about the Cannady case and your brother's affair with Red Banshee?" Hector dove in with a more hot button subject.

"Cannady's plans for Meta-humans are something out of Nazi Germany. He wanted us all to be resources of the state, under the

- 149 -

direct control of certain members of government, and any and all children born from Meta-humans would be monitored and secluded from normal humans. I don't have to tell you what that kind of government creates," K-Force stated.

"Slavic Union of Belarus and Kingdom of Libya," Hector responded, wincing at two of the worst examples of such programs. The end result was a history of the oppressed rising up and slaughtering their tormentors and becoming the oppressors. Another end result would be a new monarchy where the Metas would be the upper class and an actual higher stock than normal humans. Another end result would be the creation of a fascist hellhole with a caste system, which would make India and Israel seem nuanced.

"Fair point. How does it feel to work with a woman?" Hector asked, since it was required by the station for him to ask that question.

"She is a Meta, which makes gender a moot point," K-Force said, deciding to be blunt and open.

"What do you mean?" The reporter liked where this was going.

"Superpowers are the true equalizer, since once you have them, who or what you are is out the window. Only one's own limits in skill will determine how high you can go," K-Force stated.

It was two hours after the busted bank robbery, and K-Force felt all hyped up with no release. So as soon as he got off shift he headed to the Heroes' gym in workout gear to use the facilities and push his body. The bank robbers were not a threat. He had held his power back, so he could actually get more of a workout from the exercise. He performed several ton legs presses and dead lifts as well a good hard combat scenario in the Holodeck or Hard Light training room. The room ran off of virtual intelligence that slowly pushed a Meta above the norm standards set and went as high as possible without killing anybody, though accidents have been known to happen.

K-Force set the device towards difficulty level eight, one versus one, and even turned up the pain, literally, so that with every mistake he made, he could feel it. Surprisingly, the computer chose a Hero who had tangled with his brother, A-Line. A-Line was the rare mixture of super speed as a prime power, but had a high level of durability and super strength. This made it so that he could withstand high levels of speed, which meant that he could go faster than most speedsters. Speedsters were a lot more limited than other supers. If one did not have a certain level of protection, they would be affected by outside interference. Adaption does not help, since the only thing it did was keep the body from pulling itself apart every time a speedster went over level forty. Air pressure, obstacles, and insects becoming embedded into your flesh—these all became issues over level three hundred-forty.

For someone who can take a sniper bullet to the dome and shake it off, that meant a high level of speed that most speedsters could not reach. Mach 20 was the highest speed he had ever run, which might not seem impressive to many since there are some who can break the speed of light. That is, until you realize the total number of known people who can do that are three, and he was eighth on the list of super speedsters.

Okay, this will be a challenge in more ways than one. My usual anti-speedster tactics I can't use since it is a not a life and death situation. Using my forcefield is out of the question. Using enough force to create a minor earthquake—nope. Strictly forbidden in the facility. Take a beating to the point that I can keep up. Sadly no, I don't want others to know how fast I can move, which means I'm going to be taking a beating until I can convincingly defeat him in any way that doesn't expose myself, K-Force thought to himself as he waited for the simulation to begin.

And when the lit sign switched to "START" A-Line knocked him on his ass before he could blink. Then the speedster danced away with that constant smirk on his face. There was also a very painful mark on the right side of K-Force's face.

Wow, they even got his cocky mannerism. K-Force's thoughts were derailed as he felt himself being flipped through the air. The world was spinning fast as he was dealing with vertigo. He could barely prepare his body or mind for how fast the blows were coming. When K-Force finally got his bearings, he felt some blood in his mouth; he had turned down his defense so he could learn from his mistakes.

I'm not always going to be in top shape, and I have to think of a way to beat him with these restrictions, K-Force thought as he tasted his own blood on his lips, enjoying the challenge.

This will be a long fight, K-Force thought and decided to up his own game. The next blow came, but instead of flying away, he absorbed the supersonic blow to the gut. K-Force realized that weakening himself so much, even in practice, was only testing his pain tolerance.

The single, playful but powerful punches didn't knock him to the floor again. A program built to mimic opponents as closely as scientifically possible reacted like A-Line would have. So instead of doing the smart thing and putting a stop to all the playing around, A-Line just went for a bigger dash and super punch, which did knock K-Force down again. Unknowingly, all that did was feed more power to K-Force. Despite not being able to fight back, K-Force quickly picked up a pattern and was able to use kinetic senses to react fast enough to dodge and block. The several times the light clone hit K-Force, more power was suffusing into his body. A-line decided to end it by using his favorite move, 'Tornado Punch.' There was one problem with that. A-line's opponents were usually already on the ropes, or they were so disoriented that they couldn't see anything coming. K-Force was neither. A-line created the little tornado around his fist and charged right at K-Force, hoping to take him out with a devastating blow, only for K-Force to move at the same speed to dash into the faux hologram blind spot and unleash a kinetic energy-empowered punch. As the faux A-line was sent flying from the counterblow, K-Force did not stop his attack. K-Force jumped after the flying object and unleashed a beam into the hologram's chest with enough force to break several ribs of the real A-Lines a result, the program ended.

"Match end in user K-Force victory. Final score is eighty-two, with room for improvement. Suggestion: have combat awareness increased. Less chance of being overwhelmed in the beginning,"

"Yeah, like super speed is something everyone can react too quickly. Especially when some can move fast enough to do a mile in one-thousandth of a second," K-Force said, as he massaged the area where the hard-light hologram hit him.

K-Force looked at himself and observed his body coated in sweat. Even his work out gear was practically painted onto his body. Seeing as he did not want to smell like a musky old dog, he headed towards the showers. While en route he noticed several stares from his fellow female Heroes, including Gyges, who looked on at him with a knowing smile.

Gyges' popularity among plus-size women and average men was easy to see. Given that she was in the green zone of being bigger than the average woman, but curvy enough to draw the eye of most men who looked beyond slim women. She was talking to some of the staff and a few Heroines K-Force had yet to meet. White tank top and purple spat leggings seemed to mold to her body. Even more so because of her sheen from a workout she had just finished. K-Force swore that she eyed him by looking him up and down. She gave him a smile before she turned from him and then stuck out her hips to show off the word "Juicy" on her leggings. Shaking off the attention of the curvy, lavender-skinned beauty K-Force decided on a quick rinse of cold water then a hot shower.

After he got out of his quick shower, he looked at his phone for any calls. It was mostly spam calls and the Homeowners Association who always tried to force him into a meeting despite his busy lifestyle. And there was one call from his mother, which confused him, but he could guess the reason for the call. Preparing himself his mother's usual antics, K-Force called Intercessor.

As soon as she picked up and asked who was calling, the young Hero replied, "Hey Momma."

"Oh my God, baby I'm so proud of you," Intercessor dropped the whole venerable Heroine act and became a proud mother who had just witnessed her son score a touchdown.

"Thanks, Mom, but it's not a big deal. It was just a bank robbery," K-Force knew his mother was only being supportive, which he loved, but he wanted support when he actually did something praiseworthy.

"Yes, it is sweetie, you did so well and acted so quickly without anyone innocent being harmed. Most Heroes your age think of the fame and spotlight and do not care about efficiency," his mother impressing how important his first act as a Hero was. K-Force just sighed and began to dress while his mother praised him.

Just let her get it out of her system. You know she is just happy for you. And take the love she is freely giving, K-Force rolled his eyes at his mother's call.

Chapter 7
Falling Upwards

K-Force was having a good time at a soup kitchen with Bronze Bomber, or BB as social media fans called her. It was apparent that she went to soup kitchens every Thursday, if she could help it. Bomber did not do this for the publicity, but she went because she wanted to help with something that she could not fix with a wave of the hand. Bronze Bomber preferred to help people on a personal level. Lost children looking for their parents, visiting kids in hospitals, cats stuck in trees—she essentially loved helping people with personal problems. K-Force didn't mind, since anything that required their attention was handled by their fellow heroes who had priority. He knew this would happen, but their only excuse was that there were few crimes that required someone of Bronze Bomber's power. And unless the police called them for backup, Heroes were not allowed to save the day unless it was a case of life and death. Bronze Bomber saw this as a plus since she had the perfect excuse to be more intimate with the common man.

What he found strange was the fact that the press didn't advertise it or tell everyone that she did these things. He figured that the media wanted to maintain Bronze Bomber's image of a teasing sex symbol and powerhouse. So, unless there was some juicy gossip scandal which fit the image, they ignored it. They wanted her to keep a sexy, diva-like persona, and apparently, her being a peppy, sweet woman who just happened to be well-endowed was boring. There were a fcw incidents where some of the less than reputable homeless men tried to grab her, but their hands were promptly slapped away, like a child reaching for the cookie jar. K-Force had a couple of young girls looking at him, but they were mostly schoolgirls with crushes.

"You seem to be enjoying yourself. I expected someone with your skill would be craving action at this point," Bronze Bomber was surprised by his lack of complaints.

"I'm just glad I'm doing something significant instead of just posing for the camera. Helping people is my objective, and this is just another way of saving and aiding people," K-Force said, as he served another bowl.

"Ah, so you wish to be useful instead of a centerfold, but you realize that's where the real money is," Bronze Bomber joked.

"We're in California. I'm pretty sure a third of anything I make will go to the state," he commented.

"Hah, that is true, although more living expenses than anything else." Bronze Bomber looked at her protégé and grinned. "I'm glad the first rookie under my wing isn't a glory seeker like most of my colleagues have had to deal with."

"I won't lie. I would love some fame, but at most I want to be useful," K-Force smiled back at her.

"Oh God, you're too precious," Bronze Bomber said, patting his head like a sister does a younger sibling. This irritated K-Force a little, but he was more than used to it.

After two and a half hours of helping around the soup kitchen, K-Force and Bronze Bomber were flying back to headquarters for a shift change. As they were flying, K-Force asked a question that had been annoying him for a while.

"Hey Bomber, I was wondering. You seem to be a very wholesome sweet person. Why do you," K-Force began to ask.

"Dress like I'm trying out for a dirty magazine," Bronze Bomber jested at his question.

"Yeah," K-Force confirmed her guess.

"Ugly Duckling syndrome," Bronze Bomber said in an offhanded manner.

"Huh?" K-Force asked in confusion.

"I used to be skinny stick figure of a girl. Had an overbite, retainer, larger than average nose, and got a zit every month. I was called a bunch of terrible names in high school until one summer right before my junior year my Meta gene kicked in. My imperfections gone, my figure blew up and all the so-called queens of my high school were jealous of me. And most importantly, I had my pick of boys and their attention. And while I'm big time now I still love having men desire me after years of being ignored and picked on," Bronze Bomber explaining her past trauma and rise to the top.

"Oh, I get it. It's like when I got a six pack from my Meta boost. I was looking for an excuse to take my shirt off, even in the dead of winter," K-Force compared. "Wanting to show the world you are beautiful after years of teasing is not unusual."

"I also love making divas feel inferior after years of enduring it myself," Bronze Bomber quipped as she let a little pettiness escape.

When K-Force got home his publicist sent him pictures of himself in the soup kitchen serving food and more articles about his statement about superheroines being a hot topic. Apparently, his statement has everyone talking about how powers equalized the playing field for both men and women. This had a lot of people going back and forth on the idea of Meta sports becoming one division since gender in this case was meaningless. While others still believed that there was too much advantage between the genders despite superpowers.

"Do you want to stay silent or add more fuel to the fire," his publicist asked.

"More truth. If it causes a barn fire so be it. Put this in my social media account. There is an old question what is heavier, a hundred kilograms of steel or a hundred kilograms of feathers. The answer is they are the exact same weight despite being made of different materiel. A man who can lift five tons is not stronger than a woman who can also lift five tons. Hence powers are the true equalizer in my personal opinion."

"Oh that's a good one, and these comments are bound to get people talking about you. However, you will have to get out there and show people what you can do, or someone is going to say that your opinion isn't going to matter," his publicist informed him.

"Not much I can do about it. I am not on the queue for the next big event. Shoot, the bank robbery was lucky enough to happen because there was an immediate threat to the pursuing police officers," K-Force stated as he began to disrobe and become Samson again.

"I know. California rules. You have to talk someone into letting you take up more chances before your star power fades away. Community service gets you more likes, but it can only do so much," his publicist emphasized.

"Understood, Royce, but you can only do so much when people from LA County steal your chances because of some backroom deals," Samson said, as he washed his face after wearing the mask for more than half a day.

As he hung up the call, Samson didn't have the heart to tell Royce and his sponsors that because of all the nonsense he was experiencing he was tempted just go to FED. Samson didn't have to deal with this garbage, because the government would not take this crap. The best example was the time when he was in Riverside. He and Bronze Bomber caught wind of a rogue Meta attacking a local city councilor. The Meta attacked because they foreclosed on his mother's house and forced her into a retirement home. This was a dirty move, K-Force would admit, but murdering a bunch of people to get to one asshole did not seem like a rational response.

Bronze Bomber was about to subdue him, when out of nowhere a Hero named Verge swooped in as Bronze Bomber got blasted into a building. Despite not being harmed by the blast, Verge made the excuse that Bronze Bomber looked like she was taken down, despite the culprit was on his last legs and got off a lucky shot. Verge just swooped in to take the last blow and took all the credit. Bronze Bomber was pissed and wanted to strangle Verge, but the public was watching and the one thing that was emphasized by the companies was to never fight in public, whether physical or verbal.

This is why Heroes get into fights, not as a matter of misunderstandings or conflict of morals. No, eighty percent of the time it was Heroes trying to reach a quota and some else stepping on their turf. Where was K-Force in all this? He was tied up with crowd control and saving people from debris, and he did a good job apparently.

As K-Force closed the door to his room, he was surprised that QuickTime was already on the couch in the living room playing a multiplayer shootout. "Hey, you're back. Thought you were going to the Holodeck for training," K-Force said. The Holodeck is what everyone called the hard-light Hologram room in which various training missions and tactics training took place.

"Some idiot decided to run a Level 4 team battle by himself," Avery paused for effect.

Samson, dressed down into his house sweats and tank top, mentally winced as he sat on the end of the L-shaped couch. The hard-light Hologram room may have been a simulator, but it packed enough force to injure anyone not tough enough to resist attacks. Hard light was just as it sounds; it gave off physical sensations of an object in every way except when it was in combat mode. All damages had a burning sensation ranging from mild sun burn to hot skillet.

"How badly was he injured?" Samson asked.

"Couple of second degree burns, two cracked ribs, and a twisted ankle. It will be a week before he's fully healed," Avery filled in.

"Did he do it on a dare or was he drunk? Because to do otherwise is just plain stupidity, unless Jackass is filming him trying to do a stunt," K-Force joked from his room.

"Sadly, nothing that fun, apparently, he was trying to impress Ceto the Cerilian princess," Avery said, as he played an online match.

"So, he is chasing after *The Little Mermaid*," Samson joked, which did get a laugh from Avery. Ceto was the princess of an underwater kingdom in the Pacific. Her people were not the top-half human and bottom-half fish from old tales. They were more closely related to the *Creature from Black Lagoon*, meaning they had webbed hands and feet, human-like faces with small snouts, and side frills instead of ears. Their bodies were human-like but scaled, except for the chest and crotch area, similar to the underbelly of some aquatic creatures. Despite all this, they were very attractive which gave way to tales of the old mermaid myths.

"It is not all that surprising they are actually big business in the porn scene," Avery replied, sort of defending the man's choice.

"It only proves that humans are more susceptible to our desires then anyone is willing to admit. There is no limit of how far the

Internet and the sex industry will go," K-Force said, as he sat on the chair next to the couch.

"Ain't that the truth," Avery half paid attention as he got the final kill to help his team win the match, which swiftly devolved into a middle school kids' swearing contest.

"You got room for one more," Samson said as he lifted his controller.

Avery said nothing as he turned the match to co-op mode, as he waited for the match room to fill.

The next day looked to be another boring day, until they were called in to stop an attack from Atomic Droid, a massive nine story tall spider centaur-like machine. It was built by a genius scientist from the 70s that ran on a fission reactor that is controlled by a mind cap. It was not the world-destroying weapon that it was years ago, but outside of the well-equipped army or group of Metas, it was extremely hard to stop, the reason being that unless the genius who was using it didn't pick one of the few Heroes who were strong against it. One the lesser-known abilities of Bronze Bomber were the fact she can eat and absorb all forms of nuclear fallout and cleanse the area five miles wide in ten minutes. Hence, she was the Achilles' heel to this machine.

Normally, a team of Heroes would take the Machine on since it was a high Beta-low Alpha level threat. But because Enteriagey wanted to promote their star, Titan Slayer, to the upper tier by him taking it on by himself. Bronze Bomber and K-Force were assigned to protect the civilians while they let Titan slayer, an equally tall mountain of muscle, clashed against the metal monstrosity. Titan Slayer's attire was pretty much pro wrestling attire—flashy green pants with special boots and knee pads, and he was shirtless, mostly because of a very high endurance and a strong healing factor. So, his broad-muscled, yellow-skinned body was not much of a concern to him. Though the helmeted mask was another factor, since few would be able to regrow a head, no matter how strong their healing factor was. Adding to the fact, Titan Slayer had long, purple hair that reached to his waist, and you would swear that he was sponsored by Vince McMahon.

Much to K-Force's dismay, he acted like a wrestler in his fights. Titan Slayer was a man who loved to make a show and spectacle of his fights and didn't care about the damage he caused. For instance, the first thing any Hero would know when dealing with a massive enemy would be to take them away from populated areas, if possible. That was what Bronze Bomber was going to do, but Titan Slayer and his company Enteriagey always believed that more flare and show would bring in more foot traffic, so to speak. While it was true, lives and livelihood should not be merely stepping stones for one company's profit.

The two giant sized figures grappled each other, which would make sense if Titan Slayer's opponent was not a robot. The problem was the machine's strength was closer to Titan Slayer's strength, and the robot had a weight advantage. In plain English, Titan Slayer was at a major disadvantage as he struggled to keep his balance. Titan Slayer gave way enough to make Atomic Droid lose balance for a second, which for the Hero to do a shoulder bash to the android's chin. While this might work on humans, machines were not susceptible to that kind of damage. This only allowed Atomic Android to get a good blow against Titan Slayer's helmeted head, which temporarily dazed the yellow giant. Then, in a move only something with no muscles could do, the android rotated its arms flipping and slamming Titan Slayer into the asphalt.

Next, in a move that proved it was not human, it spun its head 180 degrees and fired red atomic energy rays into Titan Slayer. In a show of grit, the giant super hero pushed through the pain and stood with his arms held out behind him. Then Titan Slayer donkey kicked the android away, which broke its iron-like hold. The blow sent the robot flying towards a crowd of gawking citizens trying to capture the show on their camera phones. Thinking fast, K-Force used one his hidden powers and created a forcefield that blocked the giant machine from crushing the twenty or so idiots trying to get views on social media. The forcefield was the pale amber color that one sees in sunglasses, and it spanned twenty feet in height and ten meters in width. Precision was not as important as making sure that no one was hurt.

"Hey, you ruined my shot," a woman with a pink pixie haircut screamed.

"Sorry, I thought your lives were more important than views and the thumbs-up you would get," K-Force snarked.

"Don't get smart with me. I could call your company and have you canceled," the self-entitled woman screeched as she tried to wield power she didn't have.

Of course I would run into one of 'these' kind of people, K-Force thought as he just ignored her and ushered the people from the combat zone. The demanding woman at first refused to leave in her own stubbornness until a police officer practically dragged her away. K-Force mouthed thank you to the woman who was not putting up with the demented woman.

Bronze Bomber looked to her assistant in mild surprise. "You can make forcefields. Why didn't you show that at the Combine or put it on your resume?"

"Well, I don't like letting anybody know my full capabilities if I can help it. It leaves one too open to attacks by people who research and find ways to take you out," K-Force replied to his mentor.

"Who would want to kill you? You haven't made a big name for yourself yet," Bronze Bomber heard of such talk before from older vets, but by the time they reached the point where they have over a half a dozen enemies.

"I got a list. I'll tell you later," K-Force said as he saw a car flying towards the police perimeter. K-Force caught the vehicle with one hand which should be impossible, but when you control kinetic force and a small amount of mass, it is easy as catching a baseball.

The two massive brutes had an all and out brawl where they were throwing, punching, and kicking each other all over the streets. They destroyed a few store fronts but would have been worse if K-Force didn't create forcefields to protect as many buildings as possible. The Android was getting the upper hand throughout the fight because every time Titan Slayer had the advantage, he would try to showboat and pull out a flashy finisher. Again, he was forgetting the android had none of the human joints, muscles, and pain receptors. It would just twist and turn in every direction to escape and pounded on him for being a cocky idiot. Though those moves were his main areas of attack, he was not completely helpless.

Titan Slayer started to show why he was considered upper tier hero of the Alpha class. The speed and strength of his blows came out faster and was able to turn the tide. Next Titan Slayer caused a small shock wave by stomping his foot into the ground to unstable the giant droid then jumped to deliver a devastating elbow to the Android's faceplate. He then performed a 'cutter' that would have made Diamond Dallas Page proud. The next move was him trying to lift the six-legged android into a powerbomb, only for the Android to wrapped its legs around Titan Slayer's waist and pummel its fist into his face, which allowed it to escape and attack.

Atomic Android decided to stop playing around with the Hero by having its shoulder panels slide away. This revealed missile pods aimed at the down yellow giant. The first few missiles took Titan Slayer off guard, but he just tanked them to show off how tough he was. Titan Slayer delivered a couple of haymakers to fight back, which caused the machine to bend in some of its legs. Then he slipped under Atomic Droid's guard and tried to end it with his patented Titan Crusher Supplex, only to be donkey-kicked by the android's hind legs. It seemed he forgot that this machine was a centaur, not a biped, which would have made that move viable. Atomic Droid turned around and showed another function—a glowing fist covering its right hand which struck like a cannon. Titan Slayer was sent flying into a massive building, then Atomic Android pinned Titan Slayer against the wall and charged up a massive cannon hidden in its chest, which was two feet away from Titan Slayer's torso. Atomic Android unleashed a massive beam attack that would have wiped out everything in its path, if K-Force didn't absorb the hit with his forcefield from a distance.

When the large flash of light cleared, the entire front torso of Titan Slayer's chest was charred and cooked. There was a huge divot in the giant mountain of chest muscles that allowed people to see inside. Almost anyone would be dead after such a blow, but the active healing factor of Titan Slayer and his durability were the only things barely keeping him alive. Considering that blast was a little less than what the US dropped on Nagasaki, concentrated into an energy beam, Titan Slayer was lucky to be among the living. Everything that was not protected by K-Force's forcefield was a melted and charred mess.

There was so much force behind the blast that super charged K-Force's energy reserves that he could knock out five Prime Times with as much power he possessed. Luckily, he remembered that he could not show that such an attack was ineffective against him. *Less people know your limits, the more unprepared they are to fight you*, K-Force thought to himself before he feigned being pushed to one knee, lifting both hands up, and grimacing his face. This gave the illusion of him being pushed to his limit.

The giant Android was charging up for another such blast, but never got the chance as the Atomic Droid was lifted off the ground by a certain blond Heroine. At this point Bronze Bomber stepped in despite not being given the go-ahead. Anybody arguing about semantics over a life and death situation was not someone worth listening to. As Bronze Bomber got the metal giant above the clouds, she made sure the huge cannon in its chest were pointed skyward but far away from any aircraft. Then she carried the massive machine into the Shadow Mountain area far away from any casualties. Only the news choppers would be able to see the fight, and less people would be hurt.

Can I survive looking out for idiots who don't understand death is three feet away from them, she thought as she slammed the giant android's front first into a hillside. Bronze Bomber was about to dive-bomb into the machine and pierce through it. Any and all nuclear energy and residue would be absorbed and cleansed.

"Don't! The military wants the robot returned, so keep the damage as minimum as possible." The warning came from her company agent.

"You got to be kidding me," Bronze Bomber scoffed. She couldn't believe what the military was requesting.

"No, I just got word from the military to not completely wreck the thing. Besides, if you beat it too quickly you are going to make Titan Slayer look like a fool," again her company agent informed her.

"Too late for that, not my fault that mister superstar couldn't stop flaunting for ten seconds. I've seen fourteen-year-old girls with more self-control," Bronze Bomber said, letting her feelings on the matter be known.

"I'm not here to argue with you. Just follow through with orders. Besides this, it has been awhile since you got any action so you could use a good fight for the cameras," the company agent retorted.

"God give me strength," Bronze Bomber said, as she waited for the machine to climb back onto its six feet. Then, as if to lead the news choppers' arrival, K-Force arrived to see the Atomic Android center all of its attention on the human that interrupted its execution of a Hero.

"Come on, you overgrown Pinto. You're fighting a real woman not an overgrown boy," Bronze Bomber said before she went into battle.

The Android fired energy beams at her from its smaller weaponry, which she merely batted aside as if it were an annoyance. Bronze Bomber swooped in and slugged the machine in the face plate which left an actual dent. The machine tried smashing her, but she was faster and more serious, so she was able put up a guard. Bronze Bomber was able to tank its blows despite floating in midair, which sent her flying a couple of meters away, but she would always come back swinging.

Despite having a strength and speed advantage the android moved at odd angles which threw Bronze Bomber off and allowed it to continue to fight. The fact that its arms, head and torso could move in any direction made it a difficult opponent for her to subdue without destroying it, since any of her fatal moves might utterly destroy the Android. Thus, Bronze Bomber was stuck gradually taking it down bit by bit. Then, as if to raise the difficulty the other hand fell away from Atomic Droid's left wrist to reveal a thirty-millimeter cannon, and it began to fire away at Bronze Bomber, actually hurting her. That surprised many, including K-Force, considering that this woman could take rounds designed to eat through tanks like a ten-year-old ate cake. She was able to shake them off, normally, and yet this was actually causing her to fall to the ground in pain as she tried to fight through it.

K-Force meanwhile observed and supported his mentor, as the assistant Hero protocols demanded. "Screw it," he said as he got into the battlefield to block the heavy caliber gun fire.

K-Force blurred in front of his mentor into a squatted position and blocked all the shots with another forcefield large enough to protect them from fire. After twenty seconds of continuous fire, it stopped once it realized that its ammunition would not pierce the forcefield. Though the penetrating force behind those oversized bullets was intense, piercing damage was always harder to resist than other forms of damage, even for him.

Bronze Bomber was able to shake off the assault long enough for her to give out a game plan.

"Distract that overpowered tin can, so I can land a good shot to take it down," Bronze Bomber told her sidekick.

"Will do," K-Force said as he jumped into action.

K-Force dropped the shield as soon as Bronze Bomber flew from behind him and began to shoot fire with a pinkish-purple energy which barely singed the fourteen-foot Android. The Android began to track her while revving up its gun to fire again, only to be hit with a super powerful knee into its faceplate, almost making it topple over. As K-Force bounced back, he recoiled off the robot face and air jumped to dodge a glowing fist swung at him.

The android was still trying to pound him while aiming its gun at Bronze Bomber, who had to move away from the enemy fire. K-Force realized that the only way to fight a machine capable of fighting a small team of Bravo and Alpha class Metas was to push himself.

Flipping to the ground, he boosted his speed with running strides which surpassed the speed of sound; something this machine was more than capable of tracking. Next, he surrounded himself in visible energy and shot toward the front torso of the metal insect centaur. This looked like K-Force was trying to do a head-on charge which most Heroes did when they got serious in a fight, only for K-Force to roll in mid-air and rocket towards a seven o'clock position. This made the glowing fist and energy beam miss their target. As K-Force was racing towards the ground, moving faster than before, it looked as though he was going to slam face-first. Only again, he rotated himself to jump between the legs of the machine. The Atomic Droid could track objects going Mach 10, but the constant chance of higher speed made it difficult to track K-Force, who was moving Mach 19. K-Force used the kinetic force from the power of the explosion that took down Titan Slayer in a pinpoint strike at its underbelly. This amplified blow actually damaged the machine enough to send it flying off of its feet. All this happened in less than two seconds with over a quarter of a mile between them. To the normal human eye, it appeared as if K-Force teleported underneath the Android and sent it flailing.

This action allowed Bronze Bomber to charge up her energy blast, actually cutting the Gatling arm of the Android body. There was yelling on the line to not damage the machine too much and wait for back up. But like her protégé said, "Screw it, K-Force, take this thing down as fast as possible. I'm not going to get pounded on for some military jarheads who want to capture and mothball a death bot."

"Got it," K-Force said as the pair was beginning to end the Atomic Droid. Without the modified thirty millimeter cannon shooting out damaging fire, it was easy for them to overcome whatever it had left. Every energy blast from the face plate was absorbed by Bronze Bomber, and its missiles were absorbed by K-Force's shields. Soon it lost two of its legs, which lowered its mobility and flexibility as its systems were trying to keep up with the two.

As it seemed the fight was going to end, K-Force realized something. This machine was so powerful the scientist made sure that it was controlled by a special helmet. The scientist who built the Android was a big anti-AI believer. The scientist made virtual intelligence with a controller to keep it under the scientist's power. The only fault to it was the fact that the controller's range was limited to a mile and a half distance. Seeing that they were in an isolated place and there were few people present, outside of the press, he looked around for anything that looked out of place, like an extra chopper, or an extra tourist. Everything looked to be on the up and up, but he couldn't help but feel like something was off. Then he saw something that seemed to wrap and blend the sky as a raptor-like bird flew by in fishbowl-like lens view. Seeing that, K-Force closed his eyes, stopped moving, and focused his senses on something that he had been developing, a kinetic sense where everything that moved within two miles he was able to sense and feel. To K-Force, it was like the world was in a shade of black, blue, and violet. Objects like the earth and plants were black, while people, animals, and vehicles were blue if stationary, and violet if moving.

With this, K-force spotted a flying RV-like vehicle that looked like it came from *The Jetsons*. This was not the time to be impressed since with this they could end the fight. So, without looking, K-Force captured the fist slamming towards him and held it for a few seconds. Then, in a feat of strength many didn't think he had, K-Force flipped the robot in a judo-like throw. K-Force didn't stop there; he let go of the machine, rushed towards the flying vehicle and stopped it in place.

K-Force knew he looked like a fool standing there with a mime imitation of pushing an invisible wall. That was until he gave the vehicle a good smack, which temporarily dropped the cloaking device it had. Then, in a show of dominance, he brought the ship down to the ground despite the thruster on it going at maximum. It was as if no momentum could be achieved, and this seemed to be effective. The Android stopped fighting desperately against Bronze Bomber, and tried to attack K-Force only to be shoulder-checked by her. As it tried to rise again, the ground seemed to suck it in as if were quicksand, then just as quickly it hardened when nearly half of it sank.

Out of nowhere a man in a mixture of combat uniform and duster arrived riding on a wave of sand and dirt. Behind him QuickTime arrived, throwing little circular EMP mines in the open wounds of the Android, finally bringing it down to slumber.

QuickTime also threw one more mine towards the area in front of K-Force, which revealed a retro, futuristic air vehicle with a design from the 1970s.

"No fucking way? A 1972 mini command center," QuickTime exclaimed as he looked at the ship that was still trying to get away. "It has the flying train motif with gamma power thrusters in cherry red and silver chrome. Does it still have ZM-6 carbine engine?"

"Naw, it doesn't have as much torque as it should. Whoever is behind this took it out for a quiet engine," K-Force noticed

"That's sacrilege," QuickTime said, looking actually pained.

"Well, some people prefer practicality over form and style," K-Force commented.

"Careful brats, this is not your dad's hot rod. There is still a dangerous asshole who needs to be brought in, so get your head in the game," Faultline said in a gruff voice as he created rock-like arches tightly around the command center to make sure it wasn't getting away.

"In our defense, this is like the 1972 Dodge charger of mobile command centers," QuickTime contrasted the two classic vehicles.

The veteran seemed gruff at the comparison, not wanting to agree with the rookies; then he noticed that the press was surrounding the conquering Heroine as it were.

"Damn vultures don't have the decency to wait and let us make sure the target's down. Those lemmings would run through a land mine to get a story," Faultline sighed.

"Think I will get in trouble for jumping in despite protocol," K-Force said as he removed his hand from the ship. With it locked down, he didn't need to hold it in place anymore.

"Protocol is a guideline. When you make it a doctrine, then it's nothing but a hindrance for people to do their job," Faultline stated, as he walked towards the now visible mobile command center. "Alright, whoever is in there better come out now, or I shall come in with less restraint. Because if you didn't notice you brought a nuclear weapon into a crowded city, which means the final solution is on the table."

Faultline was not wrong; nuclear weapons created such a danger to the general public that labels of terrorism and traitor could be used. Having a weapon that could wipe out a city meant that by any means necessary lethal force was allowed.

That was all it took, since Faultline had a decent body count. The man who stepped out of the vehicle was the upcoming genius multi-millionaire Barry DeMotte. He was a weapons contractor for NATO who didn't have any criminal record outside of drunken and disorderly conduct.

"Mr. DeMotte, why the hell would you do something like this?" Faultline didn't really care, but was curious about the man's reasoning.

"If my memory serves me right, it is not about us or Ms. Bronze Bomber. It is about Titan Slayer sleeping with his wife," QuickTime said in a tone that sounded like he came from Oxford. "Exactly. If that bastard thought I would not retaliate for him screwing my wife and trying to cuckold me, he had another thing coming," DeMotte growled in a Dutch accent.

"Okay, I actually sympathize with him," K-Force muttered.

"Really?" QuickTime looked shocked.

"There are lines you are not supposed to cross, and another man's wife is one of them." K-Force made his feelings known.

"I'm with the kid. If anybody tried to screw my wife, I'd stomp a hole in them but that's neither here nor there. If he kept this personal, then we wouldn't care. But he stole government property with a nuclear core that could have taken out half the city. So, you are under arrest for a long time if I have my say," Faultline said, as he encased the man's hands in solid stone.

Elsewhere, a bald, thin yet muscular black man sat at a table in his office and looked over his establishment. It was a mixture of nightclub, hidden brothel and drug den to more discerning clients. He would have a DJ, dancers, and foam parties for the younger crowd, and all of it was seemingly legit. Any drug dealers found on the premises were tossed out with a broken arm or black eye, something to remember that there would be no selling in his territory unless they wanted to be put in a hearse. It brought too much attention from law enforcement, and that was bad for business. To many, he was just a law-abiding nightclub owner since he enforced this strict anti-drug policy in his club. To those in the know, he ran a mini-Gomorrah underneath it all in a secret section. He took care of the prostitutes and only asked for a third of their monthly profits for rent in a protected environment. They also had the services of Eric Folley, a Meta-human whose powers could cleanse anyone of drugs and diseases, and this meant he was essential for this type of establishment.

The bald club owner did this for practical reasons and little bit because of his own mother was a stripper and prostitute while trying to raise him. Many hookers wanted to work for him since he took far less than most pimps and gave effective health policies. He allowed them to build their own nest egg without micro-transactions. Because of this, many were willing to work for him and only the best were allowed in. Also, any drugs sold were pre-approved by him and certain suppliers. He had them displayed like candies in a movie theatre, and they included the names and locations of dealers and a voucher for quality. With this system, dealers benefitted since many would go searching for that supplier.

This system worked so well that he expanded it throughout the Great Lakes area. All it took was a little management and brutality to push away would-be parasites. While he was not some grand scale villain, he was notorious for catching bodies of Heroes and villains. Mickey the Moocher was one of the most dangerous people alive for his power absorption ability and his analytical mind which devised plans and contingencies. If he got his hands on you, he would drain you of your powers and ability. And, somehow, he always had a power ready to defend him, in spite of any supposed restriction of his powers.

As Mickey looked upon the club as a reflection of his growing empire, his phone began to play Lady Marmalade. He rolled his eyes at the fact that his prankster of a son had played with his phone again.

Good song though, Mickey thought as he answered his phone.

"Ah Mickey, we might have a job lined up for you," a mysterious feminine voice with a slight French accent said.

"Might?" That was unusual. They only called him if something dire was about to happen or there were a Hero for whom they had lost control.

"Shield user, we are not sure if he is strong enough for us to be concerned with. But we might need your services to make him disappear," the feminine voice informed him.

"Ah, is this your way of saying keep my schedule open?" He was beginning to understand why she had called him.

"That's why I like working with you. You know how to understand subtlety in words and actions," the mysterious female voice purred.

"Easy Yasmin, our rendezvous is within a week," Mickey warmly stated as he loved meeting up with his on-again off-again lover.

"Can't wait, but still please be ready if need be," the mysterious woman named Yasmin reminded him.

"Would love to but can't. Bombarda is planning something big and gathering her minions. I'm already having trouble around the

Michigan-Canadian border. The Meta Mafia are doing something big, and if I left, they would take advantage since I'm one of the few people who can stop her and any actions against us," Mickey explained.

"Damn that vulgar witch, always causing more trouble than the Heroes. Fine, but we may need your expertise before all this is over," Yasmin growled under her breath at the mention of her adversary.

"You know my consultation fees are half-off for my fellow conglomerate members," Mickey said, as he knew how something like this could snowball into a bigger problem.

Chapter 8
Known Quantity

"You know you have an annoying ability to say just the wrong thing to get headlines," Avery said, half-jokingly as he read from his laptop, reading the latest headline. Samson's little comment as K-Force was somehow a big no-no. For the past week somehow their comments were controversial.

Now in their condo lounging and streaming some TV, Avery was a little jealous of the free publicity that Samson was getting. Samson was portrayed as controversial, despite many agreeing with him and viewing his comment as a fair assessment. There was so much sympathy that Mr. DeMotte was sent back to Belgium where he only got three years on house arrest.

"How is saying that 'a guy who sleeps with another man's wife is a douche' a bad thing," questioned Samson, half-watching a cheesy sci-fi film from the 80s.

"Superhero unity they call it. We are supposed to present a unified front—not point out each other's mistakes in view of the public," Avery recited the rule in an annoyed tone.

"I'm not going to let an obvious wrong go unanswered. That fight was all because he couldn't keep his pants on," remarked Samson as he tried to watch the film, but he was sure that he wouldn't finish it.

"We are not priests or politicians. We have sex outside of marriage. Hell, we are another version of celebrities alongside actors, athletes, and models. So, having people throwing themselves at you is a lot of temptation, and she was a model. Besides, how was he supposed to know she was married at the time?" Avery decided to play devil's advocate.

Samson just rolled his eyes, unlocked his iPad and began searching for the previous tab which held the information he wanted. "First off, no, we are not. We were protectors of the people first. The media made us celebrities, and we accepted it because we wanted money."

"Secondly, here, catch," Samson said as he tossed his iPad in a soft, under-handed throw.

"What are you trying to," Avery stopped scrolling through the Internet and read the article that was being ignored by most local press outlets. "Barnard DeMotte introduced them at two different parties as part of an international function. Meaning that,"

"Titan Slayer knew that she was married and off limits but went for it anyway. So now I have more sympathy for the guy who tried to squash me in the giant robot than the asshole who most likely brought us a lot of grief by losing one major sponsor," Samson said, pointing out how bad the situation really was.

"Oh crap, how bad is this going to be?" Avery knew how poorly some people and organizations would react if mildly offended. "I know that the consequences are going to be big but, how big?"

"I don't know? Ask Holmes. He will more than likely tell us. All I can say, the repercussions are not going to go well for anyone," Samson said.

'Holmes' was the nickname he used when Avery would become super genius. It was still Avery, per se, but it was as if he went to Oxford and Cambridge and was top student in both universities. The change between the two personalities, for lack of a better term, was noticeable. Gone was Avery's homebody attitude and then entered a highly intelligent man with an air of etiquette. The image was only ruined by the power metal band T-shirt and shorts.

"I do say my dear Samson, that you are quite right about the implications and ramifications of this sordid tryst between Titan Slayer and most likely soon to be ex-Mrs. Loéila DeMotte. This is only a hypothesis, but there is a high likelihood that many backers in Europe will be hesitant about getting close or even trusting Heroes around their spouses. And they will make sure to put a squeeze on our European counterparts for Titan Slayer's lack of judgement. This will have an eighty percent chance on making things hostile between the United States and our allies in Europe," Avery said in extremely educated tone.

"And all because some guy couldn't say no," Samson rubbed his temples. The backlash from all this was greater than anything that robot could have done.

"Indubitably," as soon as Avery said that, the intelligent look on Avery's face dimmed a bit as he shook his head to return to normal. "Did I just say induba, er, indutab, no, that isn't right either," he said.

"Just stop. It is a word I have trouble with also, so don't beat yourself up over it," Samson tried to reassure Avery.

"Even though I said it, that seems a long way of saying that with Titan Slayer being a man whore, the Capes in Europe will feel a penny pinching, which in turn means ugly American strikes again," Avery spoke in more relaxed, layman's terms.

"True, and the term is 'slut.' Whore is someone who gets paid or exchanges for favors. A slut is someone who can't keep their pants

- 178 -

on, despite knowing better," Samson corrected as he began to watch the movie again.

"And how is that any worse," Avery said, not understanding why that mattered.

"A whore at least has some restraint," Samson pointed out.

This got Avery and Samson laughing, before a phone call reached Samson's phone. Samson, seeing that it was his mentor, answered, "Yeah, Boss."

"Yes, Mr. Brewer, we need your expertise to help us search false transactions crossing company lines," Bronze Bomber said, as if it were the typical business call.

"Got you, Boss lady, I'll be there in ten," Samson confirmed. He understood the code she sent.

"What happened?" Avery was curious as he saw his roommate rush to his room.

"Human Trafficking crossing the border, and since I'm called up, that means there is Meta or Meta-level protection involved which the border patrol can't handle," Samson said as he went to his room to change into his uniform.

Avery was actually curious about the incident since the last thing that happened to him was stopping a pair of rapists. While important, stopping a human trafficking caravan crossing the border seemed even more important.

"Need back up?" Avery was about to close his laptop to lend a hand.

"Hopefully not, but if so, I got you on speed dial, so to speak," K-Force said as he walked out, making sure nothing was missing.

"Wish me good luck." K-Force walked to the false wall and pressed his hand on the photo image of a tropical coastline. The wall opened up to an underground tunnel that led to a hidden area where he could slip in and out without being spotted. This was typical for most Heroes who lived in public areas.

"See you on the six o'clock news," Avery said in an offhanded tone. This meant he was confident in his roommate's safety.

As K-Force slid down the pole like a fireman, the wall closed back into place, leaving not a trace of evidence that it was ever opened.

It took K-Force five minutes to arrive at Sky High Industries' local branch in San Alonso where he met Bronze Bomber, fully fitted and ready for some action. The usual smile was suppressed by an almost eager look on her face. While Bronze Bomber may have liked being an up close and personal Heroine to the people, it was obvious she was eager to take down a Big Bad.

"Alright, the rookie's here so we can begin briefing, and it is going to be a doozy, to say the least," the business lady stated. This lovely older woman was Ms. Carrano, a brown haired woman in her early thirties who looked hungry to climb to the top, trying to reach that CEO position. The good news was that she was smart enough to keep hunger in check and think rationally. Not run her employees into the ground and forcing subpar work.

"First, this caravan has a couple of refugees from half of Central America and the Grand Columbian Civil War, so a lot of press is going to look at your actions under a microscope. Our Intel from the CIA tells us that it is a cover for the cartels and Mexican mafia human trafficking ring, and that many of those refugees are meant for the sex trade to be spread around the US," Jessie said, showing her team slides and relevant information to help things to go smoothly.

"How are we supposed to tell a human traffic from the refugees?" K-Force asked to distinguish who to protect and guide.

"Just look for the group with the most women and children trailing behind. They use it to make sure there is enough separation from the other groups and allows them to escape if any American patrols would be concerned with the fifty thousand trying to enter, not the five thousands that mysteriously disappear," Bronze Bomber stated.

"I'm guessing there is bribery in there somewhere." K-Force knew how these matters typically ran course.

"Yes, we have no idea who is in on it, but we do know that there is a group that is supposed to enter near Calexico in Imperial County," Bronze Bomber said.

"So, what is our job exactly?" K-Force asked.

"Border Patrol wants you two there covering them in case their Intel about a pair of Meta-humans are true," Ms. Carrano gave the relevant information.

"This sounds like a Federal Heroes job. Why aren't they handling this?" K-Force knew this was more of the federal side of the Hero work.

"Because Governor Fulson has forbid Federal personnel using excessive force on innocent travelers just trying to reach a better life," Bronze Bomber groused.

"He says, from a gated white tower," K-Force mumbled.

"I heard that. But until the government gets him to undo the proclamation, they are forbidden to take action on the border. While companies like us are free to do as we want, since we are a strange merger of law enforcement and the private sector in which he cannot control," said Bronze Bomber as she tried to keep her sidekick's head on straight.

"Are the rules of restrictive combat still in place?" K-Force asked, knowing the answer.

"Afraid so," Ms. Carrano said in a tone indicating she didn't like it either.

"Great, it doesn't matter that these are people with no conscience about to kill everyone, including the hostages, but if we accidently kill any of them we will be suspended," Bronze Bomber replied. She massaged her eyes in a way to stave off the growing migraine.

"I think that's the point. Governor Fulson sided with Cannady, and we all know what their stance is on *people* like us are," K-Force sighed as he look towards the ceiling in a silent prayer for strength that he knew he was going to need.

"We don't like it either, but we have no choice in the matter since it is easily a state of emergency. So, all we can ask of you is do your best without causing too big of an incident," Ms. Carrano emphasized that point to them as hard as possible.

The two Heroes stood up almost in sync and said together, "Understood."

The worst part of stakeouts was the waiting. Typically, waiting may be the worst part of customer service house calls, but stakeouts amplified this by a factor of twenty. This meant being given an inconvenient timetable between certain hours to expect service, with any luck. Case in point, for K-Force's mission, the timetable was between 10:00 AM to 6:00 PM. This also meant that until they actually arrived, even over an hour late, K-Force had to sit there waiting for them. Like all intelligence, it must be taken with a grain of salt, and it might be right on target or full of crap. And after waiting for almost nine hours, K-Force felt that it was the latter.

An hour after nightfall something finally happened. A group of four thousand refugees were being ushered and pushed towards the border, and this was not a group desperate families being catered over. He saw a group of pretty young mothers, teenage girls, and children. The make-up of this group just screamed flesh trade of non-consent. The line of followers seemed to stretch almost a mile, and all around them were the typical assholes with guns. There were also several cargo trucks waiting nearby, meaning they planned to pack these people in and spread them across cities, to illegal brothels, sold to special customers, or hidden in various other jobs. A small border patrol of three vehicles drove towards them, which seemed stupid and foolish without some major backup. That was the case until two border patrolmen stepped out towards the head of the caravan. In turn a man walked up from the caravan with a suitcase that just happened to cause the two corrupt patrolmen to grin.

"Wait, everybody, we can't take them down until they take the goods," said the lead officer of the bust. This appeared to be the right move until a raspy voice sounded across the frequency.

"It seems we have a group of rats to take care of. Well, it is a better use for my creations than to guard a bunch of future hookers,"

"Shit! We have been made," K-Force said in a soft tone to Bronze Bomber. Despite the fact the Border Patrol was made, there was no need to let them know that they had Meta.

"And I recognize that voice, if they go out there now, they are going to lose a lot of men and women," Bronze Bomber said, as the leader stopped the transfer and nodded his head for a henchman beside him to gun the cops down.

"We have been made! Move, move, move!" the captain yelled, as he ordered the Border Patrol troopers to the site of the exchange gone badly. At first it looked like they had everything handled. They had several armored Humvees and two six-wheel monsters with machine gun placements. They had more than enough fire power to handle a small platoon. That was until several heavy-cloaked cartel guards began acting weird. They twitched for a few seconds, then swiftly attacked the Border Patrol. The gunfire did nothing as the cloaked cartel begin jumping about like grasshoppers and ripping the border patrol apart. The gunfire seemed to be ineffective as the cartel forces seemed unstoppable. This was until a lucky female officer with a small grenade launcher hit one of the hyped-up cartel guards, only to reveal they were machines.

The robots were humanoid in shape, with no faces except glowing green eyes. Their bodies were gun metal and had the musculature of a marathon runner with clawed hands and feet. In a creepy way, the machine moved in a smooth, unnatural movement towards her, only to be blasted back by a pinkish-purple beam that sent it flying away, though the beam seemed more intense since it melted the robot where it was hit. The Border Patrol was shocked to find that they were hidden behind a wall of golden energy, as a forcefield protected them from any fire and assault from the machines. The big surprise was the fact that they could also fire out of the energy field, which was an entirely different level of control than the simple wall of energy.

Bronze Bomber fired off at any Machine men attacking the Border Patrol. The Machine Men all looked towards the greatest threat and tried to attack her, but it obvious she was out of reach. She destroyed them from a distance.

"Enough. Take the merchandise hostage. That will get the blonde bimbo to land," the raspy male voice. As he said this, a shield was placed around them blocking off all attacks. "Damn shield wielders. This is why we kill those annoying parasites."

K-Force chose to ignore the proof of the old theory that forcefield wielders were being hunted. He made sure that the hostages and Border Patrol were protected, as Bronze Bomber flew about melting the machines to slag, since she did not have orders to restrain herself except for living targets.

"Come out, Aztech. I know these tinker toys are yours," Bronze Bomber stated, looking at the convoy.

"Ah, Bronze Bimbo, again we meet as I hoped. We meet for the last time as well, since I have you within my grasp," Aztech replied. At first K-Force could not see where the man was until three cargo trucks in the caravan began to coordinate towards each other. Then, in assembly combination and rotation, the trucks began to form a contraption of some kind.

I swear if this is another giant robot, then this guy has no imagination, Bronze Bomber thought. She had fought the mad genius several times before, and each time she caught him, he was either deported to Mexico for trial or used by the US for projects for Special Forces. In two months he would somehow escape and be a bother to her in the future. Aztech was in Bronze Bomber's Rogues Gallery just because he could not handle a woman kicking his ass on a regular basis.

As the transformation finished, like always, it was a giant robot, though this one was different. Somehow, five semi-trucks were able to transform into a crab-like tank, for lack of a better description. The metal behemoth, made the Atomic Droid seem puny in size comparison, each of its six legs were twelve feet in height. On the crab like shell center were three machine gun-like placements that rotated on each side where the legs were attached. There was also a Gauss beam cannon on the front that, without fanfare, was fired once the transformation was complete. Bronze Bomber tanked the hit from the crab behemoth until a strange energy wave hit her. This had a strange effect of making her body shudder with actual pain. Bronze Bomber felt her very being was being pulled apart and being put back together again. To add injury to insult, the energy wave that hit also knocked out her powers for a few seconds.

"Painful, isn't it?" Aztech said in a satisfied tone, as he watched the bane of his existence. "The Karakinos might not win any beauty contests, but it was an absolute beauty to take down a puta like you."

As Bronze Bomber tried to stand up, the Gauss cannon unleashed a powerful round towards her. Energy weapons, explosions, radiation, and gas attacks were next to useless against Bronze Bomber. She ignored or absorbed all of those types of attacks. Melee against someone of greater strength was the only thing many people knew capable of harming her. Even then, it would take time for someone to wear her down because of her special alien metal skin. A scientist theorized that it would take a significant amount of power concentrated to a fine enough point to break past her defenses. High-end Gauss weaponry has the right amount of power and penetration to handle all three requirements very well. Bronze Bomber's ion energy field usually stopped such weaponry from harming her. The unknown energy wave stripped that layer of protection as the flawless bronze metallic skin began to tear.

"For years I have been looked down upon because I could not take out a bleach blonde bimbo. Now all that comes to an end and people will fear the name Aztech," said the mad genius as he began restlessly firing upon the metallic Heroine.

"You can't be serious. Is he monologuing," scoffed a patrolwoman that looked on from behind the forcefield and could not believe what she was seeing.

"He is a supervillain. They have a need to brag and insult their opponents, victims, and peers. It is why Professionals are the hardest to fight, because most put their egos aside to get the job done," K-Force said in a tired tone.

Just great, another aspect of my power I'm going have showcase, K-Force thought to himself as he left the policewoman's side. Now, with the ultimate cover, he was able to push back the machines with explosives along with the plasma rounds and other heavy riflery.

"Hey, get back here! We need the shields to survive," a border patrolman said out of fear.

"Relax. I have the shields on automated. Unless I pass out or die, these stay up as long as I want them," K-Force said before he rushed towards his mentor.

Bronze Bomber, for the first time in a while, was nervous. This mad genius had done it. He had actually figured out how to disrupt her powers, something she didn't think was possible. The only reason she was alive was because of her bronze armor-like skin, which was a two-way defense. It protected her from practically all damage, as well as contained her ion-generating body when she really charged up her energy. When her powers were at full swing, she radiated energy that was not healthy towards others—almost like radiation, it mutated organic life. Aztech's energy waves were screwing with her power. He was making her vulnerable enough to high caliber bullets, which were causing her internal damage.

"It has been a few years since I had a concussion. Can't say I missed it," Bronze Bomber mused darkly as the bullet fire was chipping away at her armor. She was for the first time bleeding from the damage, only to be saved by a robot that was thrown into one of the turrets. This surprised her, as her rookie was able to appear in front of her and take more enemy fire. K-Force just stood there taking everything as if it were more an annoyance than the devastating weapon that it was.

While his back was to the crab monster he put a shield behind him to block off and absorb as much energy from the assault. Then he grabbed Bronze Bomber by the waist and said, "Sorry, but it is the only way."

Before she could question his meaning, Bronze Bomber was tossed away into the energy field protecting the Border Patrol. One of the few remaining robots tried to charge in as well, but was rebuffed by the forcefield in front of them. Bronze Bomber was helped to her feet by couple of Border Patrol; she was still recovering from the beating she took.

"Miss, are you stable?" the patrolman asked.

"Yes, just give me a few minutes to recuperate," Bronze Bomber replied, trying to steady herself as she tried to stabilize the energy inside her.

"Can your rookie handle the walking soft shell buffet?" a patrolwoman asked.

"Easily," Bronze Bomber said calmly. "Aztech built the thing to crush me. He was arrogant to believe that it could easily kill my sidekick as well."

"Oh, like someone using a Xeonite machine to kill you, when it is only effective against Xeanoids like Ms. Marvelous," the patrolwoman said as she began to understand.

"Exactly," Bronze Bomber confirmed.

K-Force was doing his best not to be stepped on by the giant crab machine while he fired concentrated kinetic energy beams. This seemed pointless. The fact was he could not singe the paint on the damn machine and was wasting precious kinetic energy. Realizing that he would need more power to combat the damn thing, K-Force mentally side-blocked the blow that was made to squash him like an ant. Again and again he took the blows to his guard as the giant multi-ton foot stomped on him. Aztech, in his mechanical crab, saw that this was the only thing having an effect on the young upstart. Aztech used every bit of power to crush the kid who was ruining his chance at revenge. He continued to attack his bronze enemy, but the shields resisted everything, even his plasma cannons. The forcefields were resilient in protecting Bronze Bomber, the Border Patrol, and human cargo that was supposed to be delivered.

Aztech could care less about the latter two objectives. All he wanted was to end the overpowered trollop who continued to get in the way of achieving his goals. And at this point, when he finally found a way around her uncompromising power and durability, this insignificant jump-up black cricket got in his way. The mad genius let his anger and frustration out on this interloper. Again and again he stomped, kicked and smashed down the virtual holder of the wall that blocked him from his ultimate goal. Then all of a sudden, the momentum switched as Aztech was thrown around like he had crashed into another car. Looking down, he spotted one of his legs were stopped by the young upstart's one hand. K-Force simply rolled his shoulders and spit some blood out of his mouth.

Mom is going to get on me for not wearing a mouthguard, K-Force thought morosely. *'Always have a mouth guard because it stops you from biting the inside of your mouth and tongue,'* K-Force mentally heard his mother lecturing him as he spat the blood from his mouth. The taste was distracting him.

"My turn," K-Force stated as he lifted the metallic foot off the ground and jumped upward to tip the metal crab onto its side. The gun tried to fire on him, only to fall harmlessly against his skin. Then, from the underside of the giant crab appeared a shotgun similar to a Gauss cannon which fired a resounding and devastating blast towards K-Force at near pointblank range. This would turn even Heroes with durability of a tank into fleshy pulp. The area where K-Force stood was devastated, as if carpet bombing of C-4 blew up the area, only for the golden tan-wearing Hero to roll his neck.

"Thanks. I had a kink in my neck that has been killing me for the past two weeks," K-Force said as he then proceeded to simply smash the underside Gauss weapon, making it explode when it was fired again.

"Stop it. You're ruining my chance of glory." Aztech was getting beyond frustrated now.

"That is the idea, Genius," K-Force said as he jumped towards the crab machine, trying to flee. But it was too cumbersome to move quickly. K-Force started to rip the housing for the device that kept Bronze Bomber in pain, only for the hull to become electrified, shaking him off. This was one of the few things his powers couldn't block since it really did not count as a kinetic force. Luckily, he was resilient to a moderate amount of damage, but it was painful. He felt his body being fried from the inside out.

K-Force almost passed out from all the pain rushing through his body. He barely had enough strength to push through the electric force attacking his muscles. He finally found the crystal-like globe that was firing off that energy wave and crushed it, which caused a huge backlash of an explosion. K-Force was sent several hundred meters away from the destruction. This was both good and bad. In a positive light, it sent him away from the electrical field that was overwhelming him, and the explosion allowed the new kinetic assistance to speed his healing, despite being electrified. In a negative sense, it also hit him with his guard down, so some of his forcefields dropped.

"Damn you, damn you, you ruined everything!" Aztech screamed, furious that he could not take his vengeance. He turned his gun towards the frightened migrants whose protective field fell away. The robots were destroyed, but that didn't mean the Mad Genius would not vent his anger on them. He wordlessly turned his functioning Gauss cannon at them and fired upon them, only for it to be blocked by Bronze Bomber. She had recovered enough to tank the blow with her forcefield up. Bronze Bomber was not fully recovered. She had tears across her skin, leaking her energy. She was also bleeding from a few tears around her chest, which seemed to be painful. She was having some trouble breathing. She was furious, and all of her cheerful demeanor was gone.

Bronze Bomber flew towards the main cannon, which was firing as fast as possible and aiming to knock her away. Bronze Bomber just gritted her teeth and pushed her way through; the open cuts and wounds burned even more as she flew towards her goal. Soon

Bronze Bomber was able to fly around the back of the cannon, and with a massive amount of strength, she punched in the bottom of the Gauss cannon. She was smart enough to rip out any mechanism that might cause it to fire or rotate. Then, Bronze Bomber flew back to get some space that unleashed a massive torrent of ion energy which seemed to light the moonlit sky.

The metallic crab resisted the blast, which made sense Bronze Bomber. After all, since it was made to kill her, it should have some kind of defenses against her power.

"This is not over—you will die by my hand. Sadly, not today," Aztech said as the crab-like machine began to pull in, half-fold its legs, activate its thrusters, trying to flee back across the border. This was a tactic used by many villains around the border. Any active Meta-human Hero, Professional or Federal, caught crossing the border without permission from the nation of Mexico would be viewed as a battalion of soldiers or weapon of mass destruction. Hence, it would be seen as a hostile action by another government, unless deemed extenuating circumstances.

In plain layman's terms, any Meta-human employed by the USA, whether Federal or Private sector, would be considered the same as a military force crossing the border, because of anal retentive bureaucrats on both sides who did not see a single hostile villain as enough of a threat to allow a chase.

That would have been the smart move, but Aztech noticed that he could not move a foot forward, despite pushing his engines. He looked back at the dirty scuffed up rookie holding him into place with one hand.

"Ah, hell no, you're not going to escape from here after all that bull we went through," K-Force said, as his Mentor behind him gave a more vicious smile on her face.

With more frantic energy, Aztech tried to escape from them, more so the very angry woman. The working gun fired upon the two super humans fruitlessly as the engines were turning almost red-hot but were not gaining any momentum. Logically, it is never good for any vehicle to go full burn when there is no traction or movement, unless you want the engine to blow out. As the engine fell apart, the compartment near the end of the shell that housed the engine sounded like someone had thrown in a couple of wrenches into a dryer.

Without the engine holding the craft up, it fell to the ground with a loud thud. This was followed by a brief sound of silence, then a small cheer from the Border Patrol, as the two Heroes went towards the powerless vehicle that given them so much trouble earlier; they carefully examined the broken mechanical crab.

"Think he has enough power to open the door to escape?" K-Force asked.

"No. From my past experiences, he never thinks that he will lose or fail enough to think that far ahead," Bronze Bomber sighed, then noticing that her uniform was pretty damaged by the attack. Despite her skin being covered in a bronze alien-like steel, the top of her white, open-back leotard was damaged from the battle. While she had only a few holes here and there, what was left covered everything that she wanted to keep private.

What surprised K-Force was her reaction to the whole thing. Bronze Bomber looked down at her outfit, pouted a bit, shrugged and went on with her business. She ignored her slight exposure and walked towards the downed machine, cracking her knuckles.

"So K-Force, feel like cracking this crab open to get to the twerp inside?" Bronze Bomber asked as she rotated her arms to loosen up.

K-Force decided to be a gentleman and focus on the topic at hand. He stripped his vest and handed it to her so that she would avoid any slip-ups. This left his upper torso open in full view to the world, but it was nothing he would feel ashamed about.

"Ladies first," K-Force said as he motioned her to get the first crack at stripping the crab machine.

They began to peel the shell of the crab like a tuna can as soon as Bronze Bomber put on the vest. All the while the Border Patrol called the ambulance and coroner's van for the dead officers and cartel members as the majority of the patrolmen tried to calm the migrants—but were unsure how to help the group knowing the migrants would only be captured and abused by the same cartel if they were sent back over the border.

As the Heroes finished peeling out the mad genius, K-Force finally got a good look at the vicious megalomaniac. It turned out Aztech looked like a Hispanic version of a doctor who chased a blue hedgehog. Aztech had a potbelly, which meant he was a natural genius; no Meta gene in him whatsoever. This was not so unusual because super geniuses, with enough drive to build or invent something beyond the average human being, were counted as Meta-humans. To fit his image, he was bald with a massive mustache on top of a goatee. Despite his appearance, this mad genius had killed several Heroes before, but due to politics and the fact that the past few governors were too lenient, he escaped severe punishment.

"Go ahead. Lock me away. I'll be out in a few months ready to end you and your little boy toy as well," Aztech sniped at his rival.

"Seriously, what is his problem? Did you dump him or something?" K-Force was getting annoyed at the man's antics.

"Ha, he wishes. It's the fact that 'Barbie' has kicked his ass more times than he likes to admit, that, and he is a misogynist as well," Bronze Bomber told her assistant.

"Ah, you know it always seems to me that people with high IQ have the most fragile egos," K-Force commented.

"Let's see how cocky you are when I have your skull mounted on my wall," Aztech fired back.

"Not this time. You messed up big time today. You see, you got caught human trafficking, which is a federal crime. Meaning, you won't get a soft pinch from the California prison system. And Uncle Sam is not as nice and has over a two-dozen evil scientists building crap for him, so no deal," Bronze Bomber said happily. She continued, "Meaning, you have nothing to bargain with. And with several witnesses of you killing Federal officers, your options are the death sentence or banishment under pain of death, meaning if we see you again after this, your life is fair game."

At that moment, the angry scientist became very quiet and realized that his safety net was gone. Funny how fast a villain's bravado disappears when they realize that the death penalty is a real possibility.

"Oh, and don't think that the cartel is going to save you. I had a friend look into the whole unknown informant. I wonder how they are going to feel about you ruining a trade deal, costing them hundreds of millions of continuous revenue for a revenge plan against me that failed," Bronze Bomber added, showing her intelligence.

"You can't do that. You're Hero," Aztech felt like his world was collapsing.

"Common misconception, being a Hero who always does the right thing above all else even if it is a determent to our health and wellbeing is strictly for comic books. While many of us are not allowed to kill you, it does not mean we won't let you fall upon your own sword," Bronze Bomber replied with a smug look on her face.

"Got to tell ya, I heard about the cartel horror stories. I don't want to be in your shoes when they find out," K-Force grinned. He always loved it when a villain finally reached a level of screwed which they could not talk or beg their way out of. At that point, he could not kill them, but he had no obligation to save them from their own mistakes.

"Look, you have to protect me. I was in on hundreds of deals. You think this is the only human trafficking going across the border? There five more this month alone, and I'm more than willing to tell you, if you keep me alive and away from any prisons connected with my associates," Aztech offered, already pleading for mercy.

"That is not for us to decide, sadly because, truthfully, I would just try to break it out of you. But that would be counterproductive," Bronze Bomber said, deciding to let go of her anger at being seriously hurt. "But those people need protection and saving, so you better tell them."

"Besides, you're not her problem anymore," K-Force said as they calmly escorted the man and handed him to the police.

"What do you mean?" Aztech was so scared that he didn't notice the police frisking him and stripping him of almost everything.

"You killed federal agents, which means the state of California has no more jurisdictions when we hand you over to Border Patrol. And you know MHEAT do not play the fancy political games when their mission is this vital," K-Force stated matter-of-factly.

"Thank you, K-Force, I almost forgot about that little fact," Bronze Bomber said, happily stripping the doctor of everything, even his clothes. The Border Patrol had an oversized prison uniform waiting for him. It was an all too real cliché that super scientists had gadgets hidden within their clothes just so they could escape police custody when the Hero was no longer around to stop them from escaping. So, for better security, all scientists were stripped of everything on their person.

Despite all this, there was a determined look on Aztech's face stating that he would come back and his vengeance would be swift.

"Get a good look, you fool's gold bimbo."

"Sorry, I just was confused if you were a man or not, considering the baby bump-looking beer belly and the fact that I need a magnifying glass to find your sorry excuse for male genitals. You can understand my bewilderment," Bronze Bomber fired back.

After this, Aztech was spitting rapid fire insults in Spanish and English as he was dragged away by the Border Patrol. His hate towards her had reached a new level of loathing, despite the fact that these new problems seemed to stem from his own mistakes and actions.

Chapter 9
Exhausting Congratulations

Samson wanted to sleep after a hard-fought battle. Keeping the shield up during the entire long stake-out equaled a very tired Hero. As K-Force, he was hounded by the press for his first real villain capture, which was a heavy hitter. The press was trying to give the whole victory to his boss, only for her to admit that she would have been gravely injured if K-Force didn't take Aztech down. This in turn made him give two interviews and have three more scheduled for the next week, along with a dozen promotions to boost his image that made him feel even more mentally drained from the day's activities. He was just about to take a shower when his parents facetimed him. During the first three rings he contemplated about just ignoring them until tomorrow when he didn't feel exhausted. However, he knew that if he did so, his mother would give him a five-minute guilt trip.

Samson set his computer pad in front of him as he waited for the onslaught of well-meaning praise. Although he loved it, and this time he deserved it, he really just wanted to clean himself, go to bed, and deal with it tomorrow. As soon as the video chat connected, he was hit with party horns and a small toss of confetti as his parents began to cheer.

"I'm so proud of you, Baby. You proved your worth today and long before most of your so-called peers. And it was Aztech, of all people!" Aaliyah cheered at her son's first notorious villain fight.

"After nine years of you two training me to keep my head, it was bound to come out the way you wanted," Samson said as he fought to stay awake.

"True, but still you were sloppy. You let your guard down. You got electrocuted because you didn't expect Aztech to electrify the hull of the reject from Red Lobster," Hakeem said, as he looked at his son with a warm expression.

"Oh, give the boy a break. It was one lucky hit. He did great, considering it had Bronze Bomber on the ropes," Aaliyah chided her husband.

"And we both know it only takes a lucky shot for something bad to happen," said Hakeem, being the more cautious parent.

This was good parenting as far as Samson was concerned. While his dad may criticize him if he made mistakes, he would support him regardless. This wasn't a deterrent, but a motivator for him to push harder, which was all Samson's father wanted. His mother was the almost endless mountain of support that would tear into him for screwing up badly, but she would be there for Samson, nonetheless.

As they began to ask him how it felt to have his first official bust, there was only one response.

"I was mentally tired. It was the long ass stakeout that felt like half the day was wasted—the fight, and the interviews which were more an oral, informal after-action report. And it gets worse—since I have to, as my agent told me, use this to get myself some buzz," Samson said honestly.

"Son, you are preaching to the choir here," his mother said, giving him a sympathetic look. "But this is the life you lead now, public image and interviews, sponsorships, et cetera. You are going to have to get used to it, but don't worry—once you get through the early rush you will have time to breathe."

The look on his mother's face showed she was not lying or exaggerating, which made Samson feel his slight headache grow into something substantial. There was an old saying that came to mind: 'Don't chase fame if you're not ready for the price.'

It was another fifteen-minute call between Samson and his family before he got another call from Bianca. His parents understood that the two had always been close and that she would want to congratulate him, so when the next image popped up as Bianca, out of uniform with a pouting face. It seemed she was in her apartment in St. Louis, Missouri. It didn't help that while it was late her time, they were going through a heat wave so she was dressed lightly. This was awkward and a bit of a tease since Samson had asked her out twice before and was given the 'I only see you as a brother' speech. So, seeing her statuesque athletic body in that light blue attire was distracting him more than he liked to admit. What broke the image was the frustrated look that meant she was mad at him and the world.

"Why the hell did you get the big break?" Bianca yelled at the camera. "I have been busting my ass in St. Louis picking up every mugger and every two-bit Gamma and Delta level Meta who thinks just because they got powers they are a match for me. While my mentor, Stormbird, treats me like I'm some bright-eyed schoolgirl who needs a babysitter. Not to mention Pervy Titan hones in on my captures as some romantic gesture. But you, Mr. Golden Boy, get blessed with a Level 6 city-sized threat."

Bianca carried on as Samson allowed her to vent. "I worked just as hard as you! Hell, more, since I actually have to work for my paycheck, while you get to sit around most of the week," she shouted. The young woman was ticked to say the least, but that was thankfully not at him. This was one of those conversations where you are not allowed to talk; you're really just there for support, with a 'Uh-huh, you don't say,' and 'I understand.' He learned this a long time ago from his dad that women don't want their significant others to fix things; most times they only wanted a sympathetic shoulder to cry on. It was how they release all that tension, the way men commonly do through games, TV, sports, and so on.

'Just be there for them emotionally, and try to understand. And only fix things when they ask or strongly hint at it. It is frustrating, to say the least, but it helps to grow a healthy relationship, regardless.' Samson was remembering his father's words.

After what seemed to be ten seconds, Samson finally got his own words into the conversation. "You are underselling yourself and your accomplishments," Samson countered.

"Yeah right, you got two big scores in less than a month," Bianca challenged.

"Correction, I got one. The other counts as an assist so dock that to half. And know how well they play off my accomplishments. Now I have question - how many Level 4 incidents have you busted since you started?" Samson asked.

"Three, but…" Bianca answered.

"And how many Level 3's," Samson interrupted, not letting her diminish herself.

"Five," Bianca said, as she began to see his point.

"Despite my big splash, you are more constant then me since you are, in a lack of better terms, in a target-rich environment. Every talking head is calling me lucky or spotty at best," Samson explained.

"I noticed. Did you screw somebody's daughter or something," Bianca joked.

"Naw, just smacked around one company's golden boy," Samson replied.

"Prime Time." Bianca remembered this conversation.

"Yep, you can guess why I'm put here of all places and dismissed." Samson confirmed his suspicions.

"Please, I figured that out a week after you were assigned to SoCal. To make sure your victory was seen as a fluke, they need to make you look bad. To do that, Enteriagey needs you in an area they control, and California is mostly their domain. They feed Prime Time major opportunities to shine while you will be seen as the bust of our draft. Enteriagey saves face, Prime Time proves he is worth all the time and money they put in him," Bianca said, proving that she is right.

"I just thought they did it to mess with me, but the whole area of control aspect didn't occur to me." Samson was surprised he didn't see it.

"And them suppressing you isn't a surprise," Bianca added.

"That weasel of an agent threatened that I would be forgotten within a year. That goes without saying," Samson shrugged it off, as he saw this coming and still didn't regret taking down the so-called number one contender. "But my stance doesn't change. You are still doing great in comparison."

"So, you're saying that I should be grateful that I'm being hounded by an unwanted admirer? And I'm being treated like I'm some wet-behind-the-ears rookie," Bianca said, trying to see where he was going with this.

"First, you are a rookie, and so am I, and no matter how much power we have, we need proven experience to be allowed to do anything ourselves. So, suck it up. Plus, I'm sure Stormbird is only preparing you for the future. You know that a lot of us rookies don't make it past the first six years whether by injury or death," Samson encouraged his oldest friend.

"I am just saying I don't feel trained since he is training Twister Girl to be the next Stormbird. I know it is a cultural thing among the tribes of the Midwest, but are they really necessary nowadays?" Bianca questioned.

"Yes and no. Stormbird, Crow, Twin Wolf, Coyote, the other members of the tribal union, are the major force behind American settlers agreeing to share the land instead of just taking it like they did in the east. So culturally and historically they are important. But in truth, nowadays it is more a ceremony to hold the name of those who defend the people. Though the purpose dropped to minor levels in comparison to the past," Samson explained.

"So, it is a big deal for the 'true people of the Plains' to have the honor for them to carry the names of their guardians. Hell, the tradition was started by Iroquois who had the brilliant idea making, the British, French and American settlers believe that Sky Tamer was alive for two hundred years," Samson continued. Bianca was surprised how simple, but effective, the ploy was.

"Both empires had only one or two Omega level Meta-humans at the time, so they could not risk it," Samson added that little nugget.

"How did we get on early United States history?" Bianca was confused about how their conversation had shifted.

"I don't know, it seems we got off subject there for a second. Anyway, don't worry about it, you are going to be fine. You have more than proven yourself to be reliable. While I have a big question mark if I can do it again," Samson said.

"What about Nega Titan?" Bianca asked.

"Restraining order or complain to your sponsors about how he makes you feel," Samson couldn't see how this was a hard choice since she dealt with thirsty guys a lot in high school.

"It seems a little too extreme especially if it gets out. You know how the media loves to blow things out of proportion. I just want him to back off, not be added to the Me Too movement. He is annoying, not a rapist or molester," Bianca sighed in frustration.

"Then the best idea I have is give him a warning saying he is getting too aggressive and that you will file a formal complaint. And get a go-between that will make the statement stick. And trust me, that sends a clear message to back down without the drama," Samson suggested.

"I think I already knew that option, I just needed someone else to say it so I wouldn't feel like a bad person," Bianca trying to resolve herself.

"Look, you are not a bad person for saying 'no' to someone you don't want to date. No person has the right to push you to be with anyone you don't like and nobody has the right to make you like them," Samson confided to her.

The phone conversation began to dwindle down to a warm goodbye with Bianca saying, "Thanks again for helping me clear my head. I don't know what I do without you."

As that conversation ended, Samson decided to get the grime off his body and let the warm shower waters heal his sore muscles. *Cheapest form of therapy after a hard day's work*, Samson thought.

As much as Samson's power protected and fueled him, there were a couple weaknesses that got past his defenses, especially if he was not paying attention. Shoot him with a lightning bolt and he could block it easily on instinct. However, when he touched something electrifying unprotected, he might be able to survive it, but it would hurt like hell.

That's why Dad said I was sloppy. Never let your shields down, especially in combat. There is always a small chance for something to overpower you when you least expect it, Samson thought about his particular weakness of not paying attention.

Active energy was almost useless against him. His father and mother tested his limits while he was growing up, and he broke his limits over and over again with the amount of energy he could absorb and contain. He remembered exploding in the middle of a Meta training facility because he built up too much energy at the age of twelve. At that time, Samson's body couldn't take a thirty-kiloton bomb's worth of energy. In the present day, that amount would barely make him blink. It seemed pushing his power reserves at an early age made them grow exponentially at an alarming rate. Passive energy, on the other hand, affected him unless he put up an all-protective shield around his body.

Samson's sister said it best, if someone threw acid at him, he would be unaffected, but if dropped into a vat of it, he could be killed, unless he was conscious and kept his guard up. The power would be meaningless if he dropped his protective shell, just because he was getting cocky.

Nice going, Hypocrite. You complain about modern Heroes of your age acting like morons, but you get the drop for being just as big of an idiot as well, Samson thought, as he began to rinse the soap from his body. As Samson finished up his shower, he dried himself off and prepared for the absolute torture of re-watching his battle to make sure that he learned from any mistakes he made. Samson remembered seeing his dad watch his harder battles when he was younger and how his sister Tamera did the same thing, but in greater detail.

People may have thought that she was nothing but a brute, but in truth, of the three Brewer children she was the tactile and battlefield expert. Tamera's actions and rage were nothing but an image to lure people into a sense of security that she could easily be fooled.

As Samson looked over the fight, he saw that he had wasted some movements, but mostly he saw no alternative other than what he did. The only real fault he could see was the fact that he didn't maintain a small protective field, since he was so confident about not being affected by anything the Mexican Super Genius could throw at him.

Luckily Tamera isn't here, or she would break every move down and explain every small misstep, Samson thought. Should I call her or not? Samson looked at his phone. Seeing it was a quarter past 1 AM, he decided to hold off until the next day.

Good, I need some sleep soon, or I am going to get irate, Samson thought. He closed his laptop, placed it on the night stand and tried to get some sleep.

The next day, Samson was trying to eat his grits and sausage in peace while listening to his sister.

"Anyway, I should let you go, but one more thing, Rugrat," Tamera said, using her favorite nickname for her baby sibling. "It was nice of you to give your top to Bomber, but next time, don't stare too much, or people might think you are a pervert."

"Is that jealousy I hear?" Samson teased right back.

"*Oh please*, she is only top heavy. I'm the whole package with an actual personality," Tamera said in full confidence.

"So you say," Samson said as he finished setting up his brunch.

"Alright and remember, stop trying to take so many hits. It might look cool, but people will start to think you are a masochist," Tamera couldn't resist teasing her baby brother.

Letting that comment go unanswered, Samson just zoned out for the rest of his meal. After having to spend so much time in his car and having to put on such a grand performance, he had decided to take the morning for himself, since he had a day off from his company. Also, after a big score it was traditional to take a small break so others could have a chance to gain fame.

Halfway through his meal, he began watching a comedy series about a super observant detective who pretended he was psychic just so he could get extra compensation from the police department.

Another call went off, and looking at his phone, it turned out to be the one sibling he hadn't been able to reach for a month. Sighing, he answered the phone and placed his grits in the microwave sans spoon to warm up later.

"Hey Omari, how's house arrest," Samson sighed as he sat at the kitchen counter.

"Over and done with, though Cannady's lawyers are not happy. The fact that they have nothing on me or attack Abigail without public outcry is probably frustrating them. They are trying every avenue to sink the court case," Omari informed his younger sibling.

"Sounds big," Samson said.

"Very big, if Cannady is found guilty of conspiracy of murder. Then the other charges will stick as well. And the current sitting president can easily charge him with treason. And, win or lose, the presidential party can win the next three elections without even trying," Omari pointed out.

"Of course it comes back to politics," Samson sighed.

"When politicians are involved, it is always about politics, though that's not why I called you. I'm so proud of your first real bust," Omari congratulated him.

"Thanks. So how's your girlfriend taking it?" Samson asked, curious to have a villain's, or a former villain's opinion. Instead, he heard a subtle Boston Irish accent.

"I loved seeing you trash that sexist bastard into the ground. Aztech is one of those I'm-always-smarter-than-everyone blighters. And he was usually on the other side of the dealings, which meant he tried to kill me and my crew." Abigail had taken the phone.

"I guess your rival companies have more open hostilities than we do," Samson commented.

"And more honestly, people from my side of the road laugh at the so-called 'misunderstandings' or 'mistaken identities' that lead to Hero fights. You idiots are just trying to gain rich territory or keep others from messing with the local hierarchy," Abigail said, making her point known.

"Yeah, I have to agree. It is also one of the reasons why I am more likely going to join Federal. If anyone tries that, they will be tossed out on their ass in a heartbeat," Samson agreed.

"And throw away all that money," Abigail said in surprise.

"If it gets me away from the press up my ass every time I step out in uniform, I'm more than willing to take a pay cut," Samson quipped. He heard her laugh as it seems she was warming up to her possible future brother-in-law.

"Hey Abigail, while I still have you on the phone I have a question," Samson continued.

"Yes?" Abigail was curious about what he wanted to ask.

"Do villains hate shield users? I mean, do they really hunt them down because, if so, I want to prepare," Samson said, remembering that comment from Aztech.

"Since you're family and not my problem, I'll let you in on a secret. Of all the powers, a forcefield is the most difficult to work around. And that is all I can say right now. If I say more, there are former associates who will put a hit on me, and once in a lifetime is more than enough for me," Abigail told him.

"I understand and thank you," Samson said as he realized he had a big target on his back.

"Not a bother. Here, Hon," Abigail said as she handed the phone to her beau.

"Thanks, Love," Omari took the phone from her.

"She is a lot nicer than the press portrays her. How come I am not surprised," Samson made an offhanded comment.

"I see the press are just as annoying as Dad said they were," Omari guessed.

"Must be worse for you since you're caught in a political shitstorm," Samson replied.

"Language, and yes I am in the middle of a political scandal. Except it is the good kind with murder, conspiracy, and backroom dealings. Not the typical Senator So-and-So caught with his pants down," Omari joked.

"I meet a few that are not out to get me but there have been several attempts for me to say something controversial. I'm lucky that this month my opinion on women and fidelity is not cancelable," Samson said offhandedly.

There was silence for a few seconds across the line. "Hello?"

"I'm thinking, give me a minute," Omari said as he tried to see the connecting factor of his and their family's life. Thinking hard enough about it, he responded, "You are not paranoid. I'm thinking the lawyers and connections from Cannady and Enteriagey, who you embarrassed, are trying to crush you with a scandal, though I believe it is truer of the Enteriagey, since you are getting more press than you should. But no matter how powerful a company is, unless they run a monopoly, they can't block out big news."

"Great, nice to know paranoia gets worse when you realize you're right," Samson groaned.

"Don't worry. Just ignore them or stay neutral in your statements and don't worry about them trying to splice up your words to misguide the public. We got Incognito to back you up though they charge extra from delving into the raw sewage that is social media," Omari said, just trying to soothe his brother's nerves at that point.

"I understand hazard pay," Samson half-joked, as no one should unwillingly go through that toxic environment.

"Also, be careful, you took down someone with clout, meaning there will be those out there who will want to take you out because of your skill and power," Omari mentioned.

"I know, but that's what they warn us before we take the oath in understanding that the more good we do, the more powerful we grow, and the more there will be those who want to tear us down," Samson shrugged it off.

"You are an obstacle dangerous enough to be seen as a threat. And with those people you're dealing with, threats are often neutralized with extreme prejudice, depending on how big an obstacle you are to their goals," warned Omari.

Chapter 10
Green Spotlight

When Aztech said that villains hated forcefield users, he was not kidding. It was a week after Halloween, almost an entire month since he had met the genius robotics maker. And he has been targeted by no less than twelve villains, which was surprising, considering in this part of the country, you are lucky you get to meet and fight one every three months. Now K-Force had a horde of people after his life, which turned the quiet part of California into a hotspot.

That also meant that K-Force's metaphorical star was on the rise, as well as his mentor who would reap the benefits of actual super villains trying to kill her as well. This in turn brought an unusual amount of super level criminals to their section of California, which meant Southern California was swimming with crime and the local supers were getting more than enough screen time. It was true that in less than a month he had fought over thirty villains who were sent to the normally quiet section of the state. This in turn created other problems; namely, the Heroes of Los Angeles were, in more courteous terms, 'visiting' the area, but in reality, they were poaching.

Normally this wouldn't seem like a big deal since the villains were being caught a lot quicker than before. This meant less property damage and lives lost, so who cared which Heroes were caught? If this was a Federation, they would not care since they would get paid regardless of who they caught. Professionals got paid by quota. And right now, all the money was headed for Southern California. The best description of the situation was made by Gyges. She described it as if you were a miner, someone who has been searching for gold for years, but never found it. You only find a few pieces, but you knew that one day, by being steadfast, all your hard work would pay off. Then, all of a sudden, you get lucky and find a substantial amount of it. But a bunch of claim jumpers come out of nowhere, taking pieces of it, saying that you have so much that you must share with the less fortunate. The poachers say this while wearing the finest clothes and riding the best horses.

This created a turf war between Heroes, which devolved into fist fights similar to sporting matches without a referee to break it up. K-Force and QuickTime were the only ones not affected by the whole thing, because they were rookies. And stealing from rookies was akin to taking money from a kid, being a petty, selfish, and a bully was rejected not only by Heroes, but by most of the public, no matter how much of media darling you are.

There were some good things that came from this influx of super criminals. K-Force and QuickTime were considered the early stars of their draft class. Each of them had taken down at least four villains—two together—which was three more than most of their class. K-Force had personally defeated six super-powered criminals, which gave him the proof that his long years of training had been worth it. And Sky High Industry loved it, but was also afraid. Apparently, they were getting more and more fame, business, and money for his and Bronze Bomber's work. It was pretty much a NBA rookie who took the team to the playoffs in his starting year. But what frightened them was the fact that these attacks were not centered on regular crimes of monetary value, conquest, or passion, such as hate and vengeance; the majority centered on just trying to kill K-Force.

That was easier said than done, as many would-be headhunters were beginning to realize with this particular Hero. K-Force was overprepared, very efficient and a difficult power to overcome. Each time they thought they had him, he would somehow surge forward to pound them into the dirt. It was becoming clearer after every fight that K-Force was trained to fight a war, not small battles.

Several men and a few women sat around a large business table on monitors that obscured the rough details of a person outside of their general shape. Yasmin set it up this way to make sure that no one looking in could identify any of the 'board members.' She also had a very sophisticated voice-altering system that made their voices sound natural, unlike those cheesy store-bought toys.

"Thank you all for coming on short notice, but as we all know, time is money so I will be brief," Yasmin started off the meeting quickly, since most of these people in this room hated having their time wasted on frivolities and some would react harshly. "Someone in this room has been stirring up too much trouble. The Calamitous Conglomerate has been losing some of our top earners and top muscles."

As one the members of this meeting turned towards a large, muscular man covered in shadow who looked affronted instead of being cowed or embarrassed.

"Don't you dare glare at me, I was ordered to get rid of that shield user, like you asked, 'by any means necessary,'" the large muscular form growled.

"That doesn't mean sending a fourth of our best West Coast operatives, DeSoto," a male in robes stated out loud.

"We now have lost tens of millions of revenue because you weakened us for other organizations. Just because you are part of the board does not mean you have the power to spend as if you are a spoiled trust fund baby," a more feminine figure in a business suit said.

"How was I supposed to know that I'm dealing with the next Captain Neutron? The little bastard always escapes by his bare teeth, and always has a trick underneath his sleeves," DeSoto shot back.

"You should have observed him more. Instead you sent in the worst match-ups against him while his mentor was there," a shadow figure that resembled Mickey the Moocher reprimanded.

"That's not the biggest concern. Within three days it will be official that he will have Green Light protocols," Yasmin pointed out.

"What? I thought our lobbyist was supposed to keep that off the table so we can proceed as usual," the businesswoman stated.

"After eight of our people attacked him and several of our competitors targeting K-Force to make us look weak for not disposing of him, the Governor had no choice," DeSoto grudgingly admitted.

"There is only so much we can push from behind the scenes. The Governor is not stupid enough to piss off both the Federal and Professional Heroes at the same time," Yasmin supplied.

"Could have fooled me, have you seen the status of California in the last few years? The policy he made has let my crew expand with the proverbial slap on the wrist. What could have changed his mind?" another male said; this one in aristocratic uniform.

"Apparently the people are getting tired of the poor treatment and removed his fellow party members. This means he has to try to

- 213 -

appease as many as possible so he can keep his job," the robed man answered.

"Do we have any new back-up candidates yet?" Mickey the Moocher asked.

"Already in motion, but let's not get sidetracked. DeSoto, we're gathered here because of your constant failure and weakening of our conglomerate is bad enough that we are thinking of placing your territory under new management," Yasmin stated, showing she was already on it.

"Have you forgotten how much I did for this Conglomerate," DeSoto was getting furious at the idea of being tossed aside so quickly.

"No, we have not, but we are warning you, there are very few failures we are going to tolerate," the robed figure said.

"You don't have to tolerate anything for much longer. I already have someone lined up," DeSoto said confidently.

"It better not be one of our heavy hitters. We can't afford to lose any more right now," the businesswoman said.

"No, it is a merc who was most eager to break our little problem, especially once he learned who the bastard's mother is," DeSoto responded, grinning darkly.

"Well, don't keep us in suspense. Who is it?" the aristocrat asked while drinking his brandy.

"The rookie killer, War Fiend," DeSoto answered with flair, hoping the name would get a reaction from the council, and it did.

"Him, you called *him*?" As he spoke, the robed figure's eyes seemed to glow red in anger.

"Yes, you wanted the problem solved. Now it will be solved," DeSoto took some delight in the man's discomfort.

"And his parents will stop at nothing to kill him. In case you haven't noticed, we sent you some of our strong men to take him down, but his family could not kill them because by law if they surrendered, they would have to be taken in. War Fiend is on the kill-on-sight list by all Federals. Also, K-Force's parents are one of the few people who can match War Fiend. Hell, Intercessor almost killed him the last time they met," Mickey pointed out the flaw in DeSoto's plan.

"Not to mention, War Fiend won't stop with just one. He will leave a mountain of bodies before he leaves the area. You know his price for a favor is carnage and about half of a small city's population," the robed figured said in disgust.

"That is an exaggeration," DeSoto said, trying to shrug off the argument.

"Not by much. That *man* is a blood hungry monster who enjoys crushing Heroes and Villains alike. And he likes to bring as much chaos and collateral damage as possible. And he will try to avoid his clients' property or people, but he has a knack for putting many in shambles by the time he is finished." The robed figure was trying to get his fellow council members to reconsider the hire.

"Calm down, I have a plan to make sure that when he attacks, the casualties to anyone in our organization will be minimal," DeSoto said calmly.

"There is too much to risk," the robed figure said, trying to stop the deployment of War Fiend before he was interrupted.

All of a sudden, the volume of all the monitors dropped, revealing a lone figure at the head the table. A diminutive female figure who was there in person gave a stare that sent a chill down everyone's spine, despite being far away from her.

"Enough," the voice was a mixture of foreign elegance. Many would call it alluring, if not for the overwhelming pressure the woman's words seem to convey, even hundreds of miles from across the country.

"How long until your plan is deployed?" the head woman asked.

"War Fiend won't be available until a week after Thanksgiving," DeSoto replied.

"Reason," the woman demanded, not questioned.

"He has to finish up a contract for rebels who are trying to capture a city," DeSoto responded, being as respectful as possible.

"I don't care about the details. I just need to know that if we okay this venture, you will guarantee that it will end our little problem," she said, as the cold pressure increased again, but this time solely on DeSoto.

All of DeSoto's bravado left him. The woman may have been smaller than him, but she could crush him like an ant. Archon was one of the wicked thirteen of the exalted Omega 37. She ruled this organization, and had dominion over many major cities and, in some cases, entire states in the western half of the US.

While there were a few states she had absolute power over, there was always someone willing to challenge her rule. California was an important piece, true; however she needed someone competent enough to keep things running smoothly. Also, she needed someone smart enough not to try to separate her empire by thinking they could get away with it. DeSoto remembered his last two predecessors who displeased Archon. One was embezzling from her, and she stripped him of everything. Archon broke him mentally and had him left scavenging for scraps with nothing left to his name. The second predecessor ended up having all the women in his life forced into prostitution, all the men were killed or put into the modern version of slavery. He got to watch all in its entirety, while slowly dying by her power, which was one of the most painful ways to die. This all occurred because that man tried to lead a coup against her and failed.

"Yes, with certainty I can end him," said DeSoto, who was sweating despite the frigid temperature he felt.

"Good, because I do not need such problems with our business rivals interfering when I'm about to add Michigan to our territory. Make sure K-Force is dealt with before the New Year at the latest, or this will be the last winter you will be executive on this board. Understood?" Archon's words made DeSoto sweat, thinking that his job would be at stake, but his life as well.

"Yes, understood, Ma'am," DeSoto replied obediently.

"Good, any other problems with this plan?" Archon said, expecting no one to answer since it was rhetorical question. But to her surprise, one of her most trusted board member signaled to her.

"Yes, Mickey?" Archon looked towards one of her most efficient council members.

"I simply propose that he and his group lay low for a couple of months after the kid is disposed of. With as much activity as there is, I think it is best for DeSoto to lay low for a while until the heat dies down. And, well, you know how Heroes take it when one of their own is down. The block will be too hot for anyone jaywalking," Mickey said, merely suggesting how to help.

"Hmm, good point. It would be best to keep business in the area to a minimum," Archon warned.

"That will disrupt a lot of my business dealings that I have in the works right now," DeSoto mentioned, needing to make up his losses.

"I'm telling you, nothing to bring the interest for any form of law enforcement. Is that clear?" the woman's voice sent a chill down everyone's spine as her orders were absolute.

"Yes ma'am," DeSoto cowed again.

"Good, now onto other business. We need to shore up against our enemies. I know that we partially chose this life to avoid office work like those worker drones we harvest. So, starting east to west, I want revenue, threats, and any news of current projects," Archon requested, deciding to take over the flow of the meeting.

As the overwhelming pressure somehow relented from the meeting, many prepared to speak as the meeting proceeded.

"I can't believe you are going on a date with Gyges. Isn't she in the top ten hottest Heroines on the West Coast," Avery said, sitting at a kitchen nook, eating a Keto chicken meal after his heavy work out.

"Yep, though there are detractors saying she doesn't deserve to be up there," Samson said as he was getting ready for his date.

"When is there not? But seriously, you go from an unknown to one of the hottest Heroes on the West Coast. Are you sure she is not just using you? After all, she just got out of a relationship with that rapper, Ashtown-B," Avery questioned curiously.

"Yeah, about two weeks ago when she caught him in bed with a pair of Laker Girls," Samson answered.

"How bad was it?" Avery mentally winced at that. With Metas, relationship betrayal often led to fatal consequences.

"Think Brenda Richie when she caught Lionel, only Ashtown-B was left with a broken leg and couple of broken ribs," Samson said in a matter a fact tone.

"I'm surprised that she didn't kill him or that he didn't press charges," Avery was impressed with the woman's self-control.

"Gyges is really into maintaining her image so she kept it to a level where she could get sympathy from the public. And Ashtown-B is a rapper, despite anyone with a brain will tell you that Superpowers throw gender concepts of the stronger sex out the window. Ashtown-B can only admit she beat him, not that he was so scared that he put a restraining order on her, or he begged for help from the law," said Samson, laughing a little.

"Isn't that kind of against gangster rap rules or something," Avery chuckled with him.

"How many times have real life mobsters used the police legally to get rid of their opponents or protect them when they have a hit out on them," Samson pointed out.

"Good point, so you expect him to retaliate in some way," Avery asked.

"I'm seeing him making a couple of albums bashing Heroes with her image as well," Samson guessed.

"You know she is only going to use you as a rebound," Avery observed. "And Ashtown-B knows you can't touch him without major backlash. So, I got to ask, why the hell would you put up with it."

Instead of answering, he merely showed the image of Gyges in her night attire. A black strapless cross wrap that had a pink ensemble to help show off her larger than average breasts and wide hips enticingly.

"Okay, enough said," Avery murmured, appreciating the figure.

"You can come with me. I'm sure I can bring a plus one friend, since she is just showing me off to her entire posse," Samson invited.

"Nope, there will be party photos of me in an awkward position where my girlfriend will think I'm cheating on her," Avery declined politely.

"Oh yes, does this mysterious girl live in *Canada*?" Samson quipped.

"Screw you," Avery laughed at how it sounded. "You met Becca on video chat before so you know who she is."

"I do, I just can't believe that you and Frigid are in a long-distance relationship and doing well at it. With you being in Sunny California and her in the windy city, that has to be a bit of a strain on the relationship," Samson said.

"Not really, once our six months of training are over, we can see each other freely. She can fly at Mach 20 leisurely, and I am building a private jet that can travel Mach 10. So, it is more like an eight-minute drive for us," Avery explained.

"Right, I keep forgetting. Long distance for some Metas is entire continents' or planets' distance. Speaking of which, Becca?" Samson exposed her civilian name.

"Crap, you are not supposed to hear that," Avery remarked. He realized it was a no-no for their profession.

"I know we know each other's name but we live together, so it is expected. But you gave your girlfriend's civilian identity out to a stranger," Samson warned.

"Relax, it is only the first name like you, but yeah we exchanged names," Avery said.

"That means more of a committed relationship, not just a fling," Samson said.

"It is what we want," Avery admitted.

"Great for you man, hope everything works out." Samson spoke with genuine happiness for his friend.

"Thanks, and I hope you and Gyges work out as well," responded Avery, feeling good about his relationship.

"I don't like to get trapped in rumors, but I feel like I am more of a booty call and nothing more. Until she gets over Ashtown-B for someone else, but I might as well enjoy it, and it will put me on her good side if I act like an adult when it is all over," Samson expressed how he felt about the whole thing.

"Good philosophy—enjoy your time together and don't worry about it when it is over," Avery approved of his roomie's thoughts.

"Besides, we both know that this is just about appearances and sex," Samson said, prepping himself not to get his feelings involved.

"Are you sure?" Avery countered. He wanted Samson to be sure about the woman's intentions.

"Gyges said, and I quote, 'Don't get too attached. You're cute and you may be fun to hang with, but I'm not looking for anything long-term right now'—end quote," Samson said.

"Well, that is pretty clear. Remember to get protection, unless you want baby mama drama and child support," Avery said as he was looking on his laptop for something to watch on V-Tube. Samson knew that there was little chance of it happening. He decided to take that precaution anyway. He took the male version of the pill and used cleanse gel, which was made in the 70s. It was a KY jelly-like substance that cleansed and purified the sexual organ, and it protected up to ninety-eight percent of most venereal diseases. It was not a cure, but it was the most effective protection outside of abstinence. And most Meta-humans would destroy a condom. It was the only way, other than the old pull-out method.

As Samson was finishing his preparations, Avery's eyes lit up when he saw his video on V-Tube's top ten trending videos.

"Yes, we made it!" Avery shouted in joy.

"Made what?" Samson said curiously, as he finished dressing and headed towards the kitchen.

"We are exploding on V-Tube. Coming in second, but those stupid pet videos can't be beat sometimes," Avery groused at the unfairness.

"Is this the fight with Ragnar's Berserkers?" Samson asked.

"Yep," Avery said as he hit widescreen on their fight.

Sidekicks who had to prove themselves sometimes worked together. And after how active their area had become, there was more than enough training under fire to prove they had what it took, though their mentors were only so far away, just in case they needed help.

K-Force and QuickTime snuck to the warehouse where a meeting was being held between the West Coast Russian mob and Ragnar Berserkers. QuickTime went to a nearby twenty story building and glided to the roof with merely a scuff on top of the warehouse. K-Force simply air-walked the distance, then proceeded to long jump half a mile to land without a sound.

QuickTime look confused for a few seconds before rolling his eyes, though K-Force heard him mutter some words in broken Meta-human. The big score was that they had found two members of the Ragnar Berserkers. These were once just Gamma-level

Meta-humans who were petty thieves, until a genius from New Byzantium invented suits that amplified low tier powers. Now they were empowered to be able to match those who once lorded over them.

Now, such a discovery would normally be such a great invention that it would be highly sought after by the best nations around the world. Originally it was made by a scientist/engineer, Dr. Kallaki, who wanted her son, a low-grade Gamma Meta-human, to have protection against the bullies who hounded him. He was sent to a school specifically built for Metas, but the student body had a philosophy that only the strong rule. After seeing him hospitalized by another student, no one was willing to punish the bully because of backing. The power of his skill meant he was too valuable to lose. In the end result, Dr. Kallaki invented a way to turn her son's "weak powers" of solar energy manipulation into a powerhouse in comparison to his peers. Her work made her highly sought after by her own government, and she created custom suits for the most loyal and skilled Meta-humans.

Where did Ragnar's Berserkers come in? Some idiot politician brought in a bunch of private military mercs from Scandinavia. Instead of having local Meta who had a sense of loyalty to their nation, they got highly skilled mercs led by a man who was successful for off the book missions. Ivar, the leader of Ragnar's Berserkers played the loyal tool for two years until the opportunity was right. Ivar and his crew gravely injured Dr. Kallaki and had stolen over thirty power suits.

Ten were auctioned off to other nations, while the other twenty were given to those loyal to Ivar. He even put a failsafe to deactivate them if anyone dared betray him. Ivar created a small force of elite Metas for hire that everybody wanted to use. Officially they were outlawed around the world, meaning that if they were caught they would be arrested. However, every nation or organization saw them as an effective black ops group for their personal use.

Why was this important? Well, the question therein lies, if a suit that amplified Meta-human powers was limited because the creator was in a coma, and one became somehow captured, how valuable was it to begin with? Keep in mind that Dr. Kallaki's work was still not fully recreated, since the imitators only lasted for a few minutes before they timed out for a recharge, while hers could last for half a day and doubled the output.

That meant taking down one or two Berserkers would come with a big bonus and fame because the users would have to fight to earn the suits. None of those in possession of power suits were easy targets. Each one was dangerous, but as a pair, they would be considered very hard targets. That is, if you didn't have a strategic genius like QuickTime.

The first thing they did was take out all the perimeter guards in a quick succession. Then QuickTime unleashed a concoction, called 'Drive crasher' smokescreen. This was very effective scrambling all electronics nearby. Anything more advanced than a mechanical gun was offline, unless they were protected like those power suits. As the criminals panicked, the two members of Ragnar's Berserkers reacted like soldiers and prepared themselves for battle.

QuickTime had already snuck inside and was taking the small fry out, as they swung their guns around like clubs, since their high-end weaponry failed. The old school guns were the only ones working, so the low rank members of the biker gangs were firing at shadows they couldn't see, sometimes hitting their fellow gang members. While others were being taken out quickly by the young duo, the Bikers still standing started to fight for the working weapons, thinking they could do better. So, infighting began between the members which caused even more chaos. This was advantageous to QuickTime and K-Force as they had finally taken out the last of the gang with seemingly barely any effort. When the smoke finally cleared, there was an image of K-Force holding the leader of the Bikers being held up by his undershirt as he hung limply.

"Now that the peanut gallery has been taken care of, let's see what the infamous Berserkers got," K-Force got a good look at them.

They both had short-sleeved, light, full body armor that had glowing, neon highlighting around the collar. The six-armed brute of the two looked to be about six feet seven inches in height. It was clear that he had not missed an arm day in years, since it appeared he had softballs in his biceps. His appearance was that of the typical blonde Viking with braided hair. The other was slim and fit, but he was a less assuming figure who was built more for speed. He had an average face, short brown hair and a larger then average nose. He arrived, flying in mid-air, ready to kill the intruders.

Instead of talking, they both charged at K-Force who looked like the bigger threat. K-Force easily jumped over the charging bull and dove towards the flier. With equally fast reflexes, the flier dodged out of the way, only to be surprised that K-Force merely kicked the air to change direction and propel him toward the flying Berserker. He used a spin-hook kick that sent the flying Berserker across the warehouse into some crates nearby.

QuickTime made his presence known with a slap to the back of the six-armed bruiser. QuickTime wanted to test his suit against Dr. Kallaki's, despite it being of the imperfect series. QuickTime saw it like being a rookie athlete getting a chance to go one-on-one with a star athlete of the same sport. Then, when the brute reached for his weapon belt, he noticed that it was gone. Looking around, he noticed the cocky, silver gray and blue-highlighted individual who was holding the belt that had his explosives. It appeared the punk got too cocky since he should have gone for his weapons. As the six-armed brute brought out his laser pistols, he noticed that they would not power up. It was as if they had no energy within them. Then to power up his tech-enhanced sword and axe, they as well were deactivated.

"What the hell!" one thug yelled.

"My little smokescreen shuts down all electronics not protected from such a device, including those metal paper weights you call weapons," QuickTime cockily told them.

The massive six-armed brute grunted, "It doesn't matter. I'm going to use your spine for a putting iron."

"That is, only if you can beat me," QuickTime stated, as he waited for the oversized brute to charge. The six-armed criminal suit hummed as it geared up for whatever attack he was planning. Then the six-armed brute charged forward in a surprising amount of speed that could be described as going from zero to sixty in two steps. A normal person would become a smear on the wall with that much force.

QuickTime quickly sidestepped and executed a perfect Judo throw by sweeping the back leg, and using the momentum to slam the bruiser to the floor. Then, in a show of flexibility, he performed and axe-kicked his attacker's chest, who blocked the assault with four of his arms. While the block was successful, the impact drove the brute further into the ground. The six-armed man was jolted but not shocked enough to lose his focus as he tried to grab his assailant's foot, only to miss. As the criminal tried to stand up, he was hit with a pair of darts that merely stuck the suit with a small amount of penetration.

Then the six-armed brute was tased as the two small darts delivered a small but painful jolt. The electric charge was twice the strength of police tasers. The brute ripped out the barbs in anger. The previous criminal flier finally recovered from his hit and flew away from the two Heroes to gain some room. Then the flier charged forward with an energy cone around him.

This probably meant that he was counting on his power to win him this fight, except for one problem. K-Force was his worse match-up possible. As K-Force parried every pass, the flier was moving faster and faster.

"Now I recognize you, you're the wannabe Mortar Shell, Derek Jorsson. Though you call yourself Starkade, I do believe that's someone else's name, so there might be a copyright claim from Denmark," K-Force observed out loud.

The flier was about to smash the dark-skinned Hero's face in, only to be struck underneath the armpit that he left wide open. Normally in this state, the flier's body would become explosive, so such a blow would backfire. But for someone with kinetic force powers, it was as effective as a gentle breeze. Derek was knocked off course and sent careening into the ground, only to see a fist flying towards him.

As the flier was being taken out, the blond, six-armed Viking charged at QuickTime at relatively normal speed, and all six of his arms were blurring beyond human sight. QuickTime leaned forward with his right shoulder facing his opponent. Despite the blistering speed, and six-arms flying at him, QuickTime expertly dodged, parried, and blocked every blow that came his way, though it looked like he was being pushed since he kept throwing jabs that seemed to do nothing but irritate the blond Viking. Then two of the Viking's fists finally got a clean hit and knocked QuickTime back by a few yards. QuickTime move with the blow which looked like him doing a spinning backflip.

As QuickTime landed almost perfectly, there was a clap as K-Force sat on top of an unconscious Derek. This drew the attention of both of them as they were surprised to see the flier was taken out so quickly.

"And he spikes the landing," K-Force joked as he clapped at his friend's acrobatics. At this, QuickTime grinned and bowed at the applause. The brute tried to rush QuickTime, only for his suit to overload and begin to blast him with a surge of electric type energy. The brute was so electrocuted that there were burns and smoke from his body as his entire torso was fried all at once. As the six-armed man fell on his back, K-Force spotted a dozen of the darts embedded into the suit.

"A bit overcooked?" K-Force commented.

"Well, I prefer my beef well done," QuickTime quipped.

Back to the present, K-Force had finished dressing up for his date with Gyges. While most Heroes would go undercover in their civilian clothes just so no one would recognized them, it was not that kind of date. Gyges wanted this to be publicly seen, which suggested he should wear more of Hero business-casual attire, which meant most identifying features were covered, but still included a mask, colors, or symbols, if applicable. Samson's getup included a long-sleeved dress shirt, worn tight around his frame to show off his athletically toned body, with various gold African glyphs on the right sleeve. He wore this with a pair of tan, modern dress pants and black dress shoes. All the while, his face mask was lowered into place so that no one could identify him. If popular enough, this attire would gain entry into the most exclusive places frequented by most celebrities. Also, these areas were considered neutral territory for everyone who was not a psycho.

This was one of those hidden rules that most Villains and Heroes stuck to without things dissolving into utter chaos, and these rules were abided by, or there would be repercussions. One of the rules being, if a Villain saw a Hero or a Hero saw a Villain, they were not allowed to fight in certain areas. They would take their beef outside or get banned. And this was not a rule of merely a few businesses, but all of them. Meaning, if they wrecked one club and were proven to be at fault, they would be banned from all of clubs and bars.

The same rule applied to schools, although those would be considered almost excommunicated by that point. In an incident during 1974, a Villain massacred half of a middle school just to kill a Hero's daughter. To say the block was hot would be an understatement. Every Villain with a connection was hunted down and killed by a group of Heroes, including an Omega who saw the need for sending a message. And the government turned a blind eye, mostly because the Villains were getting more and more reckless and ruthless. So, the representatives of both sides came together in secret to keep society from dropping into a warzone, and agreements were drafted.

During that treaty, one of the agreements was that certain areas were off limits, including churches or places of worship, schools, clubs, bars, and theme parks. Also, they were not allowed to attack any Villain or Hero family members. If they were discovered doing so, they would be cast out from their community, and the victim would have free reign to exact vengeance. This was why Red Banshee was so screwed. It looked like she broke the treaty, which meant she couldn't have any help or support from anyone. This was the worst position for most modern Villains; no support meant easy capture or death, if they were unlucky.

This turned out to be a blessing or curse depending upon the perspective of it, since there were also street fights between Heroes and Villains, as well. Hero against Hero, or Villain against Villain, due to the lack of inhibition caused by alcohol and hormones, the lack of inhibition created a cocktail of drama that spiked up revenue for those places, as people would typically gather to catch a glimpse of another fight or battle. That, and BMT always stood by at these places to stir up trouble.

"So, where is this club gonna be?" Avery asked

"DeJa Blues," Samson replied.

"Okay, pretty big and expensive club," Avery turned towards his roommate. "You sure you can afford such a swanky place? I heard their special steak medallions cost about eighty bucks a pop."

"How much of a bonus did we get bringing in those two mercs? Remember, they were on the wanted bounty list, and we brought back one functional suit and a half-fried one," Samson mentioned.

"Three hundred and fifty thousand dollars," Avery answered.

"I just got notified by my bank that a half-hour ago I received $175,000 in my account, meaning I'm more then well-compensated for our work,"

"Fair enough, but how much of your signing bonus you got left? I mean, the upgraded computer game tower, AMC's latest Javelin, and the freaking Dodge Red Hellcat which you plan on driving. You know that if you drive that to the club you can never drive that as Samson right," Avery warned.

"First off, I still have $2.3 million left, meaning I spent less than a fifth of it. The Hellcat was from my new sponsor, Dodge. They like me and my so-called image and the fact I have nabbed more Villains in a month than most rookies have in six months. A bright up and comer as they say," Samson explained that he was spending his money wisely.

"You lucky son of a bitch," Avery complained a bit at his friend's luck.

"Oh, shut up. You got sponsored by Xoni and got the latest Game Station for free. Not to mention because you wouldn't shut up about it, you also get the next upgrade for free and a twenty percent discount on all their products. And don't forget more than half of these fools are after me because shield users are a hated commodity," Samson shot back.

"Okay, I admit the fact that you are being targeted is kind of a blessing for the rest of us, since we get more targets, but still, ease up on the money-spending," Avery said.

"Relax—everything I got recently, except the Javelin, is from local sponsors and gifts from people for saving them, by protecting their homes and businesses from being collateral damage." Samson shook off any concern.

"So, you're saying you are actually being careful with your money, unlike every other athlete in existence spending like it was never going to end," Avery commented.

"I read about too many celebrities, producers, musicians to do the same thing. Hell, I invested it in a couple of banks and made sure they were not in a partnership, so if someone tried to pull a Madoff, I would be protected," Samson clarified.

"Speaking of protection, I heard the governor has finally admitted you are being targeted, so you're unofficially under the Green Light protocol," Avery informed him.

"Finally, he tried to avoid it as if someone was asking for child support payments," Samson sighed in relief.

"It was getting ugly, and many Heroes and law enforcers were wondering what the holdup was. It wasn't until MHEAT's threat to do an investigation about the whole affair and what was impeding him from executing his duties," Avery stated.

"And, as we all know, no politician likes to be examined, because there is a chance for anything unrelated to be found and bring him in even deeper crap," Samson added. "So, before I leave, how many hits did our latest bust get."

"After clearing it with the DA office, we got over thirty-five million views in a week," Avery answered.

"It is official, we have gone viral," K-Force grinned wildly, as he high-fived his roommate. "And we could not have done without the excellent camera work of your drones."

While they were fighting the Russian Bikers and two members of Ragnar's Berserkers, Avery as QuickTime recorded their fight and excellent takedown. Despite the great camera work and editing, no stations nearby wanted to see it; they said the public wouldn't be interested. As if to prove them wrong, QuickTime put on his private streaming channel and they were the top trend for the week.

The big media broadcast didn't seem to understand that while they may swing opinions one way or the other, there was always a market for content creators. Especially since they both had the respective companies backing them up along with all their internet traffic.

"And despite all this, we have some old school fools who get on us promoting ourselves on V-Tube. Because in this business they are salty that we found a minor loophole to get our names out there," K-Force groused, recalling the last time they did this; almost every analyst decried them having a V-Tube channel.

"They're just mad that we were born later and able to use this technology while most of the old-timers and hall-of-famers didn't have the opportunity that we have now. Sounds like a bunch of salty boomers to me," Avery stated as he began to respond to a couple of comments. He wanted to show that they were interactive with the channel.

Soon K-Force's phone alarm went off. "Hate to cut and run, but if I don't leave in the next ten minutes, I might have to get a speeding ticket to get to my date on time."

"Aren't we excluded from speeding tickets?" Avery seemed to recall that they were excluded from any and all minor traffic violations.

"On duty, not off," K-Force said, exiting towards the underground garage.

Chapter 11
Dating Interlude

As K-Force drove in his black and gold Dodge Hellcat he actually laughed at the fact that this was, for all intents and purposes, his work car. As Samson Brewer he could not drive this car because it would draw way too many questions. People would try to put two and two together if he drove the same car in public as K-Force.

This all made him think of how things had changed since he was younger. The Internet made it both harder and easier to be a Hero. The chances of being caught or found out by people who were very lucky or had deductive reasoning were high. This was why some of the Pro Heroes chose to become public figures, forgo the secret identity and become full celebrities; the fear of being caught limited them. This was a danger for those with family because they would never know who would attack their kin just to get back at the Hero. But it also made it dangerous for anyone stupid enough to try it, because Heroes would have full amnesty to kill them.

That little nugget was added after Heroes were reinstated, because the Villains kept attacking former Heroes' families. The government at the time was too corrupt or too stupid to be effective enough to stop it. The Hero community official stated they would go on strike or become renegades unless it was put into law to help protect their families. And with the Omegas leveraging their support, the US government had to concede. Because of this, very few Villains were willing to cross that line since it wasn't just one Hero, but a whole community, that would hunt them down.

"Because judgment without mercy will be shown to anyone who has not been merciful," James 2:13-16

This verse is what Heroes used to justify this amendment to their rule and guidelines. Its meaning was quite clear; pass that line, and all bets were off. No one was going to save you from their wrath. That was the reason Senator Cannady wanted to have someone innocent murdered to remove the law and help put Meta-humans under more governmental control. And this was probably why he picked Fringe, because he was one of the few Villains crazy and willing to do so for the fun of it. Currently he was fighting with everything he had to win his court case, which at this point didn't look good for him. Hence he was trying to be sentenced as a traitor to the government, which might put him in prison for life.

Though K-Force sincerely doubted it would save him, he orchestrated an attack on an Omega's family members who were essential to national security. K-Force was pretty sure that Sunna would leave the nation if the man was not executed, and letting her leave was a political suicide, no matter how many politicians squawked about being against 'legalized vigilante thugs.' One Omega left the United States before, and it tanked the economy and trust in American money. The nation seemed more vulnerable, and the US had to increase the budget for the military since they needed to fill the hole left by the Omega. Canada and the Neo British Commonwealth gained even more wealth, as he was accepted by the British who were seen by the world as more stable.

Meaning they may just hand Cannady over to her since she has been more than patient and reasonable. And they can't risk such actions happening again, no matter how much pull or dirt he has, K-Force thought happily. He knew by his religious background and his profession that he was supposed to be above such behavior.

However, the dirty senator tried to kill his brother; there was only so much clemency in him.

These thoughts brought to mind Fringe's last moments, as the angry embodiment of the sun melted him from the inside out. One V-Tuber explained in excruciating detail how Sunna turned the sociopath from Newark into a human roman candle. The fact that she could boil someone enough to melt him from the inside out, while making sure his brain was still active, seemed like an actual hellish experience.

Though at the end he seemed shocked and in disbelief that he would die and looked around for someone to save him, K-Force thought as he stopped at a red light. *I guess Night Raven always stopped other Heroes from killing the psychopath to save them from going down some dark path.*

K-Force laughed at that and saw it as the self-righteous rhetoric that it was. A little mercy to others is important, but when that same person escaped imprisonment and continued to kill into the hundreds of thousands, then it was time to end the madness.

Shaking away such thoughts, K-Force decided to focus on more immediate problems such as how he was going to handle Gyges and her three friends for their first date. As much as he was excited to date her, it was clear that this was mostly a paparazzi date. It was nothing more than saying that she had already moved on from Ashtown-B. This also meant he had to impress her friends, since if even one disliked him, this would be a short dating window. K-Force thought about all the lessons his father taught him about dating women and how to think of it as a battle situation.

Okay, remember that she brought her friends for three reasons. One judgement, while the decision is ultimately hers. Their opinion can sway the final decision to either direction. Second reason is the fact that she wants to come from a place of power by bringing friends gives a layer of protection and boost to public opinion if anything goes sour. Final point, they are there if he is a boring date so she can still have a fun night out if he is a dud, K-Force could hear his father's words in his mind. He was only ten minutes away from the night club and cocktail bar.

Also remember that you are not completely defenseless, as you have power as well. And that is the fact she is not the only woman in the world or the only option for me. You have been getting numbers from normal women and several other women from the San Alonso area. Even if she was only willing to date you for a short time, there more women out there, so, remember not to demean yourself for her because it gives her too much control on, not only your relationship, but also yourself. K-Force remembered another little kernel of truth.

It is not just bad boys that women are attracted to, but men with confidence. You can be kind and helpful as well, but remember no one respects dirt, and a woman will not love it either. So, don't be afraid to say 'no' or walk away without letting too much of your pride cloud your judgement. K-Force was brought out of his musing as he spotted an artful blue sign that read "Deja Blue." He had to wait in line as he drove to the front. It seemed that he and Gyges weren't the only celebrities attending that night, which meant a two to three-minute wait for said celebrity to exit the car and wave to the crowd and press.

K-Force sighed, looked at the mirror and made sure he was presentable. This was his first interaction with the public that wasn't a press conference or an event party with the in-the-know. But this to him was more difficult since this was a more natural and intimate moment to see if he had the charisma to work with the crowd, and the diplomacy to handle the paparazzi. Lately they had been less toxic than the mainstream media.

A soon as K-Force stepped out of his Dodge Hellcat, many people were looking to see if he was a celebrity, or some rich old dude, or a trust fund baby. The crowd was surprised when a Superhero appeared in front of them.

"It's K-Force," a female voice shrieked from the long line of patrons who were waiting to get inside.

K-Force was surprised by this reaction. While he was in the headlines a lot more because the attacks were more focused on him, K-Force was also barely into his third month as a Pro.

I guess the more work you show to the public, the bigger your name gets, at least locally, K-Force thought as he smiled and waved towards the gawkers and the people who wanted to see him. But before he could go towards his fans, the press approached him with the usual, what you are driving, who you are wearing, et cetera.

"So, tell us, are you here alone tonight?" a gossip reporter asked.

"Not quite. I have a date with someone, but they will not arrive for a bit," K-Force replied.

"Really, who?" the same gossip monger asked.

"I'm not allowed to say. She wants to make a big splash. To get the full effect, she has to be a surprised so I'm not going to ruin that," as K-Force finished saying. They pressed on, trying to get him to squeal, but like his shield, he refused to budge. Seeing that they would get nowhere fast, another reporter who wanted to ask a serious question jumped the queue.

"Bernard Forsythe for KMZ 12 News, I just heard that you are now officially under the Green Light protocol, could you explain what that means to you, and what was the incident that pushed it to be activated," a second reporter butted in.

"Well to me, personally, it means I am under direct assault by a large organization which in essence, put a green light on me. Which means I am being targeted with extreme prejudice, so to keep me alive and healthy, this allows me to have more leeway in my battles from now on," K-Force answered what his company had scripted for him.

"You mean, you can kill them legally," the news reporter accused.

"No, unless they are such a great danger to the public, I am still not allowed to cross that line. At most, I am allowed to put them in traction to the hospital," K-Force retorted.

"Isn't that an excessive use of force," Bernard seemed to be more activist then reporter.

"No, if someone draws a gun or lethal weapon upon police, they are allowed to fire upon that person to protect their own lives or people around them. I'm still not allowed to kill, but I am given the right to use that level of force, so I am within my rights and the rights of the criminal life are still upheld," K-Force explained, getting annoyed with the man's antics.

"That still sounds like Hero brutality." Bernard refused to see reason.

K-Force looked at this idiot and mentally checked out since nothing he would say, even with all the facts being there, would quell this anti-police and anti-Hero kick.

Five bucks he says I'm a fascist promoting a system that harms a citizen's right, despite the fact these people are out to kill me, K-Force thought.

Then an idea popped into his head. "Anyone here have a pen and paper?" An old school paparazzi man handed K-Force a pen and a little yellow note pad, out of curiosity. K-Force grabbed their attention by stating, "Before I reply, I am going to do a little magic to show that I know what he is going to say."

K-Force made sure the four press gossip mongers were paying attention. Once he was finished, he handed the message towards the older gentleman, and turned towards the annoying glory seeking reporter.

"The Federal and Local Government have found proof that there is an official target on my head," K-Force said with a grin.

"So is every other Hero. This doesn't allow you to use excessive use of force," Bernard accused him again.

"True, but the others don't have certified proof of having a large organization putting a bounty on their head. And don't ask the price since it will only get amateurs trying to do so as well. Last thing SoCal needs are a bunch of greedy fools thinking they can grab some easy money," K-Force stated calmly.

"Oh please, that's just an excuse to extend more brutal control of the populist. That borders on Fascism which you seem to be in favor of, and isn't being complicit in these actions a betrayal of African Americans." This reporter wanted to catapult his career to bigger things than what could be considered BMT material.

"Alright, Mr. um, I'm sorry, I didn't get your name," K-Force said as he turned to the man who he had given the note to.

"Gus, and I didn't give it to you, so I will let it slide," the old school paparazzi said.

"Thank you, will you read the note I gave you? Out loud, if you would," K-Force said with fox-like smirk.

Gus was curious what the young punk wrote, but couldn't help but guff at what it said. Then he gleefully began reading a few lines that would deflate that self-absorbed twat who though he was too good for people like them.

"K-Force wrote, and I quote, 'He is going to call me a fascist for defending myself from lethal force and somehow make it about racism, despite it having nothing to do with it,'" Gus said.

This got a laugh from anyone nearby who heard it as the young Hero predicted the whole retort as if he were psychic.

"How did you? Did you read my mind without permission? This is a violation of my civic rights," Bernard accused, in order to save face.

"First off, assuming any law enforcement measure will always directly affect minorities, because we are supposedly more likely to commit a crime, is in itself racist. Secondly, I have no psychic powers, period. It's just that people like you are so painfully predictable that you rarely deviate from the same script for anyone who doesn't think like you do," K-Force stated as he walked away, not giving the man a chance to retort.

The reporter started to blast off insults and accusations of every type, more than half of which were prewritten.

"No mind reading required, if your opposition is so predictable you can set a clock by him," K-Force said calmly, though every fiber in his being told him to punch that waste of space. Then, as a final insult, K-Force shut down any communication with the man as he tried to answer other reporters' questions.

At this, Bernard shouted and tried to get a word in, but he was absolutely ignored. Many patrons in line started heckling him and told him to get lost. Especially when K-Force started writing autographs and taking pictures with fans; he even answered some questions. The big moment was when he lifted a crowd of patrons and fans about five feet into the air with his forcefield. This had them all laughing and cheering, but they were disappointed when he had to stop because he could not violate any rules about using his powers on civilians.

Luckily, Bernard had moved away by now so there was some sort of peace while K-Force interacted with the crowd for a while longer. One underaged girl, who should not have been allowed in the club, stole a kiss from him. K-Force immediately held his hands up and gently pushed her back a couple steps with a soft forcefield which he set to feel like a pillow. Hopefully, this would give the message to the excitable young lady that he was flattered, but not interested. There were the typical catcalls and comments, but K-Force was sure that the kiss was seen as an unexpected surprise move made by the young lady, not him; so he should not get any real flack. Though knowing how the press liked to make anything a hot button issue, he knew there was going to be some heat.

"Not that I am not flattered, but I think that's as far as we can go without lawyers present," K-Force said to her, hoping not to hurt her feelings. He silently hated how sensitive the world was that even if he did not do anything wrong, he would still be accused of inappropriate behavior.

I swear what happened to innocent, excited fan interaction or just talking to a woman without being accused of unwanted attention. Oh right, because of a couple of asshats, the rest of us have to suffer for their mistakes, K-Force thought.

As he got a couple more fan shots, a limo rolled up with his date's entourage. First, was a good-looking man who appeared to be half-white and half-Native American. His long, black hair and sharp Native American features gave him an almost movie star quality. With him being the typical tall, dark and handsome individual, he looked straight out of a romance novel cover, featuring a lonely, pioneer woman with a sexy, Native American man in a passionate embrace. Next came his date, who had been given the name Yellow Coyote. This was a name of a strong Alpha-level Hero of the Comanche. As tradition of many tribes, the best Meta-human warriors carried the names of notable war leaders who protected them from other tribes and ever-expanding European descendant settlers.

Yellow Coyote was someone who kept her identity secret by wearing a stylized wolf head dress that covered the top-half of her face. Her spandex tight costume was well-padded around the vital areas with a nice balance of yellow on black. Her gloved hands had tungsten claws on them. Yellow Coyote's powers were the abilities of every animal that ever existed, which made her very powerful, since this included dire beasts and legendary beasts. Though tonight, she merely wore a mostly yellow and black-highlighted cocktail dress with a plunging neckline. Her tawny brown hair reached her shoulders while her face was covered with an elegant wolf mask, more fit for a masquerade than fighting crime.

Another woman who exited the limousine was a petite black woman with short, dark hair and a one-shoulder strapped, warm-gray, slinky mini dress that drew attention to her hips. She looked already a little buzzed and seemed eager for the night. K-Force knew that she was going to be the wild one of Gyges' crew.

Finally, his own date, Gyges was wearing a sheathed, long, white sleeveless maxi dress, split to the waist. What made this dress lewd was the area around her hips which was held together by threads in a "X" pattern, giving the illusion that she was not wearing anything underneath. The dress was showing off her curvy body in a very appetizing way. This was why she was considered a role model for plus-sized women, who she encouraged to take care of themselves and not to be afraid to show off their bodies. Added to this were her high heels which brought in more allure to her legs. She was out that night to kill, regardless if K-Force was a boring, worthless date.

I know money and power attracts the type of women who are willing to sleep with the rich and famous, but seriously, Ashtown-B, you could look at porn to kill the urge. Especially if you have that waiting at home for you, K-Force thought, looking at her walk towards him while rolling her hips for the camera and a couple thirsty guys in the crowd.

I know I'm just an accessory to show off that she has moved on, but does it make me a bad person that I'm willing to accept it for attention from a good-looking woman? K-Force looked at Gyges talking to the press, while giving him a sultry look.

"Don't care," he muttered underneath his breath.

Chapter 12
Should I Stay or Should I Go

A little while later, they were in the cocktail section of the nightclub which filtered most of the music from the next room. K-Force was all for blasting music to dance and have fun; however the bass should not be so loud that his feet were practically getting a foot massage. To save his ears from the damage of staying too long in the club, K-Force decided to shield himself from the bass. This had the effect of messing with people's voices around him, but he preferred not to get tinnitus. Though with Meta-human biology, he wondered if tinnitus was a medical problem that he could get.

As they sat down, Gyges started the group date by introducing him to her posse, who seemed eager to meet him.

"Oh girl, you were right, he is cuter up close, though maybe a little too clean cut. Tell me, Baby, do you have any tats or scars on you?" the short-haired woman said as she openly examined her friend's date.

"You only get to see if this date doesn't go so well between me and Gyges, but I may have a few," K-Force smirked.

"Why do you want to keep them private? Don't want people seeing something bad like an old gang tattoo," Amber seemed to throw caution to the wind as she began to question K-Force.

"The one with no filter for her mouth is my old friend, Amber," Gyges remarked. She had the good sense to be slightly embarrassed by her friend's antics.

"Charmed, I'm sure," said Amber. She flashed him her side profile to show that she looked like a fitness model on Twitter.

"Something like that, and please, if I was in a gang then I would have a lot more clout and a bigger fan base," said K-Force, who held back rolling his eyes.

"He is right, you know, former criminal-to-savior is a big draw for a lot of media," Gyges said, coming into the conversation.

"And I think Blue Crusader had enough copycats trying move on his claim to fame," K-Force said, remembering how some Heroes hated copycats, especially those who had found their own schtick to fame. Copycats included those who falsely pretended to be something they were not in order to steal a Hero's thunder.

"He's a former Crip, right?" asked the male Native American who was somewhat interested in this conversation.

"Big one. Practically ran Los Angeles before he found religion and decided to help the neighborhoods he used to terrorize," Gyges stated in almost disbelief. The former kingpin who became a man of God was at least more admirable than half of the reasons her peers had joined.

"Moving on, I have a burning question for your friend, Yellow Coyote," K-Force asked as he put on a mask of seriousness.

"Which is?" inquired Yellow Coyote, who was just enjoying her drink.

"How did you not get disowned by your family by coming here?" K-Force said without losing his poker face.

"What?" Yellow Coyote nearly choked on her Long Island Iced Tea from the shock. Joseph, being considerate, gently patted her back so that she could collect herself.

"Last time I checked, isn't New York and California the new Sodom and Gomorrah for those from Texas?" K-Force's comment actually got a laugh from Yellow Coyote as she had heard the exact description from her grandpa.

"After the way the governor has been running things, you're not that far off," the handsome Native American quipped, but his superhero girlfriend elbowed him. "What? It's true."

"First, my folks understood that for me to make money I had to go where the opportunity was for me. My dad said it like this - if the only team willing to draft me was in L.A. then he preferred that I play in L.A. than for me to give up my dream." From Yellow Coyote's tone this was a halfhearted joke, which meant it was true. "Secondly, I am more Comanche Traditional so the Christian symbolism doesn't hit as much, despite me being from Texas."

"Understood." K-Force grinned as his hope for a good icebreaker had worked.

"I guess I'm the only one not introduced. The name's Joseph White Raven. Pleasure to meet you," the handsome Native American said as he realized that he had not introduced himself.

"K-Force, though I'm pretty sure you all already know that," he replied in the same manner.

"Hard not to, you've been all-over San Alonso County. It seems that whenever a new villain pops up, you are there taking a beating and crushing them into the ground," Joseph commented.

- 246 -

"Speaking of which, why the hell do you do that?" Amber asked, not caring if it was appropriate or not.

"Do what?" K-Force said, confused by her question.

"Intentionally, let yourself get pummeled to drag out your fights?" Amber clarified.

"Yeah, trust me, if I had the option, I'd go Mike Tyson and knock their ass out in the first round, but I have to drag it out or my sponsors feel cheated," K-Force answered with a put-upon voice.

"So, you have to allow yourself to get beat to keep your sponsors happy," Amber understood what he was saying; it was just the logic behind it wasn't clear.

"The one time I decided to go for a more efficient route was against a Blood gangster enforcer named Tracy 'Driller' Thomson," K-Force began to explain.

"Oh, I know him. He is supposed to be a Beta-level all-rounder. Very dangerous, since he actually has some training from the Marines before he became a mercenary," Yellow Coyote interrupted by putting in her two cents.

"He put two Heroes in the hospital," Gyges said, remembering how Tracy was very skilled and dangerous, despite his hood background and lack of flashy powers.

"Took him out in twenty seconds," K-Force said as he pulled up his phone searching for something.

"What?" There was a collective gasp from the group.

"No way. You're exaggerating. This wasn't some mundane bank robber or gang banger," Gyges said; she knew K-Force was good, but he couldn't be that skilled. That was, until he handed her a private recording which showed the entire fight between the two. It was almost a minute of Tracy grandstanding. Then, when the actual battle began, Tracey pulled out his illegal plasma gun while dropping his special smoke bomb to obscure the vision of his opponent and cause a coughing fit. Then, Driller tried to sneak up on his opponent, only to see K-Force was unaffected. Driller tried to shoot him to make space between them, but it seemed that plasma was not as effective as it was to most Metas. They merely hit the target and barely stained his suit. With a devastating one-two combination, he laid the guy out.

Gyges watched the whole scene again. She knew what made Tracy Driller so dangerous was his ambushing techniques and his ability to set almost perfect booby traps. And he was taken out with barely an effort.

"How? He plans out his attacks to the point that if you're not careful, he can take you down." Gyges knew this because he openly threatened to abuse any Heroine he defeated to prove his skill, so the company reps gave her the data to prepare for him. Gyges passed the phone to Amber, who watched the scene play out, with Joseph looking over her shoulder.

"When you get right down to it, his style of fighting is Zoning, which means he uses traps and attacks from a distance. The only reason I won was because he figured a rookie would be easy pickings. So, I rushed in and cold-cocked him," K-Force explained.

"So, exactly like a Mike Tyson fight," said Joseph, who looked unimpressed until he noticed the face mask K-Force wore actually morphed to cover his eye in a reflective lenses.

"Your mask changes depending on the situation." Joseph sounded impressed.

"Air filtration and protective lenses are just a few functions, but yes," K-Force confirmed.

"So, they order you to put on more of a show." Amber was also impressed.

"That's the nature of the business," Yellow Coyote sighed, looking tiredly at her drink.

"What? You girls do the same?" Amber asked, surprised.

"I have the same deal, though it's more of me dodging and throwing insults at my opponents. I have several comedians helping me with my insults, which actually is a favorite feature for most college age slash adult men and women," Yellow Coyote sighed. While she liked being sassy, she hadn't signed up to be a comedian.

"I on the other hand have to project the veneer of 'untouchable queen' or 'top bitch,' I merely float in place or glide about while I block practically everything coming my way. I admit I am a bit of a diva, but I'm not that one egotistical tramp on every Real Housewives series," Gyges remarked, not liking her persona either.

"You're not that bad." Amber tried to ensure her friend but a small, mischievous smile escaped. "Yet."

"Trick, please, you're more of a diva then I am." Gyges gave Amber the stink eye.

This dissolved into a minor verbal catfight between the three women, bringing up minor or old examples and mistakes to chastise each other. K-Force and Joseph kept mostly quiet and let them have at it, knowing that saying anything except that they were going the restroom or to get a refill would drag them into it.

As soon as they got 'who-is-the-bigger-whatever' out of their system, they calmed down and began to act like friends again.

"Amazing," K-Force said, watching the women finally calming down.

"What?" Joseph who was looking to say anything but not get involved until he knew tensions died down.

"How women can go from zero to a hundred and back to zero so fast," K-Force commented.

"Not that surprising. Men do the same, only it's passing insults towards each other like it's nothing," Joseph said. "My sister and her friends do the same thing."

"True, but you have to admit, women seem to go for the jugular sometimes," K-Force looked at the women of their group. "And almost never forget the insult."

"Facts," Joseph couldn't help but agree, but remained thankful the women were not interested in their small talk.

K-Force received his drink, which turned out to be a Moscow Mule. As the waitress passed out their drinks, he spotted her a fifty-dollar tip.

"Generous," said Gyges as she watched her date.

"I can afford it, and it makes us a priority to her and any hangers-on who want a fat tip as well," explained K-Force as he took a sip of his first drink of the night.

"As a former cocktail waitress, I can say I would be extremely attentive to a table that drops a fifty early, even if it wasn't mine," Amber laughed.

"I guess being a Hero is more lucrative than my job," Joseph said with false sorrow.

"That mostly depends on three factors which are the three P's," Gyges started to explain.

"Popularity, Productivity, and Power," Gyges said in unison with Yellow Coyote and K-Force, who had this drilled into them by their companies as well.

"I think I get it, the more popular you are the more you get paid. I have seen actors who are ten times the better actor than the others, but are paid less. And productivity, we all know a couple of directors who make absolute schlock, but they produce money-making films which get high returns. But how is power factoring in?" said Amber, showing that she wasn't as 'superficial' as she played off.

"The more powerful you are, the more valuable you are, because they are Heroes, seen as essential to national security," Gyges continued.

"Is that so important?" Amber asked, since she was not quite seeing the point.

"Not until the ban on Meta-humans, Heroes were made during the mid-sixties to early seventies. There was a call to remove or lower the amount of Meta-humans. It was turned down when the politicians realized that it would almost quadruple the national budget," explained Gyges, showing that she was very well informed.

"How much?" Amber said in anticipation.

"Sixty-five billion dollars annually, and that's without inflation," Joseph butted in.

"What was it before?" Amber asked.

"It was 17.5 billion," Joseph said flatly.

"Holy Crap, what were our grandparents thinking," Amber laughed at the craziness that the Superhero was banned; it seemed a terrible idea all around.

"Something about how they couldn't trust Heroes, despite the whole coup being orchestrated by politicians," Gyges sighed.

"Anyway, tell me Joseph, what do you do, if you don't mind me asking?" asked K-Force, trying to get away from politics, since he hated the subject.

"Data analyst and stock trader," Joseph said with pride.

"Trust me, it is not as exciting as the *The Wolf of Wall Street* made it out to be," Yellow Coyote teased.

"Ah sweetie, you know the only butt I want to snort coke off would be yours," Joseph kidded. This cracked Yellow Coyote up, which indicated that she liked a crass style of humor. But given the material she liked to sling at her enemies, it was not all that surprising.

"It is nice to know that something will stay sacred and in the bedroom," Yellow Coyote quipped back.

K-Force looked towards the other non-Hero at their table and asked the same question.

"Me?" Amber asked in a fake, coy tone. K-Force only nodded, saying yes and gestured to her to answer his question. "Well, a Professional Donor, which means I have the perfect body for donating DNA and bone marrow to help create clone organs. My job is to exercise and stay fit. I am an A-negative blood type, which means, while valuable, I am not top tier rarity, but the extra forty-five hundred dollars a month is a great boost."

"Extra, what is your regular day job?" K-Forced asked.

"Hair stylist," Amber replied sweetly.

"I heard about that. People just stay in relatively good health with no drugs, smoking, good cholesterol, and only donate to the medical companies, and they get paid until the mid-forties for top quality DNA for top quality organs," Joseph clarified.

"Hence, this is one of the two drinks I am having, not only tonight, but for a month," Amber shrugged.

"That would be hell for Ashtown-B. He would turn into such a little priss if he could not get wasted every week," Gyges complained about her ex.

"Considering what we know about him, self-restraint is not one of his strong points," K-Force commented as he remembered the tales of drunken stupor and the 'Molly' caught in the rapper's car.

This got Gyges laughing a bit, and she gave K-Force a somewhat warmer look than before.

Good move, but don't let that be your only move, K-Force thought as he began his mission to get to know Gyges.

The next hour was somewhat a success. The one lesson his father had taught him and his brother was the fact that women liked to vent, so never try to fix a problem unless asked to. The assignment was to be a sympathetic ear when wanted and a strong rock for her to lay against for comfort. So, K-Force did this and looked for ways to sneak into their conversation, and at times take over, which was a sign of being confident.

After that little ice breaker, the date moved along better than K-Force expected, when she actually pulled him onto the dance floor which made him feel more at ease. He was known to be the blunt one of his siblings, so he was always worried that he might say something offensive. However, the dance floor was where he felt most comfortable. While he had to possess high amounts of coordination to perform as a Hero, dancing was a natural thing for him.

K-Force wouldn't say that he was the best dancer. That title went to his sister who performed ballet until college. Something her fans would be shocked to know that the hardcore hot-blooded Ratel loved to dance and watch the ballet.

K-Force laughed as he made it to the dance floor and watched Gyges begin to sway her hips to the song, and the way she moved those big hips did something to him. Luckily, he was able to match her move for move, and he was even able to do simple dance partner moves which looked impressive but were small compared to those who often danced together.

Gyges laughed happily as her date showed that he knew how to dance closer to her style. "How?" she asked.

"Had a lot of Cuban and Brazilian friends. I had no choice but to learn," K-Force answered before the music became too loud for him to talk to her again. Soon for almost four more songs they danced together, which made Gyges smile in joy. K-Force guessed the big bad rapper didn't know how to dance, unless it was only bump and grind style. While things were progressing well, the fifth song became a slow one, which made Gyges excuse herself and drag Amber to the bathroom.

Seeing that she left the dance floor, and Yellow Coyote and Joseph were getting into the slow dance, K-Force decided to head back to their table. *Relax, you're doing good, she was genuinely surprised and happy, and she even got a little dirty in her dancing, so she is not turned off by you,* K-Force's thoughts were sidetracked by a drunk, scantily-clad, blond girl who appeared barely legal to be in the club.

"Hey sexy, smooth moves, want to give another girl a whirl before your 'friend' gets back," the inebriated girl draped herself over him.

"Sorry, I have my dance card filled for the night, but I'm sure you can find a lot of other guys who will be eager," K-Force said. He was no fool. He knew this was in public and any camera shot could screw him, so he kept his hand well away from the girl unless necessary.

"I prefer to have a big strong Meta like you protecting me from all these thirsty men who like nothing more than for me to spread my legs," the drunk blonde nuzzled into K-Force's chest, trying to start something.

"And I prefer not getting arrested or accused of molesting a girl who is only sixteen." K-Force wasn't going to sugar coat his opinion.

"Wait, you can tell, I mean, uh, I have no idea what you are talking about." It seemed clarity finally hit the drunken girl.

"Mmmhmm," K-Force said in a tone that all black people seem to do. Soon as he tried to walk away, the girl grabbed his shoulder and looked worried.

"You are not going to tell, are you?" the party girl looked nervous, since she knew K-Force wasn't buying it.

"This is one of those victimless crimes I really don't see the point of dealing with. Just be careful, because there are some crazy ass people out there you are not ready for," K-Force was trying to be nice to her, since she wasn't hurting anyone.

"At least you're more understanding then my brother. And cuter too, maybe?" again she tried to flirt with him, which was becoming far more annoying than flattering.

"Go, before I tell security to scan your ID," K-Force warned her. This got the underaged girl scampering away in heels she hadn't quite mastered yet, all the while looking around for any security who would look at her suspiciously.

"I don't need my face plastered on TV for underage scandal," sighed K-Force as he headed back to his group's table, right before the music changed to a more upbeat tempo. He was able to get everybody a refill except Amber, who was limited to one drink because of her side job.

Alcohol was not a big deal for most Meta-humans since they possessed a high resistance towards most alcohols. He himself was measured to be able to drink three bottles of Everclear to feel even the slightest bit drunk, though he would never tell his parents that he and Bianca had tested themselves over spring break at a party in Daytona Beach.

Soon the group started to reform at the table again to relax and recharge, and a plus was that Gyges snuggled up to K-Force more than last time.

At least she feels comfortable around me, K-Force thought as they got into a new conversation in the Meta community of who was dating who or just screwing. Amber tried to bring Bronze Bomber into it.

At that point he stood up for his boss by pointing out in the past two months he had worked for her, she had been the most wholesome Hero he had met. She preferred helping lost kids, cats up trees, flying busted cars on the freeway to dealerships or auto shops. Bronze Bomber was the type of Hero who prefers to be close and intimate with the community. This surprised the lot of them, though Amber did ask one question.

"Then why does she dress like that all the time? Not to mention flirting with every cute man that catches her eye. And her sex life is notorious," countered Amber, trying to defend her opinion.

"While she does like to flirt with guys, she dates less than most Hollywood starlets. In truth, she told me that when she was young, she was always taller than most girls, had big feet, was skinny as a rail, and had bad acne. Than all of a sudden the Meta gene pops in, and she began to fill out. And she had her pick of boys and as a guy I won't hold it against someone who goes boy or girl crazy when they start lining up for you." K-Force had friends who were Metas or Mundanes and each one got on him for not taking advantage of more girls when he was in high school.

"I confess when I was in tenth grade I got my Meta-human upgrade, and I was with another girl every other month," Joseph admitted.

Amber tried to get support from her friend but that was a stone wall as well. "I was a step away from looking like *Precious*, so don't expect me to judge her." Gyges was no longer on the media line calling Bronze Bomber loose. She had met the woman, who was actually very sweet.

"Speaking of which, I think y'all's judgement of what makes someone loose is far too judgmental. Just because a woman enjoys having sex and feels no shame about it, doesn't mean she is a terrible person," K-Force rebutted, deciding to throw out his own opinion.

"Oh, and you got a better version?" Gyges looked towards him.

"Sure, if a certain someone sleeps with another person while in a committed relationship, then they are a slut, or, if they knowingly sleep with someone who is married, engaged, or in a long-term relationship. Beyond that, it is not anyone's business unless they are spreading something around." K-Force laid his thoughts before everyone to pick and muse over.

"You realize that includes men in that definition, right," Gyges grinned at her date, seemingly liking his point of view.

"Ladies, I think you can agree that most men are dogs, when you get right down to it," K-Force said bluntly, which got a collective laugh from them.

"I'm with K-Force on this one. Most guys brag about cheating on their girlfriends or seeing two women at the same time. Male or not, that is 'ho-ish' behavior," Joseph added, while grinning along with everybody else.

"Glad to see your blunt nature is not just for show, but still, did you have to be so crass?" Gyges commented to K-Force, though she didn't sound turned off by his attitude.

"I never found dancing around a topic when people need to be called out, a good thing. It only seems to encourage more terrible behavior," K-Force laid it out.

"Okay, Big Shot, who is the biggest one in the Pacific region?" Gyges challenged.

"Red Dragoon," K-Force replied, after a few seconds.

"Second," Joseph agreeing with him.

"Seriously?" Yellow Coyote was surprised how quickly her boyfriend had agreed.

"Eight kids and five come from four different women, and only married to one," Joseph pointed out.

"Seriously, you'd think he was trying to rebuild the Meta-human population," K-Force said as he thought about the infamous man whore of L.A. The only reason he was still married was because his wife seemingly was using him as a beard for her own tastes.

"Speaking of which, could you explain where Metas come from?" Amber asked innocently.

"Well you see, when you get mommy or daddy with the Meta-human gene and," Gyges said in the tone of a parent explaining things to a very young child.

"Shut it, Heifer, you know what I mean." Amber said, playfully pushing her friend.

"But really, you will need to be more specific," Yellow Coyote giggled with the rest of them.

"Okay what I mean is where do all these Meta-humans come from? I mean, most of y'all were practically nonexistent until Caligula. Then all of you come from out of nowhere. At first, you were small to non-existent in numbers. Then all in a span of two thousand years, you number in the hundreds of millions spread across the world?" Amber questioned.

"Oh that. Well, I'm not sure you want to hear that since it is long and complicated tale, and you wouldn't want to be lectured," K-Force dismissed, as he drank more of his drink.

"First off, screw you, I may not be interested in educational pursuits, but I'm not some video ho who only thinks about money, fame, and bling." Amber accused him of dismissing her.

"Okay, but do you want the short explanation or the long one," K-Force replied.

"How long is the long one?" Amber asked.

"About twenty minutes while the short one can be summed up into five," K-Force answered.

"The short one then because I don't want it taking up an entire night, I came to have fun, not to get a lecture." Gyges took the decision away from them.

"Alright, are you two okay with this," K-Force asked the other two members of their group.

"Sure," Yellow Coyote didn't mind.

"I'm curious myself. I just took for granted how everything became this way," Joseph replied.

"Well to start off, there were three basic reasons why we are so widespread, despite being a small population. There were sprouting points, war, money and prestige," K-Force started.

"What do you mean 'sprouting points,'" Amber asked.

"Well, to put it bluntly, for some strange reason around the world, we humans began developing superpowers. Though since it was so widespread and around the same time period, many don't know if it was a single source or widespread phenomenon," K-Force explained.

"You wouldn't believe the crazy theories that came about with people trying to figure it out," Yellow Coyote commented.

"There was the Jesus' Blessing theory, which stated that the first recorded Meta-humans were around the period near Jesus' death. Many believe it was the final blessing that God gave mankind to surpass their normally weak forms," K-Force repeating the old theory.

"I can just imagine the headaches that caused," Amber said. She knew how people would use something like that as an excuse to be assholes.

"No more than the others," Yellow Coyote added her two cents.

"The Horny Omega theory," Gyges laughed at her 'favorite' one.

"The what?" Amber was confused, as if she didn't hear correctly.

"It is actually called the Progenitor Theory, but the idea is still the same. An Omega-level being flew around the world, impregnated a bunch of women across the planet, despite the fact that Meta-humans have DNA proof that each strand of Meta-human DNA comes from a different source, not some super Caucasian variety," K-Force said.

"And there is the nerd theory, that aliens gifted us with this power by experimenting on us," Yellow Coyote wiggled her fingers for emphasis.

"Like the pyramids," Amber said in a dull tone.

"Hey, the fact pyramids appear across two non-human cultures proves there is a connection," Yellow Coyote defended.

"Let us leave the conspiracy theories for later, like until we're drunk or high enough to consider that one," Gyges rolled her eyes at her friends' alien conspiracy theories.

"Considering we saw a Reptalis twerking her tail off on the dance floor, it is not too outrageous of a theory, originating in the 1940s," K-Force said.

"Apparently, they see it as a mating dance for a specific male they wish to mate with," Yellow Coyote added.

"Funny, so do I," both men said together which cause them to look at each other, then burst out laughing.

"Men," Gyges rolled her eyes.

"If we weren't so easily controlled, imagine how dangerous we would be," Joseph pointed out.

"That is actually a dangerous thought. Imagine how much worse things would be if they didn't think about sex every thirty seconds," Yellow Coyote said in mock horror.

"And, finally, there is the Myth and Legend theory," K-Force decided to continue.

"Oh, I know this one. People believed that maybe in the past, all the ancient religions or legends were based off of Meta-humans of the past. And information and stories were exaggerated over time and made them Gods," Amber answered like an eager student.

"Correct, now you know the starting point. Do you really want to know how we got so widespread," K-Force said, trying to shorten the lesson.

"Yes, I'm still confused how you guys are so all over the place but not a bigger population." Amber was eager to find out.

"First, there is no guarantee that Meta-humans are born from a mixed marriage. Hell, even Meta-human couples only have an eighty-five percent chance of that happening," K-Force said.

"That and most of us are Delta or Gamma-level," Joseph added

"And secondly, the main reason we are so widespread is sadly because warfare increased our numbers dramatically at first," K-Force continued.

"How does using you guys as soldiers increase your population?" Amber asked.

"Before gunpowder was invented, or more accurately, before World War I, even a trained Delta Meta-human could crush hundreds of soldiers. Therefore, one Meta-human was more valuable than any battalion of highly trained soldiers, and less expensive in the long run. So, the armies of the world were willing to give these individuals money, power, and mates to grow their military might." K-Force stopped as he received a refill of his drink. He tipped the waitress and sipped from his glass. As soon as he quenched his dry throat, he continued. "Soon they became champions of the army as they would decide battles and conflicts of state—depending which nation had the most powerful ones."

"Of course they were those Meta-humans who wanted to rule over the weak rulers, right," Amber seeing where this was headed.

"Of course, back then, might made right, and swords, spears, and arrows weren't going to do much," K-Force said.

"But if that's the case, how did the rulers not get kicked off the throne?" asked Amber, knowing there were more regular human rulers early on.

"Simple, benefits and marriage to the royal lines," Yellow Coyote answered.

"Despite what Hollywood portrays, most people just want the wealth and prestige. Actually ruling the nation is too tedious for most people," Gyges entered in her own opinion, showing what she knew as well.

"Exactly, give someone enough political power and riches, and they don't care about ruling the nation, though this became a moot point since most of the early Meta-humans were wedded into royal family, so they more or less had royal blood. Sadly, this brought about a mixture of power, an instability because what happens when your little brother becomes stronger than you," K-Force led Amber to answer.

"You don't have to tell me. Hidden power plays and assassinations," Amber sighed at how predictable humanity was, with powers or not.

"And outright fratricide," Gyges added.

"Though the bonus for women was the fact that if they were powerful enough, they could not be bossed around by anyone," Yellow Coyote said with a grin.

"Obviously this could not keep happening, so many governments decided that Meta-humans need to be controlled, either by removing them when they are young, or making them loyal to their country. Those with loyalty to their nation were rewarded with riches and some power. Though the level of power given is usually determined on how powerful a Meta-human truly was. A state Meta-human is automatically given the rank of Lord, which meant they were of the peerage," K-Force said.

"And of those who didn't get with the program?" Amber asked, but knew the answer.

"They had better watch whatever they ate or drank unless they wanted to be dead or at least very ill. Though, that is not much of a guarantee since most poisons are just indigestion for the most of us," Yellow Coyote was again showing that she knew more then she let on.

"So, there were no Meta-humans taking over countries after that point?" Amber was confused.

"Hell no," emphasized K-Force. There always were high level Beta or Alpha taking over areas because the nation was too weak to stop them; or he or she killed the opposition. Things got more complicated around the early medieval age when women were willing to sleep with a Meta-human to gain a Meta-human child. Whether for wealth or to have the blood of the Gods flowing through their family veins, we don't know, but it seemed to explode across the world."

"There were changes to law that allow Meta-humans to have multiple spouses to extend each nation's power. Especially Meta-humans who could help build infrastructure or benefit the people more than just crushing armies," Yellow Coyote said.

"That is why polygamy and state-funded babies is a thing nowadays," Gyges added.

"While the need for warriors has gone down, the need for productivity and boosts to industry will always be valuable," Joseph added.

"And only men can take advantage of it." Amber scowled.

"Viscera with her three husbands would disagree with you," Joseph held up his hands to placate any anger towards his comment. "I'm not saying that most of the powerful Meta-human males don't take advantage of it, but female Meta-humans make up a solid third of who uses such arrangements."

"So, men are blameless and we should excuse such things," Amber said; she did not like hearing how such things are ignored because everyone does them.

"No, men should be held up for such things if they abuse them," Yellow Coyote surprisingly spoke up. "This is a system that is more beneficial for women in the past than now. The government pays an extra thirty-five hundred dollars a month to help with raising a child with the Meta-human gene. Therefore, mothers have a lot to gain, as well, such as education stipends with no debt."

"How do you know this?" Gyges was surprised at her friend.

"I have an aunt who just uses her kids who are Meta-humans. She lives off of them. After my aunt graduated from college, she received money from the local casino as well as a government paycheck for two kids. She gets paid ten grand a month and plans to be a baby factory to keep her lifestyle," Yellow Coyote stated. It was clear that she was red-pilled to the point that women would abuse the rules for their benefit as well.

"It is like she said. The nation gave such benefits to women who were willing to raise Meta-human children since they were a valued resource. And they were reimbursed, usually in triple, one way or the other. It got so bad, the poor families would offer their young daughters and even their wives to be impregnated which was a boost to their standing and money to be well off," K-Force explained.

"But men are the only ones who took advantage of that back then. I'm sure you couldn't name one woman who willingly turned themselves into baby factories to gain power and prestige. Or have a bunch of husbands because they wanted to have a court of Himbos," Gyges made her statement known.

"There were quite a few women. There were many famous female leaders being Meta-humans who had multiple husbands since no religion or culture forbade it. Or at least because they were not strong enough to pressure them," K-Force said

"Yeah right, name four," Gyges challenged.

"Arabella of Spain, who had two husbands and four consorts and about twelve kids in all," K-Force said.

"The tyrannical Queen Adjua of Unshati was infamous having an entire of harem of men and no husbands. And she only allowed ten of her kids to survive, because she was scared that her own children would overthrow her," Yellow Coyote helped.

"Hell, there are two more who are even more so notorious that they are tropes for such actions," K-Force added.

"You're kidding." Amber was interested now.

"Does the phrase, Fertile Myrtle, mean anything or how about a river of children," K-Force asked.

"I know I'm going to regret this, but yes, I have heard about those," admitted Gyges, waiting for the other shoe to drop.

"Mertyl Joan Sigismund was a high level Alpha. To Germans she was also called Great Mother Mertyl or the Mother of Germany,"

"I'm guessing she had a lot of kids," Amber grinned.

"Try about twenty-five over the forty years of rule. And twenty-two became Meta-humans as well," K-Force answered.

"Twenty-five," the girls said in unattended union.

"Four husbands and ten lovers, and all these children had multiple lovers as well so by the time after the Napoleon Wars they had so many they thought they could take on the whole of Europe," K-Force said.

"Hah, that's nothing. The Great River Mother of the Lakota, a mighty Omega class woman who never married but always had an entourage of young men, gave birth to anywhere between forty to fifty-four kids," Joseph stated proudly.

"Over fifty, how in the world could her body stand it," Gyges said.

"Remember Meta-human women have a higher ability to have many children with no complications and longer life spans," Yellow Coyote showing expansive knowledge.

"But how is it forty to fifty-four children." Amber was not understanding how one woman could have so many.

"Even I know this. Many people who want clout among the tribes always say that there are direct descendants of hers so we have thirty-two proven bloodlines and twenty others who have strong claims," Joseph said.

"Okay I'm guessing that created a surplus at times didn't it," Amber was seeing the problems it could cause.

"It varies from country to country at times, but yes, and this also created wars since any nation who had a large number of Meta-humans or gained a couple of Alphas would war with their neighbors tried conquer them to expand," K-Force said.

"I guess that make sense, but how does that play into things? It sounds like there should not be even more than two percent," Amber was confused as the math didn't add up.

"Remember, these people are sent to war mostly to fight and kill other Meta-humans. You got to remember we were called Champions, so their jobs were to take out the enemy Meta-humans. And unlike today, those battles were more brutal and more likely to result in deaths. And as many wars and battles took place back then, you can understand that Meta-humans were killed," K-Force explained why they weren't more wide spread.

"The World Wars and Vigris Invasion had the most Meta-human deaths in the history of the world. I think at this point we just recover to stable numbers," Yellow Coyote clarified.

"But those events happened so long ago. How is it that you're not bigger than before," Amber still couldn't figure why their numbers were so low.

"You remember the warlords, robber barons and tyrants," K-Force asked.

"Yeah," Amber had a feeling she already knew the answer.

"They are still around. It's just we called them Villains nowadays," K-Force explained.

"So, the fighting never really stopped," Amber said, realizing the truth of their world.

"Nope, we are still fighting the same battles just under different names," Gyges sighed.

"God, this is heavy stuff," Amber said in shock.

"Told you this was not good idea for a fun night out," Gyges felt annoyed at being ignored.

"No not that. It is eye opening, but not as much of a bummer as I thought it was. I thought there was a secret organization trying to bring you down, or you guys were not as fertile as everyone thought," Amber said morosely.

"Now that is conspiracy theory that has more meat to it than you think," Yellow Coyote was about to go into one of her theories.

"Nope, stop right there. I came here to have fun, drink, and get on the dance floor," Gyges dragged K-Force to the floor, almost making him drop his drink. The curvy woman would not be denied as she pulled him to the floor with the latest club hit from Valentina, which had been blaring for two months now.

"Don't have to tell me twice," said Yellow Coyote. She merely looked at her boyfriend Joseph who was getting up to give her his arm so that they could walk back to the dance floor.

Amber didn't need an excuse to join right in as she began to dance and magically lure over two different guys who were obviously trying to get more than just her number.

As they danced to two more club bangers, Gyges pulled K-Force close for a slow dance which meant that she liked him enough for him to be close to her body.

It seems the night went well...Hello... K-Force's train of thought left him when he felt her grope his butt. Then she gave him a coy wink as she moved his hands lower on her hip.

Chapter 13
Pressure Pushing Down on Me

K-Force was stuck sitting and waiting for his appointment with his shrink. Whether the purpose of the appointment was to vent or have an introspective analysis, he didn't know, though the very idea that they ordered him to participate in the session pissed him off, in a way. The purpose of the session wasn't for a genuine reason, like for the nightmares he had been having. Oh no, the point of this session was that he had nearly crippled a villain Battle Hound. It probably irked some white tower idiot saying there was no need for such violence, when said criminal had just killed thirty-two people in one day. And the fact that he was on the Green Light protocol meant that he could not be touched.

Deciding that looking at his phone was the better option while he waited, he preferred not to listen to most press analysts saying that his actions were too severe and that he just proved the Green Light protocol only encouraged such behavior among Heroes. Even the governor tried to go with it by saying why he was so hesitant about giving it out. Luckily, the more mentally balanced groups and press sided with him. They stated the fact that he had stopped without killing the man was a huge show of restraint. Most police officers would just gun down an assailant for a tenth of what Battle Hound had done. All this happened because he felt that if he took out the supposed big bounty on K-Force, he would gain money and respect the world over.

No, better stay away from that media nonsense, though it is nice to know that more people side with you than the criminal, K-Force thought as he tried to zone out. He decided to read his favorite web novel turned published book, *Rouge Champions*. It was about a pair of Meta-humans appearing in the world, similar to *Sword and Fantasy*. It was interesting since their powers gave them a huge advantage; champions like them were purely divine beings and very rare. Not to mention, their powers sometimes broke the preconceived rules of their new world.

What really impressed K-Force was the fact that the Hero was not angsty, cold to everyone, a jerk, or a bullheaded idiot who rushed in and relied on luck, but he was a charismatic and ruthless fighter while his companion was a cold-blooded tactician at times. This made him a rarity among book heroes, but a better one, in his opinion. They didn't allow dangerous enemies to escape, if possible, and they killed those that were too dangerous to live. They would sometimes lose or fail, but that made things better since, in real life, not everything was going to go their way.

As K-Force finally settled into his book, the secretary called to him, "Dr. Quinton is ready to see you now."

Looking at the secretary, it seemed she was more professional than he was expecting for a therapist to the Heroes of Southern California. He saw so many secretaries who looked to be, for lack of a better term, someone's side chick. This one looked to be pretty enough, and she exuded professionalism. Not paying her anymore attention, K-Force walked in on a man not that much older than him. He wore business casual attire with gray slacks, a white sports jacket and a pink shirt. He had sandy brown hair, and his appearance screamed 'Yuppie' within K-Force's mind. Despite this, he threw such thoughts away and decided to let this individual show *that* he was before applying any judgement.

"Welcome Mr. Brewer, or do you prefer K-Force?" the doctor said, as he began his session.

"I'm guessing that since you are government approved and since you know my name, you have my file," Samson said, relaxing himself after realizing how much the psychiatrist already knew.

"Yes, good assumption," Dr. Quinton replied.

"Well, call me Mr. Brewer. I prefer to use my real name when I'm off the clock. I don't want to become one of those ego-driven idiots who throw away their old self for a cooler persona, or those who get so lost in character that they forget themselves," Samson sighed as he eased into his seat.

"In that case you may call me Dr. Quinton, if that makes you comfortable," the doctor offered.

"Actually, yes, since I don't know you well enough to be familiar with you," Samson said as he mentally prepared himself to get this over with.

"Understood, though I have to ask, is 'identity crisis' a major concern for you?" Dr. Quinton asked.

"Nothing major, just something I like to keep in mind. I don't want to become so absorbed by my persona that, when the day comes to retire, I forget who I am and where I came from." Samson had seen enough old Heroes who just couldn't let it go.

"Yes, that is something several of my clients have to deal with. Would you like to discuss that?" Dr. Quinton said.

"No, I prefer just to say what needs to be said and move on with the rest of my day," Samson said.

"Fair enough, from your files, it appears you are having trouble sleeping, and it seems to be stemmed from guilt. You have also been having nightmares lately. Does that have to do with recent events?" Dr. Quinton queried.

"Yes, but not the one you are thinking of," Samson responded flatly.

"Really? What makes you think I don't know which event has brought you here?" Dr. Quinton asked.

"Because I asked to come here, seeking help for my failures to people who counted on me. Not some murderer who I put into the ICU," Samson answered directly.

"Really?"

"Hard to feel guilt towards someone who has little to no empathy towards others," Samson remarked, feeling no shame in his answer.

"Very well, tell me what has you so disturbed," the doctor asked his patient.

Samson decided that since this was a corporation private practice that he would drop the whole persona. He figured that a lot of therapists believed the more comfortable their client felt, the more open they would be.

"I can take my mask off without my identity getting revealed, right?" Samson inquired.

"But, of course. We are deep inside a government building which means you will have complete anonymity from the outside world. You have nothing to fear. This is a safe place," Dr. Quinton assured him.

Removing the mask to his persona of K-Force felt a lot heavier in the past few weeks. But, then again, Samson was about to head home for the Thanksgiving week off. Normally he wouldn't be given so much time off, but with the amount of production and fighting he had been doing lately, Sky-High Industry decided that he had more than earned it. His violent outburst had him secretly suspended by the local government.

"All right, Doc, get your pen and paper out because this is a bit of a build-up for the past three weeks." Samson began the tale of his crappy month.

K-Force was there again for the third night in the row. He didn't want to be there, but his conscience would not let him leave, even though every bit of logic told him that it wasn't his fault; that it could happen to anyone. But, no, he had forgotten one of the cardinal rules that he had made with his brother and their friends; never rely solely on your powers for everything or use them as if they were the first and last resort.

It was the same burned-out apartment building, once five stories tall but reduced to a charred husk of what it used to be, though his memory kept telling him that he had saved most of the people from any real damage, his mind refused to let him rationalize the whole event. Soon stomping footsteps were coming from the building, just like the past three nights. He was not as religious as most of his family, but he had seen and read about demons and monsters that his father had to kill. Samson knew from experts that ghosts were rare and that this was all of his guilt haunting him, not the souls of the victims he had failed to save.

The figure walked toward him. Samson felt dread for the pain to come. A small figure with a soot-covered face and dead blank eyes stood before him in a pair of dirty pajamas that were partially burnt. There was a voice whispering and slowly getting louder, as the body of the small child was walking towards him. It became louder with each step.

"Why couldn't you save him, why couldn't you save him, why couldn't you save him, why couldn't you save him," sounded the pain-filled sob of a mother as she held her baby boy. She came rushing at K-Force, almost screaming in the end, despite the fact that she could barely speak above a whisper. She was in so much pain and in the process of a mental collapse.

"Why couldn't you save him, why couldn't you save him, why couldn't you save him?" The mother's voice became more distorted as the burnt, crippled apartment building began to morph into the woman's face with hollowed-out eyes.

Then at the end of the dream, every time the small innocent voice, probably belonging to an old childhood schoolmate entered Samson's mind. The dirty, innocent corpse looked at him with dead eyes crying black ink and asking the same question.

"Why couldn't you save me," he said in a small child's voice, cutting deeper than the ranting from the mother, since he was the only person he couldn't apologize to. Then the mouth opened up large enough to swallow him whole, but at this point, the emotional pain was so intense that death seemed like a good alternative.

It was there that Samson awoke with his heart feeling like it was beating a thousand times per minute. As well, there was a noticeable slight sheen of sweat, despite his previous night's activities. He didn't shoot out of bed screaming and yelling like they did in the movies. Instead Samson's eyes shot open, and he was breathing like he had just run three miles. Looking over, he saw that his date from last night, Gyges, hadn't given him her real name, which was common for most Hero Metas. Many believed that an exchange of names caused a closer intimacy that would deepen the relationship to a level more than friends with benefits, but not quite the level of lovers, by Meta standards. As Samson lay awake, he remembered that he was still K-Force and held that thought all the way up until he was leaving Gyges' extravagant condo. Her place was made for three people, but it was obvious that she could afford it.

Luckily, K-Force didn't have to worry about being tired, as he only really needed three and a half hours to be fully rested. Apparently when he was completely at rest his body sought out any momentum large enough to charge him, which could be anything from nearby cars to the very rotation of the earth, as once noted by a scientist who had studied and theorized K-Force's power. Either way, he recharged faster than most people, so he was stuck there next to the curvy lavender-skinned woman.

Looking over, K-Force saw that Gyges' top was free and open to the world, giving him enough detail to see in dawn's early light that her areolas were a dark shade of purple. He also knew, despite her small belly sticking out, that she was very well put-together, although she was not a swimsuit model like most Meta-human women. Seeing that she wasn't grabbing for him, K-Force decided to take a shower before leaving her apartment, hoping the waters would help remove the memory.

Instead the incident was playing through his mind clearly, no matter how much he tried to bury it. After his patrol in Riverside County, K-Force was on his way back home driving his 2017 AAMC Eagle when he spotted a couple of fire trucks going by. He thought, *Why the hell not—extra credit couldn't hurt.*

And, with that, K-Force drove to the back of the nearest secluded parking lot and changed. The office building parking lot was almost empty except for the janitorial staff and a few people crunching nighttime shifts. K-Force made sure to stay behind the building and away from the road, cornered in that one blind spot that all parking lot security cameras have. Then he looked around to make sure no one was around as he air-ran towards the sirens.

When K-Force finally arrived at the emergency site, it turned out to be a burning apartment building, a mixture of his greatest weaknesses. For one, his shields only worked against active forces. Burning flames was a passive force since it was not being thrown at him or exploding. So his automatic defenses wouldn't work on him at all, unless a back draft hit him. This meant he would have to use shields manually, which drained his powers.

Eh, no problem. I got more than enough power to handle this, K-Force thought to himself.

As he got near the firemen, he heard an argument between the fire chief and one of his men.

"There are still five people in there. The sonar drones see them on the upper floors," the fireman said to his boss.

"The flames are far too dangerous for anyone to go in there," the fire chief pointed out in return.

"Just let me go in there with two other men," the fireman pleaded.

"And what, turn five lives lost to eight? No, I can't risk losing you until we calm the flames down," the fire chief denied.

"They won't have time," the fireman said, becoming more frantic.

"Mind if I try? I'm pretty fireproof and I move faster than you guys, and my shields are useful for protecting people," K-Force offered.

"Get out of here, Hero! This is no time for your publicity stunts. People's lives are in danger!" The fire chief wasn't in the mood for any showboating.

"Do you see any cameras for me to show off? I'm here to help, and I can do so without additional loss of life," K-Force assured him that his help was genuine.

The fire chief didn't like it, but he had no other choice. "Fine, but if you try to monkey shine for the cameras and hurt those people, I will be sure to make your life miserable."

"I wouldn't respect you if you didn't," K-Force said as he made his way to the building.

As he said this, a female firefighter handed him a special pair of glasses that patched him into the network of the sonar drones. Now he knew where all the remaining people were at.

"Okay, my name is Gracie, and until you get those people out of that building, I'm your boss, understood?" The female firefighter left no room for discussion.

"Crystal," K-Force confirmed with no lip.

"Good, head towards the fifth floor, that's where a family of three are stuck. And don't break any walls, unless I tell you to. We don't want to bring the whole building down," the firewoman ordered.

"Roger, not being a dumbass bull in a china shop," K-Force said as he jumped toward the fifth floor which had a window for him to get through. While hopping in place in midair, he compressed his force beams to carve the window frame off the wall; then pulled it to the empty area below. This made a huge burst of fire spring up his way, but with his shields active, he went right through them.

Following the female firefighter's instructions, he was able to get the mother and her two kids off the floor using a slide with bumpers. Luckily, he remembered to smother out the flames so that they would not hurt the survivors. Next was an old woman with an oxygen tank who could barely move because she was half comatose on meds. This one K-Force gently brought outside and handed to the paramedics to make sure she was being cared for.

The final person they found was someone K-Force thought he should have left there. It was a green-haired 'Karen' who expected him to help carry all of her stuff out of the building. And to make things worse, she was an anti-Hero person who said she didn't need a jump-up cisgender freak saving her. Not wanting to deal with her crap, he simply grabbed her and force-slid her down the slide. She threatened to sue him, but there were laws which prevented such things, so it was so much bull to go along with her hot air.

Just as he was about to leave the building, the female firefighter called to him. "K-Force, we found another one."

"Where?" K-Force shouted.

"He is on the fourth floor. He was so still that our sonar drone couldn't pick up on him until now," she reported.

"Guide me," K Force said as he jumped back to the building. "Let me guess, he is in the part of the building still on fire," K-Force groused.

"Got it in one, and you have to go slowly since that section could fall apart with too much force," the firewoman ordered.

"Alright." K-Force jumped through a blown-out hallway window. He ran towards the apartment door that was still locked.

"It is safe to knock the door down?" K-Force asked.

"Yes, it is not load-bearing but the child's room is, so you have to think of something else," the firewoman warned.

Acknowledging her words, K-Force covered his hands with his forcefields and ripped the door out of the way; then he walked into a raging inferno. The whole place was ablaze with fire, and he was glad he shielded himself with a layered forcefield to make sure that any falling debris or flames could not burn him or his suit. Sadly, the heat was another thing entirely. While he could resist, it felt like being in 120 degree weather in Arizona with no shade. Ignoring his discomfort, K-Force activated his mask by pressing one of the hexagon shapes adorning the mask. The mask expanded to cover his entire face so that he could see and breathe easier. Then K-Force began to look through the apartment, ignoring everything except the young child and making sure not to bring down the structure.

"Where is the kid?" K-Force frantically searched for the child.

"Second bedroom door on the right of the kitchen," the firewoman informed.

Responding to the instructions, K-Force moved as quickly and smoothly as possible until he reached the child's bedroom door. Said door was blocked by the upstairs neighbor's fridge which had fallen through the ceiling. Normally he would just chuck it aside, but keeping in mind structural integrity and his timer, he had little ability to do it safely. K-Force decided quickly just to lift the thing to the side of the hallway that wasn't damaged, but the loud, protesting creaking made him think again. K-Force was starting to panic, looking for a solution only for him to mentally slap himself. K-Force moved the fridge back to the upstairs floor from where it had fallen, and he held both the fridge and the ceiling with pillars made of hexagons. Then he slowly opened the door towards himself, seeing a little soot-covered figure passed out on the floor. This put a fire under his ass to get him moving. Seeing as he only needed to get the child out of the building, K-Force cut open the window to the boy's room and created a slide down towards the paramedics.

As soon as K-Force made it to ground floor, away from the flaming inferno, he carefully rushed the child to the EMTs who were stationed as close as possible to the building within safety parameters. The EMTs spent the next ten minutes trying to revive the child, but no matter how hard they tried, they could not bring him back from the dead. The nail in the coffin was the mother breaking past the barricade, rushing towards the still form of her child. Her cries cut deeper than anything K-Force had ever felt before. Then, as if to make him feel worse, the mother looked at him with tear-stained eyes mixed with mascara and asked, begged, accused him in all one little phrase.

"Why couldn't you save him?"

In the present time, Samson had just finished telling the doctor about that terrible day that kept him up many nights.

Dr. Quinton looked on at his patient and told him that this was very common among Heroes, firefighters, police, EMTs, and doctors. They felt the world was on their shoulders, as they had been given the honor and duty to save people, and when they could not save them, they felt like complete failures. Because mistakes were oftentimes beyond their control, this racked them with guilt. It was a special kind of survivors' guilt mixed with PTSD. Luckily, this death was not because he made a mistake or got cocky; for those with that type of guilt, it was almost impossible to forgive themselves.

"I was informed that the child," the doctor began.

"Nathan. His name was Nathan," Samson interrupted. He wouldn't allow anyone to dismiss the boy's name.

"Nathan was dead for over ten minutes before you arrived. The smoke suffocated him," the doctor said.

"I know that!" Samson raised his voice in frustration; then he calmed himself as he collected his emotions. "Sorry Doc, it's just no matter how many times I tell myself that fact, my mind won't let me move on."

"This is common in your profession. You are a member of people who were dedicated to saving the lives of others, and when you fail that mission, in your mind you feel responsible because it was your self-appointed purpose," Dr. Quinton explained the man's feelings.

"Exactly," Samson confirmed.

"The trick is to truly understand that despite your powers and gifts, you are a mortal just like everyone else. You will fail again. You will make mistakes. That is a part of life, and you have to live with it as well," the doctor tried to soothe his guilt.

"But I'm a Hero. I'm not allowed to make mistakes. If I do, people die, people who are my responsibility. People who rely on me to save them," Samson almost whispered the last part.

"This is true but so do police, EMTs, doctors, and as you saw yourself, firefighters. You are not the only one with this type of guilt. In fact, I think the drone operator is having a tougher time with this than you," Dr. Quinton said, trying a different tactic.

"What?"

"This is just speculation but it was their job to scan the entire building and find all the survivors and get them out. Whoever is in control of the sonar drones are probably hating themselves for missing a small child, despite there being a margin of error for their equipment." Dr. Quinton used facts to help explain his point.

"I guess I am not the only one dealing with this," Samson said as he began to feel a little better knowing he wasn't alone with this guilt.

"Yes, though I don't think that was the reason for your outburst earlier this week, was it," the doctor assumed.

"No, it was a part of it," Samson looked towards the ceiling, trying to find the right words. "It was more a build-up with more crap that seemed to end with me snapping, and well, forcing my visit here today."

"Then, please continue. The sooner we see the catalyst, the sooner we can explain your outburst," Dr. Quinton said.

Samson then decided to relay to the doctor his actions at the other event. Despite having the authority to act as he did, this event led to him being put on probation for two weeks.

The next incident was the day after Samson failed the rescue of the little boy, Nathan. He thought that maybe some partying and alcohol would be enough to clear his mind or at least suppress it enough to get on with his life. K-Force knew that this was a bad idea, but he was not sure how he felt after day prior. And he was not going to bring it up with them, as he did not want to kill the group's vibe for the night.

As K-Force watched Gyges dance with a happy and a very thirsty Latino, he just sat back and drank his tall glass of a Kamikaze to soothe his worried mind.

"You sure you are okay with that?" Yellow Coyote asked. As if she was in disbelief at the fact that K-Force didn't react to his date dancing with another man.

"They're dancing, not screwing, though the grinding is getting close to dry humping. Besides, I believe we are in that stage where we are just having fun, having no commitments," said K-Force, barely paying attention.

"Are you sure?" Yellow Coyote questioned.

"I believe when a woman says 'Let's not complicate it yet with labels,' I think it means that she is not ready for anything formal," K-Force replied.

"That sounds about right." Joseph agreed with K-Force's opinion.

"Oh come on, she's just waiting for you to be more assertive," Yellow Coyote urged him.

"I don't think so. Besides, didn't she just get out of a bad relationship," K-Force replied, not about to jump the gun.

"So?" Yellow Coyote countered, not seeing how it was pertinent.

"So, she said she wanted space to do what she wants, and I am in no position to demand or act on anything. Besides we're not exclusive," K-Force responded, laying down facts as he knew them.

"And yet I know for a fact you two are burning a hole in the sheets, so why not make it official," Yellow Coyote said, not seeing the problem.

"Because she was out with some R&B singer three nights ago," K-Force said, pointing out the hole in her theory.

"*Please*, she's interested in you. You just got to show her," Yellow Coyote dismissed.

"I will, but I have to find the perfect girl for the test," K-Force said to get her off his back.

"What does that mean?" Yellow Coyote was getting suspicious.

"A little test to check and see if she is interested in me," K-Force calmly replied.

"Oh, I got to hear this. What is the test?" Joseph asked eagerly.

"Simple, I dance with another woman. If Gyges gets jealous or overly interested that means she wants me." K-Force put it out there.

"I know this one, you go out on a date with another girl, and if she reacts to that then she wants something deeper, but if nothing happens, then you are just a booty call or a sex friend at best," Joseph said.

"What is the point of that?" said Yellow Coyote not liking the idea.

"It is applied psychology. When something is easily obtained, less people usually want it. But the harder it is to obtain, or more coveted by others, then someone will see the value and will want to fight to keep it," K-Force answered.

"That's wrong," Yellow Coyote said with a disapproving stare.

"Oh, and making me guess for a month and a half is fair," Joseph added, seeing nothing wrong with K-Force's way of thinking.

"It's part of the fun. You know we like to be chased," Yellow Coyote defended.

"Fun for who?" said Joseph, making his feelings known.

"In the past, yes that might be true. However, to be blunt, nowadays it is a minefield, for us being accused of being perverted or accused of sexual harassment when we're only trying to be considered friendly," K-Force stated flatly.

"Oh you're just exaggerating," Yellow Coyote dismissed.

"No, he is not. I've seen enough guys being accused of wrongdoing at work just because they were flirting with the wrong girl," Joseph agreed, seeing where his new friend was coming from.

"Are you sure you are not biased?" Yellow Coyote accused.

"Love, you know me, if a guy harasses a woman in any true way, I would step up in a second. But saying he harassed a woman by saying she was hot with a group of guys in private is ridiculous. I have heard women talk about men in almost as dirty a manner when they think men aren't around," Joseph asserted his point.

"I'll admit locker room talk is universal, and I heard some very hateful women use this against innocent people to get what they want. But you guys are by far being too overly cautious," Yellow Coyote insisted, not seeing the big deal.

"Think of it like this, there is a large display of cake, and each slice is delicious in various ways. But in that hundred pieces of cake there are five pieces that are poisoned. In that situation, how eager are you willing to eat a slice without a little precaution? Yeah, there is only a five percent chance of something terrible happening, but that is still something that floats in your mind," K-Force laid it out.

"Do guys really think like that?" Yellow Coyote was surprised.

"Nowadays, yes because as long as there are spiteful people who will use such a thing as a weapon, it makes it hard for unconfident, inexperienced, and shy men to open up and without that fear." K-Force was talking from experience.

"But how did things get so bad? The number of toxic people didn't increase or change that much," Yellow Coyote asked, finally seeing the issue.

"No, but the rules of the game did. Nowadays someone could have their entire life destroyed with a word, without proof, which is only fueled by today's toxic culture," Joseph calmly informed her.

Their small conversation was interrupted by a commotion which was taking place on the dance floor. From the looks of it, it was an infamous nightclub brawl, as a small group of thuggish black men were pushing people away so their leader Ashtown-B could get to his target. Ashtown-B looked to be angered and drunk, a terrible combination. He went up the guy who was trying to bump and grind on Gyges and cold-cocked him, while one of his boys held the poor sap in place.

K-Force was willing to let it slide until the idiot got into Gyges' face with a gun. Despite guns being as effective as an inflated bat to Gyges—K-Force felt that he should go down there and try to stop this before Gyges lost it and put all four of these idiots in the ICU.

As he got closer, the crowd either tried to leave or pulled out their phones to capture the insanity for the sake of views.

"Never mind that you could get shot. It's true, society is way too soft when clear and present danger does not get people to react properly," said K-Force as he pushed his way through the crowd.

As he got closer, he started to hear their argument, and it was pretty clear.

"Get that gun out of my face, or I'm going to use your ass as a silencer," Gyges threatened.

"Step, bitch, I dare you. The word is that you can't use your powers to attack innocent humans unless there is a crime. Unless you want to be arrested and ruin your precious image," Ashtown-B shot back.

"That doesn't count if I am being openly threatened, you feckless pussy," Gyges insulted her ex.

At this point the rapid and colorful use of the N-word was being thrown back and forth. And it only got uglier from there. They went into each other's shortcomings and embarrassing habits. For instance, apparently Gyges had more porn than most guys, while Ashtown-B left skid mark drawls around the house when he came over. On and on it went, until it came to the point of why they ultimately broke it off.

"It is nice to be with someone who's not a flirting whore every time she goes out." Ashtown-B tried to turn it on her.

"I flirt, but I don't drop my panties every time I got a craving for every Tom, Dick, and Harry fan that walks my way." Gyges got into his face not caring about the gun.

"Well, maybe I prefer someone who doesn't feel like I'm plowing a cow, you overgrown heifer," Ashtown fired at her.

"And I prefer someone who can last longer than three seconds, quick shot." Gyges returned a blow right back at him.

That seemed to be the final straw as Ashtown-B pulled up his gun, only for his arm to be stopped. Looking around at who would dare try to stop him, he saw that it was K-Force who appeared from nowhere and grabbed hold of the rapper's arm, careful enough not to break the rapper's arm, but firm enough to make it go limp, cutting off the blood flow.

"Let me go, you overgrown cape-wearing motherfucker" Ashtown-B cursed at K-Force, who looked more bored at this drunk idiot's attempts.

"Hey dumbasses, get this mofo to let go," Ashtown said as he began punching and kicking at a flesh-padded wall of muscle. His posse tried to help by throwing punches at him as well, which was just as ineffective. Soon, they were grabbing furniture and smacking him with it, yet the furniture either bounced off or broke on contact with K-Force, who looked unperturbed about the whole thing.

At this point, Ashtown-B's arm finally dropped the gun as his finger went limp from the pressure. His arm's circulation was being cut off. K-Force caught the weapon in his other hand before it hit the floor. Then K-Force let Ashtown-B's arm go as he almost surgically pulled the gun apart by removing the clip, popping out the one bullet left in the chamber, and ripping off the chamber of the gun to make it inoperable.

"Gyges, let's go! We don't need this heat," K-Force said, trying to escort her away.

"No, this mofo needs to go. We were here first, and we're not swinging guns around like a lunatic." Gyges said, wanting to get into this.

"Fair point, but I don't think security is going to care, so let's just go before we get kicked out or get put on BMT." K-Force tried reasoning with her.

"Fine." Gyges gave her ex a look and began to leave. "Let's go. I don't need a pre-mature rapper ruining my night."

As K-Force was guiding them towards their table, Ashtown-B called back to K-Force, who immediately turned back towards the drunk rapper, seeing that he had pulled out a knife. Ashtown-B tried to stab K-Force in the eye, only for it to bend as it could not get past K-Force's small forcefield.

Of all the instinctive protections, K-Force had his eyes, heart, throat, and crotch almost always protected as a main priority. This meant the asshole could have shot K-Force in the eye with the gun, and it still would have been just as ineffective.

Ashtown-B would not stop and kept stabbing at K-Force, which did nothing, until the blade broke.

"Cheap knife," K-Force quipped with a smirk that stayed in place until the rapper grabbed another gun from a member of his crew. At this time, security finally showed up and told Ashtown-B to calmly put the gun down and leave. This was far more lenient than K-Force would have been. Instead of doing the rational thing and doing as the bouncer said, Ashtown-B, still drunk and angry, aimed at them and fired towards the security and the crowd behind them.

The sound of a gun in the nightclub going off was heard, but thankfully, despite the wild firing, no one was hit. A wall of golden yellow hexagons stopped all the bullets. After hearing the gun's click, Ashtown-B tried to reach for another gun, only to be knocked out by a blow to the back of the head.

K-Force looked at the surrounding posse and gave them a none-too-friendly look. "Y'all done or should I knock all your asses out and leave you to the police?"

"Naw, man we good," one of the posse members said as the other two nodded as well, putting all their hidden weapons on the floor for security to confiscate them.

Joseph, being the first to walk toward K-Force commented, "Well, that killed the mood."

"And now I'm being sued for excessive use of force and put on probation for irresponsibly using my powers," K-Force recalled, pissed at the situation.

"I have to agree, that seems very excessive, especially with over six video feeds showing that you used as minimum force as possible," Dr. Quinton agreed.

"Tell that to the D.A. who seems to hate Heroes, considering the crazy crap he has pulled," K-Force commented.

"I cannot comment on that, though your frustration with the man's actions is understandable. But I think we are only at the tip of the issue that caused your outburst of anger," Dr. Quinton said, seeing what might have been a trigger point.

Samson kept quiet as he knew that these incidents were adding weight to the straw that was holding his temperament from breaking.

"Tell me about what happened to your friend, QuickTime."

Taking a deep breath, Samson released some of his left-over anger and resentment. When the tension left him, he was able to talk about it. "This is what happened on that day." K- Force deflated as he recounted that day.

Chapter 14
Pressure That No Man Can Ask For

Samson was on edge as he sat at home while his own company fought against the ridiculous persecution. And despite the political razzle dazzle, most people with the Internet saw that the uncut footage sided with him. What also hurt the D.A. was the fact that he didn't arrest the perpetrator for having a gun, despite state law making it near impossible for ex-cons to own one. This was going to go in his favor no matter how the D.A. tried to swing it.

No, the thing that was pissing him off was the BS lawsuit about assault and battery charges and injuries. After the so-called gangster rapper woke up from his hangover and mild concussion, he charged Samson as K-Force for breaking his arm and massive head trauma. This was a lie since the only massive trauma and damages were to his ego. Ashtown-B's lawyer was laying it on thick and trying to paint it as a misunderstanding that went too far. The fact that his client was drunk and in possession of an illegal fire arm, which he fired at other people was supposedly irrelevant. According to Ashtown-B's lawyer, Samson used force against Ashtown-B, which put the rapper into the hospital, and therefore Samson should be held accountable for the incident.

If this was a rationally sane state, or even Northern California, this court case would have been thrown out as the measure of a desperate man trying to save face. But this was the southern half of California where hating any authority was the cool thing to do, even when the criminals were in the wrong. In this part of the country, 'F- the Police' was almost a motto that they lived by. And Heroes, despite being popular, were just the authorities with flare.

Not to mention, there were some who saw this incident as Meta supremacist action against a poor defenseless human.

Samson had stated multiple times even before he became a rookie that he hated and loathed the Meta supremacist and saw them as 'a pox that needs to be cleansed from the earth.' But that mattered little to people who wanted to see him raked across the coals. K-Force didn't make it better by ripping his accuser on social media. Even his manager didn't know whether to lecture him or tell him to continue because it was building support from K-Force's fans and the public.

K-Force gladly resumed the flame war, because in the public eye turning the other cheek didn't work. In a media-driven society this allowed false narratives to be built. K-Force was all ready to fire a message across to the bow of Ashtown-B's ship. Ashtown-B had the nerve to call him and every black Hero an 'Uncle Tom' because they helped put minorities away.

Samson replied under the callsign 4realK-Force:

"First off, I doubt you ever read *Uncle Tom's Cabin*, since the character died to protect two black women who were sexually abused by their master. Second, I been to the 'hood' you love so much—more in the last three months than you have in the last three years. I donated money to that same neighborhood which you, after three albums in the last five years, have yet to do. Third, that bouncer you were about to shoot was a black man with two kids and a third on the way. So who is more a supporter? Someone who talks a big game and does jack, or someone who actually puts his money where his mouth is."

While tame compared to the filth sent his way, it hit harder because he left links to actual proof of his statements. K-Force was out there practicing what he preached. And the final stab was to tag under a picture of Bronze Bomber actually playing with kids at the Boys & Girls Club saying, "That suburban white girl has done more for the community than you."

That set the Internet aflame and it was true, but Ashtown-B fans acted like K-Force had said he was going assault Ashtown-B's mother. While others, including a few of his critics and fellow rappers with beef, jumped to K-Force's side since they viewed this as an open area to attack.

Avery, who read, and helped edit the comment, laughed at the response it was getting. He himself was all for backing his roommate and future tag team partner. Duos were uncommon but were always huge sellers, almost as much as teams. However, for that to happen, a process had to be gone through, very similar to that of major sports teams. The fact that they worked so well together was a plus, and both of their companies were on very good terms. It was the reason why they were made roommates, despite being from other companies.

This made sense to them mostly because they filled gaps in areas which the other lacked. Samson had great battle instinct, but as far as strategic planning went, he was no Napoleon. Also, Avery was the info guy who had weakness for almost every Villain in the area and the major ones he wished to avoid. Avery proved he was the best when the time came for detective work in their training. As far as Samson went, his combat prowess, brute power, and versatility made up for whatever Avery lacked as QuickTime. They figured since they were cool with each other and had worked well together, they might try to become equal partners, when the rookie trials were over, that is.

Both their mentors trusted them, so the fact that they were going on their patrol route together wasn't strange. They had proven themselves again and again, despite their young age and inexperience. So, on this day, they were patrolling San Bernardino County, and it was quiet except for one incident where an idiot threatened a twelve-year-old girl with a Dire Beast as a pet. This was no housecat breed of Dire Beast but a full-grown lynx which almost gutted the man. It was up to K-Force to pull the steel-clawed and fanged lynx off of the man, who had a syringe and a gun; meaning he was up to no good.

When the police arrived, they thought this was an animal attack situation and might have to take the Dire Beast away, since they were seen as too dangerous, despite these beasts being more obedient than regular pets. That was until QuickTime pulled up the file on the fact that this man had been under suspicion of three missing children, and the syringe was filled with a concoction called Spice Pax. This was a new-age date rape drug that put the subject in a semi-conscious state and increased their sexual desires by eight. This drug was extremely illegal to have in possession. The moron tried to claim the syringe belonged to K-Force; a desperate cop-out denial that it was. But K-Force calmly asked the police to dust the syringe for the man's fingerprints and DNA, and if not easily located, he would gladly submit his own for testing.

This was the standard protocol in California, just to make sure that no one would get framed for a crime, despite how blatant the crimes were at times.

"You know, I think we need body-cams just so we can skip those bullshit accusations," K-Force said offhandedly.

"Why do you think I always have camera drones? It is not for the free publicity and my V-Tube numbers," QuickTime said. This made K-Force give him a look for such a blatant lie.

"I'm calling bull. You have a Diamond Button at home," said K-Force, calling his friend out.

"Okay I admit, some of it is for the fame, but it is mostly to make sure any flimsy lawsuits deteriorate before they begin. No amount of lawyer talk is going to change video evidence with no signs of tampering," QuickTime admitted.

"Imagine what that would mean for the common Heroes who don't have three degrees in engineering to make our own," K-Force joked.

"That's not a bad Idea. You think there is a market for it," asked QuickTime.

"In this anti-authority and metahuman environment lately, yes," K-Force said in mild disgust.

At this point QuickTime realized that there was a market for his drones whether they were used for law enforcement or to help self-promote the Hero, it was a money maker. Because these were for both the government and entertainment industries, his prospective clients would have deep pockets to cover any of the replacement or repair costs.

"With the current means of production and materials, I can bring in forty to forty-five grand for a pair of drones. And charge extra for reinforced armor or wave-shielding on certain types. And every year I can make more advanced versions and charge more for the new versions of my work. But to make it fair, I could make the older versions cheaper for those on a budget so that, within five years, newer models could be cheap enough to bring into the common sector. There are many who would love a virtual intelligence drone for recording, especially those of a more action-oriented lifestyle," QuickTime's *Sherlock Holmes* personality detailed.

"I think I just helped you make your first million-dollar idea. But better check and copyright it before some other genius or greedy corporate stooge tries to say you stole their idea or research," K-Force joked.

"That action has already being researched, as we speak. By the time we get home everything will be ready to be sent to the government. As of right now, no one has a working prototype which means, while several people have been working on it, none have proof of the concept or work," responded QuickTime. His educated voice actually sounded excited at the prospect of earning his own funding for his work projects.

This was the big dream of most super geniuses; they would come up with enough money to fulfill their needs to do their research. The only problem was that many didn't focus on legality and ended up getting ripped off or cheated by some wily corporation who, with enough lawyers, could take their work. Some lost everything they built, and others became villains on a hunt for revenge, if they were sponsored by companies. QuickTime's company Lunglomerate had enough lawyers who would hunt down every legal loophole. This made such actions nearly impossible, and Lunglomerate received the publicity and money to protect their inventor, though they may pull him off of patrol duty to help meet production or work on an upgraded version of his work.

"Thank you for reminding me about the legal issues and awakening me to the profitable possibility of my work," QuickTime thanked his friend.

"No problem, I just saw the need for something like that in our world." K-Force shrugged it off.

"True, and because of it I'm giving you five percent of the profits from it," QuickTime added.

"Sweet, my first stable stock, maybe I can retire now," K-Force joked. As the two went on their eight hour day shift patrol, there were minor incidents, but they decided to ask the police if they wished for assistance. If they said 'no' the two would move on, but if asked to standby just in case, the two would be nearby if the need arose.

Hence the second incident that got their attention that day was a naked woman who was on a drug-fueled rampage. Normally the police could handle it, but this was a Meta-human which meant there were only two types of drugs that could cause such an effect.

Of the many benefits of being Meta-human, one advantage and disadvantage was the fact they were resilient to nearly every poison, including narcotics. There were few drugs that had any harmful effects on Meta-humans, meaning that most of the harmful side effects would be so microscopic in effect that most Meta-humans would ignore it. Therefore, certain drugs were made for Meta-humans for medical reasons; otherwise they would be ineffective when needed for procedures like surgery.

But like every other medication in history, if it gave pleasure, relieved pain, or supplied a good trip, then it could be expected to be abused. And as one reformed drug dealer's current preacher put it, Meta-human drugs were the best because they were so strong you just needed a few grains of it to get a high equal to a whole bag of crack. This meant easy transport and marketing, but the only problem was due to it being so concentrated, those who ignored the warnings would overdose easily.

And in those cases, when it was given to Meta-humans, drug-fueled madness was more dangerous than a wild Dire Beast.

"So which do you think it is, Sukka Cane or Spiced Pax?" K-Force asked as he watched the very good-looking woman toss a cop car thirty feet, which he caught with his forcefield.

"Considering that she is calling for every man to screw her and is attacking anything that gets in her way, I say Spiced Pax," QuickTime said, back to his usual self.

"That means someone thought it would be a good aphrodisiac or tried to make a date rape drug. Either way, we have to deal with it," K-Force said in mild disgust.

Spiced Pax was a weird and dangerous drug since it could turn anyone into a horny nympo or frat boy. Its original form was Paxionia, a drug that was made to cleanse and flush the system of harmful chemical substances. And, like Viagra, which started out as a blood thinner, it caused a subject to be very aroused, except it affected both genders; mitigated by the fact that this was not the main purpose of the drug.

Then another scientist tried to change Paxionia into Viagra for both genders. After all, who wouldn't want to make a multimillion-dollar drug? They succeeded but it was more an illegal narcotic than over-the-counter bedroom aid. Lucid Spiced Paxionia, or LSP Spiced Pax for short, in low doses made people lower inhibitions and brought the primal need to breed. It also had an almost acid-like trip to the whole experience, even for the diluted dose of five milligrams per two cups of water. Higher doses could cause cardiac arrest or overdose. In a Meta-human, the primal side would become so strong that the higher the dose, the more horny and primitive they would become. This became so intense that their only single desire would be to breed, and addicts would take anyone who suited their desires until their needs were met. This could include grievous harm or death for the physically stronger Meta-humans, who didn't care about their partners' health.

A heavy sigh escaped from K-Force, as he was disgusted with this result and couldn't believe he was hoping it was typically stupid people experimenting on drugs rather than a date rape. "You got your tranquilizer ready?"

"I'm afraid not. This woman appears to be deep in her thralls and she's a Meta-human, which means a more concentrated, larger dosage is needed. I have the amount, but I have to administer it manually," said QuickTime back in control.

"Right. I'll keep her pinned while you give the right amount of mixture to knock her out." K-Force prepped his powers.

"It will take me three minutes, can you," and before QuickTime could finish the statement, a translucent forcefield of golden hexagons were erected in front of the primal woman. Soon there were four more made to keep her in place and even a roof to keep her from jumping out.

"Your ability with forcefields always seems to impress me, but why didn't you try to handle her physically? You're by far strong enough, and I know you don't like to play your hand of your full abilities," said QuickTime, being mildly impressed.

"This is the most efficient way, and I'm pretty sure most intelligent people can assume I can do this. Also, there is no way I'm going to be caught by the press touching a naked drugged woman. That will bring a headache, regardless of how essential. So I'm exhausting every avenue before I have any contact with her," K-Force said flatly.

"You don't have to tell me...parasites and slanderers in all." QuickTime, not being rushed, began properly preparing the vial for the appropriate amount of the enhanced sedative.

All the while, K-Force was calling every available Heroine strong enough to handle this lust-driven Meta-woman. He knew that this protected him in two ways, especially since he recorded it, showing that he had tried every avenue out there. He asked for his mentor, who was busy with a bust in Ventura that required her powers. Yellow Coyote was busy at a photoshoot that she would have loved to leave but was forbidden to do so. Then K-Force tried Federal Meta-humans hoping they would send in a female operative. The only problem was that they saw it as far too minor of a problem for them to waste their time. They told him that this was not a violation of any kind, and he had full permission to handle it as cleanly as possible.

"Well?" QuickTime wondered how long they would have to wait.

"Looks like I'm going to be on top with the gossip magazines for a while," said K-Force as he really didn't want to proceed.

"We could give the physical restraining part to SWAT members," QuickTime pointed out.

"They have no one who is as strong as this woman that can get here within a reasonable amount of time." K-Force breathed hard in exhaustion on the subject. "Screw it, fine, let's do this." K-Force visually went closer to the woman who had already beaten her hands bloody trying to break the forcefield.

A heavy sound escaped K-Force's lips as he dropped the field, and the hormone-possessed woman charged forward, toward QuickTime. He was momentarily caught off guard but danced around her clumsy attempts to capture him. Said young woman was an athletic brunette with a slim and slightly curved form but a tone as if she were a fitness model. The only thing that remained of her clothing was a bra that somehow had hung on.

"Come on, Sexy, you know for a fact that you dress so skimpily because you want it," the young woman said.

"I never thought I'd ever hear that from a woman," K-Force said from behind her and kept her in elevated full nelson. This was to cut her strength into half as she had no ground for purchase to use her immense strength.

That did not stop her from struggling and shouting lewd slurs. Half of the things she said made them blush from embarrassment and the other half made them angry because the drugged woman said some very offensive stuff. Luckily, she was finally injected with the sedative to calm her down and after a minute she fell asleep. K-Force gently laid the poor woman down so the paramedics could take over.

"What took you so long?" K-Force complained.

"A drug-enhanced super strength Meta-human kicked me straight in the crotch," QuickTime gasped.

"And you didn't have that armored?" K-Force was surprised.

"Not well enough, I suppose," said QuickTime, visibly in pain.

"How could you not? That's the area most guys protect first, outside of their head," K-Force said as he reinforced that area despite having a near perfect shield.

"A design flaw, I assure you. I was so concerned with vital areas of my armor, such as my head, neck, spinal column, and auxiliary cavity that it slipped my mind to reinforce my reproductive area," QuickTime's educated voice said.

Right before K-Force could reply, he got a call from Gyges. He hadn't heard from her in almost a week after the incident. Apparently, he was getting ghosted, which was unexpected since she was there and knew that he didn't escalate that confrontation, despite what Ashtown-B's lawyer was trying to portray. Sighing, K-Force tapped the lower right hexagon on his mask which connected his phone line.

"Hey Gyges, thought you forgot I was alive," K-Force couldn't help but sass.

"There were circumstances that made it hard for me to reach you," Gyges defended.

'Yeah, the press and the gossip mongers who call themselves reporters who might damage your image' is what K-Force wanted to say, but he wanted to make sure that his emotions were left out of this. Getting angry was not going to help their burgeoning relationship.

"Okay, then why are you calling me now," K-Force really didn't feel like being bothered but kept being polite.

"We need to talk," Gyges said.

Those words are never followed by anything good, K-Force thought as he realized where this was going. But considering how impersonal it felt and the way she kept him at arm's length the whole time it shouldn't be that much of a surprise.

"So when do you want to meet," K-Force said as he was looking to get this over with.

"Right now would be good," Gyges said.

"Sure, give me two hours. I have to finish my patrol first," K-Force explained.

"No, I meant come see me right now," Gyges demanded.

"I'm working. I can't just drop everything," K-Force responded.

"Oh please, you're in my county. It is not going to interfere with your patrol." Gyges dismissed his worries.

"I have a feeling that this is not going to be a quick chat, so to speak," said K-Force, restraining his frustration.

"Just get here soon, or I will promise you, your situation will be worse than playing hooky from your job." With that, Gyges hung up the phone to clarify her statement.

At this point, K-Force was getting ticked off at her threat. He knew that their relationship was either sunk or sinking at this moment.

"Dude, just go," QuickTime said as his more laid-back personality was returning, which meant he was either resting the *Sherlock Holmes* side of his personality or he had already overstretched his mental abilities for the day.

"You sure, man?" K-Force didn't like leaving in the middle of a shift.

"No worries, I have two hours left. If I need backup I'll call you," QuickTime said.

"Okay, but be sure to call when there's trouble. Don't," K-Force started to warn.

"Don't showboat because that is why most rookies die in their first six years." QuickTime in his more mellow voice repeated the same rule that was hammered in both of their heads by their mentors.

Seeing as there was nothing more to say without being an annoyance, K-Force jumped high into the sky once more and did his stride jump to air-run across the sky towards Santa Ana.

Dr. Quinton interrupted because he wanted to be sure he had a clear picture of the whole scene.

"How did that make you feel?" Dr. Quinton asked.

"You got to be more specific, Doc, because that is not going to help." Samson was confused what the doctor was getting at.

"What about the whole situation?" Dr. Quinton asked again.

"Still not helping," K-Force replied.

"Can you put your feelings into words?" Dr. Quinton seemed to ignore the statement.

"What feelings? And before you go 'all my feelings' that is not going to help sorting out how I feel. I need specifics to focus on, and asking to sort everything at once is just going to be a huge block in my brain," countered Samson. He had dealt with psychologists before and felt sometimes it was important to give them structure.

"Very well, let's put it in order, why did you hate dealing with the drugged woman?" Dr. Quinton relented.

"Because it feels like the press is trying everything in their power to put me in a bad light. It feels like they resent me for not being able to ignore my achievements, and I barely give them anything to slam me with. So they pick at the smallest thing, not to mention back a lawsuit which by every measure should be thrown out," K-Force said in annoyance.

"Are you sure that you haven't caused the hostility?" Dr. Quinton was making sure that his patient was honest with himself.

"Not really, unless that's me saying I won't comment on something without context or facts and that I refuse to support unrepentant crooks," K-Force laid it out.

"No, to the first, that is actually a rational way of thinking things through, and I can see why they may see that, with you being obstinate, but you are hostile when it comes to all criminals they wish to bring up for sympathy. Do you hate criminals so much that you are willing to damn them all, regardless of the reason for their crimes?" Dr. Quinton asked.

"Convicted child molesters, rapists, and serial murders deserve no sympathy." K-Force left no room for argument.

"Not all criminals are like that."

"True, but those who are usually the ones that I am supposed to show sympathy for," K-Force said.

"You're exaggerating," Dr. Quinton said.

Instead of arguing, Samson brought up five Villains they asked him to support in their own way, and one was convicted of molestation, another killed a child, and the other three had body counts in the triple digits.

"You were saying?" K-Force awaited his rebuttal.

"Very well." The doctor gave him that one.

"It is not like I'm not sympathetic towards those that deserve it, such as Mr. DeMotte, a super scientist who got screwed over by the system and corporate backers—defenders of nature, people, and causes that get ignored—those who lose their home, family, and jobs and are desperate. People who are pushed by circumstance to be the way they are. But when you harm anyone else, especially a child, you lose any and all sympathy, no matter the reason." K-Force was showing where his line was drawn.

"Let's come back to this topic later since we are departing from the main issue. How did Gyges' demand make you feel?" Dr. Quinton was wanting to move on to a more productive subject.

"That whatever relationship we were building was coming to an end." K-Force was not hiding his feelings.

"How sure were you about it coming to an end?" Dr. Quinton asked.

"Whenever in the history of relationships, has the phrase 'we need to talk' ever led to anything good?" K-Force said in a dry tone.

"Understandable reaction, but how did that make you feel?" Dr. Quinton was asking a typical question of his profession.

"Kind of sad, but relieved at the same time. I felt I was always on eggshells with this woman," K-Force admitted.

"How so?" the doctor questioned.

"It seems whenever I did something wrong she compared me to her ex and felt the need to nag me to do better," K-Force answered.

"So, do you see the fact that your relationship failed because of her being overbearing," Dr. Quinton said, trying to get into his patient's head.

"Not really. I think she was still far too hurt and rushed into another relationship, when instead, she needed time to recover from her last one." As Samson said this, he actually saw a surprised look on Dr. Quinton's face. "Just because I'm built like a typical jock meathead, doesn't mean I act like one."

A laugh left Dr. Quinton's lips as he couldn't help but feel slightly ashamed at his own preconceptions. "Sorry, my fault, but still, that is a very mature way to look at it. I'm guessing that it did go smoothly when you two went on a break."

"No. Not in any sense of the word." K-Force shook his head in emphasis.

"Do you know why I called you here?" Gyges said as she gave him a disappointed look. She was wearing nothing but panties and a bra, covered by a robe.

Definitely wasn't for a booty call, K-Force thought as he stood in front of Gyges getting comfortable in her robe.

"I'm guessing it has to do with your ex going O. J. Simpson on both of us," said K-Force, getting right to the point.

"On you, everything was under control until you stepped in," Gyges accused.

"The fact he had a gun in your face says otherwise." K-Force was pointing out that it was going downhill before he got there.

"*Oh please*, Ashtown may say he is from Oakland, but he was raised in San Francisco. He was born in the worst area, but his daddy became junior executive when he was five years old and moved out. He visited his cousins over there and hung out, but he is as gangster as a scrub from Toronto," Gyges retorted, playing down the danger.

"So, he is a fake gangster, normally, but alcohol has a way of making normal people violent," K-Force said.

"He wouldn't have started anything if you didn't antagonize him," Gyges blamed him again.

"How is disarming him and trying to walk away antagonizing him?" K-Force rolled his eyes.

"You challenged him, Idiot," Gyges said.

"No I walked away. You felt the need to needle him again. You wanted the last word which pushed him over the line," K-Force responded, pointing out the facts.

"Oh, so, now it's *my* fault." Gyges was about to let him have it.

"No, the blame is mostly on him since he acted like a temperamental fourteen-year-old instead of a rational grown adult." K-Force was trying to point out the obvious truth.

Gyges wanted to argue that point, but it was what she wanted. Though she wished she had the final word on the matter.

"Fine, that's not the point of me calling you here," Gyges said, not seeing a way to argue about it.

"Which is?" K-Force stood waiting for the other shoe to drop.

"We need to go on a break. The way you acted was not acceptable by anyone's standards. And until you control yourself, I don't feel like moving forward with you," she said.

"Don't lie. This has nothing to do with my behavior. It is about how the press is hounding me and trying to make me look like the bad guy, despite the video footage of the whole incident. You want to protect your image until all this blows over." K-Force didn't feel like being lied to.

"Are you so shallow to think that you did nothing wrong? You gave the man a concussion," Gyges accused.

"That man was shooting wildly at security and the crowd. I had every right ending that before someone got hurt," he defended.

"And if you let me take care of it, there wouldn't have been any trouble. I would have handled it without all the drama." Gyges raised her voice to make a point.

"You act like I had the option in that situation," K-Force retorted.

"Yes, you had an option of just staying out of it," Gyges said.

"No, I had no such option." K-Force raised his voice, then spoke in a calm tone. "If I stayed back and let you handle it, you would have been pissed that I stood back and that I didn't defend or at least stand with you. So, I picked the option that meant I cared and was man enough to take this heat."

"This wasn't about me, but your fragile male ego to prove that you were in charge," Gyges dismissed his point.

"Trust me, if it was my fragile male ego, all of them would be in the hospital eating food through a straw," K-Force glowered a bit.

"God, you're impossible. I swear all you men think of starting a fight, and when you do it, it has to be a grand display to prove how tough you are," Gyges accused.

K-Force wanted to shout at her that wasn't the case, but realized that would not help his argument. Then a thought occurred to him; she didn't care if he was right or even if she was right. She just wanted to win the argument. He could bring up the point that when he tried to separate them, she was the one throwing insults and egging Ashtown-B into starting something. Seeing that continuing on at this point was pointless, he let all his anger and frustration leave and resigned himself just to walk away.

"How is me standing there, not doing anything other than letting him attack me, a grand display?" K-Force was genuinely curious about the logic behind this.

"You challenged him by doing that," Gyges accused again.

"Refusing to fight is challenging someone," responded K-Force, still not seeing the problem.

"You used your powers too," Gyges began.

"Before you started, I only used my power when it came to the crowd and security's protection. Even without my shielding abilities, handguns are too weak to hurt me, let alone a knife," K-Force added.

"How dare you interrupt me? Do I look like one of your bimbos you can," Gyges erupted in a barrage of insults. She blasted him with every insult imaginable, though K-Force noticed that most of the insults seemed to be related to Ashtown-B. Since this had stopped being about him, K-Force mentally checked out and let her vent, seeing as he refused to let her get a rise out of him anymore.

She is not worth the anger and frustration. Let it go, K-Force thought as he controlled himself while she tried to push his buttons.

"You know what? Leave and don't come back until you learn to control yourself," Gyges said, dismissing him.

K-Force wanted so bad to point out how hypocritical that was, but he thought it was better to leave and let her have the last word than deal with her crappy attitude. So, instead of saying anything, he got up and left her condo, though he did have the satisfaction of surprising her by not reacting the way he should have. K-Force refused to let her anger and resentment latch onto him and calmly left the room. But once out the door, he ran away fast as possible to get away from her before she could insult him again. This meant he was in the stairwell before he heard her muffled voice about to curse him, although she couldn't see him. Once he was out of the building, he air-ran away from Gyges' home.

His phone rang, which he thought about not answering, thinking it was Gyges trying to tell him off, but it was emergency call. When he answered, he felt a large lump of guilt hit him in the gut.

"Shit, I knew I should have finished patrol with him," K-Force said, as the alert guided him back towards San Bernardino. At that, he was sure he would be lectured about breaking multiple windows nearby. Luckily, he could legally claim it was an emergency. It took one minute for K-Force to get there, but he was too late to do anything.

Outside of San Bernardino, about a third of the way to Hesperia out on the open road, there was a large crater with two bodies, a large one that looked vaguely familiar and smaller one that was far too recognizable. QuickTime looked like something had shifted his body to the entire left side of his skeleton. His bones at certain points broke through his skin. The other person was in even worse shape. The unrecognizable brute was a mixture of white pieces of marble-like stones that were charred and covered in a blue viscous substance that smelt of blood and gore.

Then K-Force realized the figure of the dead man was Curbstomp. It would seem that there had been a great battle, but whatever happened had left QuickTime crippled and the white stone brute dead.

"Dammit," was all K-Force could yell as he pressed for a Medevac, but noticed that it didn't send a confirmed signal. He tried again but found that it was not working. K-Force examined the transmitter in his suit for any malfunctions and noticed that he was in a dead zone.

Not wanting to waste time, K-Force had to move almost three miles away to get a signal. He hit the Medevac signal to reach someone to help his friend. Then once the signal was confirmed, K-Force raced back to QuickTime's side, frantically looking up at the sky for a helicopter to appear.

"Don't worry, man. I got ya. I got ya."

Chapter 15
Breaking then Mending
Part 1

"I'm guessing seeing your friend injured by a Villain angered you greatly," Dr. Quinton said.

"Not as much as the vultures trying to say that QuickTime used an unnecessary amount of force, despite being put in a medical coma so that his body can heal," Samson grimaced.

"I'm hoping there is not a group so self-righteous and idiotic to say that," replied Dr. Quinton with complete disbelief.

"Channel 7 News, San Alonso," Samson answered.

"Of course, them," Dr Quinton responded, rubbing his temples at how vile some media personnel had become that they would desecrate a young man who had almost given up his life. Furthermore they were calling him a criminal because he had killed the man about to murder him. "I have to surmise that they didn't like the fact Curbstomp was killed in the fight."

"No, they tried and failed to paint him as the bad guy, but the backlash from it was insane since it was clear that there was no way for QuickTime to survive without killing Curbstomp. Especially with the crime scene report confirming that QuickTime had been tortured for a little while." Samson was trying to swallow his anger.

"So there is where you resolve to hold your anger back?" the doctor asked.

"Not really, a lot of my rage was pointed at myself for not following protocol and not staying with my patrol partner." Samson was being honest about his feelings.

"It was not your fault. No one knew that Curbstomp would show up." Dr. Quinton tried to dissuade his guilt.

"Yes, but I was being targeted by criminals all month. Even I knew there was a chance of attackers setting up a trap for me," Samson pointed out in shame.

"There was precedence for caution but not proof for it," Dr. Quinton explained.

"That's what Bronze Bomber said, but she and Faultline chewed me out. And I had to pay a big fine for leaving him in a lurch, despite both of us agreeing that it would be okay," K-Force replied. "It was Battle Hound who pushed me over the edge."

It was nine days before Thanksgiving and K-Force was angered because he was under strict supervision with his mentor. All the trust he had gained was washed away, and it would be a while before he got it back. The lapse of judgement had been three days prior, which felt like forever as much as the press hammered home his screw-up, along with their failed campaign to paint QuickTime as an example of Hero brutality.

In their scan of Santa Ana, they got a report of someone robbing an armored truck with plasma weaponry which had already injured six officers. The department asked for Meta-human assistance as SWAT was dealing with a drug bust with Spiced Pax which required their immediate attention. The criminals who were responsible for the destruction were Trigger and Battle Hound, a pair of mercenary assassins who later heard about the open bounty on K-Force's head and decided to go after him. Trigger had the gift that he could manifest weapons from the fat from his body. For this reason he was one of the fattest Villains out there, but also one of the skinniest, depending on how much he used his power for the month.

These weapons included those not generally open to the public, such as plasma weaponry, which was one of the few weapons known that could take out a majority of Meta-humans, or at least hurt them. There was Battle Hound, whose claim to fame was explosive energy, more thermochemical in nature, that sent him rocketing to great heights and speeds with considerable maneuverability. He used this power in two ways; he could fire from his hands or turn himself into an explosive shell and wipe out anything from a bunker to an entire city block.

Because K-Force's shields were more effective in containing his explosive power, Bronze Bomber ordered K-Force to keep damages to as minimum as possible. This was not something K-Force wanted to do after the week he had been having. He wanted to hurt someone, and this greasy, long-haired, Arnold Schwarzenegger-accented ass hat was a therapeutic punching bag. The dirty blonde was wearing a commando-like uniform with boots, cameo pants and a military green tank top. The professional look went away with the fact that this dude looked like a long-haired Metalhead from the eighties. Bronze Bomber flew to chase the gunman who pulled out a plasma rifle from his side and began to fire at her, driving her away. When the two were twenty feet apart, K-Force finally got a good look at what was on the olive-green tank top.

"Seriously, metal band Rammstein," K-Force commented.

"Yes, got a problem with them?" the merc growled.

"Nope, I just think they don't want to be represented by a merc," K-Force quipped.

"True, but how would they feel about being represented by this," The merc exploded forth in a flying fist charge. K-Force blocked the blow with his arm and tried to punch back with the other, but the man propelled himself away with a blast from his feet.

"Good reflexes, but you're too slow to keep up with me. Why don't you just drop dead so we can take the 180 thousand dollar bounty from your hide," Battle Hound said with another blast.

"That's the only way you are going to get it with a weak ass attack like that," K-Force said.

"Well, let's turn up the power then," the merc said

The battle went on like this for a time while explosive punches and kicks were flying towards K-Force, who neatly blocked and tried to counter, but failed. That was until the golden and black Hero felt he had enough power to do some real damage, so when Battle Hound tried to escape from another failed attack, K-Force jumped after Battle Hound and caught him in the gut. This sent him flying backwards, and K-Force didn't stop there, as he fired his force beams to pin the explosive fighter, long enough to hit him with a flying shoulder to the chest. K-Force also landed a powerful uppercut to the jaw that sent Battle Hound flying away from the bridge.

When Battle Hound oriented himself, he was angry for being caught off guard. The mercenary charged up his fist and fired a torrent of explosive energy, only to be blocked by a golden-yellow hexagon grid which was followed by another blow, but this time a kick to Battle Hound's side. K-Force was venting to let his anger out but noticed that he did it a little too much as he was losing power.

Seeing that he had to end this quickly, K-Force landed to the one part of the bridge where there were the least amount of cars. The mercenary hated being knocked about so he decided to charge for his most powerful attack. When he unleashed the blow, it caused a great blue plasma blast that had enough power to send a shuttle in orbit five times over. At first, the haze from the heat warped the air for a bit, but when it cleared, K-force was none the worse than when the fight started.

This only infuriated Battle Hound more as he flew as high into the sky as possible, until he was smaller than a speck. He then flew straight toward his target at immense speed, looking like a small blue comet, with a large, glowing aura. He was going to destroy the bridge overpass and everyone on it, just to take K-Force out.

K-Force realized that he needed to reinforce everything nearby to withstand the blast and block off everything else that he could not stretch his power over. So, when the impact came, there was a huge explosion surrounding the nearby area. The height of the blast rivaled the smallest skyscraper. When the explosion cleared, the only thing affected was a section of the sidewalk. Everything nearby was slightly singed by the heat. No one was worse for the wear, and K-Force received a massive amount of power from that attack, something he hadn't received since his fight with Primetime. With the power K-Force possessed, the Hero felt that he could actually send this guy flying somewhere between Colorado and New Mexico.

Better tone it down. I don't want to shatter the man's body on accident, K-Force thought as he slowly regulated the power into his reserves.

"Why, won't you just, DIE?" Battle Hound yelled and charged towards his hard target again, with both fists out in his blue blast shield. The blast shield was supposed to make him invulnerable from any harm, since it used kinetic energy which he built up and added fuel to his explosion. He always figured once he got really going he would be damn near impossible for anyone to stop. It took Hyperman going all out to take him down, and even then the Omega-level Hero had a tough time doing it. Sadly he couldn't have known that; while his powers were good, they were at disadvantage.

First, the Hyperman fight was not as grand as he remembered it. Hyperman was told by his agent to stretch the fight out, saying that early-round knockouts were not as impressive. So, Hyperman played with the explosive merc as a way to play up to the crowd and media. While near the end, Battle Hound did gain enough power to hurt Hyperman, it merely meant it felt like a slap. It stung, but had no real bite to the blow.

Secondly, K-Force's powers manipulated and controlled the kinetic energies while Battle Hound merely used them up. It was just a bad match-up between the two, where one had full advantage over the other. Their clash proved the fact that K-Force absorbed the blow to the point that there was barely an explosion of energy. K-Force caught one of the man's fists then began to pimp slap back and forth across the man's face three times; then put the man in an armlock behind his back. Battle Hound tried exploding multiple times to escape, but he felt all his powers almost drain away whenever he tried to move away from his target. And the lock was getting more painful as K-Force kicked the back of the man's knees to make him fall into a kneeling position, putting more leverage and power into the hold.

As soon as Battle Hound saw the power dampener cuffs come out, he knew he was going to prison. He figured he would be taken down by an Omega or an Alpha-level veteran who could keep up with him. But a rookie like this was taking him down like some chump. No, he would not stand for it. He fought the best. He was Battle Hound, the A-class Meta-human and this upstart barely took any damage taking him down. The damn bridge was hardly scraped by his attacks.

No, he would not be embarrassed like this. Battle Hound saw a female reporter taking pictures despite the rules of them not being allowed near an active combat scene, which they ignored half the time. This gave Battle Hound an idea, as petty as it was. He researched the fact that this brat was already on thin ice with some of those in authority because of a scuffle in a nightclub. If he allowed a reporter to die while apprehending a criminal, the media would bury his name and fame as recompense.

"You still fail, you little punk," Battle Hound growled.

"Really, I'm not the one who is about to go to jail," K-Force said as he was about to put on the power dampener hand cuffs.

Instead of answering, Battle Hound used his free arm to fire one last blast at the female reporter, which blew her in half. K-Force could do nothing as the top half of the reporter's body fell over the overpass in the traffic below. There were screams of horror and disgust, which only made the Meta-human merc laugh.

"Not much of a Hero when you can't even save a weak Mundy," Battle Hound laughed.

It was at that moment all the anger and pressure put on K-Force broke his temperament. From his perspective, K-Force saw the world blur as he audibly snapped the man's arm. Half of the Meta-mercenary's teeth shattered from his mouth. The blow was strong enough for Battle Hound to get free, but he was fearful, because he knew that he had pushed the wrong button on the wrong person. He tried to blast away only to be cutoff in mid-flight and decked back into the overpass hard enough to crack the foundation.

That's impossible. When I'm in flight, nothing can touch me. Battle Hound felt one his greatest protections fall away as he slowly got back to his feet in great pain. He felt his right arm swing limply.

He saw K-Force rush towards him, and he reacted in fear, using most of his energy and turning it into a blast to kill the guy, or at least distract him long enough to escape. This was futile as K-Force rushed through it unharmed. K-Force slammed a fist into Battle Hound's left side, causing him to collapse and start foaming blood out of his mouth.

K-Force was willing to continue, before Bronze Bomber started to hold him back and was yelling at him to snap out of it. It took a few seconds for K-Force to collect himself, but the damage was already done.

"So, here we are, me getting suspended pending an investigation with the DA trying to railroad me for using excessive force even though the guy openly admitted that he was after the bounty on my head. It was still seen as Hero brutality."

"I see that it wasn't that incident but an accumulation of other things being put upon you." Dr. Quinton was able to understand where the anger cultivated.

"Being haunted by a failure to save a true innocent, being bad mouthed by the local insane government… the constant bad mouthing by the press because I'm not allowed to have a different opinion, or the right to stay silent… having to deal with some relationship drama… and a petty asshole who just killed someone to piss me off," Samson said dejectedly.

"While it is true that is a lot to take in, but it is part of the life you chose," the doctor reminded him.

"Yes, but when does becoming a Hero mean having the whole world against you for doing your job? When did doing the right thing become a crime because someone is a celebrity? When did the word of a repeated murderer or felon become more viable than someone who stood by the law?" Samson questioned in frustration.

"I know, it seems maddening," the doctor started.

"That's putting it mildly," Samson mumbled.

"But you have to put yourself at a better standard, as you are a Hero now. That means you are held to a higher example," Dr. Quinton tried to remind him.

"Hard to do when they paint you as the bad guy," Samson said.

"You really think you did nothing wrong?" Dr. Quinton asked.

"Not at all, but I refuse to take blame for doing my job. That's like being reprimanded for arresting a known drug dealer for peddling drugs." Samson was refusing to budge.

Dr. Quinton sighed as he knew that this wasn't going the way his higher ups wanted, at least not quickly. For right now, he was going to have to do it slowly since the man had a solid sense of right and wrong.

"Our time is almost up, but I suggest you unwind to release your anger, healthily. Maybe leave the area for a bit, since you are not able to patrol or apprehend anyone," Dr. Quinton said.

"Way ahead of you. Since I'm officially off duty, I'm going home to visit my folks for Thanksgiving," Samson answered.

"That's good, family will help you calm down and see that maybe all this pressure you feel is self-placed. Not the world around you trying to crush you," Dr Quinton said as he shook the young Meta-human's hand and began to escort him to the door. As Samson left, he saw another patient waiting but paid them no mind since whoever visited Dr. Quinton was not his business. That was, until he noticed that in walked his mentor's rival, Wraith Queen.

Though she was in her civilian uniform, he had seen her several times out of her attire. She wore a professional business suit dress that looked to conform to her body which, like her public personality, was the opposite of Bronze Bomber. To say Wraith Queen had hips was an understatement as she could give video queens a run for their money. Shaking his head to clear it of those thoughts, Samson put on his mask and was about to leave the room.

"I think you were in the right," Wraith Queen said in passing.

This caught Samson by surprise so he turned to face her. "What?"

"The club and the bridge overpass were not your fault. You were just doing your job and making sure the casualties were kept to the minimum," Wraith Queen said before entering the office of Dr. Quinton.

Samson didn't know why it made him feel better but it did, knowing that at least some of his peers had his back. It meant that he wasn't by himself out there in Cali.

Chapter 16
Breaking then Mending
Part 2

It was the day of Thanksgiving, which meant a day full of Pro Football and Meta Ball. Tamera and Aaliyah of the Brewer household were talking to Omari's new girlfriend Abigail, while the men were making the food because Omari's mom was a bad cook, and his sister wasn't up to the same level. His mother and sister were giving Abigail questioning on the level of interrogation. While Samson was wary around the woman, he felt she was a good person overall, though he was not the best when it came to judging women to date if Anita and Gyges were any example.

Samson and the men were going introduce Red Abigail to a Louisiana style Thanksgiving dinner. Hakeem was whipping up his famous rotisserie red chili and orange glaze turkey, buttermilk cornbread with sausage, and corn fritters as stuffing. Omari was using a receipt of his grandma from New Orleans, which included sweet potato bisque and a family secret brisket that had won his uncle a few barbeque competitions. Samson himself was always good at preparing desserts, such as his beignets and peach cobbler. He was also known to throw down with vegetarian gumbo, braised greens, and seasoned cauliflower. While making dinner, they made small talk between the three of them.

Samson was waiting for the right moment to ask his big brother for a big favor. While everyone was being nice not to talk about his suspension, he knew there was some disappointment there. But he had to do this, since it was just the start of clearing up his mistake and getting back into his peers' and companies' good graces.

"Son, I heard that you got another offer from a mega-corporation wanting you to join them," Hakeem said.

"Yeah, I heard JP Morgan offered 260 million dollars. My friends think you're crazy as hell for turning that down, though the majority thinks you're being noble. If you ask me, it is because they are sports fans who don't want their teams' best players bumped off by accidents," Samson said as he guzzled down a cocktailed brew.

"Yeah I didn't really feel like being owned to the point that they would tell who should I breed with and have an option to put any of my kids on contract. Apparently, our family is of high potential for greatness, considering all three children are alpha-level or projected to be so. It makes me think they are seeing a thoroughbred," Omari said as he finished glazing the smoked beef and laid them on the huge serving plate.

"Tell me about it, though the government can't force us, they are hinting that they want another child from us since your mother and I are physically in our forties, despite being near sixty myself," Hakeem said, looking in his liquor as if the answer lay in there.

"Won't they try to buy you out from the hospital instead?" Samson asked.

"Not since said company owns the hospital, which is owned mostly by the teams I heal. Not to mention that every athlete would throw a fit that their security to having a long successful career was taken from them," Omari said lifting his own drink.

"Doesn't that make you just as controlled as the others?" Samson asked his brother.

"To put it bluntly, I'm LeBron James on the Cavs so everyone is kissing my ass to make sure I stay. They allow me to help lower and mid class instead of being exclusive to the 2% percent. Which would happen if I took any offer other than that? Hell, I'm, as the news put it, 'first public healer above Gamma-class that has not been swept up by the government or corporate in 65 years.' And that's worldwide, not just the States," Omari replied.

"So, you can, per se, help family out, right?" Samson said with a bit of desperation in his voice.

"Hell, you couldn't stop corporate healers from doing that, and those couldn't be more monitored than the FCC." Omari opened the door.

"What about friends of the family?" Samson was hoping badly that his brother could help Avery.

"What is this about Sam?" Hakeem could sense something was wrong.

"Dad, I, I have a friend who needs help badly," Samson's head was hanging down as if he was responsible.

"What happened?" Their father needed to know if he could help in any way.

"You know how much Heroes my age want to be drafted by the big companies and corporations and make huge amounts of money," Samson began.

"They treat you like you're the number one draft pick for a year or two before you get labeled as a prodigy or a bust." Omari was filling in what he knew.

"Well, I don't think athletes try to bump off the competition," Samson said through gritted teeth.

"Son?" Hakeem was getting worried now.

Samson's eyes were filled with tears of anger at this point "Look, my friend Avery was put in critical condition, and he might not be able to walk again, let alone be a Hero, so please help him."

"There's more to it than that. You said that a Hero had taken him out or was partially responsible," Hakeem was getting worried.

"I have video proof that Primetime and his company brought Curbstomp over to cripple QuickTime," Samson vindicated.

"Show us," Omari said in all seriousness.

"After dinner, I have a feeling that this would ruin our night," said Hakeem, feeling that a topic this heavy would kill everyone's appetite. He wanted a good Thanksgiving with the whole family before the drama ruined it.

"Omari, are you willing to help," Samson almost begged his elder brother.

"Sure Sam, just let me tell my staff. I will be making a detour before going back to Crescent City." Omari assured him that he had no problem helping.

A wave of relief fell from Samson's shoulders as he knew his brother would be willing to help. The fear was Omari would not be able to because of some bureaucratic bullshit.

Dinner was more toned down as each of the family got to know Abigail better. While his mom, Aaliyah, was more than eager to grill her some more, his dad cut the crap out quick. Omari and his girlfriend were grateful, seeing as the woman was relentless.

Samson trying to be the 'good' little brother, decided to play a harmless little prank.

"Don't worry, as soon as you give mom some grandkids to spoil, she will forget all about your criminal past," Samson teased.

At this statement, K-Force felt his shield drop and a hard slug to the shoulder. Samson was used to his brother making him vulnerable when he felt that his little sibling needed to remember he still could get his ass kicked. But that was fast; what usually took a minute or two was now a mere second.

He got stronger, but how? Samson thought as he rubbed his shoulder, still grinning that his little comment served its purpose.

"Speaking of which, how soon can I expect some grandbabies?" Aaliyah began.

"Mom?" Omari really didn't want to contend with this conversation.

"Don't you '*mom*' me, boy. You nearly died trying to save this woman, and it has been almost half a year. Put a ring on it, and put a bun in there when you're done," said Aaliyah, making her feelings known.

At this, Tamera started laughing as her brother's expression went crestfallen; she loved watching her brother take the heat for once. Her parents, her mother more so than her dad, wanted her to settle down because her little black book was going to need a third volume the way she was going through boys.

This broke the somewhat quiet mood over the table and got everyone talking again. This led to siblings lightly ribbing each other by telling some embarrassing stories, including how Dad caught Tamera with a boy hiding naked in her closet; or the fact that Samson's date farted during his first dance, and like a gentleman, he became the fall guy and was called "Stinkson" for half a year.

When the good times were over, Samson gathered everyone into the family den with a computer linked to the flat screen. Once

Samson synced the two devices, he showed the family the incident that sent QuickTime to the hospital.

The scene was cut from three images on separate monitors. There was a large monitor screen in the center.

"Where did he get these images from?" Omari said.

"Invisible recording drones, three to be precise. It is how he gets great images for his company on V-Tube," Samson replied.

"He is a V-Tuber?" Hakeem rolled his eyes.

"Free advertisement and it brings in a lot of publicity and connects with his fans on the Internet," defended Omari.

"I swear you kids are becoming more fame hungry every year," Hakeem shook his head.

"Dad, look at the video first. Then explain how things were done when Elvis Presley was considered a deviant for wiggling his hips," Samson commented.

Instead of commenting that he became a Hero during the seventies, he decided to keep quiet, look at the video, and soon became enraged. The video showed everything in beautiful high definition 1080p. QuickTime was flying back from Hesperia towards San Bernardino, when a tire from an eighteen-wheeler hit him in the chest.

This made the Hero tumble from the sky and crash land into the ground. One of the cameras focused on where the object came from. Standing near the wreckage of an eighteen-wheeler was Curbstomp, a brute made of white stone marble that looked to be carved instead of built. The driver in the cab was crushed to death. It seemed Curbstomp and the eighteen-wheeler had a head-on collision. This was obviously to get other people's attention and call the nearby Hero.

"Okay, you mangled up art piece, you just bought yourself an ass-kicking," QuickTime threatened.

"Don't count on it, wimp. Just because some computer says you can beat me doesn't mean you are good enough to do so!" Curbstomp shouted, bashing his knuckles together.

"Wait, you killed the driver to prove that the machine's findings were unverified." QuickTime couldn't believe anyone was this petty.

"If by unverified you mean full of horseshit, than yes," Curbstomp growled.

QuickTime audibly groaned at this over-muscled rock-like tank's stupid excuse to pick a fight. "Heavenly Father above give me strength."

QuickTime heard the lumbering brute begin to charge towards him as if he were a bull. Not feeling like dealing with this meathead, QuickTime threw some explosive daggers to Curbstomp who was chasing him now. Despite the knife bombs being stronger than the ones he usually used, they did little except irritate him.

"Hmm, a more penetrating weapon would be more effective," QuickTime said in posh tone when his *Sherlock Holmes* side took over. Another dagger flew from his hand toward Curbstomp. The white stone mini-giant ignored it until it turned into a drill and dug deep into his marble-like skin. This made Curbstomp wince in pain. Soon, three more drill daggers charged him, causing him to instinctively cover himself with his arms. The daggers dug into them as well, only this time, he shrugged it off as he looked even more enraged. He began ripping parts of the road and the total eighteen-wheeler, throwing them at QuickTime, who actually had to work to dodge the objects raining as fast as bullets. Curbstomp was able to knock him out of the sky. QuickTime never realized that the brute had such good aim.

After a few acrobatics and destroying a couple targets that got too close, QuickTime showed that he had more tricks up his sleeve. QuickTime snapped his left hand and the daggers embedded in Curbstomp's chest exploded, leaving bigger gashes and cracks in the walking pillar's body. The reaction to it was a cry of the typical "I'll kill you." However, instead of QuickTime trying to play keep-away, he rushed forward and began to go hand-to-hand. After dodging several grabs, QuickTime tossed a couple of small balls which contained pepper bombs.

At this point, everyone saw that QuickTime had everything handled. In fact it seemed while Curbstomp was trying to rub the pepper from his eyes, QuickTime inserted a mini speaker on Curbstomp's back between the shoulder blades. Then, when it looked like Curbstomp recovered, QuickTime touched his thumb to his pinky, which sent a debilitating sonic wave which dropped Curbstomp to his knees.

Just as QuickTime was about to finish the brute and call to have him taken in, a blur slammed into his back. The blow was pretty bad as it looked like what happened when a car hit a normal person from behind and sent them flying instead of being run over. QuickTime was sent tumbling across the ruined road, tumbling like a ragdoll. His suit was actually ripped from the impact. Despite all this damage, QuickTime was able to recover enough to move after a few seconds, only for the blur to knock him and a couple of teeth out.

The blur turned out to be a massive figure in a black outfit with a skier's type of mask to hide his entire identity. Looking around to make sure nobody was nearby, the figure angrily walked towards the stunned brute. Curbstomp was trying to remove the sonic weapon that was giving him a massive migraine. The black-outfitted figure shot energy beams from his eye sockets and blasted the device from Curbstomp's back.

Curbstomp was able to collect himself after thirty seconds while the large black figure of a man waited impatiently for the massive brute to get to his feet steadily.

"Well, am I going to have to cripple him myself, because if so, then our deal's off," the black figure stated.

"Alright, alright it's not like I had to deal with my brain being turned into mush," Curbstomp moaned in pain.

"Like you would know the difference, now go do your job or I'll do it myself," the black figure commanded.

"Fine, you don't have to tell me twice," Curbstomp said before he looked at the limp form that had given him so much trouble. "Besides, I'm going to enjoy this."

The white stone marble man began to systematically crush QuickTime's left arm and broke the right leg into three parts. As the final touch, he shattered the lower spine, making sure QuickTime would be confined into a wheelchair for the rest of his life. "There, and now I expect the rest of my payment up front."

"Oh don't worry, you'll get payment," the hooded figure said as he moved closer to Curbstomp and removed his mask from his face. From the middle camera, you could not see anything but shoulder-length dirty blond hair.

"Wait, aren't you," was Curbstomp's last words as a massive amount of force was blasted into his face and actually made his torso blow up.

"Keep the change," the black-suited figure said, before making a call. "Hey, Mister Smythe, the job's done."

"Yeah, QuickTime is out permanently, and Curbstomp is nothing but a pile of rubble. What? He is already on his way? How? The area is a dead zone for signals," the black-suited figure said. "Fine,

I'll leave. Don't worry, I made sure there were no witnesses to testify." The man with the dirty blond hair put on his ski mask like a tactical cover and ran away at an extremely fast speed. Three minutes later Samson as K-Force appeared and was looking frantically at the carnage.

Back at the Brewer House, the family and guests were disturbed and disgusted. While the main camera couldn't see who it was from the back, the other camera caught the culprit at the side. Though his hair was in the way for some of the shot, Samson had Incognito clear it up and match it to eighty-four percent probability of it being Primetime.

The data showed the match was based on the shape of the body and face, as well as the energy signature of the eye beams. Despite the proof, it would not be taken seriously because there was footage of Primetime doing autographs at a promotional event in LA, at the same time. This meant that any lawyer could use a clone frame up which was a common defense nowadays. There was no DNA evidence or fingerprints since Primetime had gloves on the whole time. The only evidence was Primetime's energy readings, which were like fingerprints for Metas, but not recognized by the court. After seeing all the data before them, Samson's family's opinion was clearer.

"So, you have proof to prove it, but not enough for the court of law," Hakeem growled in disgust.

"Yeah, they were thorough enough to have a double to take his place so he would have an air-tight alibi. And you need at least a ninety percent confirmation to start an investigation," Samson said in depressed voice.

"And the definitive evidence is his energy signature, which is inadmissible in court," Omari rubbed his temples.

"Oh God, can't believe I thought that little shit was cute," said Tamera feeling physically disgusted.

"I been telling you looks and title are surface area. Whatever the job or position, there is always corruption," Aaliyah spoke from experience.

"Do you know why he would do this?" Abigail asked.

"Claim jumping," Samson replied.

"What?" Abigail was more confused.

"Claim jumping is when a Hero takes another Hero's territory," Omari explained this dark side of Hero world. "For Professionals, the amount of crime and TV spotlight is all that matters, especially when money is involved, which is why those with little or no crime go to someone else's territory for more Meta-criminals to bust for the cameras."

"It is like trying to steal their land or gold," explained Abigail, seeing the same attitude on her former side.

"Which at this point makes 'Heroes' start a fight and turn ghetto," Tamera said bluntly.

"Tamera," Hakeem chided.

"A bunch of people fighting over turf like they own it instead of just living and working there, that's the epitome of ghetto, only Heroes don't wear unified colors," Tamera defending her statement.

"Nice to see that even Heroes have to deal with this crap," Abigail gave a dry comment.

"So, what are you going to do with this information?" Aaliyah asked her youngest.

"Show it to Avery as soon as Omari gets him back on his feet, and I already have Incognito putting Primetime and Entcriagey on their watch list," Samson informed his mother.

"It is not enough, but it is a start. I'm going to warn the others about Enteriagey employees. I seem to recall several of my former colleagues dying or becoming crippled only to be replaced by Enteriagey employee," Tamera added her own suspicions.

"Keep me posted. I can't start an investigation against such a large company, but as soon as I get something concrete, I will take it to the IMRB*," Hakeem stated.

"You think it will need to go that far?" Aaliyah knew that was severe, even by their standards.

"This is not the first time a company went this far, and if caught, it might fall out into a miniature war," Hakeem said.

"Not to mention, it allows those of the villainous persuasion to try to recruit or remove those they deem a problem," Tamera said.

"True, but it is a problem we will have to face or let the corruption seep further into our community," Hakeem said, resolute in his decision

November 25

It was three days after Thanksgiving that Samson was able to get his brother to come Santa Ana with him. Abigail said it was an opportunity to see the infamous Orange County and decide to make a mini-trip of it after her man was done helping Avery. While getting Omari to help was easy, it was difficult for Samson to get Avery's company to allow him to use his brother's gifts to heal Avery. Some bureaucrat saw it as a violation and believed that it would be bad press to allow him to do so. That meant going around the idiot to Avery's parents. Avery's mom has been by her son's side for two weeks, looking over him with his girlfriend

Frigid, which she was glad to see, though the ice-powered Meta was not happy to see him.

"Easy Frigid, I'm only here to help Avery," said K-Force as he raised his hand in peace.

"It's because of you that he is here," Frigid growled. It turned out this girl was very protective of her boyfriend.

"Now, dear, I know you're angry," replied Avery's mom.

"He left for some booty call with that pastel fat bitch, while Avery was fighting for his life. You were supposed to be his partner and you left," Frigid began.

"Snowbird," a raspy voice was heard. They all saw it was Avery awake, despite the drugs in his system. "Let him speak."

After the bed was raised to a more comfortable position, Avery was ready to speak to K-Force. "And I told him to go. K-Force wanted to stay and finish the patrol,"

"It doesn't matter. He still should have stayed," Frigid insisted, glaring at Avery.

"We are both partially at fault, but that doesn't matter now." Avery's voice was dry. It seemed the drugs were really messing with him.

"You said you could help?" Avery's mother asked, being hopeful.

"Not me, specifically, but my brother Dr. Brewer can help," K-Force said.

"Avery has three doctors monitoring him. What can your brother do that they can't," Frigid challenged.

"Snowbird, his brother is a helper in the A-class," was all Avery could get out before a cough that ripped through his body. "I saw footage of him remaking an arm."

At those words, Avery's mother rushed forward put her hands on K-Force's chest and had a pleading look in her eyes. "Please tell me you can contact him."

"He is right outside, but he needs your permission to help Avery. I tried going through Fletcher & Jameson's Limited, but I was blocked because it would be bad press if you were associated with me anymore," K-Force explained.

"God save me from idiots who think about the company more than my well-being," Avery said in raspy voice.

"You can't be serious," Mrs. Monroe, Avery's mom said in disbelief.

"Mrs. Monroe, you will find that in every company there are those who will do anything for the bottom line, despite it might be detrimental in the long run," Frigid groaned. Because she was part of the same company, she became wary about her health if she ever got injured.

"You don't know the half of it. So can I bring my brother in? He can't legally walk in without Avery's or his mother's permission," K-Force asked.

"Yes, yes, please let him in. I want my son able to walk again," Mrs. Monroe was eager to see her child healthy.

K-Force quickly leaned out the open doorway and motioned his brother forward. The healing Meta-human, calmly walked in and examined the patient. Doing a quick glance over the patient, he handed Avery's mom a small contract.

"I need one of you to sign so I might proceed with the healing process. Because of certain laws I am not allowed to do anything more than examine your body until I have signed permission," Omari explained, as he handed her a clipboard and lease contract.

"Pen." was all Avery said. He wanted this pained, drugged, and broken body over with.

"I think it would be best if you mother did it, for binding purposes," Omari said.

"What?" Avery was confused and mildly insulted.

"What he means, sweetie, is the fact that you're in a lucid state and some crackpot will use that as an excuse to bash him in the press in some way," Avery's mother said.

"Precisely." Omari questioned.

"Edna Monroe, Minnesota Senate."

"Your mom is a senator?" K-Force asked in surprise.

"I didn't want to seem like a spoiled rich kid like my peers were," Avery said in mild embarrassment.

"Like his father, Avery is a self-made man who prefers to work for everything he receives in life," the senator said as she read the short two-page document of an over-glorified permission slip and signed it on the dotted line.

With that, Dr. Brewer got to work using his powers and winced a bit at the extent of the damage to the young Hero. He saw everything that was obvious and some things not so obvious. While the medical staff caught six bones in his ribcage being broken and a collapse lung, they didn't catch the minor puncture in his lungs which could have led him to drown in his own blood or have future breathing problems. The legs were not just broken; it was shattered to the point that there was no way they could, even by modern science, make it work again. It would be best to amputate it to save Avery from an infection. The arm was a list of torn muscles, broken bones, and dislocations; while it would work again, it would never be the same. The worst part was the fact that the damage to his spine would render everything below his waist lifeless, and he would be confined to a wheelchair for life.

"Now, you will feel some discomfort as you will not feel anything below your neck for a while, mostly because to completely fix you we will to have align several of your limbs. Little bro, if you will?" said Omari as he gestured to K-Force.

"Sure," K-Force said as he ripped the cast off of Avery then wrapped Avery in his forcefield to keep his body aligned. Then, a soft glow left Omari as his power flooded Avery's body. There was a disturbing sound of bones jangling and snapping back into place. The process seemed a success as Avery's breathing became clear and less haggard. Avery's face seemed tired and drained but restored to full health. When the full healing session was done, Avery's body looked to be in perfect condition, though the monitors were going off after such a rapid change.

A doctor and nurse rushed in to see what the problem was and tried to push everyone out. K-Force calmly accepted their instruction, but Avery's mother put up more of a fuss. Frigid threatened to turn a handsy nurse into an icicle if Avery didn't calm her down. Omari stayed because he was finishing his work, despite a doctor trying to elbow her way past him, which felt like she was trying to move a truck. When he was done, Omari calmly left the room and let the doctor examine her patient. After an hour, a shocked doctor came out and looked in utter disbelief.

"What did you do?" the doctor questioned.

"Hello, my name is Dr. Omari Brewer. Nice to meet you," Omari properly introduced himself.

"Dr. Brewer," Avery's doctor face implied that she recognized his name. "Oh!"

Recollection hit her as she realized why her patient, who looked like he was run over by a Mac truck and survived, was now in pristine health.

"My God, I heard about your power. After seeing the results in person it is a whole utter experience," she said as her look of interest grew. Omari had seen this before - doctors had written a couple of papers about how his healing gifts worked. But those were preliminaries; the hard copy medical thesis won't be out until February.

"There is another patient I would like for you to heal," the doctor asked with a gleam in her eye that looked like a child with a toy.

"Love to, but can't. I am under a strict Friends and Family clause with my powers. Only my hospital's patients, certain pro team athletes of the NBA and the NFL, and executives of said organization can freely be healed by me," Omari tried to explain the actual wall of red tape that prevented him from doing such a thing. "Because QuickTime is a roommate and friend of my brother, I am allowed to heal him. For anyone else, you will need to go through my office to get permission since they control who I may and may not heal."

"More the pity, but I'm sure we can convince them to allow us to borrow your time," she said as she tried to lead Omari away for a more private conversation.

K-Force just watched them walk away as he slowly turned to look at his friend's girlfriend, who looked less ticked off but had a look that she was still trying to stay mad. The Minnesota senator had an aid that looked frantic. From the bits and pieces of their conversation, it seemed she was needed back home. It was a look of anger and frustration as it seemed she wanted to stay and make sure her son was back to full health, but politics don't cater to politicians.

"Get me a flight around nine, but if this is some hogwash bill or grandstanding, I'm going to be a nightmare for Miller," Senator Monroe growled.

It was a little later that the doctor returned and explained that Avery was fine and set to leave. They had to remove the tracheostomy and colostomy tube from him. And with this, they wanted to keep him overnight for observation, which was the standard practice. Once the medical staff left, they let the women crowd around Avery, who were happy to see him well again.

K-Force decided to read on his phone while he waited to be called or dismissed. His brother was brought in and they profusely thanked him for his help. Omari accepted their appreciation but left because Abigail wanted to have a lunch with him. Then after another half hour, the women allowed K-Force to leave, with Senator Monroe hugging and thanking him for saving her boy. Frigid pouted while thanking him, but she made it clear he was a long way from getting into her good graces.

"What if I have proof that it wasn't by chance but design that QuickTime was taken down?" K-Force said

"What?" Frigid and Avery said together, as well as a third voice from the door who happened to be the last person he wanted to hear about this.

"My son was part of a," and before the senator could say anything, K-Force covered her mouth with his hand and closed the door. Then he slowly brought her towards Avery's bed. He then created a dome of yellow hexagon energy to protect them from outside listeners. Once he was sure they were secure, he released the older woman who looked very angry with him.

"Sorry ma'am, but we can't have people overhearing this unless you want a second shot against him," K-Force pointed towards Avery.

"Very well, but where and how did you get this proof?" Any warmth Mrs. Monroe had was gone.

"Recorded on a device at a secure location, and how, I'm sure Avery can guess," K-Force turned to Avery.

"My drones, Brah." Avery mentally slapped himself for forgetting them.

"Got it in one," K-Force confirmed.

"So, do we know my attacker," Avery asked.

"Yes and I have a pretty good reason why," K-Force said

"Which is?" queried Avery.

"Claim jumping," K-Force said bluntly.

"Are you serious? All of this was because of some turf war?" Frigid said in anger.

"A very rich and profitable territory," Avery said, seeing the reason.

"I'm lost, what is claim jumping? Did my son find an oil field somewhere?" Mrs. Monroe was getting more confused.

"Heroes of the Professional level get paid by the number and types of criminals, not to mention they get more press swung their way. The area we patrol has seen a big boost of criminals lately which mean more of a chance to get sponsors and a gain profit for smacking villains around," Frigid began.

"So because some greedy schmuck wanted more revenue, my son was put in critical condition," Mrs. Monroe finished.

"Sadly, mom, yeah," Avery confirmed.

"And there is very little chance of me seeing it since I have to fly home soon," she said, turning to her son with a look that said she wanted no argument. "As soon as you see the film, send it to me on our secure website."

"But mom it's too,"

"This is a mixture of corporate craziness and power-hungry politics which I deal with more then you. And I have proven I can keep my emotions in check, but if you think I'm going to sit here and worry senselessly about who attacks you, you are insane," the senator stared directly at her son with the look mothers give their children to obey.

"Alright, alright, I'll send it over as soon," Avery started.

"As soon as possible," the senator finished for him, leaving no wiggle room.

"Yes, mom," Avery sighed, knowing that no matter how old you get, if you have a good mom it will always be hard to say 'no' to them.

November 30

DeSoto was waiting for a caller so he could finally remove the biggest thorn in his back. While the media, with a little funding from him, were trying to cancel the bastard, it all failed as most of the public didn't buy as much as he wanted. For at least until February his business would go back to normal with expected losses.

That is, as long as I can remove those roaches sneaking in my territory and thinking they can get away with it, DeSoto mentally growled.

Then the phone rang with the caller ID showing it was his employee.

"What color is the sun that rises in the West?" a gruff, gravelly voice asked.

"Black. Glad to see you're on time," DeSoto answered.

"It is not easy getting a pocket nuke as they do on TV. I had to call in a lot of favors, but it is set on January 12th," the gruff voice said.

"Why so late?" DeSoto asked.

"I'm weaker around the holy holidays. It is a consequence of my powers, but don't worry about it. It will be done or your money back," the gruff voice responded.

"Why are those bombs so important." DeSoto was perplexed by the plan.

"It is because Bronze Bomber somehow knows a way around my magic and can hurt me, so she would be a problem. With nuclear material in the area, they will call her. And with this, I take out K-Force with little effort and any other Hero who has the misfortune of attacking me," the blood thirst was audible in his voice.

"You're so confident, but be careful. He has taken down many of my employees who were considered top tier," DeSoto warned, as he couldn't fail again.

"Hmph, none of your people were me. None of them were War Fiend."

Chapter 17
San Alonso Massacre

Samson took advantage of his down time as he was suspended. Some people felt he should be expelled from being a Hero, though luckily that was only from the fringe groups. Since this was the age of every phone having a camera, footage surfaced of Battle Hound not in handcuffs, yet killing a reporter. This meant the lie that K-Force was beating a powerless man in handcuffs was false, though there were those that claimed the footage was edited. Ashtown-B's trial was more dragged out, but that was because celebrity lawyers were slicker than others. For some reason, the judge allowed them to bring up the incident with Battle Hound as a history of violence, despite it being irrelevant to the case at hand. It was getting so bad that there was blatant jury tampering, until the judge was removed due to misconduct unbecoming of someone of his status, which meant he took a bribe. The next judge, Ms. Mendez, was a fifty-year-old woman who didn't take any bull from anyone. Think of a Latina *Judge Judy* with a bit more street cred, and you have Judge Mendez. Apparently, she used to be gang member when she was young but turned her life around.

With her in the driver's seat, the trial ended in five days because there was nothing substantial to prove that Ashtown-B, or Ashley Burnson, was innocent. He had to pay for damages, was found potentially liable for the PTSD of those he had fired at the bouncers and the security.

Even though he was acquitted in both trials, the governor decided to punish him as much as he could for mild excessive force, which was a suspension until February 3. This got him cheers and jeers in equal measure, but his word was law until he was removed.

Despite all this, there was an old saying that the only bad press is good press at for celebrities, which for Samson was true. K-Force became a nationally-recognized name again and popular in several areas, especially his home region. Hero fans were begging to bring him home, saying that they take care of their own. Most were calling out the Governor Fulson as owned by criminals because his rulings within K-Force's trial, and several others, were unusually harsh against Heroes. Governor Fulson tried to state that he believed Meta-humans, especially Heroes, had far too much sway in society, only for a senator in Louisiana to point out that Meta-criminals had been given very easy sentences. Fulson almost always ignored very serious crimes, such as murder and destruction of property on a large scale. That was a bit of exaggeration, but in essence, it was true because he did allow some the more violent offenders and major flight risks into the least secure prisons, which they escaped from easily.

The news station which formerly employed the deceased reporter, sided with K-Force as well as most of their other branches around their country, so he was being seen in a more favorable light by many. His toys, costumes, even his Hero jersey and varsity jacket were big sellers during the Christmas holidays. Sky High had backed him, since many felt that he was being railroaded for some strange reason and were rewarded for their loyalty, and customers protested with their wallets by buying more of their products and merchandise.

Speaking of the Christmas holidays, his brother proposed to his girlfriend by creating a fifteen carat tanzanite with a halo made of half-karat sea-green sapphires set in a white gold band. This ring was estimated to be worth more than six hundred thousand dollars. To say she was happy was an understatement. Abigail's mother joked that she would be willing to marry him for a ring like that.

When their mother, Aaliyah, asked if this was what Omari wanted, he answered, "I've known her for more than a half a year. I did somethings that I'm not proud of, nearly died to save her, and stood up to someone who could've turned me into ash. I think it is safe to say I love her and I'm willing to go the extra mile for her," Omari answered.

Suddenly, K-Force had a new sister-in-law who, with the help of both families, was deciding when, where and who should show up to the wedding. You could never have seen the cluster of chaos a Hero/Villain wedding can be. There were the typical problems such as location, time, and expense.

Here is hoping Abigail doesn't turn into a 'Bridezilla,' Samson thought, as he tried to adjust to having a new member of the family. But that was a minor concern in comparison to a bunch of Meta-humans meeting and a chance of them bringing their beef, especially with alcohol added to it.

Better have it outside of the city limits. Less chance for property damage, Samson thought as he went across the daily news which brought him to the grease-oiled-up, tan meathead.

It was no big surprise that Primetime had taken QuickTime's spot while he was injured, even though QuickTime made a full recovery. They insisted to keep him on leave to recover from the traumatic experience, which would be true for most people, but the side effects of QuickTime's power could ignore most traumas because he could separate the pain and memory. Though they did have proof of Primetime's involvement, all of it was circumstantial because despite having video to confirm with ninety-two percent certainty that he was the second attacker, this still wasn't enough to bring him in.

That was because of shape shifters, clones, and extremely good masks had been used to frame Heroes before. There was an incident where a Hero named Deluge was executed because he was spotted at a murder scene of a Presidential candidate. With only video and witnesses to the crime scenes, he was indicted and executed without any DNA, fingerprints, or motive. He had an alibi, but he didn't want his daughter and ex-wife caught up in it. A month later, a Heroine who didn't believe his guilt found an underground lab filled with robots. One of the robots had dried blood of the senator on the bottom of his boot with a skin-mask that looked like Deluge.

The scientist was currently doing life in prison, and a new law was made for Meta-humans of the Hero profession that no crime could be placed on them without empirical evidence. Witness statements were not enough anymore. So all they had was proof that couldn't be taken to a court of law because energy readings were not admissible, in spite of being as distinctive as fingerprints.

QuickTime and Frigid saw this as a learning event and were cautious of being anywhere near Enteriagey employees, since they couldn't trust the company or clients if they got bigger than them. While QuickTime's mother wanted nothing more than to burn the company down, she had to play it cool as she slowly hampered every move Enteriagey made by pushing the bill to get acceptance of energy signatures as evidence, since it was the only available evidence to convict Primetime.

There was another factor to QuickTime's assault which seemed to uncover how perfectly everything was set up. For example, K-Force being called away by his girlfriend seemed to be timed perfectly in order for the ambush to take place. Whether Gyges was in on it or just a patsy, it didn't sit well with them.

January 12
San Alonso

Nearly all the Christmas decorations were put away, except for a few left over from people who were lazy, or from those who wanted to keep the season going for a little bit longer. Either way, this suited K-Force just fine. This meant War Fiend was at full power without the holy atmosphere and spirit of the holidays affecting him. It didn't really suck him dry of power but it did make him feel like he had a cold coming on.

Now War Fiend could enact his plan since he had two of his biggest obstacles called away to the state capital to stop a major bomb threat. There was a call to inform the police of the three pocket nukes in Sacramento, and to prove he was serious, he exploded one ten miles away from the city. This got about every alphabet agency combing the city to find them, which led to a lot of head bumping and infighting among them. The only smart thing they did was to call Bronze Bomber, who was the closest Hero who could handle the situation. Bronze Bomber could fly the nuke out of the city to absorb it into her body. One of the lesser known abilities of Bronze Bomber was the fact that she could eat and absorb all forms of nuclear fallout and cleanse the area. She was assigned to America's anti-nuke division because of this reason.

With her out of the city, the other problem was Faultline, who was also removed by sending him to fight his nemesis in Colorado. He had fought the vicious bastard once and didn't want to do so again. Faultline had made the very ground War Fiend was standing on become like quicksand and sunk him a hundred feet into the ground. When War Fiend finally hit rock bottom, he had to tunnel his way out, which took over two months. He had to dig his feet into the bedrock to finally move, then dig with his bare hands through miles of rock, clay, and stone to get to the surface. Although his powers wouldn't make it possible for him to die this way, since he didn't need air to survive nor food and water; he still felt like he was suffocating and starving for the entire two months it took to dig his way out.

It took him half a year to get over the trauma, and to that day, he had a great phobia of going underground, for fear of having to repeat the experience a second time. Now that they were gone and couldn't stop his rampage, War Fiend decided to enact the second part of the plan which was drawing K-Force out by crushing and killing any civilian and Hero that got in his way. All the while he planned on calling out K-Force to come die so that he could make his mother, Intercessor, pay for breaking his horn. Once he got confirmation that both hindrances were deposed, for the next three hours he began his rampage through the city.

To everyone else it seemed a fairly normal afternoon; a partly cloudy sky with a cool sixty-eight degree temperature, which was considered brisk in this part of the nation. That was, until a massive explosion caused by a building full of people seeming to collapse on itself. At first, people thought they were demolishing a building until those nearby heard screams of terror and pain from the rubble. They were able to realize the gravity of the attack when the rubble fell away, and a giant of a man at least ten feet tall stepped through the rubble.

War Fiend was a massively broad man with an astonishing height. The best way to describe him would be a bear-like body builder with huge arms and burgundy wine-colored skin. The iris of his eye was obscured by his yellow pupils. His armor was unconventional, but when practically nothing on earth could hurt him, protection was secondary toward looks and functionality. His chest plate looked like an evil knight's armor or what you might find a demon wearing, all in dark jade-like green that glistened of any blood that landed on him. His arms were bare to the world, and the armbands around his biceps were fitted with gauntlets that look like a bear's claw. His uniform was highlighted by black trim around the edges of his armored long boots which had blackened spikes on the kneecaps. Lastly, he donned a spartan-like helmet with one steer horn sticking out of it, as the other horn appeared to be broken or hacked off.

As the demonic being stepped from the rumble, he grinned at the people around him, who looked like sheep before a slaughter, especially those with phones in their hands.

"Time to reap for the power that was given to me, I'm sure you would be glad to pay it for me," War Fiend said to the crowd before summoning a massive claymore-like blade with a curved tip coated with flames, giving it an eerie look. The final touch was the whisper; the tongue was foreign and obviously demonic and anyone who heard it felt the intent. "Feed me. Feed me blood."

And with the swing of the blade, he lopped off the heads of men and women close by. Screams ripped through the air. As the brute began to rampage through the streets, he began killing anybody he could get his hands on. Men, women, old and young, none were spared from his huge blade. It was wholesale slaughter of twenty people before the police arrived. And they too were killed with only one escaping, but not before he tried to ram his car into the ten-foot giant in dark armor.

War Fiend merely grinned at the man's feeble attempts to stall him in any way, but he just walked forward, felt the car crumple his shins and walked onto it, as if it were made of cardboard. This was what he wanted from the people. Besides blood and death brought about by his carnage, he needed the feelings of despair and dread. These fueled War Fiend's power and made him stronger. The more chaos spread around him, the more his powers grew, but these pitiful victims were not nearly enough for him to grow in power yet. That was, until a pair of Heroes stepped up to stop him. The one on the left called himself Super Bass, and the one on the right was his partner, Empress Hornet.

Both of them were Alpha and Bravo-class respectively from Los Angeles, which meant they were poaching from the locals hoping to gain more fame bypassing the red tape that was bureaucracy. Super Bass had on modern club wear in a blue and purple pattern, with an open vest. Empress Hornet wore a tasteful cross-strap bikini in a yellow and black color with a hint of brown surrounding it. They at first looked scared but decided to chance it and confront the demonic mercenary.

"Stop right there, you punk and prepare for," Super Bass started.

"Can we skip the drivel. I'm here for a real opponent and Hero who has yet known defeat. And you are not K-Force, which means I'm not interested," War Fiend yawned in faux boredom.

"Hah, that hothead. I'm not surprised that he's the cause of all this," Super Bass said.

"Hah, please, it's nothing personal, but someone has put up a lot of money because he's too big of threat," said War Fiend, again trying to dismiss the little Hero.

"Either way, you won't be seeing him, because you will deal with me first. Super Bass," the Hero introduced himself, striking a pose that was more cheesy than anything. Then he unleashed a wave of sonic screams towards War Fiend.

The reverb from his cry would make lesser Villains wince in pain, but War Fiend saw all this as mere annoyance. The sonic Hero fired off a wave of sound that caused the air to ripple in its wake but only seemed to splash against the armored chest. This caused Super Bass to look on in slight shock. Even if the force of his attack did nothing, the sound would typically have some kind of effect. War Fiend merely gave a dark grin and walked towards the pair, warming up his sword arm by swinging the blazing piece of metal as if it were nothing.

Super Bass tried to up his power, and this time the ground rippled as it cracked under his waves of sonic energy that swept towards the demonic-armored giant of a man. Again the sonic energy did nothing as it seemed to splash harmlessly against War Fiend, who kept walking towards the pair with nary a worry. Super Bass tried again, holding it as long as he could, but it seemed there was nothing he could do to deter the blood-splattered Villain. The footsteps were getting louder, and he seemed to stomp his large boot prints into the ground as he stepped towards the young and soon-to-be-dead pair. As soon as he got fifty feet from his target, Super Bass unleashed a massive wave that destroyed windows for over half a mile, cracked the walls, ripped crevices almost a half a foot deep. Cars within the blast radius crumpled in on themselves and were flipped hundreds of yards away, and this force was held for a solid minute. It was a force that could carve a cave through a mountain, yet all of that power did nothing to War Fiend as he got within distance and grabbed hold of the Hero, stabbing his sword right through his stomach. He then lifted him high into the air as the razor-sharp blade and gravity cut him into twain; the people who were still stupid enough to stay and watch screamed in horror at such an easy disposal of a Hero, causing great fear and despair. That made War Fiend finally feel he had more than enough power to kill his target.

Empress Hornet was in total shock at her partner's butchering, and she was not being able to save him. She was his ride, so to speak, and helped him move about. The big lummox that he was, Super Bass was not that mobile. But he forgot to warn her about the last attack and high-powered sound hurts like hell to an insect, especially to someone who inherited super senses along with her amplified hornet mimicry powers. Seeing Super Bass struggle to stop the sword slicing through his body was going to haunt her nightmares.

"Well it has been a couple of years since I pulled the wings off a bug, but let's see if it is still just as fun as when I was a kid," War Fiend grinned darkly.

Empress Hornet zipped away from the brute as fast as possible, not wanting to share the same fate as her recently deceased partner. But she also couldn't run away, for she was being watched and televised by others. If she fled, her career and credibility would be shot and all the hard work, ass kissing, 'casting couch' deals, would have been for nothing. Though she was not going to fight this monster alone, Super Bass may have been an idiot trying to fight a borderline Omega-level Villain.

"This is Empress Hornet. Super Bass is dead. I repeat, Super Bass is dead, and I'm fighting a high-level Alpha criminal, War Fiend," Empress Hornet was dodging all the thrown debris and crushed cars nearby while she called for assistance. "I need back up. I repeat. I need back up NOW!"

"Understood, just stall him long enough for back up to arrive. ETA three minutes," the responder said.

"Understood, just get here soon, I can't hurt him and I'm pretty sure that he will go after citizens if he loses interest in hurting me," Empress said, giving her opinion as she fired her venom stingers which bounced off War Fiend's frame.

"Copy, we will get help as fast as possible." The Hero Headquarters dispatcher assured her.

Empress Hornet decided the safest route to handling this monster from a demonic nightmare was strafing shot and blows. She had heard this War Fiend couldn't fly, so she did not have trouble fighting while keeping out of his range.

First, Empress Hornet brought out her stingers which grew out of her arms and wrists and were known to pierce through a foot of temper steel and dose them with venom of various types, hoping that one would work. Sadly, despite her being able to shoot her stingers out at three times the speed of a regular bullet, all they did was annoy the demonic brute. With his armor and magical forcefield, it was more like smacking a bug off the windshield of a car. It was annoying, because it may cause a stain, but it was not effective. The only sting that worked was a gas-like substance which only made his healing abilities activate. While he didn't need to breathe, the gas seemed to seep into his skin surprisingly as a poisonous oiled mist. And the biggest surprise was this little buzzing was to hinder his movement by destroying the ground he walked on.

Empress Hornet might have been rated lower Heroine, but she was no fool. She had heard all about War Fiend being on the top-ten list of criminals that she wanted to avoid. He took delight in the deaths of Meta-human Heroes or criminals, not because he hated them, but because it was almost as if he got off on their deaths.

"Annoying pest, come down here. Or are you too scared to face me head on?" War Fiend beckoned.

"No, I'm not stupid enough to charge at someone as powerful as you without a plan," she yelled back, as she continued to fly around and away from him.

She was flying far too fast and out of range for his anti-air weapon to work against her and decided to play off of the one thing Heroes were obligated to consider when playing this tactic—aim for civilians. The best part was that people were idiots and always trying to find a way to get famous on social media, or just watch a deadly battle.

"A mixture of sheep and lemmings the lot of them," War Fiend said out loud.

"It would be best for the gene pool to remove them from the equation." War Fiend charged at the crowd of bystanders.

Empress Hornet tried to disrupt the man's steps, but it was too late. He began to use his main power which meant that once he was in motion he stayed in motion, and nothing and no one could stand in his way. He bulldozed through a crowd of onlookers, adding dozens of more innocent deaths to his rampage. And it didn't look like he was going to stop.

Empress Hornet hated that he maneuvered her into a corner and knew that she had to fight him head on or somehow hurt him enough to pull his attention towards her and away from civilians.

Let's hope the ultimate lance does the job, or worst case scenario, my leg becomes an accordion, the wasp-themed Heroine thought as she flew hundreds of miles into the sky. Empress Hornet transformed her right leg into a chitinous, piercing black blade, one the greatest defenses in the Meta-human world. Nathan Sparks called her to test a new armor to be able to fight a Xenonian like the Ms. Marvelous family, and with this attack; punched a hole right through it.

Then, with a deep breath, she began to dive bomb at a speed equivalent to Mach 10 with a piercing sword-like kick that should at least pierce or cut into her opponents' flesh. When maximum speed was met, she dove right into the center of where the man's gut would be. When the ultimate sword and the ultimate shield met each other, the forces fought against each other for a few seconds, as if they were battling themselves. Empress Hornet's power folded in on itself, and her leg crumpled and cracked like a rice crispy treat, but instead of marshmallow, it was muscle fibers holding her leg together.

The Heroine stopped screaming after a few seconds, as the pain made her pass out, which was less fun for War Fiend, though he did enjoy the suffering that was coming off of her.

"Ah, the sensations of war, fear, despair, suffering, and death, all fuel me and push Astaroth's War Fiend into heights of power." War Fiend grinned at his new prey collapsing by his feet.

"Now, for K-Force to show up before those witches from Oregon or Washington show up," War Fiend muttered to himself.

War Fiend was extremely strong, almost impossible to stop once he was determined in a course of action. But strong magic, or something of a holy or divine nature, could still hurt him. The

Mystical Shaman in Oregon or the spiteful Witch who used a rare magic force was more than strong enough to actually hurt him and beat him, if he was sloppy. Seeing as his target had not arrived yet, he decided to push the issue, as he was on a timetable and he had an hour before any real magical backup might arrive. War Fiend picked up the partly shattered Heroine Empress Hornet and moved towards a man with a camera pointed towards him. Seeing the man had a large, wet stain on his pants meant that he would do anything to stay alive.

"Hey, dickless, get your dumbass over here and make this broadcast live," War Fiend said.

"Ye, yes sir," the camera man said in fear.

Soon, across the city, on all the local news channels, whether live TV or online, the confrontation was played across all the new outlets. This was ratings gold, even if people were dying.

"Okay, everyone I'm War Fiend, and if you couldn't guess I'm the bad guy," War Fiend said in a dark amused tone. "And I already took care of two of your brightest and youngest out. Now I want K-Force here, or else. Why? It doesn't matter, but if you must know, he has become too good at his job lately, and it is my job to make sure there is always enough job openings for up-and-coming superheroes, by removing the old one. And if he isn't here in these next fifteen minutes, I'm going to take my time and enjoy this sweet, fresh Heroine."

The Heroine was still out cold from the pain and shock of her leg crumpling in on itself. Empress Hornet's face was shown to the camera as the giant, meaty hand lifted her head for the world to see. The demonic mercenary's dark grin told everyone what he was going to do, which was not a bluff. He had sexually assaulted several Heroines over the years and had gotten away with it, because he never stayed in the same area long enough for an Omega-level Hero to catch him. This was the best way for him to gain power because when he left his victims alive, they would become constant batteries of feeling, fear, despair, and mental suffering for all their days. This was a treasure trove for one connected to an abyssal plane of power, which was an entity all in itself.

The one time he ran into the current Ms. Marvelous he had lost, since she had enough power to surpass his strength. Even she was able to take him down at the height of his power with one punch. And she wasn't going full power, which meant that he couldn't match her in brute force. Not to mention, she was faster than him, so he could not hit her, no matter how hard he tried. The only reason he escaped was because of his magical amulet that allowed him to transport to a predetermined place, namely his home base.

Now that his demands were made, he knew the young Hero would come flying in, like an idiot. War Fiend could kill the little idiot trying to save the damsel in distress and add insult to injury. He would enjoy creating another beacon for him to draw on. That was his plan, before he was smacked hard enough to send him away from Empress Hornet. A purple and gold figure stood tall and was ready to throw down with a cocky grin on his face.

"I'm sorry K-Force has been grounded for being a naughty little boy. But I can play with ya," Primetime said.

Though the blow only knocked War Fiend away a few steps, it did get his attention. It was something his natural defense could not shrug off.

"Finally, someone within my own weight class," War Fiend said. But just before he could grab his hostage, a shadow swallowed her into the ground and moved her away.

A woman in a Goth-like black and purple armor appeared, floating above the both of them with a grimace of distain on her face. Wraith Queen may have become Professional but her clothes still spoke to the Goth background of her early years. Her black and purple-highlighted metal-covered corset lifted her pert chest while showing little cleavage. Her arms and legs were covered in dark gray and silver metal gauntlets that reached to her elbows and boots, and traveled mid-thigh with a kilt-length purple skirt. Her skin was deathly pale and her facial features were hidden in her hood, with the exception of white, glowing face paint in the shape of a skull.

"Don't worry, pretty. I'll get to you after this little turd learns the hard lessons in life," War Fiend said cockily.

Primetime, too eager to continue bantering, decided to jump-punch in the dark, helmeted face of War Fiend. The massive merc just grinned as his head was turned with the blow. War Fiend unleashed a blow which made Primetime take a few steps back. Primetime touched his face as he actually felt the pain from that strike.

"There is always someone higher on the totem pole," War Fiend said as he unsummoned his sword. He wanted to enjoy the scrap as a warmup for the real fight ahead of him.

Soon, the two massive forces clashed in the middle of Santa Ana. Back and forth, they tussled by throwing punches and blows that tore the very street they were standing on. Shockwaves and their bodies tumbled across the landscape, destroying everything in their wake. Wraith Queen used her power to evacuate the civilians who still refused to leave the battleground. There were those angry with her for moving them away or ruining their shot.

"Go back if you want, but if you die, it is on you," she told them in a bored and disappointed tone that most Goths master in high school.

She didn't even care about new reporters after they tried to sue her for saving them. She decided if they wanted to die for their art, she would let them.

As she came back to a nearby rooftop, Wraith Queen looked on at her ego-driven protégé though she felt more like a babysitter. Her people made her look after their new golden goose who was supposed to be the face for the next ten to twenty years. Scientists projected that the young man could grow to peak Alpha, maybe a borderline Omega, so they wanted one of their biggest headliners and employees to look after Primetime.

One problem, despite have his ass delivered to him twice, and almost losing in the semifinals, he still thought of himself as invincible. Flukes, he called it, as if he could dismiss being knocked out cold for an hour. She wanted to train Primetime properly by smacking him around with the one thing that was a weakness to eighty-eight percent of the Hero community - magic.

Her powers allowed her more than the ability to move and teleport wherever shadows existed. She could morph and manipulate them to take form of anything. Swallowing the light over a city block to blind her opponents, she could use this power to attack with rare force or enhance some magical spell. She freely used magical powers, giving opponents great bouts of pain or fear, and these were only a few of the things she could do.

Wraith Queen's job was supposed to guide Primetime and keep him safe. This was made all the harder by the fact that he didn't listen. It had nothing to do with her being a woman; he was just an arrogant little skid mark, whose few battles with villains were won by his powers alone and a stroke of sheer luck. Wraith Queen wanted Primetime to run into someone stronger and would let him hit rock bottom to learn his lesson.

War Fiend was not the lesson she wanted him to learn. The man was a murderer. He did not care for the delicate balance that was an unspoken rule between the two sides. Pros do not kill or permanently hurt Villains, and Villains matched them in that respect. War Fiend was one of the outliers, and he was strong enough to toss aside most Heroes. He could escape those that could actually take him down. She should help Primetime, but, like she thought, maybe an objective lesson was needed. Soon she heard a thump beside her, only to see K-Force standing there.

"Why are you here?" Wraith Queen was mildly surprised.

"I choose Empress Hornet's safety over my career. Besides I'm only kicked out of the Professional track. The Feds would hire me just to piss off the current governor for his crappy policies for the last six years," K-Force stated.

"Ha, wish I had your confidence, but I should warn you, my company agent is telling me to hold you here so Primetime can win the glory," Wraith Queen said in a sardonic tone.

"Sure, but Primetime is not going to win," K-Force said with certainty.

"What do you mean?" Wraith Queen knew several reasons why this was so, but she was curious to hear his reason.

"War Fiend is a professional merc and trained. Before he slaughtered his comrades to gain power from a high demon prince, he was a Russian marine force turned merc. While Primetime's fight skills seem to have improved since our last bout, let me guess, he's still relying on his power," K-Force knew the type.

"Very much so," Wraith Queen admitted.

"Primetime also has no experience fighting magical opponents who are infamous for going around almost any defenses. He is letting the guy pound on him, believing he can get high on his own hype. So Primetime is ignoring most of the shots he has taken, just so he can play up for the remaining cameras nearby how tough he is. Primetime is going to give the people a slugfest to make this battle more epic. War Fiend is the king of that style of fighting," K-Force pointed out.

"Number three?"

"Primetime is already winded. The guy needs to work on his stamina and conditioning. It seems that he never pushed himself in training, always relaying on his power to see him through," K-Force finished.

"And you do?" Wraith Queen retorted, not believing it.

"Twice a week, even on suspension I try to break my limits by using a dampener wristband I use to keep myself sharp," K-Force said.

"Just like Intercessor." Wraith Queen had seen that type of training before.

"And my father and sister too. I was taught from an early age never to rely solely on a weapon or tool because it might be taken from you or fail you. And even if it is heaven's tool, a fool with a divine weapon is still a fool against a real warrior," recited one of his mother's mantras.

Wraith Queen looked on at the young Hero who didn't feel like these Ivy League graduates. This felt like a child soldier who was raised with compassion, but with steel in his spine.

Again the blond bimbo lucks out with a great rookie who knows what the hell he's doing, Wraith Queen thought, as the no holds barred fight between the muscle-bound Meta continued. While technically stronger, Primetime lacked the ability to put War Fiend down or even try to capitalize on the opportunity when it presented itself.

Primetime was able to send the big brute flying a couple of times, but it did nothing to the demonic giant. As soon as Primetime felt that holding back wasn't going to work, he finally unleashed his full power that could put craters in mountains. These were the blows that he had been working on since his battle with K-Force and Azougue. Those two were somehow able to withstand his punches, only because he held back. Now, against a highly dangerous individual that had the rabid label, this meant that he could do anything to him to win. Because War Fiend was such a monster and killer, there would be no penalties, which meant no more holding back. The blows echoed and sent miniature shock waves as each punch landed on the demon who felt each blow a lot more now. War Fiend was even surprised that one of them dented his armor, something that only could be done by elite Alphas and Omega-level Meta-humans.

"I guess it is time to quit playing with him," War Fiend grinned. As he charged forward an aura of power surrounded him. Primetime saw it as a stupid move by a knucklehead, only to be tossed aside. This left Primetime with a shocked looked on his face. As he tried to punch his opponent he felt something slow down his jump forward while War Fiend shoulder-charged and sent Primetime flying through three buildings. This was followed quickly by War Fiend seeming to turn up the speed and was soon right on top of the young Meta-human.

"I admit, you are pretty strong," War Fiend lifted the dazed Primetime, who was now familiar with the old forgotten sensation of pain. "But strength is not the only thing that makes a warrior," War Fiend said as the glowing aura that covered his blows, punched his opponent repeatedly, over and over again, until he felt the Hollywood pretty boy's nose get crushed.

Then he tossed the almost whimpering fool through a couple more buildings. War Fiend began to systematically break down his opponent. He charged at a high-rate speed and began crushing his little playmate. The fight degraded even worse as Primetime tried to fight back, but every blow he threw was off-target and flailed more like a scared teen than a powerful Hero.

If any professional fighter or coach was watching this, they would realize that the fight was over because Primetime was desperately trying not to lose. K-Force had to give him credit for not running like a coward, but to still keep fighting under these conditions was not an intelligent move. Several times Wraith Queen asked for the chance to relieve Primetime and pull him out of a battle he couldn't win. But their agent/handler said that making sure K-Force didn't interfere was more important, which K-Force couldn't believe what he was hearing. He looked at his so-called captor and didn't want to stop the fight, mostly because he was secretly enjoying Primetime getting the beating of a lifetime. It came to the point that War Fiend actually walked over Primetime, stomping his boots. Each time he did, his bones would break and a scream escaped Primetime's lips.

"I think it is time to tell your agent to shut up and save Primetime," K-Force rose to his feet, ready to tag in.

"You're right, I don't think my handler is working rationally here," Wraith Queen charged up her magic for another teleportation spell.

Without saying a word, K-Force used his built-up momentum to jump toward the War Fiend, who was about to stomp on Primetime's head like an overly ripe pumpkin, only to be stopped by K-Force who blocked and absorbed a large amount of kinetic energy from it.

War Fiend looked down in surprise at what stopped him and grinned at his target finally showing up.

"*Finally*, I'm on a tight schedule so be a dear and drop dead for me," War Fiend said in a condescending tone.

Chapter 18
Going Gonzo in San Alonso

As K-Force lifted the metal-plated boot from Primetime's skull, the shadows swallowed the rookie and whisked him from the battlefield. With him gone, K-Force decided to unleash as much pain as possible on this tank of a butcher and pulled the big brute into a split. This was boosted by War Fiend who tried to kick K-Force away. Normally, War Fiend's power and durability would protect him, but he overstretched his own muscle, not an outside force. This had the added effect of embarrassing the demonic man, while hurting him a bit.

This ticked War Fiend off as he got to his feet, skipped the 'foreplay' and charged forward. When he slammed into his target, K-Force merely slid a few feet and shook it off. This raised War Fiend's eye, in that he felt no one should be able to ignore his attack. Again he punched with his dashing ability on the twerp, who negated it by jumping a few feet back on impact. This should be impossible, because the rule of his powers, beside immense strength and durability, was that once he was in motion, his body stayed in motion, unless he stopped himself. But this brat seemed to be able to take it.

This soon became the least of his problems as the first blow was returned, and it actually lifted him off his feet and sent him tumbling backwards. The blow was side-aimed at the top of his chest. When War Fiend got up, he looked even more surprised as he felt that blow, and it was equal to his own blows.

That's impossible. He is not Xeonoid or Omega who can control an aspect of reality, War Fiend thought as he got to his feet and tried to rush down his opponent. K-Force put his guard up and took the three blows that would kill any Meta without a high defense. War Fiend was getting disturbed as he was getting blows that were just as strong as his own. While War Fiend was a former marine, he was rusty in hand to hand when it came to combat because he was so strong he didn't need it as much. Now, he was regretting it since this kid was using kickboxing moves that surpassed any of his previous combat skills.

Most high-powered Metas had little use for hand to hand or combat tactics. Again, neither did he, but he was someone who could take what he threw and give it back. The fight was getting more and more grand, and soon there was a large crater in the middle of the street. It was growing more and more damaging with each blow that increased in power. K-Force would have loved to get him out the city, but every attempt to toss him was blocked, almost as if another force was keeping the miniature giant pinned to the earth. So instead, K-Force decided to keep going until he either gained enough force to beat him or tired out. Despite how unstoppable this demonic merc presented himself, there were upper limits to how much damage he could take.

K-Force and War Fiend eventually backed away from each other, which left observers surprised. War Fiend's armor was a lot more damaged than many had ever seen it, while K-Force was no worse for the wear as he was able to block every blow on his arm and shoulder, and he was able to counter hit. In considering brute force, everybody believed War Fiend was stronger, but K-Force's durability and skill kept him in the fight.

While separated, K-Force decided that it was time to make sure this monster didn't escape, so he put up a ring-sized football field over a hundred feet high. This seemed appropriate since he had never seen this beast jump half a foot.

I guess when you specialize in brute force and defense so high that only the top tier Alphas and Omegas are your only threat, mobility is not your main concern, K-Force thought as he closed off the area.

"You're actually trying to keep me from escaping you, ha," War Fiend's dark laugh almost seemed cartoonish until it became clear that the man was a ruthless murderer.

"It's so you don't try to grab someone, when you know you can't win, like Hyper-Man two months ago," responded K-Force, knowing that was a sore spot.

"You little shit, I'm going to bash that smart mouth of yours through your ass," War Fiend said, his eyes seeming to glow red.

Again, the massive brute charged forward and again he merely made his target sidestep and take half the damage from the attack. The fight was getting more destructive, but no one was near enough to get caught up in it, except reporters in helicopters, drones, and rooftops nearby. Those who were watching saw that it was becoming more and more clear that K-Force had the advantage in this fight. War Fiend refused to let his target get the better of him and called forth his sword, gleaming and coated in fire again.

"Let's see if you can take this," War Fiend challenged as he charged forward, only for K-Force to jump away from the blow of the sword. The more the demon merc swung his sword, the more K-Force back-pedaled from the attack.

"Afraid?" War Fiend grinned as he finally had the upper hand.

"Nope, just not stupid enough to think my powers can trump magical weapons." K-Force had learned that lesson hard from his father, who told him many stories of how magic trumped regular superpowers any day.

K-Force was a lot more cautious than most would be with his power, but he was not stupid enough just to sit and take an attack from an unknown weapon. Instead, he waited and watched for an opening to attack. With his immense strength, War Fiend could move the blade in near-supersonic levels, like his fists. With his power, he could increase the cutting force even more. Normally, this meant you would have to dodge the cutting wind attacks from the blade as well, but luckily, only the blade was magical, not the air-cutting attacks. Also, K-Force was faster than people expected since he never needed to use it because he was never pushed.

K-Force ducked quickly into War Fiend's guard and gripped his wrist, though he had to use both hands as the man was tripped off balance then pushed onto his back. K-Force used the opportunity to twist and break his grip upon the blade. Whatever force that refused to let War Fiend from being lifted from the ground didn't seem to keep him from tripping. When K-Force touched the blade, he felt a large amount of mental anguish and hate wanting to be wielded. So disgusted he was by this weapon, that he threw it far away from War Fiend, who quickly rose to his feet and raised his twisted hand.

It seemed the damage he gave War Fiend healed as the demonic merc popped and twisted his wrist back in place with almost no signs of pain, though K-Force could see the fiend's anger at getting damaged in that way.

"Got any other tricks, or can we end this?" K-Force felt somewhat confident after getting rid of the magical item.

"Just one." War Fiend grinned.

That grin felt ominous, so much so that K-Force saw a faded, magical snake pass, then on instinct or pure luck, he jumped to the side, while the same blade had thrown away was suddenly cutting a clean slice through K-Force's arm. Resisting the urge to look at his wound, he saw a phantom-like chain pull the blade back to War Fiend, who darkly chuckled at his wounded opponent.

"Impressed?" War Fiend said as he tossed the blade into the air away from him and the ghost-like chains quickly wrapped around the hilt of the blade and brought it back into his hand. "I can't be separated from my weapon. Though, good try on your part, I don't think I ever met someone who ever gave me this much trouble who wasn't an Elite. I guess that's why they want you dead. You are too dangerous to be allowed to grow."

With that, War Fiend in his off-sword hand fired a chain at him, which K-Force dodged by quick-stepping away. Quick-stepping consisted of a small burst of speed he used to move at high speed in a small area. Long distance he was not that fast, but within a mile he could move as fast as most super speedsters.

Though the move seemed to surprise War Fiend, he quickly sent out two more chains, only for a forcefield to be placed in front of him. Logistically, this didn't matter since they easily ghosted through walls, though it did clue War Fiend in.

"You can see them, how?" War Fiend soon figured out as he said it. "Right, you're the Mage slayer's son."

Mage slayer was the nickname Armory gained for himself since he was infamous for killing all powerful magicians who wanted to rule/remake the world. Hence, he was considered a danger to anyone with magic.

"You know, it was because of that damn sword he gave to your whore of mother that I lost my horn. Maybe taking something precious from them would ease the pain," War Fiend said as he rubbed the stump of his left horn. Then he fired three more chains, and K-Force dodged as fast as possible around the mercenary. K-Force tried to get in close, but War Fiend used his swords as a flaming shield to block attacks.

K-Force realized that he would have to chance it to get a good shot in. So, gritting his teeth, K-Force plunged through the flames and tried to ignore the heat. As his shield thickened to protect him from the damage, slammed a massive punch right to the side of the helmet. Though the helmet protected him, the punch made War Fiend slide across the ground on his back for twenty feet.

Despite the impressive blow, it was a major mistake. K-Force punched with his injured right arm and it allowed War Fiend to wrap the chains around said arm. Then he squeezed it as he pulled K-Force off his feet and slammed a huge fist into his gut. K-Force did moan but only from the pain of his arm being squeezed.

"Finally I have you where I want you." War Fiend grinned darkly as he held the annoying Hero by the neck. Then he dismissed the sword once more as he pulled K-Force close enough to smell his foul breath, which smelled like rotten chewing tobacco and sulfur.

"I'm not going to let you die easily for your embarrassment of me. Before you get absorbed into my blade I'm going to break you first," and with that, War Fiend slammed a massive punch into K-Force that sent him flying away, then tumbled roughly across the street for a few hundred meters and slammed into a building. Then the chain still wrapped around his damaged, bleeding arm and was pulled him back towards War Fiend again. Next, War Fiend decided to use K-Force as a human paddle ball by slamming him into the gut and sending him out into the air, then bringing him back with chains to punch him back out again. War Fiend did this several times and counted each time his fist connected, as if he were trying to break his record and the Hero at the same time.

K-Force's arm was going through the worst pain from the crushing force from the chains, and the fact that it was being stretched out of his socket made things worse. More and more blood started to leak out from his wounds, which were dripping at this point.

Boom. "18." Another massive punch landed, only to get reeled back towards War Fiend's huge fist. Boom. "19 and," War Fiend seemed to wind up for a massive punch that would have killed a lesser Meta-human. Boom. "20." The last hit was so strong that actual shockwaves blew away debris and caused an explosion that was equivalent. This would have wiped out an entire section of San Alonso, and yet the shields still didn't drop. Everything within the field was tossed around and uprooted, as if a massive hurricane tore through this entire area. Then, the chain flew out to its maximum length, which seemed to be a mile, and dragged K-Force hurtling back into the ground with a big human-sized imprint of his body into the asphalt, about five times the size of wrecking ball dropped from the same height. K-Force wanted to scream in pain when the last pull of the chain popped and twisted his arm out of place, but he refused to let this monster leave the area, so he kept focusing on the wall he erected.

War Fiend was enjoying himself, deciding to do an old favorite of his which was digging up the road with someone's face. So, the demonic merc slammed the rising Hero back into the dirt with his massive foot. He grabbed him by the neck, rammed his face into the ground, then tilled the road with his makeshift plough. This usually was meant to rub in how outmatched his opponent was, while making a statement that War Fiend should never be messed with. When he was finally done, War Fiend lifted up his surprisingly strong opponent. War Fiend wanted to look in the young Hero's eyes before he killed him and sent his head to the Southeast MHEAT headquarters to his father. The young man's right arm was absolutely wrecked, with blood flowing down to his pants which surprisingly looked like they were only scraped. The only real clothing damage was the cracked mask with an opening which exposed a part of his face. War Fiend thought about removing K-Force's mask for the world to see but decided to let him die with it on as a respect to a worthy opponent.

As War Fiend held K-Force by his head with one hand, he summoned the fire-coated blade ready to stab through him, just like the wimp earlier that day.

"I have to thank you. You are the most fun I had in a long time," War Fiend said as he raised his blade to strike, only for K-Force to grab the monster thumb that was holding his head. K-Force broke it by bending it all the way to the back of War Fiend's hand which released him from War Fiend's grip and made the villain lose his concentration with his chains. This released K-Force.

As K-Force landed on his hunches, he struck out with a raising knee charged into War Fiend's crotch. While this was covered and protected, the blow was so strong that it left a big dent in the crotch plate, causing the blade to fall from War Fiend's hand. Then he rolled and jumped away until his back was up against a literal wall. As War Fiend recovered from having an impromptu vasectomy, K-Force looked over his own injuries. Despite all the absorbing power, he felt that many punches with that much power was like wearing a helmet in football practice. Yes, he was protected but he still felt some bells ringing here and there. The fact that he was actually being grinded into the street meant that he needed to concentrate more. He should have been able block this, but he needed to keep the Field up so that the merc couldn't run away. The wounds on his left arm and right leg were scrapes, in all truth and honesty. The right arm was broken beyond normal repair. His shoulder was popped out, and he was sure that his elbow was crushed by the chains' repeated use of him as a yo-yo.

Remember this - pain is there to remind you of your mistakes. Only when you let it stop you from doing what needs to be done, does it become weakness, K-Force thought as he began to regain his breath. He looked towards his opponent who was approaching to block out the sun with his large frame. Instead of running away, K-Force charged up his fist, getting ready to unleash the mother of all left hooks.

"You're still willing to fight, hah! I'll give you this, you are a lot braver than most of your pampered counterparts," War Fiend spoke calmly, but it was plain to see that he was more than a little pissed and wanted to kill K-Force on a more personal level. "But do you still think you can win."

"Yes I do,"

"Oh, and why is that," asked War Fiend. He closed in as fast as he could, at around three hundred miles per hour, only for K-Force to sidestep and unleashed a glowing fist to the face. The blow was strong enough to actually lift War Fiend off the ground and send him flying back.

"You duck and run when things get tough, when you experience pain, people like you run away or get others to do your job to avoid it." K- Force started to visibly allow the energy of his power to flow all around. "Me, I respect pain, understand its lessons, and never run from it. It is not a question of who's more powerful, but who can deliver the most pain before the other party quits. And it is not someone who ducks out like a punk."

This actually infuriated War Fiend being disrespected as such, and in public, since he knew cameras were rolling. He couldn't walk away now, which meant he had to kill this kid and fast. As he rose to his feet War Fiend felt and saw something that he had not seen in a long-time, his own blood.

How strong is this kid? War Fiend thought in fear.

K-Force took a deep breath and released a lot of tension in his body and focused on the target in front of him. He knew he would lose if he used anything less than lethal force. Well, I'm already in trouble for breaking my parole, so killing him shouldn't be too much of a problem since he has a kill order for most of the US.

K-Force dashed in a zig-zag pattern from different directions as he rushed towards War Fiend, who was trying to keep track. As soon as K-Force came near him, War Fiend would time the attack perfectly and he would gut him, or at least seriously injure the young Hero. That was until K-Force kicked the air in front of him to reverse momentum, causing War Fiend to miss his attack. K-Force used the overswing to duck into War Fiend's guard and strike right into his exposed armpit. Despite the pain, War Fiend sent out his chains again to entrap K-Force once more.

This tactic succeeded again as it wrapped around K-Force's left bicep, but instead of retreating, K-Force went towards War Fiend and swept the man's leg from underneath him. While War Fiend was on his back, K-Force wrapped the chain around his sword arm as well and twisted the entire arm until it was at a breaking point.

"You are not going to do, ARGGH!" War Fiend was writhing on the ground in pain. K-Force was standing on his back, holding War Fiend's arm in place, then popped and twisted his arm free from his shoulder by kicking the joint and pulling it the wrong way. Then in a quick succession, he snapped his elbow by bringing it down over his knee. The move was brutal, but at this point, K-Force didn't care. He wasn't going to die because some people were too sensitive.

"Now we are even," K-Force said, unconsciously rubbing his limp arm. K-Force wanted to end it right then and there, but he knew that whatever spell or magic item might send him away if he ever came into danger was going to activate if he went for the killing blow. So, the best he could do was to injure War Fiend so badly he could be taken in by MHEAT.

K-Force waited for the massive man to stop rolling on the ground in pain. In what seemed like a few minutes, he realized he was right on the money about the man not being a big fan of pain. It took War Fiend a few minutes to try to get to his feet, but he was enraged at what was happening to him. Even if he was injured, the magic in him should have been able to heal or soothe his wounds by that point.

This brat is not normal, even by Meta standards. He has something to hampers my powers, thought War Fiend, who was furious that he would have to retreat, and that he couldn't win as confidently as he expected. "Tactical retreat for now and next time take him out as quickly as possible."

War Fiend saw the wall about three hundred yards away and figured he could plow right through it with no problem, only to find out it was harder than he originally thought. Once he reached a hundred miles per hour, he started to push into the golden-yellow wall of hexagons, but he was slightly pushed back.

"That's impossible, nothing can stop me," War Fiend said in disbelief as he looked at the only cage that could contain him. He tried to run another wall at his max speed of over seven hundred miles per hour, only for the wall to briefly flicker than return back to normal. No, it actually looked stronger, almost like it was magic.

"Magic?" War Fiend accused.

"Like I'd tell you anything," K-Force said with his own blood lust flaring in him.

War Fiend, seeing the only way out was to kill the brat, called forth his sword again, but in his left hand, since the right was still broken beyond repair at this time. He charged at K-Force with full intent to kill the young Hero, but his opponent was too nimble, even with just one arm. And his counter attacks were getting gradually more painful. The punches that got through actual hurt him, and he could not return any of the pain, despite how desperate he was becoming. Strangely, there was a lot of low kick focus at his right leg.

Then, as if Astaroth was helping his avatar, K-Force got cut across his arm, allowing more blood to flow. He needed this, and he felt the hope from the viewers, the people nearby watching in despair. This was needed to turn things more into his favor. So, after getting a small foothold War Fiend charged forward to take back the battle. K-Force simply did a small front kick aim at War

Fiend's right leg, near the kneecap, which caused it to bend inward and caused War Fiend to fall forward.

As War Fiend fell forward, K-Force grabbed the back of his head, then slammed an energy-charged knee strike into the man's face. This shattered the helmet and his nose which laid the demonic merc down. This was not the end, as K-Force jumped over a hundred meters into the air to deliver a massive axe kick that drove War Fiend into a fifty-foot crater into the ground and caving in the mercenary's armor, which seemed invincible.

The man was knocked out cold, with bile released from his stomach, and it was safe to say that K-Force had won. But despite being filled with that monster's energy, he was still mentally exhausted from the whole ordeal. He lowered the shield as it was not needed anymore and hopped out of the crater, looking for the nearest raised sidewalk to sit.

He found the closest perch which was next to a retro ice cream malt shop that promised gluten-free milkshakes and vegan options. As he sat, he noticed another shadow that seemed to grow before him. Wraith Queen in her gothic regalia seemed to study him as if he were an interesting experiment.

"I am impressed. I thought you were just blowing smoke when you said you train with pain," Wraith Queen said as she looked down at the very strong rookie.

"Most do, since few are willing to seek pain unless it is a kink of theirs," K-Force said in a slightly ragged voice.

"Trust me, in the crowd I hung with in the '90s, I knew quite a few who were into that sort of thing." Wraith Queen grinned and decided to stand next to the tired-looking Hero. It would not do well for her to sit down like a normal human being. "So, why didn't you finish him?" Wraith Queen wondered why Armory's son had not taken the killing blow when presented with the opportunity.

"Remember him teleporting away whenever anyone has a lethal blow against him? It did seem an unconscious action, so whether a passive spell or magical item, I will check in a few. But right now, I need a breather," K-Force said, taking a few deep breaths.

"I'll say, so how long until your arm is back in working order?" Wraith Queen asked.

"I give it a week. The magic from the cut of that sword seems to block any healing attempt from my body." K-Force was seeing why so many died by that monster's hand.

"Question?"

"Ask, but can't promise any answers," K-Force replied.

"Fair enough, you were able to see his chains. Something that many can't do unless they have magic within them," Wraith Queen stated out of genuine curiosity.

"Yes, I have magic, but minor in the grand scheme of things," K-Force admitted.

"Magic sight is very useful. Few have access to it, but I understand. 'Minor' as you put it," Wraith Queen said to the battered and bruised but still handsome Hero who looked like he could use a cigarette or vape. Then she saw her protégé hobble towards his tormentor who was brought low for the first time in his criminal career.

"Yo, Prime, stop. He is still magically active. Strike him now, and he'll teleport away." K-Force tried to stand to stop him.

"Shut up, I'm going to end this bastard myself." Primetime, the battered and still healing Hero, was about to drive his fist through War Fiend's face only to hit blackish-green flames, leaving nothing behind except a large, human body print and a pissed-off, slightly signed form.

"Whelp, there goes all my hard work," K-Force replied. He lay back on the ground wanting to say 'screw it' and just rest for a bit.

"You're not upset?" Wraith Queen was surprised that he wasn't angrier.

"At this point, I'm too sore and tired to care. As long as War Fiend is away from this area and innocent people are safe, I'll take that as a win," responded K-Force, not wanting to do anything for at least an hour.

With this, Wraith Queen laughed loudly at how a nonchalant rookie had taken down one of the most dangerous villains alive.

February 6
San Alonso

Bronze Bomber was not pleased to be in San Alonso, especially with her old rival. This wasn't a friendly rivalry, as with most Heroes. This was a drag-out, 'I will cut you if you cross me' rivalry. She tried to bury it, but Wraith Queen seemed to have an axe to grind and wanted to bury it in her, which is why calling her to a Meta-human bar in Santa Ana was unusual. When she walked in, there were Meta-humans, Hero fans, and paparazzi. They could barely get through the front door; the strict no press rule at this bar drew a large crowd.

It was run by a former Hero who could talk to machines, so he could shut down anything with recording function, unless it was a fan. And at the moment, she was walking towards her LA counterpart. After sitting down at corner booth, roped off to prevent any fans from disturbing them, they stared at each other in a not-so-subtle way of dislike. After getting the preferred brand of alcohol, Wrath Queen decided to break the ice by saying, "I want K-Force."

This caused Bronze Bomber to cough her whiskey out. It took her a while to get herself under control, but she looked on at her rival.

"I'm not his mother so you're more than welcome to him, but isn't he a little young for you?" Bronze Bomber scoffed.

"Not like that, you uber Bronze Bimbo. What makes you think I was trying to get into his pants?" Wraith Queen slightly glared.

"The last two boys you dated were in elementary school when 9/11 happened." Bronze Bomber had intentionally emphasized 'boys.'

"Fine, there is some interest in that area, but he would benefit more from someone who can help him with his powers," Wraith Queen mildly admitted.

"Oh, and what can you teach him that I can't?" Bronze Bomber said, drinking her whiskey.

"How to use his magical talent," Wraith Queen said calmly, then cracking a grin at Bronze Bomber, she realized she had something over her.

"What magical talent? His powers?" Bronze Bomber asked.

"No, those are from the Meta-human gene. That move War Fiend does that people think is telekinetic actually involves magical chains that he can control with his mind, and K-Force can see them," Wraith Queen explained.

"Wait, you knew this and never told anyone?" Bronze Bomber said.

"This was my first time seeing War Fiend in person," Wraith Queen replied, seeing that as enough explanation, as not everything could be captured on camera.

"Okay, so how are the magical chains relevant?" Bronze Bomber was not seeing the significance of it.

"He could see them because he has a natural, magical sight, meaning he has an untapped gift that I could teach him to harness. This could be a chance to push him to a higher tier if I taught him how to harness that magic and add it to his arsenal." Wraith Queen was eager to be useful in her mentorship.

"As your own apprentice?"

"That little turd is nothing more than a babysitting job my company stuck me with. I'm his third mentor in six months, and the only reason I lasted longer than the others is because I let him hang himself. I don't care about him screwing up since I made it clear that I would only save him, not take blame for his mistakes," Wraith Queen groused, being honest in her opinion on her sidekick.

"That is a bit cold," Bronze Bomber said in surprise.

"You got the real golden child attentive, professional, and humble enough to accept help. I got the little idiot who thinks because he was dominant in his little world that reality would be the same." Wraith Queen was not holding her thoughts back.

"You forget that I'm from a different company, and last I checked Enteriagey and Sky-High Industries were not on the friendliest terms," Bronze Bomber said.

"That's why I am warning you that we as a company are going to poach him. Sorry," Wraith Queen said, not really sorry at all. She expected her rival to be mad, but instead Bronze Bomber was laughing out loud and actually trying to catch her breath.

"Ha! Ha!" With a snort, Bronze Bomber added, "You are going to have a tough time. He made it perfectly clear that he wanted nothing to do with anything between LA and San Francisco;

something about not wanting to be put on the waiting list for work and spending ninety percent of his time trying to be relevant for the press." Bronze Bomber drank confidently, knowing that her sidekick was not going anywhere.

"He will be paid more than your company can provide," Wraith Queen offered.

"Doesn't matter. This boy is not in it for money nor is he fame hungry, so that is not an incentive to him." Bronze Bomber finished her whiskey in amusement.

"Now I know you're full of it," Wraith Queen countered. She could not believe that anyone could not be swayed by money.

"Go ahead and ask him, and don't be surprised when he turns you down." Bronze Bomber decided that she was there long enough and nothing Wraith Queen would say would matter at this point. "Thanks for the beer. Talk with you later when you fail," Bronze Bomber said, leaving a fifty-dollar bill as a tip on the table.

February 6
Unknown Warehouse in Oakland

DeSoto was angered and he could not believe they were going to kick him out; after all he had done for the conglomerate.

"How is this my fault? Nothing we knew indicated that Armory and Justiciar would produce not only another Alpha-level Hero, but one that could beat a borderline Omega-like War Fiend," DeSoto questioned, furious at being removed.

"Of course, we're not letting you go because of that. None of us knew how skilled or strong K-Force is. In fact because of that display, we mostly forgive you since losing some of our operatives was inevitable," Mickey said calmly.

"The reason we are kicking you out is because you got caught bribing the governor," Yasmin stated coldly.

"Yes, what was it in the newsroom that made you a person of interest? You were physically threatening the governor to have K-Force expelled from the state. And now he's free of all charges and punishments, easily won both lawsuits, and practically untouchable for at least two years before the fervor dies down," the businesswoman said in a mocking tone.

"You made it hard for us to do business, and now the governor, his cabinet, and party are in question because of his actions. Now we have no real leverage since the investigation will be during election time," Mickey accused, bringing the main reason for the expulsion.

"Exposed, DeSoto, you and your recent actions have exposed us. What makes us the best group of villains is the fact that no one knows we exist, which is why you're going to be taking the entire fall while losing your connection to us," Archon said in a cold manner.

"But,"

"I'm not your mother, so I don't want to hear it. You're at fault, so you will deal with it, but if you mention us, your mother and every member in your family will be seeing one of our associates in a nonfriendly manner." Archon made her final thoughts known before disappearing.

DeSoto was livid, but he knew he stood about a snowball's chance in hell against the woman.

"Understood? Good. Since you have been an asset until now, I will allow you to get your affairs in order before you will be released," commanded the boss lady, before she disappeared. The others saw this as the end of the meeting, and one by one they left.

"You have until the end of the week. Don't make the chairwoman regret it because you won't live long enough to do so." Yasmin was the last one to leave as the holoimage conference ended.

When the hologram meeting was over, DeSoto's anger was unleashed as he trashed the room and everything in it; all the years of sacrifices and work that he had put into this organization and they dropped him as soon as he became inconvenient. He would get back at them and make them pay, but first, before he could make any open moves, he needed to move his family away from this area to safe zone.

As DeSoto left the Wharf and the Conglomerate warehouse, he made a call on his personal phone that was protected from any outside interference. After he was sure he was away from any nosy lookouts, he waited for the confirmation of a woman with a southern drawl.

"Hello," answered a mysterious, southern female voice.

"It is DeSoto. I'm in."

About the Author

LeRoy Carter Smith is an author and artist living in the Las Vegas area currently. His first novel *Meta World* has been years in the making and is soon to be available worldwide.

Printed in the USA
CPSIA information can be obtained
at www.ICGtesting.com
LVHW041050191023
761555LV00002B/23